Praise for Cara Bastone and *Just a Heartbeat Away*

"An utterly satisfying and delicious read. One for the keeper shelf!"
   —Jill Shalvis, *New York Times* bestselling author

"Emotionally intense and real, *Just a Heartbeat Away* touches the soft place in your soul. Cara Bastone's debut novel will warm you from the inside out and stay with you long after you finish the book."
—Christie Craig, *New York Times* bestselling author

"Gorgeous, brilliant, with characters so unique and real they leap right off the page. It's a master class in achy breaky yearning. Don't start this one late at night unless you don't need to do anything the next day except for pre-ordering the next one."
   —Sarina Bowen, *USA TODAY* bestselling author
                    of the True North series

"*Just a Heartbeat Away* is a beautiful slow-burn romance. The chemistry between Sebastian and Via absolutely stole my heart!"
                    —Molly O'Keefe, award-winning author
                    of the Riverview Inn series

Also by Cara Bastone

Forever Yours

When We First Met (prequel ebook novella)
Just a Heartbeat Away
Can't Help Falling

Look for Cara Bastone's next novel
Flirting with Forever
available soon from HQN.

CARA BASTONE

can't
help
falling

HQN

HQN

Recycling programs
for this product may
not exist in your area.

ISBN-13: 978-1-335-01339-2

Can't Help Falling

Copyright © 2020 by Cara Bastone

This edition published by arrangement with Harlequin Books S.A.

For questions and comments about the quality of this book,
please contact us at CustomerService@Harlequin.com.

HQN
22 Adelaide St. West, 40th Floor
Toronto, Ontario M5H 4E3, Canada
www.Harlequin.com

Printed in U.S.A.

For C A-S.
Thanks for sharing.

can't
help
falling

CHAPTER ONE

"STALE POPCORN, LUKEWARM hot dogs and flat beer. What more could a man want from life?" Tyler Leshuski flung an arm around the back of Matty's seat and tilted his face up toward the cheerful squint of the early-June sun that was belatedly trying to make up its mind between spring and summer.

Matty Dorner, freshly seven years old as of this morning, peered dubiously into Tyler's cup. "I dunno, Uncle Ty. I think I like orange soda better than beer."

"That's because you've never had beer," Tyler replied, knowing he was about to receive—yup, there was the sharp flick to the back of his head smartly administered by his best friend. Tyler, grinning, tipped his head backward and viewed Sebastian upside down, sitting in the row behind him. "You rang?"

"Will you kindly quit talking to my seven-year-old about beer?" Sebastian asked.

Tyler opened his mouth to respond, but the slight, pretty woman tucked under Sebastian's arm beat him to it. "Matty knows beer is a grown-up's drink. There's no harm in learning about it from Uncle Tyler."

"See? Listen to the woman." Tyler quickly sat back up, feeling strangely deflated even though Sebastian's girlfriend had sided with him, as she often did. Via DeRosa was sweet and thoughtful and loving. There was no arguing with the fact that she was downright good for Sebastian and Matty, who'd both endured enough loss to tide anyone over for a lifetime. After Sebastian had lost Matty's mother, Cora, in a car accident almost five years ago, Tyler had wondered if his best friend would ever be himself again. The old Sebastian. The one who laughed easily, played rec basketball and every once in a while, hired a babysitter so that he could go out and have a beer with his oldest friend Tyler.

In the half a year since Seb and Via had gotten together, Tyler had seen more glimpses of the relaxed, open, fun-loving man Sebastian used to be than in the previous five years combined. This was a good thing, Tyler knew. He just wished that he was around for more of it.

Hell. Matty's birthday party today was the first time he'd seen the kid in almost ten days. There used to be a time when Tyler hadn't gone more than twenty-four hours without shoving the kid's wiggling toes into a pair of tiny socks or cramming a waffle down his throat while they bolted out the door, late for Matty's school.

There used to be a *reason* for Tyler to be around. Now? Not so much. There was more than enough supervision for Matty these days. Via was officially moving into Sebastian and Matty's house in three weeks, when her lease ran out. And then Seb's house, practically Tyler's second home, would officially become a place where Tyler rang the doorbell while he waited outside on the porch for someone to answer.

"Did I miss anything, Matty?" Joy Choi asked anxiously in that high, clear voice of hers as she slid into her seat, her pigtails tucked under the Coney Island Cyclones cap that matched the one on Matty's head.

"You're back!" Matty practically shouted in his best

friend's face. "I was worried you'd miss the seventh-inning stretch. That's the best part."

"Matty, Matty, *Matty*." Tyler shook his head in mock disappointment. "The best part is obviously the actual baseball. Besides, it's only the fourth inning."

"Right, Uncle Ty," Matty agreed, nodding his head sagely before turning back to Joy. "Did you get any snacks?"

Tyler chuckled to himself. The kid obviously knew the best way to shut up an adult. Agree with what they say and move on.

"Thanks for taking her, Fin," Seb said from behind Tyler. "Was it any trouble?"

"None at all," replied the woman whose voice never failed to make Tyler's pulse trip over its own feet. Facing away from her, toward the ball game, Tyler tried not to pay attention to the hairs rising on the back of his neck as she settled next to Sebastian. Tyler couldn't figure out if it was better or worse that she sat behind him.

If she was in front of him, he could at least keep an eye on her, though he knew it would mean he wouldn't watch a second of the game. But behind him, she became a disembodied voice, the sound of which practically haunted him, if he'd believed in that sort of thing. Behind him, she became all sultry Louisiana drawl—smoky cloves, lavender and sage. The woman had the kind of voice that told a man exactly how her mouth tasted.

Tyler shifted in his seat and did not turn around. The only thing more potent than her voice was her face, and he didn't need to turn around to call it up, perfectly, in his mind. Moon-pale skin, eerily light eyes and plush lips. Gah. *Baseball, baseball, baseball*, he reprimanded himself.

He wasn't here to swan around about a woman, no matter how painfully beautiful she was. No matter if it made his feet sweat in his perfectly matched Nike socks to know she sat behind him, gorgeous and dangerous, like a gemstone tiger come to life. He was here because it was his quasi-nephew's seventh birthday and because a minor league baseball game was the second-best way to pass a warm day, preceded in Tyler's mind only by the bike ride down Ocean Parkway that led to said baseball game. Well, he amended internally, maybe the *absolute* best way to pass a warm, sunny day was indoors, tussling under the covers with some warm, sunny woman.

The hairs on the back of his neck rose yet again, this time forcefully, and he wondered, uncomfortably, if the woman sitting behind him somehow knew that his thoughts had turned to sex. Serafine St. Romain claimed she was psychic, which Tyler wholeheartedly rolled his eyes at. He didn't believe in that kind of thing, and was naturally skeptical of people who did. But every once in a while, like right now, with the bright sun warming his baseball cap, when his skin gathered into goose bumps, Tyler just sort of…wondered if parts of her claims could be true. Could she read his thoughts?

"Yes," her voice said from behind him, low but clear and just as sexy as always.

"What?" he asked, jolting and spinning around to face her. "What did you say?"

And then he was facing her and there was no looking away from the unabashed attractiveness of that high-cheekboned, clear-eyed, plush-mouthed face. He felt like he was suddenly staring into a solar eclipse.

"Via asked if I'd texted with Mary today. I said yes," Fin responded dryly, though she smirked as if she knew exactly the reason his stupid heart had just fallen down the stairs. But she *couldn't* read minds, he reminded himself.

That was ridiculous. It was just coincidence that her voice had broken through his thoughts at that particular moment.

"Right," he said gruffly, before turning back around. Then he quickly turned to her again. "Why were you texting with Mary?"

One of Serafine's dark eyebrows rose up her forehead, further framing her large, light eyes. "Because she's my friend."

"Right," Tyler said again, just as dumbly as the first time. He turned back around and put his eyes on the game, feeling all sorts of bothered. He hadn't known that Serafine and Mary texted each other. It was stupid that it bothered him. It was stupid to feel like Mary was his and Seb's friend, not Via and Serafine's friend. But, dammit! It was he and Mary who'd dragged Sebastian back to life after Cora died. It was Sebastian and Tyler and Mary who'd laughed until they'd cried and then just plain cried together all those nights. It was Tyler and Mary who'd coordinated meals for Sebastian and done the grocery shopping and traded off babysitting without Sebastian even having to ask them.

This time last year and it had just been Sebastian, Mary and Tyler at the annual Cyclones game they always went to for Matty's birthday, riding bikes down the parkway to get there and scarfing processed meat and snow cones until the sun threatened to go down and they had to bike home.

But Tyler had to admit that things were changing. This year Matty had even ridden his own bicycle, instead of in a seat on the back of Seb's. Mary hadn't been able to make it, busy as she was at her shop these days, and the extra ticket had fallen to Joy. But the biggest change of all? Last fall, Via had tumbled into Sebastian's life, and she'd plunked her best friend and foster sister, Serafine, down along with her.

Thus began the new era. Dawn of the Age of Serafine.

Jurassic, Triassic, Serafinaceous. Tyler pictured mist gathering at the opening of a cave, a man discovering fire. But then the man looked up, saw Serafine St. Romain in a bikini made of mastodon fur and promptly burned the shit out of his hand.

He shook his head at himself. This was the new era where Tyler went ten days without seeing Matty or Sebastian and when he did, there was a sexy psychic making ants crawl over his skin.

Tyler attempted to relax, smiling at the coaster car of screaming Brooklynites that whirlwinded alongside one end of the outfield. The field was right on the edge of all the Coney Island roller coasters and every three minutes or so, thrill-seekers swirled over the far outfield wall on a bendy, bright red track. Beyond that was the silvery ocean with its whitecaps and thin stretch of yellow sand.

An airplane painted a skinny line of bright exhaust over the water, cutting the sky in two. As he watched, a pop fly momentarily made it into the frame of Tyler's vision. There was nothing more New York than that view. A baseball, an airplane, a roller coaster filled with screamers, the scent of caramel corn mixing with the briny ocean.

God, he loved Brooklyn.

"We'd like to thank everyone for their attendance this fine June day," the smarmy announcer said over the loudspeaker, slightly slurring with what was most likely one beer too many. "But as today is our yearly Parent Appreciation Game, we'd like to particularly honor all the mothers and fathers in the crowd right now."

The crowd clapped and cheered as tepidly as they had for everything else that had happened so far.

"Stand up, Dad!" Matty said, twirling on his knees on his seat so that he could see Sebastian.

Sebastian shook his head. "I'll just wave at the crowd."

"Come on, Daddy!"

Sebastian pursed his lips and stood up reluctantly, jamming his hands in the pockets of his jeans. Tyler grinned down at Matty. The kid knew the exact power of the word *Daddy*. He used it rarely, as if appreciating the raw wattage of it, knowing it would get his dad to pretty much agree to anything these days.

"Let's hear it for the parents! You'll notice behind the dugout we've got the parents of the players. And here, we get to see the players' appreciation."

At that, many of the players climbed the fence between the field and the crowd, blowing kisses to their parents and tossing balls and stuffed animals to the crowd.

"Tyler…" Matty said, a question apparent in every squished-up line of his face, so much like Sebastian's.

"Yeah?"

"You don't have kids, right?"

"Matty!" Sebastian said in surprise from behind them. "I can't believe you don't know the answer to that!"

Tyler laughed. "Matty, don't you think that if I had a kid you'd have met him by now?"

Matty turned to Joy and the two of them shared a serious look. "But sometimes parents don't ever see their kids. Especially dads."

"That's true…" Tyler responded carefully. He knew better than most just how true that was. And he suddenly had the baked-potato-sized stone in his stomach to prove it.

"So, you might have a kid I've never met."

He couldn't argue with Matty's logic. "I guess I see what you're saying. But I don't have any kids, Matty. *And if I did have a kid, I'd never pretend like he didn't exist.*

"Why?"

"Why what?"

"Why don't you have any kids?"

Because Leshuskis aren't meant to procreate, he thought, almost matter-of-factly. Being a good father, you had to have genes like Sebastian. Patient, selfless, willing to put up with the mess and disorder of a still-developing human. Tyler was comfortable enough in his own skin to know that that wasn't him. It hadn't been his father either. Arthur Leshuski had been impatient and exasperated and, on the rare occasions that he actually bothered to see Tyler, apparently always right about everything. Tyler didn't care to have a kid and find out just how like his father he really was. He preferred to leave that particular skeleton strung up in the family closet.

"What is this, a therapy session?" he joked. "I thought we were supposed to be watching baseball." He pushed Matty's cap down his face again, very aware of the three adults sitting behind him, likely listening to this entire conversation. He would have had this conversation in front of Sebastian no problem, but he barely knew Via and, in his mind, Fin was still in her fur bikini, sucking his awareness into the black hole of her hotness.

"*Can* you have kids?" Matty asked, fixing his hat and staring doggedly up at Tyler.

"*Matty!*" Sebastian leaned forward and took his kid by the chin. "That is a very rude question to ask someone!"

But Sebastian's reprimand was offset by the fact that Tyler was laughing his ass off.

"Uncle Tyler always says I can ask him anything!" Matty protested indignantly.

Tyler waved his hand at Seb. "It's fine. He's right. The kid can ask me anything." He focused his attention back on Matty. "But for the record, your dad is right. That's not something you should go around asking people. And also for the record, yes, as far as I know, I'm perfectly able to have kids if I wanted. I just don't want to."

Matty narrowed his eyes at Tyler. "But why *not*?"

Tyler sighed. Matty could be like a puppy with a slice of dropped bologna. He knew it was best to just answer. "To tell you the truth, I don't like kids very much."

Matty's lips pushed out indignantly. "You like me."

"That's true. I like you. Also, I love you. But you don't count."

"I don't count? Why?"

"I don't know. Because you're cool. And because I knew you when you were the size of that chihuahua over there. You were just a tiny, whiny baby and so helpless that I just had to love you. It wasn't my *fault* that I loved you."

"So…you're not ever gonna be a dad?"

"Not if I can help it, kid." There was a beat of silence and Tyler felt the hairs on the back of his neck stand up and dance the hula. Dammit. He was too aware of her. He resisted the urge to smooth them down.

Tyler glanced back down at Matty and frowned. He wondered for a moment why the sudden font of questions. All because it was Parent Day at a Cyclones game?

"What makes you so curious all of a sudden?" Tyler asked, nudging Matty with his elbow.

Matty shrugged sullenly, pulling his own hat down this time.

This was new. The Matty that Tyler knew was always effusive and sweet and guilelessly talkative. Tyler sighed. All sorts of things were changing.

Joy leaned around Matty, looking nervous, but joining in the conversation for the first time. "We were just talking about cousins is all. I have a lot of them."

"And I don't have *any*," Matty cut in, sounding like he'd woken up on Christmas morning to discover he'd gotten graph paper and mechanical pencils when the rest of his friends had gotten trips to Disney World.

"Ah." The pieces fell into place. "But if I had kids, you'd consider them your cousins."

Matty shrugged again. A little less sullen, a little more sheepish.

At a loss for what to say, Tyler would have turned around to Sebastian for the assist, but he didn't want to face Via, the woman with all the answers when it came to kids, or Serafine, who'd laser off his manhood with one haughty glance.

"Good thing you have Joy, then," Tyler said. "She's as good as family." He nudged Matty again and then leaned toward Joy. "And for the record, Joy, Matty's not the only kid I like. You're pretty cool too. And my little sister. She's older than you guys by a few years, but I like her too."

"Okay," she said, nodding solemnly and looking relieved.

"Besides," Tyler continued, looking down at Matty, "you're as close to a kid as I'll ever get, Matlock. So, in a way, you're kind of like your own cousin."

Matty pursed his lips, but this time Tyler saw that it was to hide a smile he wasn't quite ready to give up. "That's weird, Uncle Ty."

Tyler shrugged. "Life is weird, my friend. The sooner you learn the better."

They fell back into the rhythm of the game, Matty's good mood restoring, especially when a pop fly landed three rows in front of them, the kids scrambling down to get it and missing it by a hair.

Tyler rolled his eyes at the middle-aged man who

snatched it up for himself and held it up to the booing crowd.

But the near miss didn't damper Matty's spirits; he was back and buoyed by the joy of the game.

Tyler, however, was bothered. He was bothered by the conversation between him and Matty, by Serafine's gnawingly hot presence behind him. By the fact that he hadn't gotten a minute alone to chat with Sebastian the entire day. The sun was pleasantly warm and the breeze was refreshing, but still, Tyler felt itchy and hot, like he was wearing a Tyler Leshuski bodysuit, like he'd had to put on a Him costume to join this family outing and it wasn't fitting right.

Antsy, his leg jumped in his seat.

"I'm grabbing more snacks," Tyler said, rising up. "Anyone need anything?"

"Popcorn?" Via asked, smiling at him and digging in her pocket for cash.

He waved away the money. "On me." He had to fight with his face not to frown at her. She really thought he'd make her pay for her own popcorn? "Anyone else?"

"Ice cream?" Matty requested, blinking innocently, as if this was everyone's first rodeo.

"Ix-nay," Tyler said with the ease of someone completely accustomed to discipline. Some honorary uncles took pleasure in spoiling their honorary nephews. Tyler took pleasure in adding normalcy and boundaries to Matty's life. "You're already getting a snow cone in the seventh-inning stretch. Anyone else?"

He let his eyes cast around the group and was thrilled when Sebastian held up his cup and jangled it around, indicating he wanted another Budweiser. They generally had a two-beer limit when spending time with Matty, but recently Sebastian rarely met the quota.

"Me too," Serafine said, jangling her own empty beer cup in the same way Sebastian had.

"Right," Tyler said, which was apparently the only thing he knew how to say to this woman today.

Without another word, he scooted down the aisle and jogged up the cement stairs, taking them two at a time. He was relieved to see that even though internally he felt as clumsy as an elephant in ice skates, his natural grace and dexterity kept him from falling on his face. He ducked into the bathroom first and was both relieved and annoyed to see himself looking perfectly normal in the mirror. It was a strange thing to be the kind of person whose internal life never, ever showed on their exterior. Tyler knew, from experience, that his heart could be shredded like taco meat and he could still manage to look unbothered and pleasant on the outside. Perhaps it was partly due to his scrupulous attention to his outward appearance, his neatly cuffed shirts and permafresh haircuts ensuring he always looked put-together. Normally, he was grateful for that particular attribute, but today it bothered him.

When he emerged from the bathroom he walked up to the nearest concession stand. Taller than most of the other patrons at the game, he had a bird's-eye view of the crowd. The first thing he noticed was that every single male head— and some of the female heads—within twenty feet were all surreptitiously glancing in one direction. He sighed, already knowing the reason for it, and looked around until he spotted Serafine.

"What's up?" he asked, sidling up next to her.

She immediately stopped her peering circle through the crowd. "I was looking for you."

"Why?"

"Three beers and a popcorn is a lot to carry. Besides,

Joy decided she wanted a water and I started feeling hungry myself."

He cleared his throat. "Okay."

They filed into the concessions line and stood side by side, a good sixteen inches of distance between them. He was conscious of the looks he was receiving, simply for daring to stand next to this exquisite creature.

In a different world, he would have already dated and broken up with Serafine St. Romain. If she'd been just a skosh less attractive, or less spooky. If she'd made his palms sweat just a bit less. If there had been just a tiny bit less smoke in her voice, he'd have had no problem asking her on a date, texting her, sexting her, charming her, hopping into bed if and when she was into it.

The problem was, he happened to live in *this* particular world, where she was a perfectly beautiful, spooky, smoky-voiced vixen who gave him heart palpitations and made him feel like a preteen who'd never even check-yes-or-no-ed a girl before.

He shifted on his feet as they shuffled up the line, trying to ignore her and at the same time memorize every second of standing next to her. He frowned at himself, wishing he could pour a gallon of ice water over his head. *Snap out of it, Ty!*

Tyler Leshuski was no inexperienced lad when it came to women, he reminded himself. When he wanted company, thanks to his extensive contacts list and the internet, it was the rare occasion that he couldn't find it. He was good-looking and smart and funny.

He watched a man bobble his beers as he double-taked on Serafine, almost breaking his own neck like a chicken.

Tyler shook his head at the poor fool, knowing exactly how he felt. There was just something about Serafine St.

Romain that made Tyler feel like his heart was wearing clown shoes.

They finally made it to the front of the line.

"What'll you have?" asked the bored sixteen-year-old girl with a hairnet on. She was the only person in a twenty-foot radius who didn't look entranced by Serafine or mystified by Tyler's place in her life.

"Ah, three Buds, two bottles of water, a large popcorn, a hot pretzel—no salt. And whatever she wants." He pointed one thumb at Serafine and didn't chance a glance over at her.

"Mmm, chili cheese fries, please, and is there any hot sauce back there?"

The girl pointed listlessly at the condiments stand and plugged the rest of the order into the register, holding her hand out for cash. Tyler wordlessly handed over a fifty.

They went to the side to wait for their food.

"What?" Serafine eventually asked him, turning to him with her arms crossed and those bright eyes burning a hole in the side of his head.

"What *what*?" he asked back, his eyes stubbornly on the kid slapping their order together behind the counter.

"I can feel your question for me. Just ask it."

He resisted the urge to roll his eyes, but just barely. He really hated all this psychic bullshit. "You got chili cheese fries."

"So?"

"So, I assumed you were, like, a vegan or something." He'd eaten with her before at Sebastian's house but had been too distracted by her presence to pay attention to what she ate.

She lifted an eyebrow. "Why?"

He couldn't help but laugh as he finally turned to look

at her. He took her in from her dark, complicated braid over one shoulder, to her makeup-less face, the silver-and-gemstone rings on her fingers and bangles on her wrists. He looked her over from her loose, embroidered top to her equally loose, embroidered pants and all the way down to what looked like a pair of velvet slippers. She carried with her the scent of sage and something else earthy. As painfully gorgeous as she was, her look screamed earth child.

"Because you're all..." He rolled a hand in the air, searching for the right word. "Organic-looking."

To his immense surprise, she actually burst out laughing. He was used to making people laugh. It was one of his favorite things on this earth. But he'd yet to make *her* laugh like that. He'd thought she was most likely one of those people who never laughed, merely smirked instead. But here he was, blinking down at a row of white teeth, her lips, so full in repose, almost disappearing in the stretch of her smile. He got that solar eclipse feeling again and when he tore his eyes away from her, a faded echo of her smile followed his vision for a moment, like he'd burned his retinas on her laughter.

"I also happened to grow up in Louisiana," she reminded him. "They run vegans out of town down there."

So, she was a meat eater. He couldn't say why that pleased him. He couldn't say much of anything, really, as befuddled as he was by her smile, her laughter. Why did he let this woman throw him off his game so much? It was annoying. She wasn't *actually* magical, regardless of what she told people. There was no reason at all for him to treat her any differently than he would any woman he happened to be attracted to. He could do this.

Determined to prove it to himself, his heart banged hollowly in his chest like a rock clanging against the side of a bucket. *Holy crap.* He was gonna do it. He was gonna finally do something about the hairs that, even now, were rising on the back of his neck. He'd been an athlete his entire life, and Tyler instantly recognized this feeling. This at-bat, at-the-free-throw-line, let-the-muscles-do-their-thing sort of feeling.

"Let's go out," he suddenly blurted to Serafine, his voice a little too loud, his eyes on the ground instead of her face.

Shit. Unfortunately, he'd forgotten to factor in the whole clown-shoes effect she had over him. Could that have been any more clumsy? He wasn't even facing her. He couldn't seem to be able to tear his eyes away from the girl in plastic gloves brushing salt off his pretzel. *Stop watching that, dumbass!*

Serafine turned to him, and, unfortunately, so did the woman next to them, obviously extremely curious to hear how all of this was going to pan out.

"Uh," Serafine said, her bright eyes on the side of his face. It became immediately clear to Ty that he'd just clicked on a swinging light bulb in a dark room, tied himself to a chair and begged a concessions line's worth of Cyclones fans to mock him.

Tyler made himself meet her eyes. He was an eye-contact sort of person, dammit! He believed in introducing oneself with his full name, in firm handshakes, in looking a person full in the face when talking with them. He'd been doing it his entire life! Why was this so hard with her?

"If you want to," he added on lamely. Clearing his throat, he tried again. "Because I want to. Go out with you, I mean."

She just sort of stared at him for a moment.

"I mean that I want to take you out," he tried one more

time. "I mean that if you're into it, I'd love to take you out sometime."

"Order's up," the kid with the food called. Ten seconds later, Tyler found himself with two arms full of food and drinks and no answer yet from Serafine. He looked down at the hot pretzel and popcorn, the beers balancing in a tray and felt like he was tumbling through the air with his arms too full to catch himself as he fell. He wanted to toss the food in the trash and bike home.

She stood there, the water bottles under one arm and her fries in the other. "Tyler..."

Yikes. He could practically see the dot-dot-dot lingering in the air after his name. She'd dot-dot-dotted him. *Not a good sign, my friend.*

FIN HAD THE dream last night. Which generally meant that today would be a foul day, no matter how flirtatious the June sun was.

It had come at dawn. Fin, twisted in the sheets of her bed, found herself trapped in a dream world with the last person she ever wanted to see again.

Her mother, painfully beautiful, smoking a long, seductive cigarette and obscured by thick layers of smoke and otherworldly blur, sat in a chair in the corner of Fin's bedroom. She looked exactly as she had the last time that Fin had seen her, over eighteen years ago.

Long black hair, just like Fin's, bright eyes that laughed cruelly at the world. Her mother, vividly gifted with clairvoyance, had always made it seem as if she knew absolutely everything.

She said the same thing she always said to Fin when she met her in her dreams. *A man will bring you down, Serafine. Just the same as he did to me. Think of the thing you want the most in this world and then sail it down the river. That's what a man will do for your life. Trust me, daughter. Trust me.*

Serafine couldn't remember if her mother had actually ever said that to her in real life or if this was her subconscious's way of telling her that time was running out for her to get what she wanted the most.

All Fin knew was that her mother had truly believed that a man had robbed her of everything she'd ever wanted. The man in question had been Fin's biological father. And the way he'd robbed her had been by getting her pregnant. With Fin.

It was ironic to Fin that a child was what had ruined her mother's life when a child was what she herself wanted more than anything.

Think of the thing you want the most in this world.

Even now, standing here in the concessions area of a minor league baseball game, Fin could feel the rejection letter in her pocket. It had come to her in email form, but she'd purposefully printed it out and chunkily folded it up to carry it with her today.

For the fifth time, her application had been rejected to be a foster parent in the state of New York.

She carried the letter with her now as a sort of reverse talisman. A reminder of all the ways the world could get in the way of this thing she so desperately wanted. Her intuition had told her to print the letter out and bring it with her to this game, and now she understood why.

Because Tyler Leshuski, Nordic blond perfection in his pressed jeans and polo shirt, had finally mustered up the courage to ask her on a date.

She blinked at him. Was Tyler funny? Yes. Did it occasionally make her blood heat when she caught him surreptitiously watching her from across the room? Sure. Was he so handsome that even now she could count at least three different women letting their eyes take a little spring vacation from their husbands? Yup.

To tell you the truth, I don't like kids very much.

It was the first time she'd ever heard him say it out loud, but not the first time she'd gotten that vibe from him. She knew for a fact that the man had dated his way around Brooklyn and had no intention of stopping.

She shifted on her feet and one sharp, folded corner of the rejection letter in her pocket jabbed into her thigh, fortifying her. There was no room for a man in her life. And there was certainly no room for a committed bachelor looking to get wet and wild.

Fin looked into those nautical blue eyes of his, dreamy and proper all at once.

"Trust me when I say that the two of us," she said, "are not a match."

She held his eyes for a second more, nodded her head resolutely and then turned on her heel toward the condiments stand.

There. That oughta do it.

Tyler was actually the second man she'd had to reject today. The first was a smarmy, pushy businessman on the Q train who'd apparently thought that just because she'd accidentally jostled into him, she might want to hand over her digits. She'd set him straight in just as resolute a way as she had Tyler. Although with the man on the train, she'd had to ignore the "bitch" he'd tossed her way, seemingly under his breath. She'd found that one had to be firm when dealing with men. Much like children.

"Hold the phone," Tyler said after a moment, striding

after her, his long legs easily catching up to her, beer sloshing over one wrist in his hurry. "That's your *entire* answer?"

She looked back over her shoulder as she pumped Frank's RedHot over every inch of her chili cheese fries.

"You want more of an answer than that?" she asked, raising an eyebrow, a kernel of dread bursting into existence in her gut. *Please don't make this harder than it has to be*, she internally begged him.

"You don't like me?" he asked, searching for clarification.

"I like you just fine. You're funny and sweet with Matty." She shrugged.

"You're not attracted to me?"

She swept her eyes over him, almost lazily. "You're attractive."

"But we're not a match. Not even for a date."

She opened her mouth to answer him but he cut her off.

"What's the issue here?" he asked. "I didn't *propose*. I'm not a bad guy. It would be fun."

Of course he hadn't proposed. That was the whole point. Not that she wanted him to propose. But the venomous disdain that dripped from his voice at the very idea of commitment...

"I'm not looking for fun, Tyler—"

"Well, what are you looking for, Fin? Because I can't figure you out."

Temper crackled inside her like static electricity. She set down her food and turned to him, dusting salt off her hands.

"First off, I was about to tell you what I'm looking for when you cut me off twice. And trust me, if you were any other man on the street, I would have already walked away from this conversation. So take it as a compliment that I'm even explaining this to you. Tyler, I barely date people at all. And I certainly don't date men with *your* priorities. I'm not looking to eat fancy food at an overpriced restaurant and make small talk while I watch you attempt to figure out how best to get my clothes off. I only like seeing movies by myself, and I'm not interested in ice-skating or binge-drinking or whatever the hell else it is that people do on dates." She sucked in a breath for more air, and watched as the color leached out of his face. "And, most important, you are never going to have kids 'if you can help it.'" She threw two quotes around those words, letting him know that she'd definitely overheard his conversation with Matty just now. "And I am looking to start a family. ASAP."

"I didn't—" he started, but she held up a hand to stop him.

She'd lost her patience. Maybe if she hadn't dealt with the man on the train that morning, or maybe if she didn't feel the eyes of other men on her right that very second, taking her confrontation with Tyler as an opportunity to let their eyes linger on her breasts and ass and face, maybe if the world was a little more decent to women, she'd have let him say his piece. But here they were, on Planet Brooklyn, where her temper still hadn't burned itself out.

"You're in your forties," she continued, "which doesn't bother me, but even at this stage of your life, you show no interest in anything beyond seeking your own comfort and having fun while you do it, which *does* bother me."

"Serafine," he started again, looking like he thought there was still a chance for him to argue himself into a date.

Nope. Sorry not sorry. She went in for the kill stroke, deciding to, mercifully, grant him a swift and final death.

"You cling to Matty and Seb instead of living a life of your own. You're charming, sure. Good looking in a Zack Morris sort of way. But from where I'm sitting, you're also a childish, too-smooth commitmentphobe. Besides, if I wanted a fling with someone—which I don't—I'd know better than to fling with my best friend's boyfriend's best friend. Is that a good enough answer for you, or shall I go on?"

TYLER HAD BEEN sucker-punched once, in the eighth grade, by a kid named Simon Sigrid. Out of nowhere, the kid had marched down the hall and socked Tyler in the face. They'd found out later that it had been on a dare from another kid and had nothing to do with Tyler in the least. It wasn't the pain that had hurt Tyler the most, but the shock of it. The realization that one could just be carrying on in one's life and then BAM, knuckle sloppy Joe right to the nose.

That hadn't been any more shocking than this had been. Tyler gaped at her for a moment before he realized that he wasn't breathing. He felt like she'd just waxed all the hair off his body in one fell swoop. He felt completely naked, and every inch of his ego was smarting.

"Damn," he said. Because it was the only thing to say. He took a step back from her. And then another. And then turned and walked back to his seat, mechanically passing out the food and drinks. He stared down at his pretzel, which he'd forgotten to get mustard for, and just passed the whole thing over to Matty, who'd enjoy it no matter what.

She was looking for more of a commitment than he could offer her. He'd always sort of known that. He didn't begrudge her that. But to tear him to shreds over it? As if it was a mortal character flaw and not a choice he'd made a long time ago. Tyler would not be repeating his father's mistakes. Even if it meant that Matty was as close to a kid as he'd ever get. He might not be able to commit to anyone, but he wasn't *abandoning* them either.

A few minutes later, he sensed the moment that Serafine

came back and sat down behind him. This time, the hairs on the back of his neck didn't stand up. There was no electricity or tripping heart. He felt entirely heavy, weighed down and slow, as if her words had been one lead blanket after another that she'd tossed on top of him.

When Simon Sigrid had punched Tyler in the hallway of his school, knocking him to the ground, it had been Sebastian who'd pushed Simon away, who'd helped Tyler to his feet, led him to the nurse's office while Tyler pinched his own nose against the blood running down his face. It had been Sebastian who'd sat there for hours with Tyler while they waited for Tyler's parents, who hadn't come.

And it had been Sebastian who'd ridden the subway home to Tyler's empty house so he wouldn't be alone after school.

But right now, at that moment, Sebastian was snuggled up with the woman he loved, his first priority no longer Tyler. Tyler was a distant third after Matty and Via. And that was the way it should be, he reminded himself. Yet he couldn't help but acknowledge that that hurt almost as much as Serafine's words had.

That once again, Tyler was the one who nobody wanted. The one who waited in the office with a bloody nose, knowing that no one was coming to get him. If he wanted to get home, he was going to have to do it himself.

CHAPTER TWO

Three months later

"So, uh, where's the crystal ball then, huh?"

Fin restrained her eye roll and merely gave the man a polite smile. These were the sorts of questions that all nervous, quasi-skeptical first-time clients asked her. It was people's natural reaction to try to figure out *exactly* how real her abilities really were. Fin had found it was best to just let people tire out their nervous energy and take the opportunity to observe them.

The man in front of her, Enzo, was an odd duck. Handsome in a rough way, a bit of a beer gut, a tough-guy swagger but nervous as a cat. She knew, at a glance, that he was the kind of person who made fun of other people's superstitions but had spent more than a night or two listening for ghosts in his own house.

"And I thought there'd be more tarot cards and stuff. Or, like, black candles. Skulls. Velvet tablecloths."

They were in a small office that Fin rented for first-time clients, until she got to know them well enough to decide whether or not she was willing to do house calls for them. The office was unadorned; nothing about the decor suggesting anything out of the ordinary.

She cleared her throat and Enzo stopped pacing and

turned to give her a glancing perusal, as if looking directly at her could be dangerous.

"I'm wearing velvet pants," Fin said in her Louisiana accent, intentionally making her voice drawlier and deeper and calmer than normal. "If that helps ease your mind at all."

Enzo's eyes dropped to her legs, and Fin detected a flash of suspicion that gave way to humor. His first reaction to her upon entry to the office had been intense attraction. But it had faded almost as quickly as it had bloomed. He was more nervous than he was turned on, completely unsure what to make of this supposed psychic.

"Wanna talk about why you're here?" she prompted.

"You can't guess? Thought you were a psychic."

It infinitely irritated her when skeptics tested her as if they and they alone were the end-all judgment of what she was or wasn't capable of. Especially when those skeptics, like the man in front of her, weren't actually skeptical at all. But rather they were scared about what they might actually end up believing.

"Enzo, you're not paying me so that I can convince you I am what I say I am. I'm here to help you. If you don't want help, this is a waste of your money and my time."

Enzo stood stiffly for another few seconds before he sagged backward against the wall. He let out a deep breath, and Fin saw that his beer gut was actually a bit bigger than she'd originally assessed. Apparently he'd been sucking in.

"I'm here 'cuz of Rachel. She thought it would be a good idea."

Rachel Giulietta was one of her best and favorite clients. Fin, who rarely, if ever, took on male clients, was seeing Enzo as a personal favor to Rachel.

"She, uh, thought it would be a good idea if I talked to you."

Enzo shrugged and started pacing again, but it wasn't the agitated pacing of before. Fin recognized it as a thoughtful pacing, still a bit nervous, but also the tick of a man searching for the right way to explain something.

For the first time since he'd walked in the door, Fin relaxed a bit.

An hour later, Enzo left the office, and Fin stared thoughtfully at nothing. They hadn't made much progress, except for the fact that Enzo had ceased his skeptical posturing. She'd only promised Rachel that she'd see Enzo the once. It was up to her to decide if it would be worth anyone's time or money for her to see him again.

Already leaning toward a no, Fin paused. She had few male clients. Generally, it was her inclination to boot them out the door. As fast and as far as her boots could boot.

For just a second, Tyler's face flashed across her mind's eye. His flayed expression at the ball game. It bothered her that it was still sticking.

"Damn" was all Tyler had said as he'd stepped back from her. Emotionally, she'd stripped him down like corn off a cob and his navy blue eyes had asked her *why* even as he'd taken two more steps away, disappearing into the crowd. *Damn* was the last word he'd spoken to her, and she'd had to convince herself that it didn't sit heavy on her shoulders like a curse.

Sure, he'd been pushy. Unappealing in his quest to get what he wanted. But she'd been cruel. It bothered her.

She heard a conversation start up on the other side of the wall and it jolted her out of her reverie. She packed up her things and decided to walk home, the air finally crisply chilly in a very satisfying early-autumn sort of way.

As she turned the corner onto Ocean Avenue a man called out to her from the corner, jogging to catch up.

"Where you headed, beautiful?" he asked, as if it were any of his business.

Mars. A funeral home. To my freaking living room where I can get some peace.

Fin wondered, for the countless time, if her answer, were she to give him one, would even matter. All he wanted was a way to ask if he could come with her. Didn't strange men on the street have anything more pressing to tend to than chasing pretty women down the block? Who had the time for that?

She knew better than to indulge him with a reply and instead shook her head at him, frowning. She picked up the pace, left him in her dust, and was practically panting with exertion by the time she made it to up to her apartment ten blocks later.

Fin didn't even have to step inside to feel the vibes peacefully spiraling out toward her. Her foster sister had an extremely recognizable energy. Calm, a little worried, openhearted, homebody energy. There wasn't a more comforting flavor that Fin had ever encountered. Via often used her key to drop in on Fin.

Fin pushed through her front door and into the welcome embrace of her private space. She closed New York out and flipped the lock.

"I love you, Fin," Via said, not even bothering with a hello as she came to stand in the doorway between Fin's kitchen and living room. "But your kitchen makes me cringe."

Fin laughed, hung up her coat and came to stand shoulder to shoulder with Via, surveying the mess.

Even she could admit that things were a little more

tornadoish than usual today. Herb trimmings were on the floor beneath where Fin had hung them up to dry the night before. A rather pungent new poultice recipe was simmering in her slow cooker, the steam from the pot humidifying the air and making her eyes sting. On the far countertop sat the remnants of yesterday's geode excavation. A gorgeous amethyst geode sat broken into three pieces, its craggy, dinosaur-like exterior belying the sparkling purple crystal on the inside. The hammer that Serafine had used to crack it open still laid haphazardly on the counter and a fine coating of rock dust stubbornly covered everything within a two-foot radius.

Two years ago, the two women had shared this kitchen and this apartment. Two years ago, this kitchen would have been startlingly spick-and-span and there would have been chili percolating in the slow cooker, not a fresh batch of burn poultice. When Via had lived here, she'd firmly limited the amount of non-food-related interests Fin was allowed to pursue in the kitchen.

But now, Fin lived alone and she was living her life in pursuit of mindfulness and magic.

"If it makes you feel better, sister, don't think of this as my kitchen. Think of it as my laboratory."

"There's a fridge," Via pointed out stubbornly. "Ergo, a kitchen." Via picked her way around the fallen herbs and poked her head into said fridge. "Have you used this kitchen to, I don't know, prepare any food today?"

Fin restrained a smile. If Fin spoke the language of magic, then Violetta DeRosa spoke the language of food. Food was the way in which Via measured her days, her weeks. Food was her way of telling someone she loved them. The woman was a true artist when it came to the kitchen. Nothing extremely fancy or gourmet, but everything was fresh and made with love and care. There was simply no other magic like a Via meal.

"I had lunch at that very kitchen table not three hours ago, I'll have you know."

Via closed the fridge and raised an eyebrow. It was like staring down a cross little cat. "Microwave popcorn and turkey roll-ups does not a lunch make." She raised a stern finger. "Even if you took a multivitamin with it."

Serafine laughed and marveled how it could feel equally gratifying and annoying to be so well-known by another.

"You're gonna need to take some serious cooking classes before you become a foster parent," Via said, settling herself at the kitchen table.

Fin felt her smile freeze in place. How to tell Via that her unflagging optimism sometimes hurt more than negativity might have?

"I've…decided to take a break from that. For now."

It was a miracle Via didn't strain an eyelid with how round her deep brown eyes became all at once. "What? You're— Wow. What do you mean 'a break'?"

She understood why this news was hard for Via to reconcile. It was no secret between them that practically since the day she was born, Fin had longed to belong to a unit. She had Via, of course. The two women had known and loved one another since they were preteens. Via had been shuffled into Fin's aunt's house as a foster kid. Fin had been shuffled into her aunt's house as a lost kid whose mother no longer was able to take care of her.

They'd become sisters before they'd become friends. Even as they aged and changed, they seemed to do so as halves of one organism, developing and altering in relation to one another.

And now Seb and Matty were becoming part of that

relationship little by little. But Fin wanted a unit in her daily life.

The thing you want the most in the world...

Fin sighed. She felt prickly and vulnerable and sad but there was no way she would have folded herself into a kitchen chair and plopped her chin on one hand if it were any other person on the entire earth. But this was Via. So, she did just that.

"I've been trying and trying for a few years now, and always the answer from the state is the same. I've changed my house to suit them, revamped my business, prepped for weeks for the interviews, had countless people look over my applications and still, it's nothing but no, no, no." Fin dropped her eyes and fiddled with her rings for a moment. "I don't understand why there's this wall up between me and the foster system. But maybe it's time that I listened."

For better or worse, the universe had bricked off access to the foster system for Fin. She figured it might be time for her to stop beating her head against the bricks, trying to get to the other side. Brute force had never been her style, and she worried that the rejection and disappointment was warping her.

For the second time that day, she got a flash of Tyler's face from the baseball game.

"A break means that you'll try again, though, right?" Via asked, her eyes still round. "You're not giving up?"

Fin sighed. "No. I just need...to try something else. Whatever energy I've been bringing hasn't been working. I can't walk the same road a hundred times and expect it to bring me someplace new, you know?"

"That makes sense," Via agreed slowly.

Via was going to continue, Fin could tell. Optimistic, unbridled love and support were about to spew all over the conversation. Fin didn't think her heart could take it right now. She straightened up in her chair and interrupted.

"You wanna tell me why you're here?"

Via's lips quirked. "You mean to tell me that you don't already know?"

"You're here to drag me over for dinner, of course."

"Glad to see you're not slipping in your clairvoyance."

Is Tyler going to be there? Fin didn't ask it aloud.

In the past, it had been a fifty-fifty chance as to whether he'd be there or not. But this would make it five Fridays in a row that Serafine had attended dinner at Seb and Via's and five Fridays in a row that Tyler wasn't there. "Sounds like a smash."

Tyler had been MIA recently. Fin could feel Via's worry over him. It had Fin leaning forward, searching for a trace of him in Via's energy.

Via's familiar form filled Fin's vision. She slightly blurred her eyes until her best friend was merely a silhouette. And there was Via's energy, mixed with and illuminated by the natural light surrounding her. Fin read the happiness there, the relaxed, eased love that Via felt on the daily. Like the tartness or sweetness of the first sip of wine, she could read, first and foremost Sebastian and Matty mixed into Via's energy. They were always prominent these days. The very first page in Via's book. The oak trees planted firmly in her heart.

With just a moment more of looking, Fin located Tyler. He was as distant as he'd been for months. Still bright, like a far star, but distant.

Almost the second she'd located him, Fin dropped her reading and turned away. "Let me just change my clothes, sister."

Via wandered out to the living room to wait. Fin closed herself in the bedroom and shed her clothing.

She always felt chilled after she went digging around after Tyler. She could liken the sensation to prodding at a paper cut that she already knew was sore. So she kept doing it, because frankly, she felt guilty as hell.

She pursed her lips. "I'm not the only reason the man is lost," she reminded herself. "Hell. I'm not even the main reason."

But she was *part* of the reason. Her words to him at the ballpark had been as cruel as they'd been necessary.

Him asking her out that day had been the equivalent of suddenly finding a stray dog sitting in her kitchen. She'd known the pup had been lurking around the yard, but to actually see him sitting there, blinking up at her like an expectant mongrel, waiting for some belly scratches...

The last time she'd seen him had been at Seb's end-of-summer barbecue. She'd stepped out into the backyard to see Tyler gunned down in a blaze of freezing water-gun water as Matty and Joy had cackled like maniacs. She'd smiled at the scene but ended up frowning when Tyler had looked up and seen her. You didn't need to be a psychic to sense the ice that had immediately formed around him.

Apparently she'd not only kicked the puppy out of her kitchen—she'd made an enemy.

She shivered and dressed herself against the chill. She didn't want Tyler as an enemy. She just didn't want to screw up her life over a man.

Fin pulled on leg warmers up to her hips, and over top of that, she donned a long, swishy dress that fell to her ankles. It was a deep red in color, bolstering and passionate. She took a few minutes to braid her long, dark hair. And finally, finally, her jewelry.

She traded out a peridot ring for a silver garnet one. Amethyst earrings and finally, a hideous necklace with large wooden beads that Matty had made for her. She'd sensed, immediately, how much love he'd put into making it, and she considered it one of her strongest and most potent forms of magic.

Dressed and ready, they made their way from Fin's Lefferts Gardens apartment to Seb and Via's home in Bensonhurst.

"Auntie Fin!" Matty shouted from inside the house the second Via's key hit the outer lock. Still on the porch, Via laughed and stepped back and let him scrabble with the locks from the inside. He flung open the door, one hand firmly on the collar of his exuberant dog, Crabby.

Boy and dog broke the threshold of the house and immediately got tangled in her long red skirt.

"Crap!" Matty yelled, dragged to his knees as he attempted to keep his dog from escaping into the dimming Brooklyn evening.

Fin laughed and held still, knowing that if she moved she'd trip over the pile of excited mammals at her feet.

Fin grinned when somehow Crabby ended up under her skirt. She lifted the hem, grateful for the intuition that'd told her to wear the long leg warmers. She lowered a calm hand to the top of the dog's curly white-and-brown head. "Shh," Fin murmured, concentrating hard.

The dog stopped yanking Matty's tightfisted hand and plunked his butt down. He still sat between Fin's legs and his tail bongo-ed a mile a minute, but he was no longer attempting to escape.

"Crabby, come!" Sebastian called, appearing in the hallway with a dish towel over his shoulder. The dog sprinted back inside, leaping over Matty and into the house. Sebastian strode forward and lifted Matty from the ground, dusting off his son's trousers. "I swear Crabby is somehow *gaining* energy as he gets older. Hi, Fin." He bussed her on the cheek and then pulled Via into a hug. "Hi, baby."

"Auntie Fin?" Matty asked a few minutes later as he sat on the steps to his upstairs and watched Fin unlace her boots. Via and Seb had disappeared into the kitchen to fix dinner.

"Nephew Matty?" she replied, using the same questioning tone that he had, knowing it would make him smile.

It worked. He smiled for a moment and then went back to tugging at the loose white strings at the bottom of his jeans.

"How come Crabby is always trying to escape? He's always trying to get off the leash in Prospect Park or get out the front door." Matty tug-tug-tugged at his pants. "Am I doing something wrong?"

Fin's already tender heart went ahead and shoved itself through the meat tenderizer known as Matty Dorner.

Fin tossed her boots into the shoe closet and turned to survey the scene in front of her with her physical eyes. Matty looked a little flushed and a little sad, one of his cheeks inched up the wall that he leaned his face against, his hands still tangled in the hem of his jeans.

His sadness, like all children, was so bright it hurt Fin to see it, like biting down on a sour candy. Most children she knew didn't tangle up their emotions the way adults did, they painted them in the broad, bright strokes of undiluted paint, and Matty was the most undiluted person that Fin had ever met. His feelings were large and intense, and thus, usually dealt with quite quickly. But this feeling was different.

She answered the question at hand, because he hadn't asked her, "Auntie Fin, why am I so sad right now?"

If he had, she might have told him. But that wasn't the way Matty's brain worked.

"Crabby wants fun, Matty. And the most fun he ever has is with you in the park. So, in his mind, any hour of the day, he wants to pull you out of the house and to the park. Even if that means he might accidentally get off leash and get away from you."

Matty picked a string clean off the bottom of his jeans and twisted it around his finger. "He's not *trying* to get away from me?"

"Definitely not," Serafine answered truthfully. "He loves you more than anything. But it's kind of like when you eat a really big slice of confetti cake at someone's birthday party and you already ate three slices of pepperoni pizza."

Matty looked up with a knowing smile on his face.

"And you get a stomach ache?"

"Exactly," she nodded. "He wants it all. Even if it means getting lost in the dark, Crabby still wants to drag you out to the park." The dog in question was suddenly back from the kitchen, tongue hanging out one side of his mouth and pushing the crown of his head against Fin's knees. She laughed as Crabby looked up, saw his boy sitting on the stairs, and bounded forward, knocking Matty backward. "The poor guy can't even help himself."

Matty didn't answer, and Fin knew that it was because he was already lost in the world that only he and Crabby knew how to enter. Gone through some magical door halfway between reality and make-believe.

A moment later, Fin was standing in the doorway of Seb and Via's kitchen watching quietly as Sebastian scrubbed at some crayon that had accidentally found its way to his countertops. Via was serving something from a slow cooker into bowls and slicing bread.

"He misses Tyler," Fin said quietly.

Seb and Via both froze, exchanging eye contact so personal that Fin averted her eyes. Sebastian sighed and straightened, towering over the countertop and tossing the dishrag over his shoulder again. He scrubbed a hand over his face, his dry palm making a loud sound against his stubble.

Wow. Fin nearly took a step back from the powerful emotion that emanated off of him.

"We all miss Tyler," Sebastian responded gruffly, "but he's MIA."

Fin bit her lip. "You haven't seen him at all this summer?"

"No. He's been in and out a little bit. It's just that he used to stick to us like glue. And now, all of a sudden, he's ducking my phone calls. Can't really figure it out."

Fin, on the other hand, could see it all quite clearly. She'd accused Tyler of clinging to Seb and Matty instead of living a life on his own and he'd taken it to heart. And now he was in the process of hurting the people who loved him best. She frowned at her own shortsightedness. She'd carried that rejection letter with her to the ball game thinking that it would fortify her. But it had been bad magic. Dangerous.

Fin's eyes clashed with Via's. She'd told Via that Tyler had asked her out at the ball game, but she hadn't given her the details on exactly what had been said. She knew she'd have to tell her the rest of the story tonight. She couldn't keep this a secret any longer.

Via cleared her throat and crossed the kitchen to link her arms around her boyfriend, burying herself in his chest. His big arms came around her easily and anyone, even the non-psychics of the world, could have seen just how much she melted him, like he was a stick of butter and her cheek against his sternum was a beam of heat.

"He's gonna be there tomorrow," Via reminded Seb. "He promised he'd be at Matty's first basketball game," she informed Fin. "And Matty's been nervous about it, so Ty said that he'd report on the game and that he'd even write a little article about it for Matty's personal use. And that no matter what happened in the game, he'd make sure that Matty sounded really cool in the article."

Dimly, Fin remembered that Tyler was a sports writer; he reported on the Brooklyn Nets for one of the daily New York papers.

A pit of something cold was yawning in her gut and she wanted to fill it up with good food and the love that emanated from this little family.

"Salad?" Fin asked, changing the subject. "Want me to toss together a salad?"

Wary of Fin's cooking skills, Via bounded between her fridge and her best friend, her arms tossed out like she was protecting a baby carriage from a runaway horse. "How about you set the table, Fin dear?"

Fin's face instantly matched Via's. Two wide, genuine smiles. She rolled her eyes and deviated to the kitchen table, the pit in her gut temporarily filling up.

CHAPTER THREE

THERE REALLY WAS nothing like an eight-thirty a.m. basketball game in some sweaty, humid gym in Bensonhurst. Surprisingly, this was not a sarcastic thought of Tyler's. He was dead serious. He loved organized sports. He loved fancy coffee, of which he currently had one in hand, courtesy of the cute barista he'd been casually flirting with for the last few weeks. And most of all, he loved Matty, who bolted to his feet the second he saw his Uncle Ty across the gymnasium, pinwheeling both arms in the air to get his attention.

Sebastian caught Tyler's eye as well from where he was leading the team of eight-year-olds through some pregame stretching. The two men grinned at one another. How many early Saturday mornings had they spent just like this in their childhoods? Lackadaisically stretching before they played some intramural sport that neither of them particularly cared about.

Tyler's happiness at seeing Seb and Matty was slightly punctured by the realization of just how much he'd missed them this summer.

You cling to Matty and Seb instead of living a life of your own.

Pretty much every single letter of every single word that Serafine had spewed at Tyler at the Cyclones game had wounded him. But had anything hurt him more than that? He wasn't sure. With one sentence she'd transformed one of the things he was the most proud of in his life to something shameful and embarrassing.

The worst part about it? She hadn't been wrong.

After Seb's wife had died, Tyler had gotten so used to letting Seb lean on him for anything and everything that he hadn't noticed the subtle shift over the years. The shift where finally he'd been the one leaning on Seb. As soon as Fin had pointed it out, it had seemed apparent and glaring and mortifying.

Seb was his family, would always be his family. But that didn't mean Tyler's daddy issues needed a seat at Seb's dinner table.

So, he'd taken a step back. He'd let Via get settled into her new house, let the three of them get acclimated to living with one another. They didn't need Tyler popping in at all hours.

But now, looking across the gym at Matty rolling into a new stretch like the floppy Great Dane puppy that he was, Tyler wondered if maybe he'd overcorrected a bit too much. Because damn. He missed that kid. He missed Seb. He missed being Uncle Tyler.

"Ty!"

Tyler turned toward the voice and immediately pasted on a smile to hide the wince. Via was standing in the bleachers waving him over. He waved back and quickly glanced away. Of course he'd be sitting with her. It would be super weird not to. But for some reason, he hadn't thought she'd be at the game.

Of course she was here. That's what good parents and guardians did. They came to their kid's sporting events. Just because he'd never had anyone in the bleachers for him did not mean that Via would ever miss Matty's game.

Tyler walked over and bounded gracefully up the bleachers to Via's seat. He was so focused on pleasantly smiling at his best friend's girlfriend that he didn't notice the woman sitting beside her until he sat down.

"Morning, Via—" The breath whooshed out of his lungs as Fin leaned around Via, her elbows resting on her knees, her dark braid swinging down over one shoulder and one eyebrow raised to the vaulted ceilings. "Fin," he choked, with what he hoped was an aloof nod.

What the hell was she doing here? She was spending so much time with the family that she was even attending Matty's sporting events these days? God. He'd taken a few steps back this summer, and apparently Fin had taken a few steps forward. The thought made him panicky.

He cleared his throat, casting about for something to say. "I would have picked up more coffee if I'd known I'd have the pleasure of seeing you two today."

Fin may have fishgutted him at that Cyclones game, but he could still be polite.

Her second eyebrow raised to meet the first and he knew that she completely saw through his facade of manners and fake smiles.

"That's okay!" Via chirped. "We already had some and I don't need any more. I'm too nervous."

"For what?" Tyler tore his attention away from the annoyingly seductive black hole of Fin's beauty and put his eyes on Via.

"For Matty's game."

Tyler couldn't help but laugh. "It's just intramural basketball."

"I know," Via said, looking a little sheepish. "But he was so nervous this morning. He's really scared the ball is going to bounce off the backboard and hit him in the face.

Apparently that happened during a practice and he's yet to live it down."

Tyler chuckled and looked out at Matty. "I can't believe he's at an age where he's finally starting to feel embarrassment. I once saw him tear the ass out of his shorts on the playground and just shrug and keep playing."

Via burst out laughing. "He's an inspiration to us all."

The scoreboard buzzed loudly and Tyler watched as both centers missed the ball during tip-off. All ten kids on the court just sort of scrabbled after it in a big, shoe-squeaking clump. He set his coffee between his feet and pulled out his notebook from under his arm and took a few notes on the surroundings, on the other team, on Matty.

"It's sweet of you to do this," Via said, nudging Tyler with her shoulder. "He's really excited about having an article written about him. By a real sports writer."

"I thought I'd give him the notebook too, along with the article." He thumbed through it to show her. "So he can see that I've used it to take notes on the Nets as well. He can see his own name along with the superstars."

He felt a bright light on the side of his face and knew that Fin was looking at him, but he didn't bother turning to look back at her. He was doing just fine ignoring her and he wasn't about to deviate from that path.

"It's so neat!" Via crowed, looking closely at a page of his carefully handwritten notes. Even when he was scribbling as fast as he could, Tyler's handwriting stayed scrupulously tidy. Just like the perfect wave of his blond hair, just like the collars of his shirts and the crease in his pants. Neatness was something that he'd learned at a very young age. At both his mother's house and his father's house, there'd been an army of employees with feather dusters and cans of furniture wax. His home life may have been trembling like it was made of matchsticks, but the homes themselves had been showcase perfect at all times.

Even as a kid, he'd transferred the same principle to his physical appearance. Clean fingernails at dinnertime, flossed teeth, a drawer of spare shoelaces in case one broke. All things he could do to keep his life strung together. Besides, he'd figured that if he was going to be imposing himself at Seb's parents' house all the time then he couldn't afford to be a sloppy houseguest. The habit had stuck. So here he was, a man in his early forties, with dress socks showing a half inch under his tidily tailored trousers, his face shaved in neat lines.

A perfectly wrapped present with no name in the card.

He glowered down at his own handwriting. He'd been so excited about the game. And all it had taken to turn it into a pity party was one sultry psychic who'd yet to even say hello.

"I'm gonna run to the bathroom real quick," Via said, stepping carefully over Tyler's coffee. "Back in a sec."

No! Tyler resisted the urge to grab the tail of her long sweater, keep her from abandoning him to Fin's chilly waters.

He glanced to the side. The space where Via had been sitting was shockingly small. He'd felt that she'd been some sort of impenetrable forcefield between him and oblivion, but really, that forcefield had only been about eighteen inches wide.

Tyler couldn't help but look up. Fin's light, ruthless eyes were on him. To his surprise, she glanced away immediately, sitting up straighter and clearing her throat.

He busied himself with writing a quick note about an accidental assist—the kid had obviously been aiming for the hoop but had arced the ball into his teammate's hands instead.

"How was your summer?" Smoke and cloves and all spice, no sugar.

He looked up at Fin, his brow furrowed. She was small-talking him? He hadn't thought her capable of so pedestrian an act. "Fine. You?"

"Fine."

They both looked back at the game. He took more notes, frowning when the hairs on the back of his neck rose up. Even though his brain and heart were done with Fin, apparently his epidermis had yet to get the message. Sitting next to her was like sitting next to a hot fire on a cold day: too hot to touch, but he couldn't resist turning toward it anyhow. He realized his knees had started pointing in her direction and quickly corrected. He faced the game. Ignored Fin.

"What kind of coffee did Christi make for you today?"

He stiffened and turned to stare at her, his mouth dropped open. "How the hell did you know the name of my barista?"

She smirked and nodded toward his coffee cup. Apparently today was the day that Christi had worked up the gumption to leave her name and number on the side of his cup.

"Ah." He hated when Fin did that. Used some sleight-of-hand trick to make it seem like she was all-knowing. "My usual," he answered her, for some reason not wanting to tell her his coffee order. He'd rather it remained a mystery to her, if she hadn't already deduced it simply from the faint fumes of steamed milk and cinnamon on the air. Or whatever.

Luckily, whoever had planned out this game was well aware of the stamina of children and they were already almost to halftime. The score was four to two. Matty's team was down.

Tyler made a few notes and prayed for Via to come back.

"Listen, Tyler," Fin started in a tone of voice he'd rarely heard her use before. It was so...normal. Nothing spooky about it. She sounded almost contrite.

He turned to her. "Yeah?"

"I wanted to tell you something."

For some reason his pulse kicked up about ten notches. He waited, dimly aware that he was holding his breath.

But she said nothing. Instead, her eyes dropped to his trouser pocket.

"Your phone is buzzing."

"Right." Extremely aware that he was answering his phone in the middle of a very strange conversation, he reached into his pocket and frowned at the unknown number. He almost rejected the call but he saw that it had a Columbus, Ohio, area code.

His blood sped up in his veins. He hadn't some-how screwed that up too, had he? No. He'd kept up his Thursday-night phone calls no matter what. Besides, she never called him. He always called her, and he had her number programmed into his phone. If she was calling it would be from her own phone. Unless it was an emergency...

"I have to take this."

"Sure."

"Hello?" he answered the call.

"Is this Tyler Leshuski?" a woman's voice asked him. She sounded firm and exasperated, as if he'd already pushed all her buttons.

"It is."

"This is Myra King. I'm calling from Franklin County Social Services on behalf of your sister, Kylie Leshuski."

Tyler stopped breathing altogether. "Okay."

He was suddenly aware of a hand on his shoulder. Via was back. But Tyler saw nothing, whirling needles pricking his vision as he listened to a woman he'd never met completely change his life.

CHAPTER FOUR

TYLER STARED UP at the same pure white ceiling he'd woken up to stare at for the last month and a half. Out of sheer habit, he inwardly chanted the mantra that had become his best friend since he'd come to Columbus. You've got the all-clear to take her back to New York. You've got the all-clear to take her back to New York. You've got the all-clear to take her back to New York.

But he stopped and scrubbed a hand over his face. Because the universe had answered that mantra. And the day was here. This evening's plane tickets were burning a hole in his email inbox. After a month of court appearances and suit coats and meetings with lawyers and social workers, he actually *did* have the legal all-clear to take his little sister, Kylie, back to Brooklyn with him. As her legal guardian.

And that was good news, he reminded himself. And terrifying news. And pretty much everything in between.

The call that Tyler had gotten at Matty's basketball game had picked up Tyler by the scruff of his neck and ker-plunked him directly into an active missing-person case. Apparently his little sister's mother had up and disappeared completely.

Their father had passed a few years ago, and Kylie had no aunts or uncles. Which left Ty. Here. To figure everything out, or whatever it was that adults did in situations like this.

The cops were almost entirely certain, from the note she'd left behind, and from activity on her bank account, that Lorraine was alive. Alive but currently abandoning her daughter. Who was not a child, but was still kid-like enough to wear a matching reindeer pajama set that Tyler had put through the laundry the other day.

Kylie herself seemed completely unworried about her mother's welfare, which led Tyler to believe that she might even know where Lorraine was. Not to mention the fact that she'd had several months to get used to her absence already.

Either way, Tyler had been stuck in midwestern limbo while the state of Ohio had figured out what the heck to do with Kylie. Apparently, the heck they'd figured was legally tying her to Tyler. And now, here he was, staring up at the ceiling, as of yesterday Kylie's temporary guardian. *Guardian.* Heh. The word sounded foreign and clunky even in his own mind.

Childish, too-smooth commitmentphobe. No interest in anything beyond seeking your own comfort.

HA. He hoped the universe was laughing so loud it woke Fin up from a dead sleep every night for a year. Two years.

This childish commitmentphobe had slapped on his best suit and practically danced the Charleston to get the judge to saddle him with the biggest commitment there was. A small, almost adult. Goodbye, normal life. It had been good while it lasted.

He imagined dateless Saturday nights. A beerless fridge. Finding a—*good God*—babysitter for the nights he had to be out late at Nets games.

When he'd first come to Columbus, his mantra had been *Please let Lorraine walk through that door. Please let Lorraine walk through that door. Please let Lorraine walk through that door.* It hadn't taken more than a week for him to realize that he couldn't possibly wish that on Kylie. Lorraine had willingly abandoned her. And even if their father had still been alive, Tyler wouldn't have wished his brand of passive inattention on any kid. Miraculously, Tyler had somehow become this kid's best bet. The mantra had morphed into *Gimme the all-clear to take her back to Brooklyn.*

After five weeks in Ohio, Tyler was pretty much ready to walk back to Brooklyn. Hell, he'd tape a skateboard to his shoes and grab the tailpipe of a semi if it got him back to his borough. He missed home.

He missed the women in sky-high heels on the subway. He missed the symphony of garbage truck–lumbering, neighborhood-hollering, horn-honking *life* that had been his constant soundtrack.

Columbus had its charms. He genuinely liked the college town. He liked the grand architecture on campus, the borderline maniacal sports fandom that one encountered in almost every citizen.

He hated, however, the plastic suburban neighborhood his stepmother's house sat firmly in the middle of. He hated the rental Toyota he'd been forced to white-knuckle all over the city. And he really, really hated the suspicious, pitying, judgmental looks of every neighbor who rubbernecked past their driveway.

They all but stopped to stare because behind this beige front door was the little girl whose mother had abandoned her. The little girl who'd hidden it for damn near *four months*, living alone, taking herself to school, eating Easy Mac she bought at the grocery store she took the public bus to. On her own. The little girl who slammed doors and all but refused to speak to her older brother. The little girl who'd made it completely clear that she did not want to go to Brooklyn with him.

The little girl in question was apparently awake because he could hear the heaviness of her footsteps upstairs, which reminded Tyler that she really wasn't so little anymore. Though he still thought of her as eleven—the age she'd been when they'd first met—Kylie was, in fact, fourteen. A difference he'd thought was negligible until he'd stepped off the plane and realized that he was not going to be dealing with a little kid, but a teenager.

Tyler roused himself from "bed," immediately forcing the pull-out couch back into its folded form and tossing the cushions back on. As uncomfortable as the accommodations were, he preferred them to sleeping in Lorraine's bed. He yanked on a sweatshirt, shoved his feet into slippers and headed to the bathroom to wash up. When he emerged, his little sister was sitting on top of the kitchen counter, her legs crisscrossed and a frown on her face, as usual.

Tyler looked much more like their father. Navy blue eyes, blondish hair and a long, handsome face. Kylie favored her mother. She had reddish hair, curly at the temples, freckles and sharp features.

"Save some for me," he requested as she poured herself a bowl of Mini-Wheats.

Holding his eye contact with a ruthless smirk, she poured the rest of the cereal into her own bowl, creating a mountain she couldn't eat by herself in a million years.

Tyler swallowed down the irritation that threatened to erupt from him like fire from a dragon's mouth. Kylie had done everything she could over the last five weeks to prove, in no uncertain terms, that she did not want or need him around. He should have known better than to go for that cereal alley-oop. She'd just stuffed the ball back down his throat right at the hoop. And she looked royally satisfied about it.

For once, Tyler was unable to restrain his sigh of disappointment. He'd really wanted some Mini-Wheats. But he said nothing as he opened up the cabinet for an instant oatmeal packet.

"Well, if you're gonna be a baby about it," he heard Kylie grumble from behind him. He turned to see her shoveling half the cereal from her bowl into his. She jumped off the counter, grabbed a spoon and was out of the kitchen before he could say "thank you."

She was eating in her room. Again.

Tyler's phone rang in his pocket and he very nearly bobbled his bowl of cereal in the mad rush to get it.

"Seb."

"Hey, man. Getting ready for the move?"

Tyler glanced at the ceiling. "Maybe? Who knows? Who knows how much it'll cost me to get her to the airport. With school, some days she'd go willingly and some days I paid her fifty bucks."

"If you were anyone else, I'd think you were kidding."

"The kid is cleaning me out."

Besides the cash bribes it took to get her to do almost anything, Tyler had taken a brief sabbatical from work in order to give this matter his entire attention. Tyler's father had left a considerable sum of money to both Tyler and Kylie, but a few more weeks in Columbus and Ty would be officially dipping into his savings to pay the mortgage on his condo. Not to mention the fact that he'd just won his petition to the state of Ohio for the legal right to start paying for *everything* Kylie-related. He didn't even know what that meant. What did fourteen-year-old girls need? Beanie Babies? Posters of hot guys? Those fancy desks where princesses in movies sat and brushed their hair at night? Some kind of mirror that opened up a direct line to Satan? How much did those cost?

Whose life was this again? Oh, yeah. It was *supposed* to be his freaking stepmother's life.

"Today's the big day."

"Yap." Tyler attempted to get excited for the right reasons. It was an incredible relief to be headed back to BK. And it should also feel like an incredible relief to take Kylie with him, simply to pluck her from this soupy mess of abandonment. But the taking-Kylie aspect of returning to Brooklyn was kind of scaring Tyler shitless. "We get off the plane at nineish tonight."

"Cool. You've got everything you need to put her up for at least the night?"

"Shit." The blood drained out of Tyler's face. "No. I've got a fridge full of rotten food from a month and a half ago and sheets for a pull-out couch."

"Okay. No worries. Look, let me and Via take care of it. We have twelve hours to put something together. We'll put food in your fridge and get some furniture for her."

"Furniture. Right. She'll need a room at my place."

"Your office will be perfect for that."

"Yeah."

He'd spent years tweaking his home office into a writer's haven. The armchair tilted just enough so that he could have his feet in the sun in the morning. The desk was tidy so that any afternoon writing he did would remain clear and concise. The blue on the walls was somehow both serious and whimsical, his best articles framed and lining the far wall. He loved that office.

"Do you know what kind of decorations Kylie would want?"

Tyler laughed humorlessly. "Slayer posters? My Little Pony bedspread? Orange shag carpet and a disco ball?"

"Well, let's just leave it up to Via, shall we?" Sebastian said, laughing. "It won't take long to get the room set up. Concentrate on getting back to BK. We'll take care of her bedroom."

"Right. God. Thanks, man. I don't know how I'd do this without you."

"It's not a problem, dude. We've got you."

We've got you. Via and Seb and Matty. Their little family. They were a *we*. Just like Tyler was now. He wouldn't be returning to Brooklyn as a one and only. He was returning as a guardian. Tyler glanced at the clock over the stove. "Look, I gotta get a move on."

"Okay, buddy. See you soon."

"I'M SORRY. *WHAT?*"

"The California PD. They found her. Lorraine. She was at a…friend's house just outside of LA."

When Tyler had been summoned to Myra King's office after his phone call with Seb, he'd expected her to have some residual paperwork for him to sign. Maybe a few pamphlets on how to cart a kid back to Brooklyn. He genuinely hadn't thought about Lorraine.

He sure was thinking about her now.

"Where is she?"

"En route, back to Columbus, where she'll be in police custody until she can make bail."

"*Make bail?* She can't come back to the house tonight!"

"Of course not," Myra said, eyeing him over her almost comically thick glasses. She had the voice of a much younger woman but the face and hair of a sixty-year-old. "Lorraine's not legally allowed to see Kylie right now.

They're going to charge her with neglect, child abandonment, a dozen other things to boot."

Tyler's mind felt both sluggishly slow and dizzyingly fast. There were seven thousand questions rotating in his head, and he had no idea which to ask first. "Jail time?" he choked out.

"Probably," Myra said, pushing her glasses up onto her forehead and pressing the heels of her hands into her eyes for a moment. "What she did is criminal. But her lawyer is good. I know him. He'll push for court-ordered rehab and probation. And there's a good chance he'll get it."

"She won't get Kylie back."

Myra's glasses dropped and her eyebrows lifted. "Are you asking or telling?"

"I don't fucking know." Tyler leaned forward, his elbows on his knees, and he hung his head.

He'd never wanted problems like these. These were father problems. Tyler wanted brother problems. He could maybe deal with *Full House*–style hijinks. But this? It was too much.

"Why would Lorraine do this, Myra?" Tyler asked after a long pause. "Drugs? Mental illness? Who just abandons their kid like this?"

Myra, apparently taking pity on him, rose up, left the office and came back a minute later with a glass of ice water. "Sorry it's not bottled. Not a lot of money running through these halls."

Tyler gulped half of it in one go, coughed and set the rest of it aside.

"It could be both, either," Myra said gently, finally answering his question. "Honestly, we might never know. Kylie might never know. It's possible that Lorraine doesn't even know."

He leaned forward again, even more vehement than before. "She *won't* get Kylie back."

"You're right," Myra said, sitting back in her seat with a barely muffled groan. "Lorraine is most likely not going to get Kylie back anytime soon. *But*, if she aces rehab, doesn't make trouble on her probation or jail time, gets a job, holds down a nice clean house, there's always the chance she could get her back in a year or two. She's the girl's mother, and the system likes to see mothers with their children."

Tyler wasn't sure what made his stomach clamp down harder: the thought of him being Kylie's sole guardian for an entire year or two, or the idea of Kylie eventually going back to Lorraine.

"A year or two." He tried the words out.

"In the meantime, we proceed as we have been. She won't be allowed to see Kylie for a few months anyhow, most likely. And once she is, it'll just mean you cart Kylie back and forth between Ohio and New York. But we'll cross that bridge when we get to it. You're going to go ahead with the original plan. Taking her back to New York."

Tyler felt that disorienting lightness associated with relief. His mind might be completely bamboozled, but his body was telling him that he was relieved that Kylie would be coming home with him still. Immensely relieved.

"Do you want to be the one to tell Kylie?" Myra asked.

"*God*, no," he answered on instinct, then grimaced. "Sorry. But maybe it would be better if you did."

Myra nodded that weathered face of hers. "That's fine. I'll be in touch in the next few days when I know more. Send Kylie in on your way out."

Tyler rose, was halfway to the door when he remembered to turn around and shake Myra's hand. "Thank you."

"Tyler, I know this is…confusing news at best."

"I want what's best for Kylie." He meant that. Even if he had no freaking clue what it actually meant.

"I know you do. And so do I. It's human nature. But when you've been doing this as long as I have, you learn that 'best' isn't a destination. It's something you have to make, over and over again."

Tyler nodded and made his way back into the hallway where Kylie was fiddling with her phone, her feet up on the bench beside her. She was smiling down at the screen but that smile dropped cartoonishly fast the second she saw Tyler's face.

"Myra wants to see you."

Kylie brushed past him. And that was it. He waited in the hallway. They said nothing to one another on the car ride home.

He was just turning to say something to Kylie, anything, when she slammed into the house and up to her room, sealing herself off from him. They had about three hours until they had to leave for the airport. They'd gotten everything packed last night and all there was left to do was throw out anything that would go bad. Lock up and leave.

Tyler decided that he'd do himself a solid and take a quick run. Something to settle his nerves.

While he'd waited for the okay to take her home, the only thing that had been keeping him sane was his five a.m. jogs through Kylie's suburb. Misty autumn runs with no one around, sleeping houses on either side, garage doors haphazardly open, occasionally an early-morning dog walker, but mostly just dawn-blue solitude.

Now, as he ran on this unusually sunny November afternoon, Tyler had to admit that there were perks to the Midwest. But that didn't mean he wanted to live there.

He ran hard, unforgivingly, feeling like if he went fast

enough, he could propel himself right back into his normal life.

Half an hour after he'd set out for his run, T-shirt sticking to him, aching for an afternoon cup of coffee, Tyler stood again on the front step of this weird, vacuous house.

It was like it sucked the essence of him right out of his chest the second he walked in. He stood on the threshold as Tyler Leshuski and then he entered and became just some primate who barely knew what to do with his two thumbs.

He'd had a similar reaction the first time he'd ever been here just a few years before. It had been a strange time in his life. Only days after their father's funeral and a week after his unexpected death. But that hadn't been the strangest part of it. The first time Tyler had stepped foot in this house had been less than seventy-two hours after he'd found out that Kylie even existed.

Apparently his father had had a second family, for over a decade, and had chosen not to even mention it to Tyler. He'd first heard the name Kylie Leshuski out of the lips of his father's lawyer, in a bright office, during the reading of the will.

Less than three days after that, he'd been here. In Columbus, meeting his little sister who was almost three decades younger than he was. He hadn't felt like himself then either. He hadn't been able to think of a single thing to say to an eleven-year-old girl. Much less a joke to make. She'd been just as weirded out as he'd been.

The whole thing had been even worse because of Lorraine's behavior. Seemingly unaffected by her ex-husband's death, she'd preened for Tyler. Basically hitting on him the entire time and straight-up ignoring Kylie. He'd only visited one more time before he realized that his presence was simply painful for Kylie. She obviously hated seeing her mother press her boobs against Tyler's arm, whispering in his ear, and it wasn't like Kylie and Tyler had had some sort of preternatural sibling connection. They were just a forty-year-old guy and an eleven-year-old with very little to talk about. Genetics be damned. Since then their contact had mostly been limited to a weekly phone call and the occasional text message.

And now this. Shoving Kylie into a tin can in the sky and taking her to a place she'd never been before. All so that he could take a crack at figuring out guardianing her.

He had to believe that things would be better in Brooklyn. Brooklyn, where he knew the way around his kitchen. Where his best friends were only forty blocks away. Where the silence at night didn't threaten to eat him alive.

Speaking of silence, Tyler stepped inside the house to find it eerily silent, except for the sound of quiet crying coming from the downstairs bathroom.

He proceeded with caution. "Kylie?" he called.

There were a few seconds of strained silence and then the lock on the downstairs bathroom turned and she slammed out, her arms crossed over her chest, raw anger cindered in her reddened eyes.

"Where were you?"

"A run." He pointed to his sweaty clothes and running shoes.

She glared at him accusatorily but didn't say anything, just let her anger singe his edges.

He almost, *almost* asked her what the problem was. But then it hit him. The deal with her shutting herself in a room with no windows and a lock on the door. He thought of the nest of blankets he'd found in the bathroom upstairs when he'd first arrived. She'd been sleeping up there the whole time her mother had been gone. Because she'd been afraid to be alone and wanted a lock on the door between her and the world.

He'd already loaded his bags into the car. She must have come downstairs, seen that he wasn't there, panicked and thought he'd left. She thought he'd left her just like her mother had.

Pain, sympathy, anger, tenderness, all of it swelled within him so quickly he almost gasped against the feeling. He wouldn't have thought there was enough room in his chest for this much emotion. His eyes zeroed in on his little sister's face, screwed into a knot, her hair messy and making her look like she was about ten years old.

She was just a kid.

"Kylie—"

"I'm not going to New York."

"Kylie," he repeated, but in a very different tone this time. "Please don't do this."

"There's no reason for me to go," she said, arms still crossed.

Feeling the same way he had watching her pour the rest of the cereal into her own bowl, he gritted his teeth. It was not the time to let his ego get in the way. "Actually, there's lots of reasons."

"Mom is back." Her face was stubborn but her voice quavered, just enough to have that tenderness swelling in his chest again. It was the first time that either of them were acknowledging that Myra had dropped a total bomb on them. "She left for a while, but now she's back. This doesn't have to be such a big deal. It's nothing I can't handle."

Or haven't handled before, Tyler finished the thought for her.

He knew that she didn't know him from Elvis, not really. Up to now, the extent of their relationship had been ten-minute phone calls on Thursday nights in which he me-thodically asked her questions about school, the seasons, and then prattled on a bit about his life before he hung up. But anything had to be better than Lorraine. Couldn't she see that? "Kylie, hate to break it to you, but you have no idea what you can or can't handle. You're a kid. You liter-ally can't comprehend it yet."

It was the wrong thing to say.

"Oh, and just because you're an adult, you understand the entire situation? You know exactly what's best for me, Tyler? Is that right? Just because you're old you can magi-cally see the future and know exactly what I should or shouldn't do, even though you don't even know me at all?"

He winced. Yikes. Way to find his weak spot and press a scalpel to it. "No, Kylie, I'm not saying I looked into a crys-tal ball and figured out that taking you to Brooklyn is the best bet. But I definitely know what the lawyer and social worker and judge all told me. Which is that it is going to be at least months, maybe a year, maybe even *years*, plural, before your mother gets custody of you again. And that's if absolutely everything goes her way. That's if she *doesn't* get jail time for neglect and abandonment."

The words *jail time* were a pin to a balloon. Tyler watched as her anger puffed out of her all at once. Her face went white behind her freckles, her arms fell limp at her sides.

He felt like dirt. No, worse than that. He felt like dirt after it had been run through an earthworm. He shouldn't have said that. Even if it was true.

"Fine," Kylie said in a low, quavering voice. "Then why can't we wait for all of that to get sorted out here? From Columbus?"

It was a young, vulnerable question. And because of that, Tyler only gave her part of the answer. He didn't say that the judge had thought it would be a good idea to give Kylie a clean start in a place where not everyone knew her mother had abandoned her. Where her grades weren't skimming the bottom of a week-old garbage can. Where there weren't people pumping the brakes in front of their McMansion just dying to get a glimpse of the kid who'd made the local news for living on her own for a few months.

Determined not to prick any more balloons, Tyler took a deep breath. "Ky, part of being charged with taking care of you is supporting you. And to support you, I have to work. My work is in Brooklyn. There's no getting around it. Dad's gone. I'm your next of kin. I live in Brooklyn. We have to go."

"I have no choice?" It was a question with a web of knives sewed into its lining.

He sighed. "On this particular part of it, yeah, you have no choice. I have no choice either. I'm as much at the whim of this judge as you are."

That much was true. Tyler had all but bowed and scraped at the feet of this judge for weeks. If the judge said, "Blow me a bubble," Tyler would say, "What flavor bubble gum?" His pride had not mattered one whit. He'd do anything if it meant keeping Kylie out of foster care, if it meant getting her out of Columbus and to Brooklyn where he could actually figure out how to do this.

He hadn't thought of his words as cruel, but the minute he said them, her face blanched and she gave him a look that could only be described as utterly wretched. She just... looked so miserable.

"Kylie—"

"Whatever, Tyler."

She turned on her heel and stomped up the stairs to her room. He winced when he heard the door slam.

CHAPTER FIVE

TYLER, FEELING LIKE he now knew very little about anything, had just been grateful to get off the plane at JFK that night.

He felt like an uneasy sailor who'd finally been allowed to get his feet back on dry land. He still might face-plant from disorientation, but at least he wasn't going to drown in the ocean.

He hadn't accounted for the fact, however, that Kylie's second day in Brooklyn was Thanksgiving. That morning he'd blinked into the judgmental cavern of his freezer and had never felt more like a sad bachelor. He was actually quite good at feeding himself normally, and though Via had stocked their fridge when she'd come over to decorate Kylie's new bedroom, he stared at all the food in hopelessness.

When he made dinner for himself, he did it with a beer in his hand and sports on the TV. He ate whatever he felt like eating, did it quickly, washed up and then usually went out for the night.

But with Kylie, he should probably at least *attempt* to make Thanksgiving meaningful for her.

God. Why did it have to be tonight?

Why did their very first dinner together in Brooklyn have to be the most symbolic meal of the year?

He picked up his phone to call Sebastian and was surprised to see a text from Via already waiting there.

Why don't you two come over around two p.m. for Thanksgiving dinner? We'll eat around four.

He closed the fridge door and sagged against the countertop. Right now, with a sullen, distant, unhappy little sister locked away in her bedroom, Seb and Via's house seemed like Valhalla.

Yes. God yes. Have I ever told you that you're a brilliant, generous, incredible woman?

Too much? Maybe.

Did he care? No.

She sent him the emoji of an eye roll next to a laughing emoji and a thumbs-up. Fair warning, the Sullivans are going to be here as well. And Fin.

The Sullivans, Seb's late wife's parents, were old hat to Tyler. He knew how to rub elbows with Art and flirt with Muriel; they both liked him. Fin, however, was another story.

It was almost like her cruel words to him at the game had been the surgeon's scalpel that had slit him clean open. Everything he'd ever felt for her, every heart-racing, warm, hot, slippery smooth feeling he'd ever had had leaked right out of him. The wound had healed adequately, if not perfectly, leaving a tough scar where she'd cut him.

He didn't like seeing her even on the few occasions he had; it prodded at the scar. But honestly, when faced with a sad little Thanksgiving alone with Kylie, Tyler would have stripped himself nude in front of Fin if Via had asked him to.

Great. What should I bring?

WHICH WAS HOW Tyler found himself standing on Seb's front porch with flowers in one hand and paper towels in the other, because he'd felt like a tool showing up with just the paper products Via had requested.

Behind him, Kylie scowled as she looked cynically around at Seb's quaint little street with its postage-stamp-sized front yards and copious Christmas lights already looped around every front window.

There was a crisp fifty folded in her pocket, which was exactly what it had taken to get her onto the train with him.

The door swung open and Tyler braced himself, knowing exactly what was about to come barreling out the door. With the dexterity of a man with quite a bit of practice, Tyler set down the flowers and paper towel, dived for Crabby's collar and swung Matty up under his arm, like the kid was a rolled-up sleeping bag.

"Long time, no see, Mickey Rooney." Tyler leaned down and kissed Matty's hair. He set him down and shooed Crabby into the house. Matty gave Kylie a shy look and then scampered down the hall.

"Dad! Tyler and Kylie are here!"

"That kid's name is Mickey Rooney?" Kylie asked as she followed Tyler's lead and kicked her shoes into the shoe closet.

Taken off guard, Tyler laughed, something he just now realized he'd done very little of with Kylie. "Ah, no. It's Matty. But let's see. I started off calling him Punky Brewster when he was going through a particularly, well, *punky* phase. And then Punky Brewster became Brew-Brew. Which eventually became Roo-Roo, which turned into Rooney-Dooney. And then Mickey Rooney-Dooney. And now just—"

"Mickey Rooney. Got it."

He studied his little sister for a second, and though he could have sworn there was the hint of humor at the corners of her serious eyes, it was gone in a flash and her sullen expression returned.

She'd brought very little with her to Brooklyn. Just two suitcases, and Tyler had been really surprised when Kylie had emerged from her bedroom that afternoon, a scowl on her fox-like face but her red hair straightened and braided. She'd worn a jean dress with plaid tights and boots.

He was as confused by it as he was impressed. He'd thought for a minute that maybe they had more in common than he'd thought, as he liked to dress up for nice occasions too, but he'd started to wonder if maybe her nice clothes were something more akin to a tiger's stripes. Camouflage. Armor. War paint, of sorts.

Her frown intensified as she looked over his shoulder down the hall and suddenly there were Sebastian and Via standing there, holding hands and smiling.

"Via, Sebastian, this is Kylie."

Kylie looked nervous and uncomfortable and shy. "You're the one who set up the room for me?"

Via nodded. "Yup. I hope you like it. I guessed on pretty much everything."

"I was just glad it wasn't pink and purple."

For some mystifying reason, that made both Via and Kylie laugh. Tyler didn't get the joke. Especially because he'd been surprised to see that Via had left his former office the same deep blue he'd painted it a few years ago. He definitely would have repainted it to a light color. Maybe not pink. But most likely lavender or something.

"If there's anything you don't like in your room, we can change it," Tyler cut in. And then, for another completely mystifying reason, his words made Kylie abruptly stop laughing, her sullen look immediately returning.

Via cleared her throat. "I suppose you're wondering who the spy is?" she said to Kylie.

"The spy?"

Via widened her eyes in a conspiratorial look and tipped her head in the direction of the living room. Sure enough, peeking around the corner was Matty in a Sherlock Holmes hat, using a pair of binoculars to spy on the newcomers, one in particular.

Kylie laughed again.

"Come on out, Matty, and meet our guest." Sebastian's voice was firm, the way it always was when he was insisting on manners.

Matty ducked away for a moment and when he came back, the hat was gone, as were the binoculars, and there was quite the look of blushing chagrin on his face. "I met her at the door, Dad," Matty said in an exasperated voice that made Tyler's blood freeze to hear.

One attitudinally challenged kid at a time, Universe.

"Well, we're very glad you're here with us, Kylie. There's more people in the kitchen. This is a new kind of Thanksgiving for all of us because Sebastian and Matty usually drive up to White Plains to spend it with Matty's grandparents. And Fin, my foster sister, and I usually spend ours together. But this year we decided to combine everybody, and every recipe, and see how it all goes. So, I'm glad you're here to see the beginning of a new tradition."

Tyler could have kissed Via when he saw a bit of tension leave Kylie's shoulders. The woman was pure genius. Making sure Kylie knew that she wasn't plunking down into the middle of a years-long tradition. That they were all as new to this as she was. *Genius.*

"How's it going?" Sebastian asked in a low voice as Via led Kylie into the kitchen, a shy Matty scampering along after them.

Tyler waited until they were definitely out of earshot. "Seb, I didn't understand teenage girls when I was a high-schooler. I certainly don't understand them as a forty-two-year-old man. I—I have no idea how to do this."

"She seems…all right," Seb said. "I mean, a little shell-shocked. But she's not like you described her, all mad at the world."

"Yeah, she only saves that for me. When we're alone together I swear she'd melt me into scrap metal with her eyes if she could."

Sebastian hummed thoughtfully. "Well, this whole transition was never going to be smooth."

Tyler said nothing. He'd kind of thought that if he got her to Brooklyn, everything *would* just sort of smooth out. *Oh, you sweet, naive little idiot.*

"All you have to do is get through this weekend, Ty."

Tyler narrowed his eyes at Sebastian. "Actually, all I have to do is get through the next four years, until she's eighteen."

"I mean that after this weekend, she'll start school and you'll both start to get into the swing of a schedule. Things will normalize a little bit. The problems you'll have to fix will be normal problems. Math homework, cliques at school, that kind of thing. Normal problems."

"Normal problems," Tyler repeated. Though, to a man who hadn't thought about math homework or high school politics since he'd been in high school himself, those problems seemed just as unsolvable. But still, he could see Sebastian's point. Right now, Kylie's issues were that her entire life was on its head and she felt completely abandoned and lost. Algebra was apple pie compared to that.

"Beer?" Sebastian asked, gently shoving Tyler toward the kitchen.

"Yeah." That sounded like heaven. But then a thought struck him. "But only if you're having one."

He didn't want to be the only one with a beer in front of Kylie.

They stepped into the kitchen and Tyler took in the scene. Matty sat at the kitchen table, shyly showing Kylie the puzzle he'd been working on. The put-together parts were assembled on one cookie sheet while the mixed-up parts were on another. More evidence of Via's genius, he was certain, so that when dinnertime came around, the puzzle could be removed without destroying it.

This was the kind of thing that experienced guardians and caretakers thought of. Cookie sheet ideas. He could do that. Give him a few days to get on his feet and he could cookie sheet the crap out of his life for Kylie.

Muriel and Art, Seb's in-laws, rose to greet him, Muriel's hug smelling of Chanel No. 5 as she always did and Art's handshake bone-crackingly assertive as it always was.

And then there—yup, music meet Tyler, Tyler meet music—was Fin, standing with her back to the sliding glass door. She had one hand tucked up under her chin and a thoughtful expression on her face as she watched Tyler. When their gazes clashed, absolutely none of her demeanor changed. She didn't acknowledge that she'd been staring at him or that now the two of them were looking into one another's eyes. Most people's faces would either have brightened or fallen at the sudden eye contact. Hers was as impassive as always.

Why had he never noticed before that the woman was

like a brick wall? Oh, yeah. Probably because he'd been too busy hubba-hubba-ing. But with his crush on her firmly mummified, he saw that she could be both unnerving and disconcerting.

It was a freeing feeling, to be able to pass a quick judgment on the woman who'd fishnetted him so soundly when he'd first met her. He was no longer under whatever spell she'd cast and it made him feel like dancing, just to test the freedom of it.

"Hi, Fin," he said, dipping his chin to her from halfway across the room. He was over his crush, sure, but he wasn't about to go on the suicide mission of a casual hug.

"Tyler," she said with that same impassive expression.

He turned his back and rubbed his palms together. "All right. Somebody gimme a job."

Via rushed in, perhaps sensing his sudden, all-consuming need for something to do. "I set up two TV trays in the other room for you and Art to chop stuff for the salad while you watch the football game. Is that all right?"

For what felt like the twentieth time, he felt overwhelming gratitude rise up in his gut for Via. He strode up to her and took the tray of salad veggies she was handing over.

"If you weren't my best friend's girl, I'd tip you over and give you a movie-star kiss right now."

"Just trying to make this a little easier on everybody, Ty," she said, giving his shoulder a quick squeeze.

Without waiting for a response, Via walked quickly to Kylie. "Kylie, would you prefer to help me with the cranberry relish or Muriel with the pumpkin pie?"

"I wanna do the pumpkin pie," Matty said immediately, glancing quickly at Kylie. "I always do the pumpkin pie."

Kylie shrugged. "Relish sounds fine to me."

Knowing for sure that he was leaving his sister in Via's

capable hands, Tyler ducked into the next room, where he had vegetables to chop and Art, who wouldn't talk through a single play of football. This was as close to perfection as his life was liable to get for quite some time. All he had to do was ignore Fin's eyes on his back.

FIN TRIED VERY hard not to watch Tyler leave the room, but her eyes were glued to the back of his neatly ironed button-down. For the first time since she'd met him, his blond-ish hair was a bit too long and there was a thick layer of short stubble on his face. Normally, he'd be immaculately shaved and groomed. It had always added to his preppy, boyish appeal.

He still looked preppy, with his pressed slacks and mint-colored shirt. But he didn't look boyish at all. He looked tired and sad and every day of his forty-odd years. He looked like an actual human instead of an animatronic J.Crew mannequin, which is how she used to think of him.

She frowned. The uncomfortable chill she always got when she thought of Tyler was intensifying, and she didn't like it one bit.

Just now, she'd felt the walls of protection and ice that he'd put up between them where there used to be rivers of nervous desire.

His lust had made her plenty skittish. But now that it was gone, it only intensified the chill of her own guilt.

She couldn't ignore this forever. Regardless of her reasons for rejecting Tyler so intensely last summer, she felt bad about it. If she didn't apologize, her eyes were just going to keep getting stuck on him, like a dam in a river. She'd tried, at Matty's basketball game. It was the whole reason she'd gone. But then he'd gotten that phone call.

And this situation wasn't any better. A crowded Thanksgiving dinner where there was so much funky juju flying around, Fin had taken her place at the very edge of the room to avoid the superhighway of emotions that ran through the house.

Especially from the newest member of the group.

Kylie.

In all of Serafine's years reading people's energy, she'd rarely met someone as guarded as the young girl was. For just a moment, Serafine got the image of the magic rose in *Beauty and the Beast*. Beautiful and fragile, and encased on all sides by thick glass. Serafine didn't even know *how* someone could go about hiding themselves so thoroughly. Secretive, guarded people generally let their true selves show in *some* way or another. But there were almost no cracks in Kylie's guard. Which made Serafine think that hiding herself was pretty much effortless at this point. She'd probably been doing it for a very long time.

Even so, Kylie was polite to Via and Muriel. She laughed when Via convinced Matty to try a raw cranberry and Matty made a face like a betrayed gremlin.

"Traitor," he said, pointing a finger at Via and making Kylie laugh again. But still, there were no cracks in her guard, even when she was laughing.

"Don't you have a turkey to baste, sister?" Fin asked Via.

The timer dinged just then and Via slanted Fin a knowing look. "Thanks. Take over for the relish, will you?"

Fin smoothly stepped in beside Kylie, not bothering to reintroduce herself. She guessed that Kylie was the sort of person who absorbed everyone's names on the first go-round. Serafine made an educated guess that on her first night in NYC, Kylie had most likely spent a great deal of time looking at Google Maps, attempting to figure out the lay of the land.

"You know," Fin said, eyeing the cranberries that Kylie was mincing, "I always liked cranberry relish from the can better than homemade."

Both Kylie and Muriel spoke up at the same exact moment. "Me too."

Fin laughed at the shocked expression on Via's face. Via made absolutely everything from scratch. Even peanut butter.

"Muriel! I'm shocked!"

"What?" Muriel shrugged one shoulder, sniffing regally as she adjusted her perfectly clean apron. "Everyone just puts a small scoop on their turkey to offset the flavor. And you always end up throwing most of it away after turkey sandwiches the next day."

"Mmm," Matty said in a blissed-out voice. "Turkey sandwiches." He grinned up at the ladies around him. "Nothing better than stuffing on a sandwich."

"That is the gospel truth, nephew," Fin said, reaching out for a high five.

"But cranberry relish from the can is so sweet!" Via insisted.

"You just have to mix in some horseradish," Kylie said. "It cuts the sweetness and makes it really good."

"That's how our dad used to make it," Tyler said quietly from the doorway, a tray of sliced vegetables in his hands.

Kylie froze and Fin caught the bright burst of emotion from her. It was a flash of lightning that the girl couldn't control. There was a streak of camaraderie in there, but it wasn't welcome. Almost like Kylie didn't *want* to be feeling it for Tyler. All this in a flash before Kylie firmly fixed her guard back over herself and her light was dimmed unrecognizably.

"Your dad cooked Thanksgiving dinner?" Matty asked,

oblivious to Tyler's subdued sadness and Kylie's discomfort. "Dad never cooks around here anymore. Not since Via moved in."

Fin watched Tyler set the vegetables aside and stride over to swing Matty up so that his little butt was perched on Tyler's shoulder like a prince on a throne. "And you're a lucky duck for that, aren't you?"

He deftly ignored Matty's question about their father.

"Muriel, is Matty an indispensable part of the pumpkin pie operation or could he be spared for a little backyard football?"

"Go, go," Muriel said, waving her hand. "Burn off some energy and get nice and hungry before dinner."

The boys were out the door in a flash and it was only when Tyler was gone that Fin saw Kylie relax again.

As she helped her dump the cranberries into the simmering water, a thought occurred to Fin. She wanted to get to know Kylie better. There was something about the girl that waved a little colorful flag at Fin. It was a feeling that Fin generally acknowledged when it came around. The universe was telling her that there was something special about Kylie and that they were meant to know one another.

Right before dinner, Kylie disappeared to wash her hands and a few minutes later, Fin found her lingering in the front hallway, looking at the myriad photos of Matty's life that Via and Sebastian kept there.

Matty sandwiched between his parents as a baby. Matty and Via's backs as they sprinted, holding hands, into the water at Coney Island. Matty and Sebastian snoozing together on the couch.

Fin could guess what Kylie was thinking without any effort.

"Lucky kid, huh?" Fin asked quietly where she leaned against the far wall of the hallway.

Kylie twisted her head, a wry look on her face. "Yeah. I thought this kind of stuff only happened on TV." She nodded her head toward a photo of Tyler teaching a four-year-old Matty to swing a fat T-ball bat.

Fin chuckled and nodded. "My guess is that this is the kind of childhood a kid has when the people who love him know *how* to love him. Know how to take care of him."

Kylie cocked her head and turned back to Fin. "Your guess?"

Fin shrugged. "Not a ton of pictures on my wall growing up."

"Me either," Kylie admitted after a minute. She looked down at her feet, back up at the wall, her eyes ricocheting off Fin. Her nervousness was bright and sour between them. "Are you, uh, as uncomfortable with sitcom Thanksgiving as I am?"

Fin laughed again. "Sometimes. But I promise that as cheesy as it all seems, nobody in there is faking it. It's just the way they are."

Kylie's shoulders came back an inch. The word *they* drew a line through the people under this roof. It put Fin and Kylie on one side and everyone else on the other. Fin found she liked being on the same side as Kylie.

Fin tipped her head back toward the dining room, where everyone was waiting, inviting Kylie to head there with her. And when Kylie fell into step beside her, it felt right.

Thanksgiving dinner passed in the expected way: too much food, deft avoidance of politics and lots of moaning and groaning over distended tummies once the dishes were cleared away. Fin, the only one there without a buddy, excused herself early and headed back to her own neck of the woods.

It wasn't until much later, when Fin, full and exhausted, climbed into her own bed, relishing the dark quiet of her apartment, that she realized the other half of her inclination to get to know Kylie.

When she'd been talking to her in the hallway and then later, seated next to her at the dinner table—the meal loud and laced with the complicated energies of each person stuffing their faces with stuffing—Fin hadn't felt that guilty chill. It was almost like interacting with Kylie had canceled out the bad things she'd said to Tyler. Maybe, karmically, if she could help ease Kylie's transition to Brooklyn, she could erase some of the pain she'd caused him with her harsh words at the ball game.

She knew that there was a kid out there, a few neighborhoods away, who needed her help, and there was a man whom she'd been feeling guilty over for months. And maybe there was something she could do about both.

CHAPTER SIX

AFTER DROPPING KYLIE at her counselor a few days later and returning home to get some writing done, Tyler's first hint that something was amiss was the fact that his doorman was bright pink and blushing like a tulip. His second hint was that as he walked through the lobby of his building, all the hairs on the back of his neck stood straight up.

There was only one phenomenon that made that happen.

The Fin Phenomenon.

Tyler turned, hoping he wasn't about to find spooky, sexy Fin sitting in one of the visitor's chairs in the lobby.

His skin tightened when he saw her lounging there, sparkly silver rings on the one hand she held under her chin. Her face was carved with shadows and gorgeous, her clothes ridiculously ugly yet somehow still alluring. Her legs were crossed, one foot bouncing, and, dammit…she wore her hair down.

In general, he had a weakness for ponytails. The high, swinging ones that women wore to Pilates classes. But there was something about Fin's inky dark hair in a solid sheet against her back that made Tyler think of getting into bed with her after a long day.

He frowned.

"What are you doing here?"

"I didn't let her upstairs, sir."

Tyler turned halfway back around to his doorman. "Thanks, Benjy. That's a good thing. I wasn't expecting her."

"I might not be a guest of yours," Fin said in that accent of hers. Smoky Louisiana sage that made Tyler have to clear his throat, no matter if he was over her or not. "But I might be a guest of Benjy's from now on. We've become great friends."

It figured she'd plant herself in his lobby and charm the crap out of his doorman. Based on the bubblegum pink of Benjy's twenty-two-year-old cheeks, Tyler considered it a holy miracle that the kid hadn't let Fin charm her way all the way upstairs. In fact, he wouldn't have been surprised to discover that Benjy had made her a copy of Tyler's key. But apparently the kid was made of stronger stuff. Tyler made an internal note to tip him even more than usual for the holiday season.

"That doesn't surprise me in the least, Serafine."

Something flared in her eyes at his use of her full name. "Where's Kylie?"

"I just dropped her off at her weekly court-ordered counseling session." He considered withholding information just for the hell of it, but that sounded like a hell of a lot of work. His shoulders sagged a bit. "Her case worker is coming to meet with her right after that. So, I don't go back to get her for another three hours."

"You're picking her up in a cab?"

"No, we'll take the train home together."

"Has she tried to do the trains by herself yet?"

He shook his head. "No. She's definitely nervous about getting lost in the city. I've been riding with her until she gets used to it."

Fin rose up from the chair, and Tyler resented it.

Stay over there! he wanted to shout at her. He was being

too nice, volunteering too much information. He was giving her an opening, dammit!

He imagined himself with a chair and a whip. In his head, Fin wasn't a lion, but that same bejeweled tiger he'd pictured her as before. Stunning and deadly.

When he'd been into her, looking at her had been difficult. Every glance in her direction had been like trying to make out an airplane that was about to fly across the corona of the sun. She'd been too alluring to him. She'd burned herself into his consciousness. But now that that was in the past, he found that he was actually able to watch her walk across the lobby toward him.

Stay back!

There was something equally fluid and threatening in the way she moved toward him. She was still that bejeweled tiger, but suddenly his chair and whip had lost air, deflating comically. He could almost picture himself as a meme, the words *womp womp* plastered underneath him.

When she was just three feet from him, she stopped and crossed her arms under her breasts. "How's she doing? Adjusting to the city?"

"Hell if I know." It had been a week since Thanksgiving, and Christmas was already looming over Tyler, jamming itself down his throat on every billboard and jingle on the radio. He'd never realized how personal Christmas gifts were before. He'd also never felt more pressure to show someone how he felt with a gift. He desperately wanted to find Kylie a gift that said she was welcome and that everything would be okay and that maybe he didn't know her that well yet, but he was trying his best.

Kylie, on the other hand, didn't seem to care to know him in the least. She locked herself in her bedroom every single moment she wasn't using the bathroom. Tyler had made up a story about cockroaches in New York City to scare her into eating her meals in the kitchen, which she did. But she didn't speak. And their train rides together were marked by the same unfailing silence. It made things...slow. The pace of his life could have easily been outstripped by an inchworm.

His only respite came when she was at school and he could lose himself in his work. He'd convinced his editor that he could still write his sports column watching the games from home and he knew enough of the players personally to be able to get quotes from them over the phone or over text or email. At some point, he was going to have to start attending the games again, hounding the guys at the press conferences after and getting home at half past two. Tyler internally groaned when he thought about how much a babysitter would cost him for a night like that. But his column desperately needed it. Lately, he'd veered from his usual witty analysis of each player and their notable plays to waxing poetic about the nature of sports in general. He was doing it to reach his word counts, and his editor was not going to continue swallowing it for long.

Not that he was going to volunteer a single iota of that information to Fin right now. Not when he could practically track the tick, tick, tick of her bejeweled tail.

"Fin, what are you doing here?" he repeated himself.

She pursed her lips. "I'd like to talk with you. Let me come upstairs, Tyler."

He couldn't help but laugh at her audacity. "You're not even going to ask? You're just going to demand?"

"Would you prefer that I asked?" Her head tipped to one side with her question, taking the sheet of her hair along for the ride.

Dangerous.

"Either way I'm not getting the impression that I actually have a choice in the matter."

Immediately, her hands dropped and slipped into her pockets. She took a step backward, a small one, her eyes softening and falling away.

In the absence of that zinging gaze of hers Tyler immediately took a deep breath, feeling as if a band of pressurized heat had just been released from around the cavity of his chest.

"Sorry," she muttered, looking surprisingly chagrined. "I've been told that I can be really persuasive. Sometimes I let it get away from me."

It was the first time that Tyler had ever wondered if she was telling the truth about her otherworldly talents. Up until now, he'd completely chalked it up as an act. She was so beautiful that anyone would find her confounding and mystifying. Psychic or not.

But right now, his heart pounding with the absence of whatever she'd just released him from, Tyler wondered if, in fact, there *was* something a little off about Serafine St. Romain.

When he remained silent, she eventually lifted her eyes again, but there was none of that persuasive, burning light that there'd been moments before. "I'm just hoping for a few moments of your time, Tyler. Then you can kick me out. If you'd rather, we can just talk down here."

She gestured behind her toward the chairs.

The funny thing was, the second she stopped pushing to get upstairs, Tyler stopped feeling the need to protect his space from her. Suddenly, it seemed ridiculous to him that he was guarding his apartment from this woman. He could sit at his kitchen table, hear her out and politely send her on her way.

"Oh, fine. You can come upstairs."

He could practically feel Benjy's disappointment. He'd no doubt been hoping that they'd air their business out in the lobby, where he could lap up every word.

As he and Fin stepped onto his elevator, his last thought as the doors slid closed was that this was almost certainly a mistake. He just hoped it was one he could recover from.

EIGHT.

Uncharacteristically nervous, Fin leaned forward and pressed the elevator button for the eighth floor.

"How do you know which floor I live on?" Tyler asked suspiciously.

"You just said it to me," Fin replied without thinking.

"No. I didn't."

Oh. As Matty would say, *crap.* Something about Tyler was throwing her completely off of her game. It'd been a long time since she'd responded to something that someone was thinking. She couldn't read thoughts, exactly. But it wasn't unknown for her to pick something like a floor number out of thin air. She'd taught herself a long time ago not to respond. It freaked people out.

Just like it freaked them out when she used her energy to get her way, the way she almost had with Tyler down in the lobby. When she really wanted something, she could look into someone's eyes and talk her way into it. If she wasn't careful, she found herself winning arguments, tricking her way into the last slice of pizza, into shows she had no tickets for. Anything she wanted.

She hated it.

Because she deeply believed in free will. She'd spent the first half of her life at the whim of her erratic, manipulative mother and she didn't wish that loss of control on even her worst enemy. She had no desire to manipulate people.

But there was just something about Tyler that brought it out of her. His smug, handsome face, that untouchable look in his eye, like he'd just hopped out of a convertible without opening the door, simply hoisted himself over the side like the rich villain in an '80s movie.

It inflamed something within Fin. Activated her desire to assert her power over him.

She realized now that his manner, his appearance, had subconsciously made her think of him as less feeling, less human than other people. She'd confused his untouchable demeanor with being unhurtable.

But the man standing next to her in this elevator was plenty hurt. She could feel the murky cloud of his lostness practically filling the space. His life had been flipped onto its side. And he didn't deserve to be manipulated.

"Um. Good guess?" she said, answering his question.

He narrowed his eyes at her. "Either you really are a psychic or you were snooping through my mail." His eyes narrowed even further. "Probably both."

She laughed at that one. "Snooping through your mail? People come up with the wildest theories to explain me."

"Some people make a good living with the use of nothing but smoke and mirrors."

She smirked at him. "Tyler, if I were cheating people out of their money using smoke and mirrors, trust me, I'd be charging a hell of a lot more for my services."

His face went long, his lips pulling down and his head bobbing to one side, as if he actually considered that to be a reasonable explanation.

"Here we are."

She thought it was actually kind of nice the way he put

out one arm to hold back the elevator doors, as if there were some head-chopping danger he was valiantly keeping at bay. It was an absent and polite gesture, one she was certain he'd performed a thousand times.

He led her down the hallway, though she could have picked his front door out of a lineup of a hundred. There was an expensive plaid welcome mat laid neatly out in front of it.

It was as ugly as her hippie pants were but in a completely different way.

Blue blood.

She couldn't help but look at his neatly pressed slacks, his fresh-from-the-Hamptons hair, wondering if she and he could *possibly* be any more different than they were. Before he even opened the door, she knew just how hard it was going to be to convince him to let her into Kylie's life.

He swung open his door, stepping aside to let her in and Fin braced herself for the inevitable onslaught of male energy that was sure to assault her. She hated going to men's homes for this very reason.

Though she was able to ignore and/or block most male energy that emanated from a man's person, his vibes were usually so strong in his own home that there was no shielding herself from them.

She imagined the scent of expensive cologne, "Eye of the Tiger" played by a string quartet, carafes of disgustingly overworshipped scotch, Cuban cigars. She imagined plaid lampshades and fur rugs picked out by some hot little interior decorator he'd been banging.

Taking a deep breath, she stepped inside and looked around.

"Oh," she couldn't help but say out loud.

"What?" he asked, obviously already on the defensive.

Fin slipped off her clogs and stretched her socked feet into the thick blue carpet of his living room. His walls were a pretty white, obviously chosen with intention, not the usual landlord beige. She spotted many pieces of Sebastian-made furniture, including a coffee table, an end table and a bookshelf along the far wall, which held more books than she'd expected of Tyler.

The couch was a gray herringbone pattern and looked comfortable and unique. She suspected that Tyler had chosen it from Mary's shop in Cobble Hill. There was, of course, a horribly gigantic flat screen taking up one wall, like the unblinking eye of Sauron. But Serafine didn't hold that against him. As she looked at it, she could almost hear the whistles of referees, the roar of crowds, the familiarly cadenced drone of the color commentators on football Sundays.

There were a pair of large windows on one side and morning light slanted lazily across the floor, a few dust motes looking right at home in the bright blur.

"I didn't know you owned." It was rare in New York not to rent.

"How'd you know I owned this place?"

"It seems obvious. Most people who rent aren't able to make this many modifications to their places. You know, they have the broken light fixtures or cracks in the drywall because they can't get the landlord to come fix them." She thought of her leaky, unusable bathtub. She liked to soak long enough for the water to turn cold, her hair floating around her like seaweed. But she hadn't gotten around to calling her super yet. Something kept stopping her, getting in the way, and each night, toothbrush in her mouth, Fin found herself glaring at her useless tub, another opportunity to get it fixed setting with the sun.

"Right." He seemed uncomfortable. "Well."

He led her into the kitchen. If she'd been surprised by the living room, she was downright floored by the kitchen.

"You cook?" she asked him, picking up on the vibes of a well-used kitchen immediately.

He raised his eyebrows at her. "Is there even a point to asking how you can tell that just from looking at my stove?"

She shrugged ruefully. "It's just…obvious. I don't know. You have all the spices lined up and a whole set of knives. And look, three different cutting boards. People who don't cook don't need three different cutting boards."

He eyed her for a second. "See? Smoke and mirrors. You're a regular Sherlock Holmes in Miss Cleo's clothing."

She rolled her eyes and he pulled out a kitchen chair, plopped himself down into it like an exhausted bag of rocks.

"I don't cook the way Via cooks," he said, scraping his hands over his face and answering her question. "But I've been successfully feeding myself since my twenties. Not so much lately."

"Via's stuffing you full of lasagna and minestrone and homemade bread?"

Tyler drummed his fingers on the table. "Her food is so good I don't have the heart to tell her that she can cut it out already."

Fin laughed, still wandering around the kitchen, careful not to touch anything. Just looking. Learning.

"Can I offer you anything?"

She shook her head.

"Tyler—"

"Fin, you've gotta tell me why you're here."

"I talked with Kylie a bit at Thanksgiving," Fin said carefully.

"No need to rub it in."

Fin felt her eyebrows rise. "She's not talking to you?"

He pursed his lips, like he wished he hadn't given that bit of information up. "She can be a bit of a closed book."

Here was her opening! Fin took a deep breath, gathering herself up. "Maybe she would open up to someone else? A woman?"

Tyler smirked infuriatingly. "Who? You?"

Her breath came out in an irritated puff. "Maybe me. I was thinking that maybe I could spend a little time getting to know her—"

"No," Tyler responded flatly and immediately.

"No?" It took a lot to surprise Serafine St. Romain, but the inarguable resolve in his voice had done it.

His eyebrows were the ones lifting now. "You and I don't exactly have a great track record."

"Look, I know I was rude to you at the baseball game." She'd planned to apologize, nice and sincerely, but she was all thrown off now, riled up by his stupid welcome mat and the organized spices.

"Rude? Fin, you tore my life a new asshole. You humiliated me in public." He paused, and again she got the impression that he'd said more than he'd wanted to. "I'm not about to invite you into my little sister's life."

Humiliated.

The word hung between them. She couldn't let that stand.

"I didn't mean to humiliate you, Tyler."

CHAPTER SEVEN

SHE DIDN'T FOOL him for a second with those big, guileless eyes and innocent set to her mouth. Tyler could still feel the way she'd looked at him down in the lobby. He had almost been able to see the hypnotizing spirals circling in her pupils. He needed to keep his footing here.

He'd let about a thousand different vulnerabilities slip out already, so he knew that he wasn't going to be able to strategize his way out of this conversation. He was man enough to admit that he was certainly outgunned when it came to an argument with Fin. He figured he had only one route. Blatant, unflagging honesty.

He gave in to the urge and scrubbed a hand over the back of his neck. Her eyes tracked the movement.

"Regardless, Fin, you're not nice to me. I'm uncomfortable around you. And most of all, I don't trust you."

"Tyler, if I could go back and be nicer to you at that baseball game, I would. I swear. I've wanted to apologize for months now. It's not like talking to you that way made me feel *good*. But I can't change what happened."

In the first crack of her impassive expression, he thought for one moment that he saw something like guilt flash across her face. But that couldn't be right. The woman was self-righteous and aloof and haughty. There was no way that she could possibly feel bad about the way she'd treated him. He was certain that he was merely one in a long line of men she'd chopped up into dog meat and fed to her pack of hell-chihuahuas.

He narrowed his eyes skeptically at her. He'd been imagining her laughing to herself about the baseball game for weeks after it happened, regaling her girlfriends with the story while she sucked away on a Cruella De Vil cigarette.

As if to prove his point, she kicked out one delectable hip, raised that imperious eyebrow and spoke again. "Don't punish me for not wanting to date you."

Rage ignited in his gut like a flamethrower being kicked on in a dark room. "You think I'm *punishing* you because my *ego* is bruised?" He leaned back in his chair and crossed his arms over his chest. "I don't even know why it surprises me anymore, how little you think of me."

"Tyler, I don't want to fight with you."

He scoffed.

She took a deep breath and rolled her eyes to the ceiling, like she was praying for strength. "What happened, happened. And either we move on from it or we don't." She took a step toward the table. He automatically stiffened in his chair. "I'd like to get past it, Tyler. And if we can't get past it, at least ignore it. Because what I'm asking for here, would be good for all of us. Trust me."

Trust her? Not as far as he could fly her like a kite. "What exactly are you asking for, Fin?"

"I'd like to get to know Kylie. Spend some time with her. I could teach her about the city a little bit. I was a transplant to Brooklyn at almost the exact same age as she is. I know a lot about what she's going through."

"You want to…mentor her?"

Fin shrugged one shoulder. "In a way. I want to be her friend. Talk to her. I feel a connection to her, Tyler. And look, I know things aren't good between me and you. But

I'm just asking for a chance to create a relationship with Kylie."

Tyler pursed his lips. "Kylie ignores me enough already. I'm not sure I want her buddying up with someone who wouldn't care if I fell off a cliff."

"Oh, for God's sake, Tyler! Will you please shelve your wounded male pride for a moment?" Her hands came up into the air in a rare show of temper. He seemed to have found the end of some rope of hers. "I'm trying to explain that I have a connection to her! This isn't about you and me! It's bigger than that!"

"Connection?" he scoffed again. "You don't *know* her! You met her once. What kind of connection could you possibly have? The unbreakable bond of how much you both enjoy gravy on your turkey?"

She huffed out a furious breath. When she spoke, it was with dangerous slowness to her sagey, southern lilt, a deceptive laziness where an East Coaster might have over-articulated. "I'm trying to tell you that literally the exact same thing happened to me as just happened to her. My mother couldn't take care of me when I was thirteen years old and she signed me over to a family member. Just like that, she was gone from my life, and I was plunked head-first into Brooklyn." She crossed her arms again. "See the connection now?"

Tyler had no comeback for that. He'd heard the word *connection* and pictured Fin waving her hands over a crystal ball with Kylie's face reflected in it. He scrubbed a hand over the back of his neck again, at a loss for what to say.

"I could actually help you, Ty. Her. I'm not just sticking my nose where it doesn't belong. The girl and I have a kinship. Or, we *could*, if you don't stomp all over it."

Even with the indisputable facts right there in front of

him, Tyler didn't concede the point. He felt ornery and exhausted. Frankly, he was sick to death of not understanding Kylie. Of being so constantly in the dark with someone he truly loved. He didn't understand teenage girls. He didn't understand what it felt like to have no parents in his life at all—though his hadn't exactly been an after-school special. He didn't understand how scary learning Brooklyn might be, and he was starting to suspect he didn't understand women at all.

It irked him that Fin, just by dint of who she was and how she'd been born, might have a speedy little highway of a shortcut to understanding and bonding with Kylie.

Honesty, he reminded himself. It was his only course of action.

"Fin, please try to understand my perspective here, all right? I have no idea how to do any of this. As in, I barely know how to talk to her, and here I am, charged with making all sorts of decisions for the girl. Case in point, who I let spend time with her. I have no experience with that at all except for my own gut." Which he was barely trusting these days. "I'm not trying to be an ass. I'm not trying to hold what you said to me at the baseball game against you, but tell me. Why, *why*, would I let Kylie spend time with someone who I've already decided is bad for *me* to be around? That makes no sense at all! This isn't wounded male pride talking here. This is me making a judgment call. I've decided not to let my little sister spend time with someone who is capable of cutting others to shreds with just a few cruel words. Call me crazy, I guess, but my decision actually makes sense to me!"

Fin's mouth opened and closed for a moment in a way that Tyler had never before seen. She looked utterly flummoxed. Her usual impassive, all-knowing expression was wiped clean from her face, replaced with this gaping-fish thing she was doing. It was incredibly satisfying. If he'd had the energy, Tyler might have snapped a photo for his fridge.

"I don't treat *other women* that way," she eventually said.

Tyler had to laugh at what he deemed the sheer ridiculousness of that proclamation. "Oh, so it's only half the human race that you treat like shit? That's supposed to make me feel better about you spending time with my little sister?"

She looked like she was going to respond right away, but instead she turned her head and looked out the small window above his sink. There was a small glass ornament dangling there that Mary had given him, but she didn't appear to be seeing it. Her eyes were lost and distant. When she turned back to him, Tyler got the distinct impression that he was actually going to be conversing with *her*, not with whatever words she thought would convince him.

"Tyler, do you have any idea what it's like to be a woman walking around this city? To get asked out by men you don't want to go out with? You reject them and sometimes, *sometimes*, they're nice about it. But I'd say ninety-five percent of the time, their embarrassment or anger or outrage turns them into assholes, okay? Do you know how many times I've been called a name because I've politely turned someone down? Called a name simply because I don't feel the same way about them as they do about me?"

He felt the blood run out of his face as the truth of her words registered. She was a beautiful woman, and he'd been around the block enough to have witnessed some truly foul behavior from his male compatriots to know that she wasn't exaggerating. But still. "You thought *I'd* treat you that way?" He was flatly flummoxed, aware enough to realize that his blank shock stank of ignorance to the issue at hand. "I thought you were being incendiary when you said that I was punishing you for turning me down. But you meant it. God. That's not what I— That's not who I— Fin, I'm not a *monster*. I know how to take it on the chin. If you'd rejected me politely, I would have been polite right back."

For the second time in their conversation, something like guilt flashed across her face. Then her chin came up and a firm sort of resolution took guilt's place, the set of her mouth turning stubborn. "Well, I don't take my chances with that, Tyler. I make myself *very* clear with a man. So there is no misunderstanding. And if he's shocked into silence or has to immediately limp away and lick his wounds, then all the better for me to make my getaway unscathed. Maybe it makes me cruel, but it also keeps me from getting called a bitch, or getting yelled at in public. Or getting followed by some guy or another."

"Men have followed you after you rejected them?" Tyler asked incredulously.

Of course, her expression said to him and Tyler's fierce decision over what to do about Fin started to crumble at the edges like yellowed newspaper.

"Dammit," he grumbled, dropping his chin into one palm and drumming his other fingers against the kitchen table.

"What?"

He glared at her. "I don't *want* to see your side, Fin. I was much happier just feeling like I was right."

To his surprise, she laughed. After a second, she pushed off from where she'd been leaning on his counter and pulled out the chair across the table from him. It was an adversarial position she'd chosen. The chair that someone sitting down for a negotiation would have selected. But still, she was sitting at his table with a begrudging smile on her face and Tyler felt more of the paper crumble.

"That's how I felt when you showed up for Thanksgiving with a beard and hair in your eyes," she admitted.

"What?" he asked, confused.

"You normally look like such a Ken doll," she said and waved her hand through the air, a casual indictment of his entire visage. "But you showed up to Thanksgiving looking scruffy and—"

"Scruffy?!" He straightened up in outrage. Maybe he'd looked a little less put-together than usual, but he'd never looked "scruffy" a day in his life. "I did not look scruffy. Yes, maybe my hair could have used a trim. But I didn't have a *beard*."

"You say *beard* like it's some sort of shameful growth."

"Men who grow beards have something to hide," Tyler said decisively and to his surprise, Fin laughed again.

"Sebastian wears a beard. And in my professional opinion, he's the least deceptive person on earth."

"Sebastian is a freak of nature."

Fin chuckled at that as well, so Tyler didn't feel the need to clarify that he'd said it lovingly.

"If it wasn't a beard that was on your face then what was it?"

He thought back to Thanksgiving and remembered that in the fog of getting Kylie to Brooklyn he'd forgotten to shave that morning. "*That* is what happens if I don't shave my face every twelve hours. It's my curse that my facial hair grows so fast."

"Sounds like it would be easier just to let it grow."

"And hide my beautiful face under a bush? A face bush?" This time her laughter was not begrudging at all. It was sparkling and genuinely humored. "You consider a beard to be a face bush?" She chuckled again. "God, that's vile."

"Good. You're finally starting to see things my way."

At that, her expression sobered. "I guess I am." She drew a quick, unseeable shape with one finger over the top of the table. She huffed out a breath, as if she were about to do something she really didn't want to do. "Look. I was rude, abrupt and maybe even cruel to you at that ball game. I understand why you might be skeptical of the time I want to spend with Kylie. So, why don't we compromise and have the three of us hang out together for a while? If you're still uncomfortable with my presence in her life, I'll back off. If you deem me to be acceptable, then Kylie and I can be friends."

Tyler was quiet for a minute, mulling over her words. He didn't want to be the kind of guy who folded after three jokes around a kitchen table, and he still felt that he had good reason to be wary of Fin. On the other hand, even if it was reluctant, he did sort of understand her point about rejecting men. She was a painfully gorgeous woman and he figured that learning how to deal with men effectively in order to keep herself safe was most likely something she'd taught herself long, long ago.

"I know you think I'm a jerk, Ty. And to you, I was. But do you really think I'd be a jerk to her? I—" She broke off and Tyler stilled when he realized that her eyes were shiny with emotion. Gone was the impassiveness he'd come to associate her with. As far as he could tell, there was nothing clairvoyant happening in this current conversation whatsoever. This was two people sharing normal words. "I had a complicated upbringing. And I think that in lots of ways, it prepared me to help out kids who've also had complicated upbringings. I could be good for her. I know I could."

He drummed his fingers again, irritated at himself for folding so easily. He suddenly threw both hands up in the air. "Oh, fine. I guess it wouldn't kill me to spend some time just the three of us."

He nearly reeled back from her when an explosively happy smile burst across her face. It changed the shape of her features from long and carved with shadow to suddenly round and high. Her teeth were a slice between her full lips, reflecting light and joy. And those big, achingly light eyes of hers had practically disappeared, all squished down into almost nothing. He was amazed that a woman so beautiful would have such a *goofy* smile.

It disarmed him.

He smiled back at her, but in a contained, cautious way. He wasn't ready to be disarmed around her. He figured that if he'd learned anything from the ball game, it was that she was never fully disarmed herself. It would do to remember that she was a woman with plenty of weapons. And she wasn't scared to use them on Tyler.

CHAPTER EIGHT

"Who are we going to pick up?" Kylie asked as their cab raced north on Flatbush Avenue, the pavement inky and slick with an ugly early-December rain.

Tyler startled from his reverie and turned to Kylie, kind of shocked that she'd spoken to him. She wasn't exactly what one would describe as chatty.

"Remember that woman from Thanksgiving? Serafine? She's coming to the game with us."

Kylie's eyebrows rose, showing just how perceptive she was. "She's a big basketball fan?"

Tyler shrugged. "I guess she just wanted something to do on a Friday night."

It had been two days since Fin had dropped in on Tyler, and the two of them had arranged for her to accompany them to Kylie's first Nets game.

Tyler's editor had been up his ass about getting to the games in person and he certainly wasn't ready to leave Kylie at home with Fin, so he'd wrangled three reasonably good tickets and informed Fin that they'd be picking her up at 6:30 for the 7:30 tip-off. He didn't usually take a cab to the games, but he figured it was probably about time that Kylie traveled aboveground through Brooklyn.

"So... She's not your girlfriend, then?"

"Um. Ah. Definitely not." He might not have volunteered this info normally, but she was being chatty and he felt compelled to share. Tyler found himself quickly summing up the situation. "I asked her out a while ago but she was super not into it. After that, my crush on her just kind of withered and died."

"So, you're friends now?" Kylie's skeptical expression said everything her simple question didn't.

"We'll see, I guess. You can tell me after tonight if you think we're friends."

For some reason, that seemed to brighten Kylie up just a bit. She looked intrigued, more interested in that than anything else since she'd come to live with him. "Cool."

They pulled up to Fin's curb and there she was standing. In the rain. With no umbrella. Tyler jumped out of the cab but she waved him away, opening the passenger-side front door and sliding in. Tyler frowned as he watched two men pause as they walked past, turning their heads so that they could watch Fin get into the car.

"Hi, everyone."

Tyler got back in the cab, a scowl on his face. "I would have called you when we got here. There was no need for you to wait in the rain."

Her braid was a wet slick over one shoulder and her cheeks were almost scarlet with the cold, water beaded on her eyelashes. But her smile was as radiant as it had been at his kitchen table. "I'm fine. How's it going?"

"Would you pump the heat in the front seat, please?" Tyler leaned forward and asked the cab driver. His question served the dual purpose of getting Fin some warm air and also jolting the driver out of his openmouthed perusal of Fin.

After a moment, Tyler became aware of his little sister's eyes on the side of his face. He glanced at Kylie in time to see her looking back and forth between him and Fin, an interested expression on her face.

He scowled. Damn. Maybe it had been dumb to let her in on his short, tumultuous history with Fin. Now he was going to be under observation the whole basketball game.

Fin looked between Kylie and Tyler, as if trying to figure out what was going on.

"Good," Kylie answered, a bit delayed. "It's going good. Are you a basketball fan?"

"No," Fin said with a resolute head shake. "You?"

"No," Kylie said, shaking her head. "I follow women's soccer mostly."

"Really?" Tyler asked. This was news to him. His job was to follow professional basketball, but he loved sports of all shapes and sizes. He'd watched some women's soccer before, enjoyed it too.

Kylie nodded, her typical sullen expression threatening at the edges of her mouth. "Not much over the last few months."

"We can DVR it if you want. I get all the sports channels."

She shrugged, like it didn't matter to her either way, but Tyler couldn't help but feel like he'd struck gold. He didn't care how tired he was after this game. He was googling women's soccer until the sun came up.

The silence in the car lasted all the way until they got to the Barclays Center.

He paid the driver and then herded Kylie and Fin around, away from the crowds, to a private entrance where he was able to flash his press pass and their tickets to get them inside in less than five minutes.

He had to admit, it was nice to feel at least a little bit cool in front of his skeptical sister and his biggest hater.

He got to feel cool again when they walked down a long, private hall, reporters and basketball players alike calling his name as he passed. It had been a while since he'd been there.

He shook hands, did a few backslapping man-hugs, and refused his usual seat in the press box, showing his mediocre tickets for the three of them.

"Seems like people really like you here," Kylie said as they made their way to their seats.

Tyler couldn't help but laugh. "You don't have to sound so surprised, Ky."

She slanted a glance at him, and he couldn't interpret the expression on her face.

He stood back to let both Fin and Kylie walk up the aisle in front of him, but caught sight of the scowl on Fin's face. He tapped her shoulder, taking care to touch mostly coat. "Everything all right?"

She frowned more. "There's so much man energy in here."

He laughed at her assessment. "You would have preferred the ballet?"

"I've never been. But from what I've seen on YouTube, ballet is a graceful, athletic sport." She sniffed, like she'd slam-dunked on him.

The thing was, Tyler completely agreed with her. And he probably knew more about the world of professional dancing than she could have possibly gleaned from perusing YouTube. Unless she'd really been scouring old YouTube channels and found…

No, he inwardly grimaced. Those videos were thankfully buried in the bowels of the internet. She'd have had to be a psychic to find those.

He outwardly grimaced. *Right.*

Figuring the fourteen-year-old and the clairvoyant could find their way to their seats just fine, he turned away from them and looked down at the basketball court. He wasn't sure he'd ever seen it from this vantage point before. Usually he was up in the crowded press box, swigging a beer, slamming some dinner and joking around with colleagues. This midlevel view was new for Tyler. It wasn't so bad, he supposed.

"Man energy," he mumbled to himself as he looked around at the crowds. There were almost as many women here as there were men. Kids too. It was a family atmosphere. Then he reflected on their walk through the back tunnel. All the men who'd greeted him, every pair of eyes that had seemed to stick to Fin's face and body as they'd walked past. No one had said anything to her, of that he was almost certain, but was that kind of attention enough to put her in a foul mood?

Shampoo commercials led a person to believe that a woman enjoyed having her every movement tracked by men who were willing to lay down in traffic for her. But maybe it grew tiresome over the years. Or—he turned and looked up at the crowd behind him, spotting Fin and Kylie settling in—maybe, in the right circumstances, that kind of attention was even threatening.

With his natural, unschooled grace, Tyler took the steps two by two, catching a vendor's eye as he slid into his seat next to Kylie.

"Whatcha want for dinner, kid?"

She wrinkled her nose at the bags of cold popcorn the vendor was selling. "I saw burritos downstairs."

Tyler's eyebrows raised and he waved the vendor off. "Twenty-five-dollar burrito it is."

"Oh. I didn't—" To Tyler's surprise, Kylie's face went

bright pink. "I didn't think it would be that much. Popcorn is fine."

He blinked at her. Not once since she'd come to live with him had she given any indication that she was aware that her presence in his life was costing him money. He would have been surprised to learn that she *ever* thought about money. Hell, she'd just accepted her monthly MetroCard without a word of thanks, as if the city handed them out to citizens for free. The same went for the lunch card she swiped to buy food at school. But he griped about the cost of one stadium burrito and she was suddenly Suzy Frugal?

He frowned in confusion and looked up to see Fin frowning at *him*. "Actually, a burrito sounds really good to me too, Kylie," she said. "I'm sure they're not twenty-five dollars. Either way, they're on me. Let's go check it out."

The girls were up and scooting past him before he could object. He lifted up to grab his wallet, but Fin shook her head at him as they went past. "It's fine, really."

And then they were sweeping down the stairs and were gone before he could say another word.

Feeling like he'd just been checkmated and having no clue how or why, Tyler stared unseeing down at the crowd below him.

He grabbed his phone from his pocket and frustratedly texted the number he'd programmed in earlier that week.

You don't have to pay for dinner just to point out that I was a dick to say that to Kylie.

A few moments passed and then his phone buzzed in his hand. An emoji with a single eyebrow raised.

What the hell did she mean by *that*? Could she have chosen a vaguer, more judgmental emoji??

He growled low in the back of his throat, grateful he was sitting on an aisle and there was no one next to him to get freaked out by his weirdo behavior. Seriously. I invited you to an event that is obviously not your thing. You shouldn't pay. At least let me venmo you.

This time the text came back quickly. Oh, good grief. Cut it out with the tired, antiquated rules on who pays for stuff. I'm happy to buy dinner. This is not a date, so quit making it weird by insisting on paying for stuff.

He glared at his phone, feeling like he'd just been slapped across the hand by a nun with a ruler. He pictured Fin in a nun's outfit and absently wondered if she was wearing her fur bikini under there.

Whatever, so she was an excruciatingly hot nun with a ruler; still, being chastised sucked. She'd even slapped him with a "good grief." She couldn't have had the decency to just swear at him like a normal woman?

His mood officially soured, Tyler did nothing more than stare at the court, watching the pregame commentators chatter into microphones and stare into insect-like cameras.

His phone buzzed in his hand. He looked down at it almost trepidatiously, and sure enough, another text from Fin.

And she's got issues around money, so don't tease her about it until you've actually figured out what they are.

He shook his head, reading the text again. Fin was telling him that Kylie had issues around money? What issues could she possibly have? Though their father had been an asshole while he was alive, he'd been a very rich asshole. He'd left behind plenty of money for both Tyler and Kylie. And Kylie's mother had been left in a very nice position when he'd died. It wasn't like she'd been keeping it from Kylie either.

He'd seen the evidence of that in Columbus. Their house was spacious and well-furnished, Kylie's clothes and belongings were all new and expensive. She had that straight-teethed, trimmed-hair look of a kid who'd had the best of everything her whole life.

He was still puzzling out what the heck her money issues could be when out of thin air, a basket with fries and an Italian sausage with peppers, onions and yellow mustard landed in his lap. He looked up to see Fin shoving a cold beer in his hand as well. Kylie followed behind with two burritos in her hands and two soft drinks pinched between her elbows and her ribs.

"I didn't realize you were getting me food too," he said in surprise. "I would have at least helped you carry everything!"

Feeling like a tool to the nth degree, he scrambled up and took some food from Kylie's arms, helping them scoot past and get settled into their seats with their food and drinks. It wasn't until they were all sat back down that Tyler really looked down at the meal he was balancing on his knee. It was the exact meal he would have scrounged up for himself. Right down to the Bud and the yellow mustard.

He glanced up at Fin, sitting on the other side of Kylie, and she instinctually turned to look back at him. "How did you know my order?"

She just raised an eyebrow at him—the same one that the emoji had—as if she were asking him if he really needed to ask.

"Right," he grumbled. "Psychic."

He accepted the napkins from Kylie and laughed when the lights clicked out and heavy bass rolled through the center, making both girls beside him jump. He was used to the before-game dramatics. He often even brought earplugs to drown out the din and allow himself to think. But tonight, he appreciated watching it all through new eyes. The eyes of two people who'd never seen this particular spectacle before.

"Wow," Kylie murmured as fire shot out of cannons on either end of the court while the home team was introduced.

Tyler felt his chest puff out, knowing it was ridiculous, considering he hadn't actually had anything to do with it. Nevertheless, he was proud to have brought Kylie here. Proud to show off one of the perks of his job. Proud that she was, finally, having a good time, and he'd been responsible for it.

After that, the game started and Tyler found himself actually relieved that Fin was there. He'd never really noticed before how insular his attention was when he was at work. He was glad that Kylie had someone to talk to while Tyler went back and forth between taking notes in his old-school notebook and muttering voice memos to himself on his phone.

He ran down to get a quick quote during halftime from an assistant coach who never told him no. The girls still seemed interested, if a little tired, by the end of the third, but they were definitely flagging in the fourth quarter.

The event was a dramatic spectacle, sure, but the game, unfortunately, was not. It had been a blowout from the beginning, and Brooklyn fans were streaming out in droves, eager to beat the rush and get on their trains home.

"Are you going to have to talk to people after the game?" Kylie asked when there were about five minutes left in the fourth.

He knew what she was really asking. *How much longer am I going to have to sit through this massacre?*

"Yeah," he said ruefully. "It'll probably take me an hour when all is said and done."

He glanced at his watch. That would put them in a cab home at eleven. Kylie's eyes widened with momentary dismay that she immediately couched behind her normal, blank expression.

"Oh. Okay."

Tyler looked back at the game. In a perfect world, the event would have knocked Kylie's socks off. She would have been so enamored by the sport, by the energy, by the buzz of Barclays, that he would have had to pry her away at the end of the evening. He'd been certain that she'd enjoyed the first half of the game and he was a man who knew when to fold 'em.

He was officially counting this as a win.

Which meant that he wasn't going to drag his fourteen-year-old sister along while he cajoled tired, disappointed players into giving him quotes for his column.

He sighed. What a pushover he was.

Not two days after he'd told himself that he was never leaving Kylie alone with Fin, he was turning to the two of them. "If you guys are tired, maybe Fin could take you home?"

He almost laughed as both pairs of eyes brightened at the exact same moment. They were obviously ready to get outta Dodge.

"Kylie, why don't you use that Lyft account I set you up with? No need to fight the trains at this hour."

"Cool." She ordered the car, Tyler helping her to decide which entrance to have it pick them up at, and then they were up. Fin was just scooting past him when Tyler tapped her wrist. She looked down at him.

"You mind staying at the house until I get back? Shouldn't be later than 11:30."

"Of course." She couldn't hide her obvious pleasure at the request.

"Thanks."

She was moving past him again and he used the wrist-tapping method once more.

"And thanks for dinner."

ON THE WAY HOME, Fin noticed Kylie messing around with the Google Maps app on her phone, tracking their blue dot of movement.

"Figuring out how it all fits together?"

"Yeah," Kylie said, absently looking up. "The neighborhoods are still pretty confusing to me."

Fin tapped Kylie's phone. "I used to do that too. When I first moved here. Only I used maps I printed off from the library computers, not a phone."

Kylie clicked her phone off. "You're not from here?"

"You couldn't tell by the southern accent?"

"Oh. Right." Kylie went a little pink in the cheeks. "Duh. I guess since Via, Seb and Tyler were all born here, I just assumed."

"Actually," the driver cut in from the front seat, "it's pretty rare to find born and bred Brooklynites. Most people are transplants."

"I can tell from *your* accent," Fin said with a grin, "that you are not a transplant."

"Nah, Bed-Stuy for life, baby."

Kylie and Fin grinned at one another at the pride in the man's voice.

"So, where in the south are you from?"

"Louisiana. I moved up here to live with my aunt when I was about your age."

"Ohhhhh," Kylie said. "It's all making sense now. I just figured you were secretly into Ty or something."

Fin frowned. "Uh, what?"

Kylie waved her hand in the air, though her cheeks were pink, like maybe she'd said a little too much. "I just wondered why you were hanging out with us. And I guess I just thought it was because you liked Ty. But now I get it. You're hanging out with me because our situations are kind of similar."

"I…" Fin was a little stymied. "I like spending time with you," she eventually said. "I guess I just figured I knew how you might be feeling, getting dropped in the middle of Brooklyn with an unexpected family member to take care of you. I had my aunt and then Via to help me figure it all out, so I wanted you to have someone too."

Kylie looked up from her phone. "I have Tyler."

"That's true."

"But he can be pretty ridiculous sometimes. The man arranges his remote controls by size. He Swiffers literally every day."

"Neat freak?"

"The freakiest."

They both laughed and Kylie looked out the window for a second. "I think it's an image thing," Kylie mused after a minute. "In order for him to feel like everything is okay, everything has to look okay."

Fin wasn't sure how to respond to that. But it kind of made sense.

Kylie swung her head back toward Fin, a sly, lighthearted expression on her face. "How much you wanna bet that he's researching women's soccer right this very minute?"

They both burst out laughing.

WHEN TYLER DRAGGED his ass into his house at 11:15, he half expected to see every drawer in his house turned over. He wouldn't have been surprised to walk in and see Fin eating his fanciest chocolate and perusing his National Grid bills. It would serve him right for letting a woman who called herself a psychic alone in his house. No doubt she'd read every label in his medicine cabinet. Gone through his bedside drawer. Armed herself in every way for a whole new set of "insights" where he was concerned.

He was not, however, prepared, to walk in to a silent, mostly dark house to see Fin leaning quietly on his living room windowsill, looking out into dark Brooklyn.

"Hi," he said, letting the confusion seep into his voice. He couldn't help but glance around the room. Besides her shoes set up next to Kylie's, there was absolutely nothing amiss.

His house looked as if she hadn't even been there for the last hour and a half.

"Hi. Kylie went to bed about twenty minutes ago."

"Okay. How was it?"

"Good. We chatted in the car a little, but she was pretty tired when we got back. She grabbed a snack and went to bed."

"Cool." He pulled off his sneakers and removed his phone and his notebook from the pocket of his coat. Both things he would need tonight if he was going to get this article down while it was all fresh in his mind. He grabbed at the zipper of his coat and the blood left his face. *Not now.* This zipper was always a little finicky. *But please, not in front of Fin.*

Whatever, it was fine. He'd just leave his jacket on until she left and cut himself out of it if he had to.

He turned back to Fin and saw that she'd risen up from where she'd been leaning. For the first time that night, he really noticed her outfit. Silver jewelry, and a big old crystal around her neck, her hair in a braid that had dried a little frizzy since it had gotten soaked in the rain. But her clothes were unusual for her. Black stretchy pants and a black tunic. How had he not noticed that before? Why was she wearing all black? It was very unlike her.

"So...did you like the game?" he asked, because apparently he was a glutton for punishment. He asked because at heart, he was just a curious little boy still. He asked because he really wanted her to say yes.

"Meh," she said, her words splashing onto him like a shower he should have known was going to be ice-cold. "It was something to see, I guess. Kylie liked it, though. She told me."

Oh. Well, that was good news.

Fin stepped toward his coatrack, sliding into her long red coat, not bothering to pull her braid out from under it. Tyler experienced the same jolt he always felt when he saw that braid. He couldn't help but wonder if it would be tensile and slick, like glass, or soft and permeable, like fabric. He may not particularly like Fin, but that didn't mean he didn't want to poke a finger into her braid.

"Are you headed out again?" she interrupted his thoughts, cocking her head to one side as she looked at him curiously.

"What?"

"You're still wearing your coat."

"Oh." He frowned down at his coat and barely refrained from blushing. Tell her the truth and look like a child who'd gotten stuck inside his coat? Or lie and risk her knowing the truth anyway?

"I...can't get the zipper. It gets stuck sometimes."

He put a hand in his hair and tried to scratch away the chagrin. He expected judgment, maybe even just a touch of scorn in her expression. But all he saw was a slight purse to her mouth, like she was trying to keep from laughing. Her eyes were bright with something that looked suspiciously like humor, but Tyler knew that with Serafine St. Romain, one simply never knew.

To illustrate his plight, he tugged fruitlessly at the zipper. "I need another pair of hands."

"You know, I've been known to have a pair of hands."

He looked up at her but said nothing.

She sighed, rolling her eyes. "Let's do this."

"Okay." He stepped toward her and held the zipper pull out between them, trying not to think of his coat as a shield. "The problem is on the inside. See? Right here? All the fabric got—"

She leaned forward and peered down the front of the coat. "Got it. Okay. You yank there, keep it tight across there, and I'll get the zipper."

He did as she said, holding the coat taut as she pulled at the tab of the zipper. But it really was jammed. She grunted in frustration, scowling up at him like this whole thing was his master plan by design or something.

"Oh. Forget it. I'll just cut the damn thing off." He took a step away from her.

She tugged him back into place by the zipper of his coat. "Don't be ridiculous. We'll get it. Just—here—" She puffed out an annoyed breath and, to his surprise, slipped one hand inside his coat. There was a dark, warm cavity between his T-shirt and the coat where he was holding out the fabric, so she wasn't actually touching him, but still, Tyler held his breath as he watched her slender, gorgeous hand disappear inside his clothing.

He fought the urge to clear his throat, instead just holding the coat out like she'd told him. She jiggled the zipper from the inside now and after a tense moment, the zip came free.

Fin stepped back, quickly slipping her hands into the pockets of her own coat. "There."

"Wow. Thanks."

By the time Tyler had peeled his coat off and hung it up, he just caught the edge of her face as she turned toward his door. Was he nuts, or were her cheeks slightly pink? Did she get embarrassed? He couldn't picture it. Frankly, it didn't seem possible.

"Well. Thanks for babysitting."

He slid back into his shoes at the same time she did hers.

"What are you doing?"

He blinked at her. "Walking you down to your cab."

"What cab?"

"The one I called for you." He held up his phone.

"Don't be silly. You don't have to get me a cab. I'll just take the train. It's not far."

"I already called it on my way home. They'll charge me if I cancel. Just take the cab. You babysat for free."

"Do you have a death wish?"

"What?" Tyler swallowed. He was just trying to be nice by calling a cab. He couldn't win with this woman!

"She's fourteen. She'll chop your head off for calling it babysitting."

"Oh. Right." He cleared his throat. "Any more advice for tonight?"

He bustled her out the door and into the elevator.

"Yes, actually."

"I'm all ears," he said exhaustedly, thinking longingly of a hot shower and his laptop in bed while he tapped out his article.

"Don't go getting super into women's soccer."

"What?" The elevator dinged open at the lobby just as he whirled on her. "How did you—"

"Tyler, that one didn't take a psychic. Kylie was the one who called it. She said, 'I bet he's gonna get all into women's soccer and make us bond over it.'"

"And I'm supposed to heed that? No fourteen-year-olds want to bond. Aren't I supposed to be forcing her to bond?"

"I don't know. I just know that she's expecting you to go all buddy-buddy over soccer, and she's dreading it. So, my advice is don't force the issue."

Tyler was fuming as he followed Fin out onto the sidewalk. He checked his phone and saw that the car was idling out front. He stalked forward, nodded to the driver, and held open the back door for her.

"You're that mad at me just for trying to give you a heads-up about this?" Fin asked, her fingers gripping the top of the car door that separated them.

"No, Fin. I'm not mad at you. I'm just sick of feeling like a dope for wanting to get to know my sister. It's pretty much been the most prevalent feeling I've had for about two months now."

She stared at him, her expression inscrutable, but at the very last second, he could have sworn something almost soft passed across her light eyes. She turned too quickly for him to really make it out, then she was sliding into the back seat.

"Dope?" she said, cocking her head at him. "I wouldn't say *dope*."

"Dare I ask what you *would* say?" he asked dryly.

She bit her bottom lip, a split second of humor in her eyes.

"Goodnight, Tyler."

He closed the door, shaking his head at her, his jaw clenched against an unexpected smile.

CHAPTER NINE

"So...NOW YOU'RE playing house with Tyler?" Mary asked Fin as the two of them sat on the floor of her fancy-schmancy home-goods-and-furniture shop in Cobble Hill. Mary had put up the "back in twenty minutes" sign, flipped the lights off and now the two of them were hiding from the view of the sidewalk behind the register counter, eating the sandwiches that Fin had picked up on her way over.

It had been two days since the basketball game and Fin was still riding high.

She'd been focusing on the time spent with Kylie, which was why it surprised her so much when Tyler was the first thing that Mary zeroed in on after Fin filled her in on the whole story.

"I'm not playing house with Tyler," Fin insisted haughtily. "I'm—"

"Coparenting with him?"

"Mary!" Fin was both exasperated and amused by her new friend. Mary had this way about her. She was all sunshine and smiles. So much so that you didn't always happen to notice the very bitter medicine she was spooning down your throat.

It wasn't very many people who could get Serafine St. Romain to take bitter medicine, but Mary Trace was one of them. Originally one of Seb and Tyler's tribe, Fin had only met Mary a little over a year ago. New friends, but fast ones too. They were both straight shooters, both experts in their fields, both business owners and they both had a certain eye for the way physical objects should look and feel in a space.

There were few home-decorating shops that Fin was drawn to; most of them were too staged, too fake. But even before she'd known Mary personally, Fin had frequented this shop, occasionally buying a knickknack.

Mary had been very vocal about her appreciation for Fin's ability to help her rearrange the items that weren't selling well. The first time that Fin had ever visited her at Fresh, she'd absently rearranged some mugs that Mary had set out a few weeks prior on one of the shelves. Apparently the mugs started selling like hotcakes. Now, every few weeks, she paid Fin for an hour of her time to come in and make sure the energy in Fresh was, well, fresh.

But first, the sandwiches. "I'm not coparenting with him. None of this has anything to do with Tyler." Fin thought for a second, wondering if that was just an out-and-out lie. "Well, very *little* of it has to do with Tyler. Most of it has to do with Kylie. And me."

Mary still looked skeptical. "It's your way of helping out or something?"

Fin picked at some of the seeds that ran the edge of her sandwich. "I'm sure a shrink would tell you that I've been rejected as a foster parent enough times that I'm desperate to help any kid who happens to cross my path. But…Kylie and I really are kindred spirits."

"Have you gotten another rejection on your foster parent application since we last talked?"

Fin set her sandwich aside this time, her appetite souring. "Remember I told you that my neighbor volunteered to look over my file?"

"Right. She said that she might be able to give you some pointers on what to change."

"Yeah. She's gone through the process and had to apply twice so she figured she could help."

"And?"

Fin sighed, feeling the fresh sting of tears in the backs of her eyes. She waited until the sting had reduced to an ache, and the ache had reduced to a dull thud before she kept talking. "The news...wasn't good."

"What was wrong with your file?"

"Unfortunately, it's not the file. It's me." Fin couldn't help but squeeze the amethyst that hung around her neck, allowing it to do its subtle magic. "I'm single. Strike one. I'm self-employed and paid mainly in cash. Even though I report it all, apparently that's still strike two. I run most of my business from various unlicensed locations, like my apartment or my clients' homes. Strike three. I turned half my kitchen into an herb garden of sorts, which to anyone coming to inspect, looks like I'm growing weed. Strike four. I believe I'm a psychic. Strike five. I'm attractive and unattached, which means to them that I've either got some secret fatal flaw or I'm just using a kid to fill the hole in my heart while I wait for the right man to come along. Strike six. I'm out."

"I think you're only allowed three strikes."

"Then I guess I'm out twice."

Mary huffed out a big breath, making strands of her blond hair puff away from her face. She looked genuinely stymied. It was one of the things that Fin liked best about Mary. She wasn't a half listener. When you were discussing something with her, her entire focus and energy was on you. "Who knew it was so hard to foster a kid?"

"I mean, honestly, I feel terrible for even complaining

about the process, considering that in many ways, I believe that foster parents should be screened *more*. Most of the people who do this are good people, but there are always some bad seeds in there that should have been weeded out. Via learned about that firsthand."

Mary set aside her own sandwich, which alerted Fin to the seriousness of whatever Mary was about to say. Mary loved eating and rarely stopped once she had started. "Fin, I've never really asked before, but what was *your* experience with the foster system?"

Fin appreciated Mary's candor. She knew her well enough to know that Mary's question came from a desire to know more about Fin as a friend. There was very little morbid curiosity mixed in. Fin didn't mind sharing her past with people who truly cared about her.

"I bounced around to a few when I still lived in Louisiana."

"New Orleans?"

"No. I was out in the bayou at the time. Hence the accent. You don't usually hear quite this much Cajun twang in New Orleans."

"But I thought you'd lived in the city for a while?"

"I did. My last two years down south, when I was technically under my mother's care, we lived in New Orleans."

Mary grimaced in understanding. "You say *technically...*"

"She wasn't around much. I was mostly on my own. The best thing she ever did for me was sign me over to Aunt Jetty."

"Her sister?"

"Yup. That's when I moved up here to Brooklyn. A few months after that, Via moved in as Jetty's last foster daughter."

"Is that why you want to be a foster parent? Because of Jetty?"

Fin frowned. She wouldn't have put it like that. Every other time she'd tried to explain it, she'd always talked about her own experiences, how she'd wanted to give back to a system that hadn't let her drown when she was too young to stay afloat on her own.

But now that Mary put it like that, with such a simple question, the answer suddenly seemed obvious to her.

"Oh." Fin laughed absently and fiddled for a moment with the amethyst necklace. "I...guess that's a big part of it. I saw the way Jetty saved Via's life as a foster parent. And Via is pretty much the most important person in *my* life. I've never really realized that I've had the privilege of seeing the system from both sides. Both as a foster kid and witnessing my aunt be a foster mother. Hmm." She turned one raised eyebrow at her friend, her eyes narrowed. "Smart cookie."

"Just something to think about," Mary said, taking a comically large bite of her sandwich and making Fin laugh.

They let the conversation float away toward lighter topics and they found themselves clicking through the webpages of a few artists and furniture makers who hoped to sell their wares at Mary's shop.

A half hour later Mary walked Fin to the door. Fin knew, without having to ask, that there was something dancing on the tip of Mary's tongue. Words she wasn't sure she should say or not.

Standing with the door to the shop wide-open, Fin leaned in the jamb. "Spit it out, Mare."

"All right, all right, I'll just say it then. I don't want to be in your business, Fin. But after knowing you just a little bit, it occurs to me that you have a bit of a blind spot—Wait. Let me start over."

Fin had rarely seen Mary as flustered as she was right

now, tugging one hand through her fine blond hair and pinching the collar of her sweater closed against the chilly December air.

"I'll just say this." Mary swiped her hand definitively through the air. "Tyler is a good person."

Fin's brow furrowed again. Why were they back on the Tyler topic again?

"Okay... Sure."

"No." Mary vehemently shook her head. "When I say *good person* it's not a meaningless platitude. I mean truly, truly *good*. I believe it to the soles of my feet."

There was a beat of silence for a moment where Fin wasn't exactly sure what to say.

"I could give you examples, if you wanted," Mary prompted.

Fin burst out laughing. "I don't need examples. I believe you. Really, I do. I'm just trying to figure out why you're standing in the cold, determined to get me to understand this."

Mary shrugged. "He's my friend. And you are too, of course. But I know for sure that he's going to treat you well, and I just want to make sure that..."

"That I do the same."

"Bingo." Mary looked a little sheepish.

Fin leaned in for a hug. Mary jolted a tiny bit, because touching was something that Fin rarely did. Touching was extremely meaningful to her, imbibed with power and intimacy, and she treated the act with care and reverence. But Mary was a natural hugger. After a stiff second of surprise, her arms were wrapped warmly around Fin. Fin could feel, pouring off of Mary and into the world, Mary's good intention. She could feel Mary's love for her. And Mary's love for Tyler.

"I'll keep it in mind." Fin took a few steps back. "See you soon?"

"I'll give you and Via a call this weekend. Maybe we need a fancy dinner on the town or something."

"Sounds great."

Fin waved and headed down the street toward her train stop, but deviated at the last second, opting to walk home instead. Cobble Hill was far from her Ocean Avenue apartment. She'd have to walk all the way across Gowanus, Park Slope and through the park. But it was a brisk December day, early afternoon, and Fin decided she felt like a walk.

Mary's words played in her head, not because of what she'd been saying about Tyler, but because of what she'd inadvertently been saying about her.

"Blind spot about what?" Fin wondered to herself, wincing when she thought of the way Mary had straight-up told her that Tyler would always be kind to her, but that she couldn't be trusted to be kind in return.

Was that really true?

It was definitely true that she valued other things, like honesty and clarity, over kindness. So, did that translate into her being stone-cold?

Think of the thing you want the most in this world...

She blocked thoughts of her mother and tightened the buttons on her coat, though she was physically warm. The picturesque brownstones of Cobble Hill gave way to the longer avenues of bodegas and apartment buildings, fenced-off parking lots surrounding public schools. When the wind changed, she could smell the noxious soup of the Gowanus Canal. People passed her, but her head was down, her eyes on each step directly in front of her. Fin didn't always love Brooklyn, but at that particular moment, with too much on her mind and so many steps to take before she was home, Fin was grateful to live exactly where she did.

"TYLER, WHY ISN'T there beer in the fridge?"

Tyler, distracted by the recipe he was reading, swam up from the depths of his thoughts. He focused on Kylie, who stood in front of the open fridge.

"What?"

He hadn't been sleeping well since the basketball game. His editor had loved the piece he'd written, but had been on his ass for more of the same, and Tyler simply didn't see how the games were going to fit into his new schedule with Kylie. He couldn't be out of the house two to four nights a week. It wasn't fair to her. But also, they needed income. For things like the beef Stroganoff he was about to attempt. And the overnight field trip fees she'd asked for this morning. And—hold the phone. Had she just asked him about beer?

He blinked his scratchy eyes and tried to catch up.

She closed the fridge and turned to face him, her arms crossed over her chest and an almost ornery expression on her face.

"Yesterday, when we went out for dinner, you got a beer."

"And…that bothers you?" he guessed.

"No. It doesn't bother me…" She let her words hang, as if he was supposed to be able to stitch together her meaning from simply that. But…yeah. He was coming up with nothing.

"Then what the heck are we talking about here?"

She squinted at him, chewing the inside of her lip. "It's because of me, isn't it? You don't want to have beer in the house because you think I'll steal it or something?"

He barked out a laugh of surprise because that thought

had simply not occurred to him. Worried she'd steal the beer? "No! No. I just—" He cut himself off, knowing that the strength of the fishing line suspending this entire moment depended on whether or not he said the next part right. "I just, I know that your mom drank around you, and uh, maybe drugs? I guess I just wanted you to know that that isn't going to happen here. You don't have to worry about that in this house."

Something went flat in her dark eyes and she turned away from him, taking two steps back toward her room.

It had been weeks of painful silences between them with Tyler stepping dubiously around all sorts of fishing lines, and in a sick way, he was almost glad to have swiped one clean in half. He'd been feeling like there was no room for error with her and that kind of precision was exhausting.

She was walking away from him; he'd said something he shouldn't have—apparently—but that was weirdly much more his comfort zone than the awkward silences in which he stewed over the perfect words to say next. He wasn't a perfect-words kind of guy.

"Wait, Kylie."

She paused.

"Don't go. Look. I know sometimes I end up saying the wrong thing…"

She turned and shrugged like, *Yeah, what about it?*

He couldn't help but laugh. "But I guess I just want you to know that you can *tell me* if I've said the wrong thing. If what I just said hurt you or made you mad, well, you *have* to tell me." He knocked his knuckles against his skull. "This is more than just a pretty place to rest a hat. I can learn, Kylie."

She pursed her lips and looked at him like he was an idiot, but the expression seemed like a win. She was trying not to smile, he was almost certain. "Yikes. You get the ladies with jokes like that?"

Tyler let out a puff of an unexpected chuckle. She'd never razzed him before. "Not lately."

She gave him a skeptical look, like she doubted the fact that he'd ever had the ability to get girls. "I'm going to finish my homework before dinner."

Okay. So. Conversation over.

Before it had even really started. He watched her go and sagged back against the counter.

The kid was a master at getting information while revealing nothing herself.

He turned back to the recipe, read it once more and started pulling things out of the fridge. For a moment, he stared at the empty shelf where he usually kept a six-pack of beer. They'd had a quarter of a real conversation, a world record for them.

CHAPTER TEN

"Hey, Seb? You home?"

"Back here!" Sebastian shouted from his place at the stove.

"Oh, is Tyler coming for lunch?" Via asked, a hostess's panic in her tone. "I don't think we have enough food."

Sebastian chuckled at the look of pure horror on Via's face. "Baby, it's fine. I didn't know he was coming so there's no way he can be offended that we didn't make lunch for him."

Fin, watching all this with a raised brow, shuffled the cards and waited for Tyler to burst into the room, bringing his ridiculously loud energy with him.

They heard him wrestling with his shoes in the front hall. When he entered the kitchen, Fin's hands stuttered on the cards.

He was...very sweaty.

It was brisk outside, probably forty degrees, but sunny, and he'd obviously gone for a jog.

Well, from the looks of things, it had been more of a sprint than a jog. His pale blue T-shirt stuck to his chest. She could see straight through it to the chest hair underneath. He wore joggers and a stocking cap, his earbuds draped over one shoulder. She'd never seen his color so high, his chest heaving in and out. She'd seen Tyler enjoy himself before. She'd seen him tease, she'd seen him loose. But she'd never seen him quite so *relaxed* before.

To her own chagrin, for just the flash of a second, Fin wondered what Tyler might look like right after he was finished having sex. It was only an instant, not longer than the irregular heartbeat it elicited from her, but the image was potent. She, for some strange reason, could perfectly picture him on his back in a bed, sheets askew, his hair damp with sweat, his eyes blurry and blissed out, one arm flung over his head, the other hand firmly clamped over the ass or breast of whoever he was with—

"Oh." His eyes landed on Fin and again her hands stuttered on the cards. "Hi."

"Hi." She wondered briefly if he was thinking about the zipper of his coat.

"Didn't mean to interrupt your tarot card reading, Via," Tyler said, snarky, but not unfriendly.

She let her irritation at Tyler rush through her, a welcome, grounding feeling. *This* was how she was supposed to feel about Tyler. Irritated.

Via laughed. "These are just playing cards. Fin doesn't do tarot. We're about to play gin rummy. Did you wanna stay and play?"

To Fin's surprise, Tyler actually looked a little regretful when he said no. "I can't. I've gotta get back, shower and get some lunch together before I go get Kylie from her meeting with her social worker."

"You could eat here," Seb suggested.

"No thanks, I— Hold the phone, are *you* cooking?"

"I can cook!" Sebastian insisted. "How come no one thinks I can cook? I fed Matty for years before Via came along."

Via and Fin made eye contact, both of them hiding their smiles.

"Right," Tyler said soothingly, as if he had no interest in

poking the bear. "Even so, I'm going to have to decline. I just came by to see if you still had that external hard drive I loaned you? I need to back up my columns. Haven't done it in a while."

"Sure. It's in the closet somewhere."

Tyler went to follow Sebastian and then paused in the doorway. "Where's Matty?"

"Joy's house," Via answered.

"And Crabby?" Tyler looked around in confusion.

Fin cleared her throat and pointed down at her feet where Crabby, usually spastic and so excited about the world he could barely live, slept peacefully.

"Figures," Tyler mumbled, rolling his eyes to the sky. "Traitor," he said to Crabby, winking at Via.

In a move that she hadn't performed since perhaps age six, Fin couldn't help but stick her tongue out at Tyler. He blinked at her for a moment before his eyebrows rose and he stuck his tongue out right back at her.

"Here you go." Sebastian came back and slapped the three-inch hard drive into Tyler's hand. Tyler, who'd still been looking at Fin, his navy eyes strangely clear to her, even from across the room, broke the eye contact and zipped up the hard drive into his pocket.

"All right, kiddies," he said. "Enjoy your burned grilled cheeses."

"Scram," Sebastian said darkly. "And don't forget basketball tomorrow."

Tyler waved at the rest and then was gone, out the front door as soon as his shoes were on.

Fin could feel Via's eyes on the side of her face but suddenly found shuffling the cards took up all of her attention. She focused her eyes on the cards, the blurring red and black dividing, slapping together, stacked neatly, newly

combined in a fresh pattern. She thought about the right-
ness of that. Those cards all mixed up together. That was
the way they were supposed to be, the only way you could
fairly play the game.

FIN HAD TO admit that the chicken curry was good. Not
grand, but good enough to have seconds. She'd been surprised to get the invite from Tyler for dinner, a few days
after seeing him at Seb's. She'd been under the impression
that she'd only be invited to do things that took place outside of the house.

She was thrilled to hang out with Kylie in her natural
habitat.

But on the other hand, that meant spending more time
in Tyler's home. Which was kind of a minefield. His energy, though not the preppy, entitled, douchey energy she'd
originally expected, was just so freaking loud.

It overwhelmed everything in the room. Swallowed everything down. Including Kylie. Serafine hadn't seen her
room, but there was very little trace of Kylie having made
this place her home.

Looking around, Fin didn't even see Kylie's school bag.
Or her shoes, for God's sake.

After dinner, which had been largely a quiet affair, Fin
would have normally volunteered to do the dishes. But she
wanted to avoid touching too many of Tyler's belongings.
It was the same idea as folding a lot of heavily perfumed
scarves. If she did the task, she'd go home with the scent of
perfume on her hands. And she really didn't want to take
Tyler home with her.

So, bad manners and all, she thanked Tyler for dinner
and then left him to the dishes and wandered after Kylie,
who was making a beeline for her room.

"Nice room," Fin said, standing in the hallway and peeking in.

"Oh. Thanks." Kylie, realizing that she had a visitor, opened the door wider and stepped back to sit on the bed. "You can come in if you want."

Fin sidled in and sat on a leather desk chair that looked out of place in the room. She realized her mistake immediately. This wasn't Kylie's chair. This was definitely Tyler's chair. A chair that he'd spent a great deal of time in. A strange electricity jolted through Fin, almost like the tingling in her arms and legs before she'd passed out when she'd been sick with the flu that one time. She stood and instead wandered over to the windowsill. But...her body still tingling from having sat in Tyler's chair, all Fin could see as she looked around was Tyler. He was everywhere in this room too.

She blocked him from her mind and turned her focus onto Kylie. "So. How're you getting used to Brooklyn? I know it can be a lot."

Fin thought of the first time she'd ever ridden over the Manhattan Bridge, her eyes on the East River so far below. It had looked far less muddy than the Mississippi. Her eyes had tracked to the side, to what had to be the Brooklyn Bridge on their right, disorienting in its instantly recognizable familiarity. Beyond that, shockingly green and shockingly small in the distance, had been the Statue of Liberty winking in the sun. She'd just gotten off the plane from New Orleans, barreling through a new city with Aunt Jetty, whom she barely knew, at her side.

She hadn't expected New York, so overbearing and rude and closed off, to give up one of its secrets for free like that. She'd expected to have to pry every beautiful thing from its clawed-off, East Coast fist. But there she was, Lady Liberty, standing at attention, a lovely shade of sage. It was fitting to Fin that she was facing away.

"Brooklyn," Aunt Jetty had said, still watching her niece with all-seeing eyes that Fin had wished she'd point somewhere else for a while. "There's psychics there too, if you're curious. And good food. Where we live there's lots of Italian food. Some Russian too."

We.

The word had hurt.

Fin's mother spoke Cajun where the word *oui* translated to mean *yes*. But over the years that yes had often disintegrated into a no. Just as Fin's *we* with her mother had slowly disintegrated into an *I*.

It had been a terribly long time since Fin had been a part of a *we* with someone. But that *we*, with Jetty, came with an entire, terrible city. It came with winters and no more NOLA. That *we* had not included her mother.

Kylie sighed, and it brought Fin back to the present. Kylie looked slightly bored, like she was resigning herself to having this tired conversation with yet another adult. "It's fine. I don't mind the city."

Fin nodded, reaching into her pocket, her fingers brushing against the small, loose crystals she carried there like pocket change. An idea struck. "Do you like jewelry?"

Kylie, surprised at the conversation shift, raised her eyebrows. Today, her hair, curling at the temples, was still flattened from where she'd worn her winter cap. "I guess. My mom has a lot of it. I don't really."

"I make jewelry. Like this." Fin pulled her crystal necklace out from under the collar of her shirt. It was a milky orange crystal affixed to a silver chain.

"Pretty," Kylie said, her eyes flitting back up to Serafine's face.

"Thanks. I make a lot of it. I sell it too."

"But I thought Tyler said you were a fortune-teller."

Fin rolled her eyes. "Of course he'd describe it that way."

For some reason, that made Kylie laugh. "How would you describe what you do?"

"I describe it differently to different people," Fin said with a shrug. "But to you… I guess I'd say that I work with people's energy. I can read them well. Sometimes it helps me see problem areas in their life that they're blind to."

"Can you see the future?"

Comfortable with the subject and thrilled with the interest she saw in Kylie's freckled features, Fin tried to explain. "Not the way you're probably imagining. More than anything I see patterns. Sometimes the paths that people take are obvious. You can often tell where someone is going based on where they've been."

Kylie's brow furrowed down hard as she stared at her own crisscrossed legs. "I've noticed that about people too."

Fin knew, without a doubt, that Kylie was thinking of her mother. She felt the cold, sharp ache of the girl's pain. Even from all the way across the room.

Fin pulled the crystals out of her pocket. There were five of them, all of them smaller than a dime. They'd traveled in her pocket for years. Each one was a different kind of crystal. One pink, one silverish, one clear with internal fingers of gold, one green and one dead black. Every day she transferred them to whatever she was going to wear that day. They were warm from her body and felt as much a part of her as her fingernails did.

"If you pick one of these, I'll make you a necklace or bracelet from its type of crystal."

There were many crystal and rock shops in New York City, one of the things that Fin loved about the city, and her personal supply of gems and crystals was hearty. Kylie, seeming to understand inherently that she was supposed to look at the gems in Fin's hand and not touch them, folded her hands under her chin and leaned over to get a better look.

"I like that one."

Fin kept her reaction smooth. She knew well enough it was no coincidence that the crystal Kylie had been drawn to was the silvery hematite. It was a crystal associated with defense. Justice. And, most hopefully, healing.

"Necklace or bracelet?"

Kylie looked up, her dark eyes slightly uncomfortable as she pushed back the shock of red hair that had fallen in her face. "Is one more expensive than the other?"

"Normally they're priced differently. But this is my gift to you. A welcome-to-Brooklyn gift."

Kylie looked like she wanted to argue but after a second, she snapped her mouth closed. "Necklace then. Please."

"I'll bring it by in a few days."

Fin slipped her crystals back in her pocket and stretched. "I should head back home."

"Fin?"

"Yeah?"

"Never mind," Kylie said after a beat. "Goodnight."

Fin paused. "See you soon."

Fin ducked her head into the kitchen, saw it was empty and clean and headed to the living room. There, stretched out on the couch, his eyes closed, was Tyler.

She wanted to creep past quickly, but something made her pause. Her eyes snagged on him. She'd never seen him in repose before. Most people curled up when they were resting. A bent leg or arms folded under their heads. But Tyler laid on his back, his legs crossed at the ankle and perfectly straight. His hands were folded over his stomach.

Fin could perfectly picture him napping like that under a weeping willow, a book folded over his face to keep the sunshine off his eyelids. How had she never noticed just how long he was?

Maybe because she'd usually seen him compared to Sebastian. Who was maybe an inch taller than Tyler and much wider, more barrel-chested. Tyler wasn't skinny, but he was a bit lanky. He had wide shoulders and narrow hips and stem to stern, he did not fit on that couch. His head was crooked up on the arm in what looked like a very uncomfortable position.

She could feel the calmness of his rest. If he wasn't sleeping, he was nearing it. Not wanting to wake him, for myriad reasons, she slipped quietly into her shoes and coat and crept out.

For the second time in as many days, Fin opted for the long walk home. It was 8:45 on a cold December night and anywhere else in the world, the sky would have been as black as a chalkboard. In Brooklyn, though, with the clouds in a thick sheet overtop and the city lights reflecting down on her, Fin had a kind of orangish night-light to walk her home. She wove down some of the more residential blocks instead of walking up Flatbush, which was busy with traffic and smoggy with exhaust. It took her an hour to get from Tyler's building in Midwood to her place on Ocean Avenue.

She took the elevator up and breathed a sigh of relief as she stepped into her own space. It smelled like sage and mint with just a touch of lavender.

Happy to be home, she went right into her bedroom and took off all her jewelry. She didn't need her talismans when she was in her own home.

And then, even though it was getting close to bedtime, she headed into her kitchen to see about her makeshift herb

garden. The scents of fresh herbs inundated her, and Serafine breathed deeply, an irascible joy rising within her.

She took down the tarragon she'd put up to dry a few
days before and carefully bottled it into two small glass
jars. One of them she'd take to Via for cooking, and one
of them she'd keep for herself. Tarragon was a useful herb
in many of the kitchen spells that Fin was learning how to
work. She wasn't much of a cook, but as she'd been proving
for most of her life, there was plenty more a person could
use a kitchen for than just cooking.

Her mind flashed back to her evening. To the meal that
Tyler had cooked for her. Good, solid home cooking. She'd
left without saying goodbye.

Frowning to herself, Fin fixed a cup of her personal
blend of sleepytime tea, and grabbed a chocolate Popsicle
from her freezer.

She settled into her living room and pulled out her laptop to watch some Netflix. Pulling up a rom-com she'd
seen a hundred times before, Fin settled back, not needing
a blanket in her hot apartment, but feeling cuddled up all
the same. She delighted in the simple pleasure of a swallow
of hot tea followed by a lick of cold Popsicle.

What more could she want—

Tyler is a really good person.

Mary's voice suddenly echoed in Fin's head and she
frowned.

Blind spot, Mary had said.

Blind spot about what? Tyler? Who he really was?

She frowned.

Going back over the night in her head, she zoomed back
to the dinner, where Tyler had barely said two words. His
hair had been perfect, his face shaved, his collared shirt
immaculately ironed. Had she let all that fool her into miss-

ing the dark circles under his eyes? The way his shoulders had sagged?

He'd grocery shopped for that meal. Fresh ingredients. She'd seen the recipe book open on the counter. He'd made it. From scratch. For his sister and for her.

Why, oh, why, did she continually think of him as a selfish person?

Tyler really is a good person.

If she'd seen a still of that night, instead of having sat there in person, she'd have seen an overworked guardian doing his best to make things all right for his sister. And honestly, his best wasn't too shabby.

He could have been serving Kylie microwaved meals, and Fin wouldn't have thought twice about it. But he wasn't. He was taking her to basketball games. He was allowing Fin to get to know her. He was grocery shopping, home cooking dinners on school nights.

Was it possible that she really thought so little of a man simply because he'd asked her out on a date months ago? It was depressing to think that all it took to plummet her opinion of someone was them proclaiming interest in her. What did that even say about her?

Fin got up, went to her coat closet and dug her cell phone out of her coat pocket. Finishing the Popsicle off in one last chunk, she huffed herself back to the couch, frowning at her phone, at herself, at this entire predicament.

She pulled up Tyler's number and sent a quick text.

I just wanted to say thank you for dinner. It was delicious. Sorry I didn't help with dishes. And sorry I left without saying goodbye.

There. Simple as that. She sent the text and waited for the weight of her uncomfortable guilt to alleviate a little bit.

It didn't.

Still frowning, she turned back to the movie and tried to lose herself in it.

She jolted when her phone buzzed a second later. She was surprised he'd texted back so quickly. She thought for sure he'd either still be snoozing on his couch or passed out in bed by now.

You're welcome. And don't worry. I didn't expect you to do the dishes.

Hmm? Maybe he was one of those people who didn't like guests to putter around in his space—

You don't exactly strike me as the housework type.

His second text came in and a yelp of outrage escaped Fin. "What the hell is that supposed to mean?" she muttered as she quickly typed the words and sent them off.

Moments later he'd texted back. Oh, come on. Don't pretend that right this very minute you aren't laying on a cushion held up by four shirtless men feeding you grapes and fanning you.

Despite herself, she laughed aloud. I think you're confusing me with Cleopatra.

She looked around her small, clean apartment. In reality, she spent a lot of time on housework, despite the occasionally rock-dusty kitchen. She very much believed in "cluttered space, cluttered mind." And though she had a lot of knickknacks, decorations and emblems around her house, everything was in its right place.

Wouldn't be the first time, he texted her.

Wouldn't be the first time he'd confused her with Cleopatra?

And then he texted her a picture of Cleopatra from an old movie. She quirked her head to one side and observed the long black hair, the golden crown and unsmiling, regal features. He thought she looked like that?

Come on, he texted, you don't see the resemblance?

She'd like to think that she smiled more than that, but then, looking back on her time with Tyler, she supposed she could see why he'd think of her like this. Untouchable, ruthless, unforgiving.

Blind spot.

Would it kill her to loosen up around him a little bit? Maybe she could hold him at, like, ten paces. She'd still be safe and maybe he wouldn't be quite so kicked-puppy.

She sighed, rolling her eyes at herself and decided to play around a little bit. She pulled up a picture and texted it to him. Better Cleopatra than this:

It was a photo of James Spader from *Pretty in Pink*. Tyler really didn't look anything like him, but at first glance they had the same preppy douchebag vibe.

You wound me, he texted back.

She laughed, reading the vibe off the text and knowing, in her heart, that he'd laughed when he'd seen what she'd sent him. It was then, and only then, that she felt some of the weight of her guilt over her behavior lift off of her. She hadn't ruined everything; she hadn't injured him unnecessarily.

She laughed again as she looked back at their texts and tried to picture having this conversation in person.

A static shock zapped her when she moved her leg against a velvet cushion and she jolted. She felt almost like she'd been jump-scared by the violins in a scary movie.

The fact was, having this jokey conversation was making her nervous system flare.

Hey, I was thinking. You need to give Kylie her own space.

The second she even typed Kylie's name, Serafine felt her blood calm. Kylie was a safe subject between them.

What are you talking about? She has her own bedroom.

No. I mean in the rest of your house. You need to let her leave a footprint on your space.

I repeat: what are you talking about.

She rolled her eyes. It was silly of her to have forgotten what a skeptic he was. Serafine brought up his home in her mind's eye. She brought a hand to her cheek when she realized that she was blushing just a little bit. Well, that sort of made sense, considering that every inch of Tyler's home was so unusually, palpably *him* that just stepping in the front door felt like stepping into his bedroom.

How to explain that to him?

Let's just say that your place is very YOU. Your energy is slathered all over every surface.

I don't know what that means, but somehow I'm positive I've been insulted.

Serafine found herself laughing again. Had she just inadvertently insulted him? She looked back at her use of the word *slathered*. She tried again.

She needs to be able to make the place her own. Otherwise she's not going to be comfortable there.

There was a long pause before he texted again in which Serafine considered getting up for another Popsicle. If Tyler were another person, she might have pushed at the energetic space between them, tried to ascertain whether he was pausing because he was searching for words, or distracted, or unhappy. But not wanting to upset the delicate ceasefire they seemed to have come to, she merely waited, attempting to be patient.

You act like I'm the one locking her in her bedroom every night. Trust me, that's all her.

Maybe make some design changes. Ask her opinion. Or change around the living room so that she can study out there.

She paused, her fingers hovering over her phone. She typed the next part in a jumble. And definitely move that leather chair out of her room. Give her something that's completely her own.

What's wrong with my chair?

Though she'd been trying her hardest not to think about what it had felt like to sit in that chair, the memory of it was unstoppable now. It was like trying not to think of a pink elephant. She couldn't avoid remembering the warm buzz of energy that had enveloped her as the back of her legs had hit the smooth leather, the wooden arms of the chair almost warm under the palms of her hands. It had been like sitting down in a dark room only to realize that Tyler was already sitting there. Almost like she'd accidentally sat in his lap.

She got that nervous-system-juddering feeling again and shied away from it immediately.

Strike that, actually, he texted a moment later. I don't even want to know what you hate about my chair. Ignorance is bliss.

Have you been steering clear of patronizing her with women's soccer?

He immediately sent her back an eyeroll emoji. Some of us call that having common interests. Tell me this, Cleopatra. Do you get off on chastising me or something?

She pursed her lips for a moment and then burst out laughing. It wasn't that the text was even all that funny. But it made a giddiness rise up within her and it burst out of her in laugh form.

She worked a few different responses in her head, but anything that was funny in return seemed too flirty.

In the end the best she could come up with was, I'll work on it.

A few minutes rolled past and Fin couldn't help but check her phone again and again to see if he'd texted her back yet. Were they done? Was he sleeping again? Damn, she should have said something sweeter. The words *I'll work on it* looked so terse as she reread them.

Her phone buzzed in her hand and she almost fumbled it.

I'll move the chair.

She blinked at her phone for a minute, turned off the movie and then went to brush her teeth, inexplicably smiling all the way to the bathroom.

CHAPTER ELEVEN

"AUNTIE FIN? ARE YOU named after lettuce?"

Tyler, sitting at Seb and Via's dinner table, nearly choked on the meatball that was in his mouth at that very minute.

"What?" Fin asked, leaning around both Mary and Kylie in order to see Matty.

"Well, your last name is St. Romain, right? And isn't this—" he waggled the bit of salad at the end of his fork "—named romaine? Just like you?"

There was a sparkle in the little boy's eye.

Tyler reached a fist across the table toward Matty. "Good one, broski."

"Please refrain from referring to my son as a broski," Seb said, restraining his smile. "And, Matty, quit philosophizing about your salad and *eat* your salad, please."

The conversation hummed on around him, and Tyler just kept eating, his thoughts whirring. Halfway through the meal, Fin got up and inched behind the table to get to the kitchen, the sleeve of her dress accidentally brushing the back of Tyler's neck as she went past. He stiffened at her familiar sagey lavenderish scent. Even though he wasn't into her anymore, that scent of hers still had a bit of a hold on him. There was just something so earthy about it.

Generally, he liked the scent of perfume on a woman. Something fancy and bottled and sophisticated. Until he'd met Fin, he'd associated the scent of essential oils with hippies, or an attempt to cover body odor. But now, he could honestly say that the scent of herbs was sexy, interesting… and just a little bit agitating. He scooted his chair in so that she could get past.

"More water, anyone?" she asked.

"Will you grab me a beer?" Sebastian asked.

Tyler couldn't help but glance at Kylie, who raised her eyebrows sassily back at him. He rolled his eyes at her.

"Me too, Fin, please," Tyler called.

Kylie gave Tyler a smug look.

"The store's been swamped," Mary said in a non sequitur, cutting off Via as she asked Matty about his day at school.

Tyler nearly groaned. Mary had this rehearsed, quasi-casual look on her face that he just knew Kylie was going to see through in a hot second. Mary was the most genuine person that Tyler knew. And by nature of that, she was also the worst actress he'd ever met. Lying? Playing a part? For Mary that was like asking a farsighted person to read minuscule print casually. Her face, though attempting to play it cool, looked exactly like she was trying to recite a cue card from across the room.

"Yup," she sighed dramatically. "The dang holiday season. I thought surely it might ease up this year. But alas…"

Alas? *Alas?* Kylie was going to sniff out this set-up from a mile away.

"It's really that bad?" Via asked in confusion. "Haven't you hired any seasonal help? You usually do, right?"

"She up and quit on me. Just like that!" Mary snapped her fingers.

When Mary had called him yesterday to complain about the unexpected quitting of her seasonal help, an idea had hit Tyler like a bread truck. The perfect solution to all of his problems.

Well. Not *all* of his problems considering he hadn't gotten laid in months, and this was definitely not going to fix that. But a huge portion of his problems would be fixed, at least temporarily, if Kylie took the dang bait that Mary was ostentatiously whipping around.

"So," Mary said, and Tyler winced as he realized that she was also now speaking in some sort of accent he couldn't quite identify. "I really need someone who can help out on the after-scho—" She cut herself off just in time. "After-*work* rush. A person who is available say, five p.m. to 9:30 or 10:00 a few days a week and wouldn't mind making a few extra bucks."

A cold beer touched Tyler's cheek and he jumped, twisting in his seat to see Fin holding out his drink for him, a wry expression on her face that told him she'd figured out exactly what he'd cooked up with Mary.

He gave her that raised eyebrow right back, picturing his own face as that imperiously eyebrowed emoji she loved to send, and reached up for his beer. For just half a second, his fingers overlapped with hers on the bottle, and he didn't feel the cold glass, the condensation. He felt only the slices of heat of her slim fingers against his, smelled only lavender.

Then he felt her flinch under him and he deftly removed the bottle from her hand and turned back around without so much as another glance her way. How many times and in how many ways was she going to have to remind him that she was completely and utterly uninterested in him? They'd finally started to get friendly, even joking around over text. He didn't need to go screwing things up by imagining electric moments between them. Tyler figured it was because he was so hard up. He hadn't gotten laid in an entire season, and now he was pretending to feel sparks when a woman handed him a beer. Yikes. Didn't get much sadder than that.

"Anyone know anyone who fits that description?" Mary prompted him, her eyes wide and slightly panicked.

Right. Crap. He'd missed his cue and now Mary was floundering. He had to get things back on track.

"Uh. Actually," he said, and then cleared his throat because his voice was rusty. "Kylie, would you have any interest in an after-school job like that?"

Kylie jolted and Tyler considered it a minor miracle that the kid wasn't rolling her eyes at the adult antics taking place. Was she actually buying this?

"A job at Mary's shop?"

"It's a really great space," Fin said casually, apparently the only one among them who could actually pull off a ruse like this. "I think you'd like it. Great energy. Cute shop and in a nice part of town. Have you been to Cobble Hill yet?"

"You'd like it," Mary prompted. Then she cocked her head to the side. "Well, actually, I don't know you quite well enough to know what you'd like. But *I* like it."

Kylie laughed at that, seemingly a little charmed by Mary. She turned to Tyler. "You think it would be all right? Legally?"

It made him sad that a fourteen-year-old thought to consider stuff like that. "Uh, we'd have to talk to your social worker." Tyler had already done so this morning and gotten the okay. They would have to get her working papers and also the social worker was putting a strict fifteen-hour weekly cap on things in order to make sure Kylie didn't fall behind on homework. "But the legal working age in New York is fourteen, so it should probably be fine as long as you can still get your schoolwork done."

"I only need help maybe three days a week," Mary

rushed in, a little overhelpfully. "So, I wouldn't be taking up *all* your time."

As world-wise as Kylie sometimes seemed, this whole scheme seemed to be going straight over her head. Anyone a little older might have raised eyebrows at the fact that Mary, apparently drowning in work and in desperate need of help, would only be looking for someone to help out three days a week. The truth was, Mary was going to have to hire someone in addition to Kylie. This was a considerable favor to Tyler. Especially considering the fact that she'd already agreed to make Kylie's work schedule line up with the Nets home game schedule and had already agreed to take Kylie home after work any night that Tyler couldn't pick her up.

Basically, Mary had agreed to pay to be Kylie's babysitter without Kylie having to feel condescended to. Tyler knew he should be buying Mary a diamond necklace for Christmas, a house in Vail, a car. She'd officially clawed her way to the top of the Best Friend of All Time list.

"I don't think schoolwork would be a problem," Kylie said slowly. "But… I've never worked in a shop before."

"Maybe we could do a trial period, Mary? Try it for a day or two and see if it suits you two?" Tyler suggested.

"Perfect!" Mary chirped, a little too loud, a little too high. She looked deeply relieved that the whole thing had gone to plan. "How's Monday?" she croaked, sagging back into her chair. Was that sweat on her brow?

Tyler bit the inside of his cheek to keep from laughing. "Works for me and my schedule. Ky?"

She blinked for a second. "Works for me too."

"Great!"

"MARY, YOU SLY DOG," Sebastian said a little while later, after dinner. The adults were reclining in the living room and

Kylie, much to Tyler's surprise, had volunteered to walk Matty and Crabby to an ice-cream shop down the block. Well, down the block by New York standards, which meant at least a twelve-minute walk.

"Oh my god. I'm *still* having heart palpitations." She dramatically clutched at her heart and sagged back into the couch where she was nestled next to Fin.

"That was a pretty good idea you two had," Via said, plopping herself down into Sebastian's lap where he sat in an armchair.

Tyler, not having wanted to crowd the ladies on the couch, stretched out on the floor in front of the TV, his beer balanced on his chest and his head propped up by couch pillows. He watched the multicolored reflection of the blinking Christmas tree lights on the ceiling and tried hard not to think about all the ways he wasn't prepared for a holiday of this magnitude with Kylie.

"Ty?" Seb said, nudging Tyler's foot with his own.

"Hmm?" Tyler lifted his head and took a sip of his forgotten beer.

"Via asked if you knew that Kylie had wanted a job."

"Oh." He dropped his head back down and watched the red-and-green lights reflect on the ceiling again. "I wasn't sure. But…I know she's got some issues around money so I figured she'd jump at a chance to earn some on her own."

He could feel Fin's eyes on the side of his face. And it wasn't the normal nudge of another person's gaze. This? This was different. Her eyes were like fingertips of ice lightly tracing his profile.

She'd been the one to tell him that Kylie was sensitive about money.

"She's got issues with money? The same kid who was

pumping you for fifty bucks every single time you needed her to do anything?"

Tyler blinked. *Right.* He'd almost forgotten that Kylie used to do that. The extortion seemed so unlike her now.

"She hasn't done that since…" He racked his brain. "Thanksgiving, I guess."

Huh. Since they'd come to Brooklyn. She'd done it all the time in Columbus but here she'd pretty much cut it out immediately. He wondered why and came up empty.

"So, how are things going with her?" Via asked softly.

This time, Tyler couldn't help but glance at Fin. She was watching him still and Tyler thought of the bejeweled tiger again. Her eyes, so eerily light in color, glittered like two aquamarines set against the twisted perfection of her braid. No. She wasn't a tiger, he corrected himself. He'd gotten it right the other night. She was Cleopatra. An imperious, untouchable queen who couldn't help but surveil her kingdom with the confidence of the most powerful woman on earth.

He sighed, his eyes bouncing back to Via. "Good," he answered vaguely. He glanced back at Fin's bright gaze and caught the almost imperceptible eye roll there. He sighed. She was right. There was no reason to hide behind machismo right now. He was among friends. Well, he was among Sebastian and Mary, true friends. There was also Via, who he had to admit had homemade-lasagna-ed herself right into friendship territory. And Fin, who was decidedly not a friend, but also wasn't an enemy anymore either.

"Hard," he amended a moment later, his eyes still on Fin's.

"Has the social worker helped you at all?" Sebastian asked, drawing Tyler's attention.

Tyler shrugged, taking a sip of his beer. "She's technically Kylie's social worker, so she pawned me off to this counselor, who put me through a ten-hour course a few weeks ago. It was pretty much useless. A bunch of pamphlets and shit like that. They all say do stuff with her, talk to her, follow through on your commitments."

"That doesn't sound so useless," Via said gently.

"I mean, the information isn't terrible, but none of them tell me *how* to do any of that shit."

"What do you mean you don't know how?" Seb asked incredulously. "You're the most tenacious person I've ever met. Ty, when we first were becoming friends, I had to *un*-invite you from my house because you were coming over too often. Where's that guy in all this?"

The group laughed and Tyler grinned. It was true. Tenacity and bullheadedness were two of the main ways that he'd gotten all the things he was most proud of in his life. His friendship with Sebastian, his job with the Nets, his beautiful apartment, his—albeit currently withered—status with women. "Eh," he grunted. "I think I left my mojo in Columbus."

Tyler sat up and leaned his elbows on his knees. He looked at no one but could feel Fin's icy eyes on his face.

"You're right that my natural instinct is to push. But I'm scared of pushing her too far." Tyler set his beer aside and scraped his palms over his face. "She did not want to leave Columbus. And here we are in Brooklyn. And I'm just tiptoeing around, holding my breath outside of her school, hoping she comes out and gets on the train with me."

He picked up his beer and gulped at it, hoping to clear the lump that had gathered in his throat. Fin's silence was unending, and he couldn't help but read into it. She was the one who'd tried so hard to be a foster parent. Who would have wanted this kind of change in her life. She could probably think of a million and two ways to reach Kylie and here he was, admitting to absolutely failing at connecting with someone he was blood-related to.

"I don't think she's going to run away, Ty," Mary said after a minute. "You might not notice it, but she sticks pretty close to you."

He looked up. The distance he felt from Kylie was so tangible, so ever-present, that Mary's words did not compute. "What do you mean?"

"Well, maybe not when you're in your own house and she goes into her room. But when you're out and about, I've noticed that she's always right by your side. Even when you first got here tonight, she was right next to you all the way through dinner."

"She took Matty and Crabby to get ice cream," Tyler pointed out.

"Because *you* suggested it," Fin cut in. It was the first thing that she'd said the entire conversation and Tyler tried not to make her single sentence be the most meaningful thing he'd heard all night. But it made his heart skip to hear it. He went back over the moment with Kylie. Matty had been begging his parents to take him to get ice cream, and they'd said no. Tyler had suggested that Matty and Kylie go together. He'd showed her how to get there on Google Maps. She'd nodded, looking nervous, but had done it anyway.

Huh.

Maybe Kylie didn't think he was the biggest fuckup on the face of the planet. What a delightful thought. He'd been thinking of himself as the one that no one wanted for so long, the idea of someone wanting only him was disorienting.

"You know," Seb said. "Not to pile on the advice here…"

Tyler leaned back against the cushions. "Go ahead and pile drive me."

Seb laughed. "But I don't think that the way you inter-act with Kylie has to be that different than the way you in-teract with Matty."

Tyler pulled a face. "Poor, poor Sebastian, you sweet, innocent soul. You will be so utterly shocked and devas-tated when Matty reaches teenagerhood. You have abso-lutely no idea that children and teenagers are completely different species."

"Obviously, but come on, teenagers are still children. I'm serious here. I'm not saying you should sit on Kylie's back and make her eat carpet fuzz the way you do with Matty."

Tyler laughed.

"But think about when it's time to get Matty to do some-thing, go to school, eat dinner, leave the park, whatever it is. Do you take no for an answer? No. You're firm. You set boundaries. You confidently know what's best for him, and even if he throws a fit, he does what you say in the end."

"The difference is that with Matty, I actually *know* what's best for him. With Kylie, I don't."

"Yes," Fin said, her head leaning on one hand, her face lit from the side by lamplight. "You do."

Just then, the front door opened. The kids had returned.

EVEN THROUGH THE chaos of Crabby bounding back into the room, his tongue askew, his tail whipping every knee and shin he scrabbled past, Fin kept her eyes on Tyler. He was sitting up, turning around, smiling at Kylie as she came in, balancing extra ice creams in both hands.

"I wasn't sure who wanted some so…"

Kylie seemed embarrassed by her gesture to the group but Tyler seemed utterly delighted. He jumped up and helped her with the ice creams.

"I got sprinkles on mine. And we chose one more with

sprinkles in case someone wanted it," Matty said authoritatively.

"Me!" Mary raised her hand in the air. Both hands on the dish, both eyes on the ice cream, Matty carefully walked it across the room to her.

"Looks like we've got a chocolate chocolate chip right here?" Tyler said, inspecting the one in his hand.

"Mine. Dibs. Called it." Fin put her finger in the air. He smirked at her as he walked it over.

"Should have guessed you'd have a thing for dark chocolate." He passed the dish to her and the same thing that happened when she'd handed him the beer earlier happened again. The heat between their fingers was unexpectedly overwhelming. Fin did her best not to touch people, because it always ended up making her feel funny. But with this moment, the chocolate passing from one hand to the other, the cold dish, the heat of the back of his hand against the pads of her fingers, it was all inexplicably delicious.

She frowned as she took the ice cream and leaned back. *Delicious* and *Tyler Leshuski* should never be in the same thought.

"Who wants pistachio?" Kylie asked. She frowned when there were no takers. "Come on. There's always some adult at some ice-cream shop who's ordering pistachio. I know one of you wants it."

Sebastian laughed. "Over here, kid."

She walked it over, and Fin began to see what a good idea this whole getting-her-a-job thing was. Kylie was a shy, insular person for the most part, but Fin had seen just how fast her energy had bloomed open when the idea of having a job had been tossed around. And even now, just having been the one to get the ice cream and to be the one passing it out, Kylie was actually standing in front of a room of adults and making jokes about pistachio ice cream.

It was clear to Fin that Kylie had been given too much responsibility at too young of an age. But that didn't mean that she didn't want any responsibility at all. Maybe giving her tasks was the way to her heart.

Fin instantly thought of a hundred different things she could have Kylie help her with at her house. Cleansing crystals for her jewelry, drying herbs, the works. She frowned and took a lick from her spoon. But all of that would require having Tyler trust her enough to invite Kylie over to her house.

It was with Tyler on her mind that Fin finished her ice cream and got up to start straightening the kitchen. Via was one of those cooks who cleaned up as she went, so there was never much to do after one of her dinner parties, but Fin liked to be the one to do it anyway.

She filled the sink with soapy water and was surprised when a pile of dishes appeared next to her. Tyler motioned for her to move aside and he grabbed the trash and the small compost bin from under the sink. He started scraping the plates into the bins.

Fin said nothing.

Tyler seemed lost in thought, at ease, and Fin felt strange, being the one who was a little flustered. There was a buzzing cloud of energy surrounding him, and Fin could neither get hold of it nor avoid it as he moved around the kitchen, putting away leftovers and wiping down the counters. She scrubbed up the plates and the few pots that were left and then drained the sink. She turned her back to the counter and watched him while, seemingly without thinking too much on it, he picked up the dishes from the rack and started drying them. She took them one by one from his hands and put them away.

His energy was like a forcefield that both kept her close and pushed her away. She couldn't read his mood, nor did she want to, but she also found that she didn't want to leave the kitchen.

She frowned and watched him as he refolded the dish towels, washed his hands.

"What?" he asked as he turned around.

She read the defensiveness on his face and purposefully dropped her crossed arms. She was sure that she was accidentally looking critical. She decided to lighten the mood.

"No comments on the fact that I did all the dishes?"

He looked confused. "You want a letter grade?"

"No. But you were the one who said I wasn't exactly the housework type."

A sparkle came into his eye. "Ah, of course. Where are your servants tonight? Gave them the night off from feeding you grapes and fanning you with palm leaves?"

"Even Cleopatra gives her servants a night to wash their golden underwear."

He laughed again, but there was fatigue in it. She didn't like that look on his face. He was supposed to look confident, amused, interested, observant. He wasn't supposed to look utterly bemused by the state of his life.

Fin shoved her hand into her pocket and pulled out her familiar crystals, the way she had for Kylie. "Pick one," she demanded.

He dropped his navy eyes to her hand and then swooped them back up to her face. "For what?"

"I'm going to make you something."

For a moment he looked pleased, then skeptical, then uncomfortable. "I'm...not exactly a jewelry kind of guy."

She couldn't help but roll her eyes and laugh. "Don't you think I know that? It's not going to be jewelry." She jiggled her hand a bit. "Come on. Pick one."

"What's it for?"

"Your energy is a mess. It's distracting. And whether or not you believe it, it's making it harder for you to connect with Kylie. So suspend your disbelief, pick one of these, whichever one draws you, and let me help you out a little bit."

He looked for a moment like he was going to argue, but then he merely shrugged and bent over a little to look at the selection in her hand. Before she could stop him, he reached down and plucked the small, clearish pink rose quartz from her hand.

She felt its weight leave her palm as she gaped. She'd forgotten to tell him to point and not pick up. It hadn't occurred to her that he'd pluck one right out of her hand.

It was the first time in almost a decade that someone else had touched the quartz. She'd carried it with her for years, using it, loving it, cleansing it, depending on it. And now, there it was, perfectly pressed between his thumb and forefinger as he held it up to the light.

She felt like he'd just plucked a loose tooth from her mouth.

"Does it mean something? Or protect against anything in particular?"

Still she gaped at him, trying to get her breath back.

"Fin?"

"Uh," she said, gravel in her throat. "Rose quartz helps transform negative energy into positive energy. It promotes healing."

"Oh. Cool." He tossed the stone in the air and caught it,

her eyes following the path the entire way. "What'll you make out of it?"

"A key chain," she said hoarsely, and cleared her throat. What was done was done. She knew better than to take it back now. She slipped her other stones back into her pocket, feeling the absence of the rose quartz, yet still aware of its glowing heat in Tyler's hand. "So that whenever you have your keys with you, you'll have the crystal with you as well."

He frowned. "Can't I just carry it in my pocket? The way you do?"

She still couldn't take her eyes off the familiar planes and corners of her crystal in his hand. His hand was so much larger than hers that when he let the quartz roll to his palm, it looked minuscule.

"...Sure."

"Great. Thanks for the gift. Not sure I totally understand it. But, uh, the gesture means a lot." With that, he effortlessly slipped the stone in his pocket, and again Fin followed the movement with her eyes.

She could practically feel the warm safety of his pocket surrounding the crystal. Her crystal. His crystal. He nodded to her and walked out of the room, and she couldn't escape the feeling that he was taking a part of her with him.

CHAPTER TWELVE

"DON'T THINK I won't tickle-torture you," Via said from where she reclined on Fin's tiny balcony that overlooked a sliver of Prospect Park. It was December and freezing, so both women were in full outdoor gear and covered up by a big blanket, but sitting on the balcony while they drank piping hot tea and chatted was enough of a timeworn tradition between them that they honored it even in the winter months. Even when a damp, cold rain had turned Brooklyn into a muted, slightly stinky version of a Parisian street painting.

"For what?" Fin demanded. Via was the only person on this earth allowed to tickle Fin, and even then, it was only supposed to be used in the direst of circumstances. Via had been firmly instructed only to use tickle torture when Fin was obstinately refusing to talk about something that she should probably let out into the open air.

"For the storm cloud over your head. Something is bothering you and you won't talk about it."

Fin said nothing, just sipped her tea.

"Did you accept that blind date your client wanted to set you up on?" Via abruptly changed the subject.

One of her clients had insisted that she knew Mr. Perfect and had attempted to play matchmaker. She'd sworn that he was a great guy.

Fin frowned. "Of course not."

"Why is that exactly?"

Fin turned her head and eyed her friend. "You know I'm not dating right now. I'm concentrating on…other things."

Once upon a time, "other things" would have been becoming a foster parent. But over the last month, Kylie had found her way into the "other things" pile as well.

"Ah. Right. You don't want a man to distract you. Which is what you told Tyler when he asked you out."

"What does Tyler have to do with this?"

"Nothing!" Via said in a voice just a note too high to be innocent. She fiddled with her teacup. "Well, I think you should go on this blind date."

"Why?" Fin asked, almost suspiciously.

Via shrugged. "I think it would help you…figure some stuff out."

"Winnie explicitly said that this guy was really charming but looking for something uncomplicated because he lives bicoastally. How would that ever fit into my life?"

Via tossed her hands up. "You don't want something casual, you don't want something serious. I don't think you have any idea what you want." A thoughtful look came over her face, maybe a little bit sly. "Unless," Via prompted, "you have feelings for someone else that I don't know about?"

Fin couldn't help but laugh. "Who on earth would I have feelings for?" Something popped up into the corner of Fin's mind, a familiar and not altogether welcome energy. She shoved it back, away, and continued on. "Have you ever known me to have feelings for someone? Real feelings?"

"Well. No. But—"

"Violetta, you *know* how I feel about having a man in my life."

"Is this all because of that dream? Your mother, the harbinger of doom, telling you that you won't be able to foster if you go on a date with an interesting, available man?" Via huffed and threw her hands up in the air. "I'm so sick of your mother. And I never even met her."

Fin sucked her teeth and let the view of the park fade in on itself, her thoughts spinning inward as she sought a way to explain. "My mother was no saint, Via, obviously. But she was rarely, if ever, wrong."

"Oh, don't give me that, Fin. Because one of the things you think she was *not* wrong about was that a man ruined her life by giving her you. And she was *dead* wrong about that. She ruined her own life by not appreciating what she had in a daughter. She's not infallible. You can't let her regrets guide your choices."

Fin frowned. To someone who wasn't clairvoyant, who didn't see the patterns and repercussions of every little choice a person made, she supposed it would seem as if she were choosing to let a superstition run her life.

Becoming a foster parent, even if she was taking a break from the application process right now, was Fin's nearest and dearest ambition. And it was a scary, unmapped maze of unknowns. And now Via just wanted her to cavalierly slap some dates on top of that? Fin would never find her way out of the labyrinth of her life if she did that. Things were complicated enough without adding a man in there. Besides, men were takers. They pursued hard, got what they wanted and gave nothing in return. Fin had a short string of casual relationships from her twenties to prove it. She didn't need that in her life.

"Name one way, *one*, that having a man would make becoming a foster parent easier."

"Oh, I don't know, love and marriage and steadier income and a higher credit score and holy moly your application gets accepted!" Via took a big swig of her tea like it was an exclamation point at the end of her sentence.

"And I'm going to get all that from one blind date with a man who lives half his life in San Francisco?" Fin asked with a wry eyebrow inched up her forehead.

"Well." Via pinched her face up. "No. Probably not. But the point isn't about the man, it's about you. Opening yourself up."

"To love?" If her tone got any drier she'd have to serve it with a side of butter.

"I know you think of yourself as a hard nut to crack. I know you're happy enough on your own. But that doesn't mean you don't need love in your life, Finny. Come on! Even you have to admit, your whole life has been in pursuit of love. What is being a foster parent if it's not a search for people to love and care for?"

"That's different. That's familial love. Of course I'm looking for that."

"News flash," Via said, rolling onto her side and yanking the blankets clear up to her ears. "Romantic love, the lasting kind, has a very healthy dose of familial love twisted up in it. Seb is my boyfriend, sure. But he's also my family. The same way you are, the same way Matty is."

Fin frowned. She could feel the truth in Via's words. It was just extremely inconvenient to her. It was much, much easier to think that romance and familial love lived in two completely different countries, and Fin could just go ahead and stay on one side of the border and never have to bother with exploring the other side.

"And," Via continued, "I know you probably don't want to hear this, but you can't just put a stopper in one kind of love and expect the others to flow freely. It all comes from the same place, Fin. If you close off part of your heart, you might just be closing off the rest of it by accident."

"How was your first day of work?" Tyler asked, nudging a reheated plate of pasta over to Kylie. Mary had dropped her off at the house about ten minutes before. Tyler had spent an evening blissfully working, losing himself in his writing. It had felt good. Natural.

He'd waited to eat his dinner with Kylie, so he dug in to his own mountain of pasta with gusto.

"Actually, pretty cool. I helped Mary rearrange part of the store and then she had me work the register while she helped customers."

She made a face that Tyler couldn't interpret.

"What's that face?"

"I like Mary's store, but there's just so much *Christmas* everywhere."

He laughed at her caustic tone. "Well, you were hired to help out with the holiday rush. That might have been your first clue that you were going to be dealing with Christmas crap."

Kylie shoved some pasta in her mouth and spoke through it. "I hope you don't have big plans for Christmas."

He frowned at her. Actually, he'd been stalling and had yet to make a single plan for Christmas, but he sensed that wasn't the right answer either, so he kept his trap shut. "What do you mean?"

"I mean…if you have really important traditions or whatever, that's cool. I guess we can do them. But other than that, would you mind if we kept it low-key?"

"I don't have any traditions. And define *low-key*."

She pushed her food around for a second and then ate another monumental bite. He couldn't look away from the half-masticated food rolling around in her mouth. Was she doing this on purpose? "I mean that I really like Via and Seb and Matty, but I don't think I can handle another awkward holiday over there. Holidays are obviously so special to their family but I just don't need everything to be so *meaningful*."

He laughed again. "I guess I see what you mean."

"Let's just not make a big deal out of it. It doesn't have to be a Lifetime special around here."

"So, no decorations?"

She grimaced. "There's more than enough of that at Mary's shop."

"No Christmas music, no advent calendars, no letters to Santa?"

She gave him a dull look. "I think he's catching on."

"Seriously, I'm going to have start eating dinner with an eye mask on if you keep talking with your mouth full."

Her eyes on his, she thoroughly chewed every bite of her food and then showed him her tongue. "Bettah?" she asked, tongue still out.

He rolled his eyes at her, trying to hide his giddiness that she was actually joking around with him. He didn't want to seem like an overeager dork and blow it.

"So, really," he clarified. "You want Christmas to just be a normal day?"

She shrugged. "Nothing special."

He wondered for a moment if this was a test that he was bound to fail. If this was one of those things where she said "nothing special" but she really meant, "Throw a huge Christmas bash. Get me a pony, bake a thousand Christmas cookies, enter us into a brother-sister gingerbread house contest."

He took a deep breath. He had instructions from his

friends to be more Tyler around her. He wasn't supposed
to be guessing what a good parent would do. He was supposed to be responding to her the way he would to Matty.

"All right, kid." Tyler leaned back in his chair. "One mediocre, unspecial, nondescript, totally forgettable Christmas coming right up."

Kylie, apparently immune to the magnitude of the moment, simply rose up to clear her plate. "Perf. I've got homework."

And then she was gone into her room. Tyler was halfway through the dishes when his phone rang. He wiped his
hands on a dish towel and raised his eyebrows when he saw
it was Fin calling him.

There was a time when he would have shaved his head
bald to receive an unsolicited phone call from her. But now
it merely perplexed him.

"Is this a butt dial?" he answered the phone.

"Do you always answer the phone using the word *butt*?"
Her tone was flat but somehow still amused.

He laughed. "Whenever I can work it in, sure."

"Why would you think I butt dialed you?" He could
hear some small clinking noises on her end of the line, too
light to be dishes.

He tried not to groan aloud at just how sagey and smoky
her accent sounded over the phone. Not good for his mo-
rale. "Because I figured if you're calling me, it had to be
a mistake."

"Actually, I'm not calling you. I wanted to talk to Kylie.
See how work went, but I think her phone is off."

He started walking down the hallway toward Kylie's
room. "I'm not sure I'm using your crystal right."

There was a pause on the other end of the line. "It's your
crystal now."

"Right. But, like, what am I supposed to be doing with it? I just mess around with it and then put it back in my pocket and forget about it."

"That sounds about right. But listen, I forgot to tell you that you have to cleanse it."

"With soap and water?"

She laughed, like he'd said something utterly ridiculous. He didn't get the joke.

"No. Put it on a windowsill that gets moonlight. Or you can bury it in the soil of a houseplant for a night. Or drop it into some salt water. Noniodized."

"You've got to be kidding me."

"What?" she asked.

"You're asking me to do *witchcraft* on my crystal."

"I'm not asking you to do witchcraft."

"Moonlight? Dirt? Salt? That's some witchy shit if I ever heard it."

"Fine, then. Forget it and just use a dirty crystal, see if I care."

There were more light clinking sounds on her end of the line. "What are you doing right now?"

"What's it to you?"

"I'm settling a bet with myself."

"What's the bet?"

"That you're doing witchcraft right this very second, on the phone with me. That you're multitasking normal human stuff and witch stuff."

"Will you stop calling me a witch?"

"Will you answer the question?"

Tyler leaned against the hallway wall, the phone to his ear and an embarrassingly large smile on his face.

She sighed after a long, obstinate moment of silence. "I'm bottling some tinctures that I made."

He laughed, loud and cathartic. "Damn, it feels good to be right."

"Tinctures aren't witchcraft!"

He let his silence speak for itself.

"Tinctures aren't *necessarily* witchcraft," she amended.

"Uh-huh," he said skeptically, utterly unconvinced. "Whatever you say, Cleopatra." He paused, eyeing Kylie's closed door. "Hey, quick question."

"Shoot."

"If a kid says they don't want to do anything for Christmas, like anything at all, do you listen or do you ignore it and do something special anyway?"

Fin paused. "I think Kylie is the kind of person that doesn't really want to do other people's traditions."

"But she wouldn't be opposed to traditions of her own?"

"I don't think she really has any traditions of her own."

Tyler paused, frowning. "That is…supremely unhelpful advice."

Fin burst out laughing on the other line and the sound of it raised the hairs on the back of his neck. He smoothed a hand over his goose bumps.

"Seriously," he groused. "What's the point of having a psychic as a friend if she can't even tell you what to do?"

Fin laughed again. He could practically hear the eye roll he was positive she was executing. "I only give the really good advice to paying customers. Will you put the kid on the line already?"

A smile on his face, he knocked on Kylie's door. "There's a phone call for you."

Kylie came to the door, looking as perplexed as Tyler had felt upon answering the call from Fin.

"It's Fin."

He held the phone out to her and watched as Kylie's face immediately brightened.

"Hi."

She closed the door in his face and Tyler turned on his heel. Back to the dishes. He paused in the kitchen for a moment, studying the small window above his sink. On a whim, he flicked off the overhead lights. A shaft of moonlight sliced the windowsill in two. Sighing to himself for being such a sap, he walked across the room, set Fin's pink crystal in the moonlight and finished the dishes in the dark.

CHAPTER THIRTEEN

FIN STEPPED INTO the storage room of Mary's store and smiled at the sight of Kylie sitting on the break table, cross-legged, flipping through a catalog and eating Chinese from the carton. In the perfect personification of what it meant to be a teenager, she looked bored and entertained all at once.

It was swampingly good to see Kylie. Fin had received another rejection letter that afternoon. It hadn't been a shock. But still. Even as prepared as she'd been, it was hard to want something this much and not lace the cocktail with hope. In the back of her mind, she'd stayed open to the idea of opening the email and finding a miracle, everything she'd ever wanted. Instead, she'd buried her face in her hands, took twenty deep breaths and decided to surprise Kylie at the store tonight. She needed to do something caring for someone who needed to be cared about.

"Hey."

Fin stepped forward as Kylie's head snapped up. "Hi!"

"Taking a break?"

"Yeah, it's actually a slow night tonight. Mary said I could take off early, but Tyler's at the Nets game so I figured I'd stick around until Mary was done."

"I brought something for you." She reached into her coat pocket and pulled out a little fabric drawstring bag that she'd sewed just for this occasion.

Kylie's eyes lit up as she took the bag from Fin's hand. "This is cool. Did you make it?"

Fin nodded. "And there's lavender sewed into the lining so if you're having trouble sleeping, you can put this next to your pillow. It'll help."

"Okay. I— Wow. Fin. I *love* them!" Kylie had upended the bag and out came the two bracelets and the necklace that Fin had made for her. All of them had the hematite that Kylie had picked out before, silvery and opaque. The necklace was a pendant on a long silver chain that Fin figured Kylie could hide under her shirt if she wanted. The bracelets were chunky and matching, made of many stones strung together.

"I hoped you would." Fin helped her put the necklace on, and Kylie slid one bracelet onto each wrist. The color suited her pale skin and red hair.

She explained how to cleanse them and though Kylie looked a little skeptical, she didn't crack any jokes the way Tyler had.

"Hey, have you done any New York Christmas stuff?" Fin asked. "We could go see some."

Kylie's smile froze. "Um, I'm actually not that into Christmas." She forced a smile on her face. "But I guess the Rockefeller tree could be cool."

Fin laughed. "Such a polite girl. But no, that's not what I meant. Here." Fin pulled out her phone and googled an image of Rockefeller Center at Christmastime. "There, now you've seen that. What I have in mind is much cooler. Trust me. Even if Christmas isn't your cup of tea, you'll like this."

"All right," Kylie shrugged. "Let me check with Mary. And will you let Tyler know?"

Fin closed the storage room door so that her phone call

wouldn't disturb any of the customers in the store and for the second time in a week, she dialed Ty's number.

"HELLO?" he shouted at top volume into the phone. The roar of the crowd nearly drowned out his words and blew out her eardrums.

"Wow. Hi."

"FIN?"

"Yes, Ty, can you hear me?"

"HANG ON." There was the sound of a door slamming, footsteps, more yelling, one more door and then quiet. "Hey, sorry. I'm at the game."

"What? I can't hear you, I've lost all hearing in my left ear."

"Oh, sorry, was I shouting?"

They both laughed.

"I'm at Fresh with Mary and Ky."

"So jelly. That sounds fun."

She rolled her eyes and suppressed her smile. She didn't know a single other grown man who used the word *jelly*. "Sounds like things are pretty dead here and I was wondering how you'd feel about me taking Ky to see the Dyker Heights lights."

"Oh. Huh. I forgot about them. I haven't been for years, but I guess they are pretty kick-ass."

"Is that a yes?"

"If she wants. What time will you have her home?"

Fin checked the time on her phone. "Ah, ten?"

"Cool. I'll already be home by then, so you can just send her up."

Confusingly, that caused a bite of disappointment in Fin's gut. Frowning at her own reaction, she made a sound of approval.

"All right," he said. "I should get back to it. Have fun."

"You too."

The line went dead and Fin listened to the silence for a moment.

She and Kylie polished off the rest of the Chinese food that Mary had provided for dinner, and then the two of them hailed a cab. It would be a mighty expensive cab ride to get all the way from Cobble Hill to Dyker Heights, but Fin didn't mind. She liked spending money on Kylie.

As Fin had known she would, Kylie used the map on her phone to track their progress through Brooklyn. Kylie shook her head, a smile on her face, as three texts in a row dinged through.

"Ty's checking up on me," she told Fin.

Fin watched as Kylie tried to hide her pleasure behind a roll of her eyes.

"Doesn't seem like you mind so much," Fin said with a small smile.

"It's annoying, but not so bad," Kylie conceded. She clicked off her phone and looked out the window for a second. "*Ty's* actually not so bad. For a while he was so freaking stiff. It freaked me out."

"What do you mean?"

"Um, like, no sudden movements. He would only ask the most boring questions, he was totally determined to pretend like this was all normal. And the neat-freak thing really bothered me for a while. I didn't even want to leave my shoes by the door. But he's started acting a little bit more like a person around me. More relaxed. More like he used to be on the phone."

"You used to talk on the phone a lot?"

"Once a week. And he was always funny. Not as weird as he was when I came to live with him." Kylie bounced her phone on her knee, looking out the window still. "It's kind of funny because I know more about him from the internet than I do from actually talking to him."

"What do you mean?"

"Well. We've only known the other one existed for a couple years. You knew that, right?"

Fin nodded. Via had mentioned it once.

"It's kind of crazy to find out you have a forty-year-old brother. So I googled him."

"What'd you find?" Fin could only pray that Ty's little sister hadn't stumbled across his dating profiles.

"Um, mostly his sports articles and stuff like that." She was quiet for a minute. "He's a good writer."

"Mmm," Fin said noncommittally. She didn't want to admit to how many of Ty's articles she'd recently read, fueled at first by curiosity and then by genuine interest. He really was a good writer.

"But it was all the dancing stuff that threw me for a loop."

Fin, still thinking about the articles, nodded absently before she did a double take back to Kylie. "What dancing stuff?"

She was suddenly inundated with imaginary images of Tyler caught on YouTube doing a choreographed dance with buddies at a wedding. Or Tyler doing the Dougie on a subway platform and slipping on a banana peel.

"You haven't seen the videos?" Kylie asked, a devilish light in her eyes. "Oh my god. You have to. Just for the outfits."

"Outfits?"

Oh boy. There was a really good chance Fin was about to see something megaembarrassing online about Ty. A surprisingly vocal part of her conscience spoke up. He probably wouldn't want her to see it, whatever it was. Maybe she should decline—

Kylie shoved her phone under Fin's nose and any thoughts of turning away from the video went immediately up in smoke. "*That's* Ty?"

Fin was utterly stunned.

Because there was a much younger Tyler, shirtless, in black tights and bare feet, leaping across a stage.

He...was a ballet dancer.

This right here, was not embarrassing. Not in the least. This was incredibly impressive. In the somewhat grainy video, he was dancing alongside a slim, lithe female dancer, also dressed in black. He effortlessly lifted her, before he set her down and pirouetted himself at least a few feet off the ground. Gravity need not apply.

Fin, mouth agape, watched his muscular arms and shoulders rise above his head. She watched the complex play of muscles at his back. The thighs that actually made her eyes bulge—

"There's other ones too. I think he's supposed to be Romeo in this one." Kylie took the phone back and handed it over again.

He wasn't shirtless in this one. But he was in tights again and the tunic he wore was open almost to the waist. She couldn't make herself stop watching the triangle of golden, sweaty skin exposed on his chest.

It was definitely Tyler. No question. Young twenties, a little bit thinner and floppier, like a puppy. But Tyler all the same. There was no mistaking that long, handsome face, his friendly eyes and light brows. But she simply couldn't reconcile her current image of him with this graceful, athletic man who radiated light.

She'd guarded herself from Tyler's energy before because she'd always been able to sense his attraction to her and it made her wary. But there was no turning away from it now. He powered across the stage on the screen. He dived to his knees, every muscle in his forearms apparent and shadowed.

His energy was nuclear, vibrant, explosively appealing as the man on the screen did what he was born to do.

His energy was undeniably golden. So gold it was almost green.

She'd always thought that if she looked hard enough into Tyler's aura, it would be red. Obstinate.

Um. NOPE.

Blind spot.

The man in this video was sweet, caring, open, brave. There was no unseeing this.

"You're drooling."

Kylie was watching her with a smile on her face. Fin figured she could either lie completely or she could minimize it. "Well, there's an awful lot of sweaty muscles in this video. I've always been a sucker for sweaty muscles."

Kylie laughed. "I thought you'd think it was funny. Like I did. But you seem…"

"Really impressed. Ballet is hard. And it looks like he was semi-professional."

"Yeah. The internet says he was pretty good before he quit to be a writer."

Fin handed the phone back. "He looks pretty good."

Kylie laughed, and Fin blushed.

"I didn't mean it like that!"

"Sure you didn't." Kylie nudged Fin's boot with her own. "Are you sure you're not into him?"

Yes! She was positive. One hundred percent sure. Tyler Leshuski was a convertible-door-jumping, collar-popping,

'80s baddie who…was really sweet to his kid sister, and actually kind of funny, and was considerate of his friends, and had faithfully honored her desire to have nothing to do with him romantically, and never hit on her, and made good curry, and made her heart skip when he shouted in her ear at a loud basketball game.

Crap.

"I…don't get crushes," Fin responded.

"Uh-huh," Kylie answered knowingly. "Got it."

For a moment, Kylie didn't look like a kid. In the dim back seat, streetlamps rhythmically splashing light across her face, Fin saw just what Kylie was going to look like in a decade. Her deep red hair twisted over one shoulder, those freckles on her nose bringing out the color of her eyes, her intelligent gaze always tinged with humor. And then, just like that, every illusion of adulthood melted away as Kylie leaned toward her window, her eyes round and childlike, her mouth opened wide enough to parallel park a Chevrolet in there.

"Oh. My. GAWD. This is what we're going to see?"

Fin laughed. "This is how they do Christmas in Dyker Heights."

She paid the cab driver, thanking him, and then they scooted out of the cab. Fin felt oddly overinflated, like if she pushed off the ground she'd take Neil Armstrong steps along the sidewalk, but she didn't want to waste these moments with Kylie being stuck in her own head. So she pushed her revelations aside and concentrated on the girl standing beside her. "Are you warm enough? Or do you want to find a place to get hot chocolate before we walk around?"

"Yes," Kylie answered dimly, her eyes still rounded as she took in the sight before her.

Fin was thrilled to have wowed Kylie so soundly.

And this was just the edge of the neighborhood.

Fin steered Kylie through the crowds of tourists, which were nothing compared to the crowds at Rockefeller Center, but were quite sizable for this rarely visited BK neighborhood. They found a hot chocolate vendor and Fin bought a hot pretzel with mustard and hot sauce for good measure as well.

The houses in this part of Dyker Heights were more mansions than houses, four-story old-money monstrosities that sat thirty feet back from the street and had century-old trees in their yards. And if anyone had any questions about just how old the money was in this neighborhood, the incredibly elaborate Christmas-light displays answered the question.

Each house, obviously in competition with one another, was more grand than the last. These were not your uncle Ted's strings of tangled lights that stayed up on the house until Fourth of July. These displays were professionally orchestrated, sheer walls of color and light. There were more lights than there were houses visible in most places. The neighborhood was as bright as noon even though the sky overhead was as close to black as it ever got in New York. And it wasn't just the lights. There were animatronic Santas that sang Christmas carols and skated on tracks around the yards, reindeer on pulleys that landed gracefully on roofs over and over again. Entire lawns were piled with white lights to make them look like they were covered in drifts of glowing snow.

"I was reading that some of these people spend around twenty thousand dollars to decorate each year."

Kylie mouthed the words *twenty thousand dollars* and kept looking, the lights turning her face a blinking rainbow of surprise as she turned from house to house. "You think that includes their electricity bills?"

Fin laughed. "I hope they do something during the year to offset the carbon footprint of this."

Kylie gave her an arch look. "If you're willing to spend twenty thousand dollars on Christmas decorations, don't you think you're probably flying in private jets and eating endangered animal canapés for dinner?"

"Yes, but they probably drive Teslas. That's sort of green."

"That sort of *happens* to be green," Kylie corrected, making both of them laugh again. They strolled on, chatting and sharing the pretzel and re-upping on hot chocolate when they started to get chilly. And Fin saw that neither assessment of Kylie tonight had been right. Kylie wasn't grown up yet, and she wasn't a child. She was in that amazing time right smack-dab in between. Teenagerhood was so often defined as a transition from one thing to the next. But it wasn't, not really. It was an age as valid as any other, Fin reflected. And Kylie wore it well.

A FEW DAYS before Christmas Tyler grimaced at the sound of his own key in the lock. At midnight, everything seemed too loud. He was late as hell, though Mary, who'd agreed to babysit, had assured him a hundred times that day that she would just be snoozing on his couch so whenever he got home would be fine.

He heard noises on the other side of the door and was surprised to hear his television on. Mary was not a TV watcher.

He stepped inside and froze, door open, when he realized that it was not Mary sprawled out on his couch but Fin. His first clue was the river of black hair that fell in a waterfall over the arm of his couch. She rustled when she heard him come in and sat up, her hair resuming its place around her shoulders and down her back.

"Hi," she said, stretching her arms over her head, though her eyes looked alert. She hadn't been sleeping.

"What are you doing here?"

Her eyes narrowed. "Mary had an early morning and I was helping her out at the shop tonight so I volunteered to take Ky home. I sent you a text about it."

His shoulders sagged as he locked the front door behind him and put his shoes and coat in the closet. He emptied his pockets into the loose change dish he kept by the door, saw his crystal in the mix and repocketed it. "Phone's dead."

"Ah."

"I guess I should get one of those portable battery packs to carry around with me now that I have a kid to care for."

"Maybe so."

Too exhausted to really say much of anything else, Tyler disappeared into his room and quickly changed into sweats. They were fashionable and euro-cut, but all the same, they were the closest he'd ever come to slouch-wear. He diverted back through the kitchen. "You want a beer?" he called.

There was a pause from the other room. He winced internally. No, she didn't want a beer. She wanted him to say goodbye and order her a cab so that she could get home before one o'clock in the freaking mor—

"Sure. Sounds good."

…Or she wanted to drink a beer.

He cracked two beers open and carried them into the living room. He handed her one and plopped into the armchair kitty-corner from where she sat on the couch, both of their feet propped onto the coffee table. "Did Kylie have dinner, do you know?"

For some reason, that question made Fin smile a little bit. Not that full, goofy grin that never failed to give Tyler goose bumps, but a small, satisfied smile that he'd rarely seen before. "She and Mary had tacos around eight, I think." She paused. "I raided your fridge for dinner when we got here. Hope you weren't saving those enchiladas for something special."

He waved his hand through the air. "All yours."

For some reason he couldn't identify, it pleased him immensely that she would eat his food without asking. It was the same jolting feeling he'd had when he'd stepped through his door and seen her hair against his couch. It was basically the opposite of the feeling he'd had whenever she'd perch against his windowsill, as if everything in his house were mildly disgusting to the touch.

"You're a good cook," she said after a minute, her tone telling him that the information had come as a surprise to her.

"And you're a watcher of crappy television," he replied in the exact same tone of voice.

She bit back her smile and used her beer to gesture at the television. "Home-improvement TV is not crappy. It's informative and uplifting."

She sniffed haughtily and he laughed.

"It's mind-numbing nonsense, and you know it."

"Oh, and I suppose all the sports programs you have DVRed are high art?"

He laughed again. "I'm not pretending to be an intellectual."

"And I am?"

He rolled his head lazily from looking at the television to looking at her. Her pale skin was a light blue in the light from the television and her eyes were strangely dark. He was used to them being the brightest thing in the room. But he could see that fatigue was hooding her eyes, and the dim room was doing the rest.

"You don't think that bingeing crappy TV kind of wrecks the whole spooky psychic image you have going on?"

"You expect me to be, I don't know, brewing potions in the kitchen and staring into my crystal ball 24/7?"

He laughed and shrugged, but didn't concede the point.

"Ty, do you think we'll ever get to the point where you realize that this isn't an image, it's who I am? And who I am is someone who reads energy *and* watches crappy TV?"

Her question twanged a chord inside him. So far, since she'd asked to be a part of Kylie's life, Tyler had felt like a byproduct of that equation. He'd been something Fin had to tolerate to get time with Kylie. But here she was, sitting on his couch, drinking a beer and asking him about the direction in which their relationship might grow.

It was…confusing.

Plus, her hair was in that sheet down her back, instead of braided carefully away, and that only further discombobulated him.

He had absolutely no idea how to answer that question so instead he asked one of his own. "Do you think we'll ever get to a point where you don't think of me as an entitled douche who thinks he should get everything he wants?"

Something flashed in Fin's eyes that was gone before Tyler could identify it. Guilt? Embarrassment? Nerves? He couldn't say.

"I will if you will?" she offered after a moment, a spark in her eye.

Tyler couldn't help but laugh. "Ah. I see. Schoolyard rules. Fair enough. No more hippie-dippy psychic, no more entitled douchebag."

He leaned forward and held his beer bottle out to her. That same spark in her eye, Fin cheers-ed him. "RIP."

They drank their beers and watched TV in what Tyler categorized as companionable silence.

The show cut to commercial, and Fin stretched, drawing his attention to her feet on the coffee table. She pointed her toes and switched the way her ankles were crossed, bringing her socked feet within a few inches of his.

He zeroed in on the feet in front of him. "Fin," he said tonelessly. "Your socks don't match." He set his beer aside, leaning forward for a better look. He could barely stand to look at what he was seeing. "Oh my god, one of them is wool and one of them is cotton."

"So?"

He looked up at her, seeing her in a whole new light. She'd always been this mystery he couldn't quite solve. Elusive and interesting and mysterious. But now, looking at her one striped purple sock and one black sock, he knew the truth. She wasn't a sphinxlike enigma. No. She was an absolute wacko. A crazy person who could tolerate the feel of two completely different socks.

She wore long, flowy pants and without too much thought on the matter, he reached down and lifted the hems of both her pant legs by a few inches.

"Hey!" she squeaked, leaning forward and kicking his hands away.

"Oh, for the love of all that's holy, Fin." He dragged his hands down the sides of his face, in full horror at what he was looking at. "One of them is a *knee* sock and one of them is an ankle sock."

She raised that insufferable emoji eyebrow at him. "I repeat... So?"

He could have sworn she waggled her toes at him to provoke him.

"Your socks are not only two different colors and fabrics, which is bad enough, but they're different lengths? That is utterly *appalling*. How can you stand it?" He gesticulated wildly at her feet. "That's my version of torture."

"God, I hope you never uncover any national secrets." She wryly swigged her beer, that emoji eyebrow still firmly in place.

He leaned back in the armchair and just gaped at her for a moment. He knew she was provoking him. But what was he supposed to do? Just sit there and watch a kitchen get made over while he knew that the woman next to him wore one sock up to her knee and one down around her heel? It was enough to make him want to tear his skin off! He stood up suddenly. "I can't look at this. No. I can't even go on knowing this is taking place. It's a travesty."

She said nothing as he stalked out of the room. Later, he'd realize that he was acting as crazy as he was internally accusing her of being, but he didn't care. He kept his shoes in neat rows on the floor of his coat closet, his toothbrush in its cup, his vegetables in the crisper and his motherfreaking socks *always* matched. It wasn't an opinion thing. It was a necessity.

"Wearing unmatching socks is like only washing half your head when you take a shower. Some things just aren't done," he informed her as he stalked back into the living room, a pair of his socks in one hand.

"Ty, forget entitled douchebag, I'm starting to think you're clinically insane."

He waved her comment away and plunked down on the couch next to her, scooping her feet off the coffee table and twisting her body to face him. He put her feet against his knees and reached under the hems of her pants legs to strip her socks off.

"Tyler!"

Sitting there, her feet in his lap and her warm socks in his hands, reality finally caught up to Tyler. He cleared his throat and looked up at her shocked eyes, her hair that had tumbled forward when he'd moved her.

"I...might be getting carried away," he said confusedly. He looked at her socks in his hands, feeling as if he'd just woken up from a dream to find himself standing in his neighbor's kitchen.

To his enormous surprise and relief, she burst out laughing. It was that huge, eye-pinching, wolf-toothed smile of hers that had been so elusive in the past, but this time it was accompanied by great, husky bursts of laughter. She shook her head at him. "You think? Clearly I broke your circuit board or something."

He stared bemusedly between the two mismatched socks in his hands. "I guess."

She leaned back and grinned at him, taking a swig of her beer and wiggling her feet against his knee. "Well? Do what you gotta do to be able to sleep at night, you psycho."

Still kinda shocked that she hadn't slapped the shit out of him and stormed out of his house for putting his hands up the legs of her pants, Tyler carefully folded up her mismatched socks and grabbed his matching pair from where he'd set them on the coffee table.

He picked up one of her feet and was starting to put the sock on when he paused, staring down, utterly delighted by what he was looking at.

"What?" she asked, wiggling her toes again.

"You have ugly feet," he said in complete amazement, incapable of tearing his eyes away.

She made a noise of outrage and attempted to yank her feet away from him, but he held them fast.

"No, no! Don't misunderstand," he said with a laugh he couldn't stop. "I don't mean ugly."

"You *said* ugly." She continued to yank her feet back.

He kept her feet firmly against his knee. "Well, I meant to say, ah, charmingly imperfect."

A smile twitched at the corners of her mouth even as her eyes shot daggers at him.

She yanked her feet once more but he held fast.

"Seriously," he said. "Ugly things are cute. Your feet are cute."

He looked down at her cute-ass feet, the knobby, irregular toes and bony ankles. She had chipped toenail polish and the tiniest little pinky-toe nail he'd ever seen in his life.

He held up one of her feet like she was wearing Cinderella's glass slipper and fully inspected it.

"Why are you getting such a kick out of this?" she demanded. Then she squinted her eyes at him, her head cocked to one side. "Didn't have you pegged for a foot fetishist."

He laughed. "I'm not a foot fetishist. I'm an everything-in-its-right-place fetishist. And that includes matching socks." He set her foot down and slid one of his socks on and then picked up the other foot, inspected that one too. "Funny feet. Who'd have known? The rest of you is so gorgeous. You know, undeniable perfection." He tried to say it matter-of-factly, so that she wouldn't mistake his honesty for a come-on. "I guess I just like that you have normal human feet."

He quickly slid the other sock onto her foot and gave his handiwork a quick pat. He set her feet back on the coffee table and rose up to walk back around to the armchair. He really didn't want her to think he'd been taking the opportunity to snuggle up on her.

She still had yet to say anything and he let five seconds pass before he chanced a glance at her.

He'd been expecting the ice of her usual gaze. He'd expected her to look all-knowing and disdainful. Maybe even to give him another healthy dose of the emoji eyebrow. But instead she'd folded her knees up under her chin, and she stared down at his socks on her feet. As he watched, she straightened her pant legs, traced her fingers over the pair of wool socks he'd just given her. He could only see part of her face, turned down as her head was, but confusingly, the part he could see looked…soft. And a little befuddled.

"They're too big," she told him, looking up after a minute, a begrudging smile on her face. "But you're right. Matching socks definitely feel better."

Holding his beer bottle in one hand, he gave her a little hand-rolling bow before turning back to the television.

They watched to the end of the program before Fin rose up and stretched.

"I'll get you a car," Tyler said, crossing the room to unplug his phone.

"Do you want these back?" Fin asked, one foot poised over her winter boots, pointing to the socks.

"No! No. They're yours. Consider them a tip for working the late shift tonight."

"Thanks." She shrugged into her coat and didn't question him when he put his coat on. He guessed that she knew him well enough at this point not to argue about him walking her down to the cab.

They were in the elevator when something occurred to him. "You have a guest bedroom at your place, right?"

She looked surprised by his question. "Yeah."

"Well, if this kind of thing happens again, feel free to just bring Ky back to your place for the night, and I'll come get her in the morning."

She stared at him blankly, her long hair squashed between her winter hat and the collar of her coat. He wasn't a parenting expert by any means and he racked his brain for what he could have said wrong. Maybe he was being presumptuous?

"I mean, only if you wanted to," he hurried to say. "And Kylie wants to. I just thought you might prefer that to having to stay late at my house and then schlep all the way over to your place at one a.m."

That blank look was still on Fin's face, even as the elevator doors slid open, and it was starting to unnerve Tyler.

"You'd let her come spend the night at my house?" she said as they walked across the lobby.

"Sure, I trust you and—"

He cut off immediately, feeling like he'd just been socked in the gut when she turned to him and put her palm on his shoulder, giving him a tight, friendly squeeze over his coat.

Though he'd just manhandled her bare feet not twenty minutes ago, Tyler couldn't think of a single time when she'd purposefully touched him, besides shaking his hand when they met. It was something he'd noticed about her. Though quite affectionate with Via and Matty, and occasionally Mary, Fin was by no means a toucher. She wasn't even a toucher of *things*. Tonight was the first night he'd ever even seen her sit on his couch.

But there she was, hand firmly clamped over his shoulder, her eyes, once again bright, lit by the white Christmas lights in the lobby. Her gaze searing and potent. Tyler felt strangely like her hand was pinning him to some sort of interrogation chair while her eyes went ahead and saw straight through to the flipside of his heart. Weirdly, he liked it.

"Thank you," she said simply before unhanding him.

He let out a breath as he strode to catch up to her, realizing that he hadn't even been breathing during that moment.

Dangerous, he thought for the thousandth time.

But this time, he wondered at just how many different meanings a word like dangerous could have.

CHAPTER FOURTEEN

CHRISTMAS WAS EXACTLY the nonmonumental affair that both Tyler and Kylie had been hoping it would be. They both slept in, and Tyler made bacon and a kitchen-sink omelet for them around eleven. Over breakfast, Tyler slid a blank envelope across the table and experienced a stab of joy when her eyes lit up over the Sky Blue soccer tickets he'd bought for her. They were the professional women's team that played in New Jersey.

"There are three tickets here," she said.

"Yeah, well, one is for me and one is for you and the third is for whoever else you want to invite. Someone from school or—"

"Fin," Kylie said decisively.

Well. That was that.

She got up and left the room and came back a second later with a wrapped gift. Tyler gaped at it in her hands. It hadn't occurred to him that she'd buy something for him for Christmas. "Thanks for the tickets," she said, somewhat awkwardly. "I got you this. But I didn't wrap it."

"Obviously Mary did," Tyler said, observing the rectangular box from one angle and then the other. No one could wrap a sharp corner like Mary.

"Right," Kylie said, sounding quite nervous.

Tyler put her out of her misery and tore open the present. He was stymied by what it was, however. It was obviously something from Mary's shop. It was a type of small wrought iron stand painted a dark blue. Was it a decoration? He had no clue.

Determined to love it no matter what, Tyler held it up. "Ah, thanks, Ky. It's great."

She laughed. "I knew you'd have no clue what it is."

He tried not to look too sheepish. "Busted."

She stood and took it from him, walking over to his kitchen counter and standing it up. She selected a recipe book and opened it, sliding it into the stand.

"It holds the pages open while you cook!" Tyler crowed as understanding dawned.

She shrugged, embarrassed. "I thought you could use it."

"It's genius!" He couldn't help but rise up and try it out himself, flipping the pages of the book and setting it back in the stand. He probably wouldn't have bought it himself, but he was definitely gonna use it. And it even matched his kitchen decor.

Unable to help himself, Tyler grabbed Kylie in a gruff hug. "Thanks, sis."

She hugged him back, harder than he'd thought she would. "Merry Christmas."

After they showered and got cleaned up, Tyler suggested they go see a movie.

"Can we go to the Cobble Hill theater?" Kylie asked, and Tyler was loath to say no to that.

They took the train and rolled their eyes through a cheesy Christmas movie. On a bolt of inspiration, Tyler tugged the back of Kylie's coat as she was walking out and motioned her into the theater next door to theirs.

"Doubleheader?" he whispered to her as the beginning of an action flick played on the screen.

"Sure!" she said in surprise.

They slinked into two seats and ducked down, not wanting to be seen. The movie was terrible, but made all the more sweet by the fact that they hadn't paid for it.

"Triple-header?" Kylie asked, a sparkle in her eye as they left the second movie.

He laughed. "Your Christmas wish is my command."

They ducked into the third movie, this one a self-serious Oscar contender already fifteen minutes in when they sat down. It wasn't four more minutes when a flashlight splashed across their eyes.

"Sir," an employee said. "Can I see your tickets, please?"

"Sure," Tyler said smoothly, handing him their tickets from the first movie they'd seen. He gave the man an easy grin.

The employee, unamused, pursed his lips. "Sir, I'm going to have to ask you to leave."

"Got it," Tyler said, tugging Kylie along with him. They waited until they got to the sidewalk to burst out laughing.

"Seb and I used to do that all the time," he laughed. "We used to spend whole days at the movies."

"I assume you used to be better at the sneaking part," Kylie said as she started strolling down Court Street.

Tyler followed after her, realizing that she was walking so confidently because she knew this area now. They were only a few blocks from Mary's shop. "Actually, we got caught as often as we didn't."

"Was it this theater?"

"Nah." Tyler shook his head. "Different ones around the city. We weren't in this part of Brooklyn very often."

"Which neighborhood did you grow up in again?"

"We grew up around the corner from one another in Sheepshead Bay."

"I haven't been there yet."

"It's a little like Midwood in parts." Tyler paused. They were having such a good time together, he didn't want to ruin it. But still, avoiding mentioning their father at all costs couldn't be healthy either. "Dad actually lived in Midwood. So, I spent a little time there as a kid."

A very little time. Basically, whenever his mother had wanted a vacation and the housekeeper couldn't stay with him, he'd be trucked off to Midwood to stay with his in-attentive father, who barely remembered which grade he was in. Tyler inwardly winced as he remembered the phone calls that he and Kylie used to have before she'd come to Brooklyn. He hadn't realized it at the time, but it had been exactly the way his father used to talk to him. Obligatory small talk.

She was quiet for a second, as she usually was when he brought up their father. "Your mom lived in Sheepshead Bay?"

He nodded. "Just long enough to see me through high school and then she was long gone."

"To where?"

"Ah, let's see. At that point she was living in Long Beach."

"That's California, right?"

"Yeah."

"Is that why you moved out there for college?"

Tyler laughed immediately, because the idea was kind of ludicrous, but he reined in the laughter when he saw the confused expression on Kylie's face. "Um. No. No, I just went where I got accepted to school. It didn't have to do with where my mom lived."

"You're…not close?"

Tyler tried to think of a way to explain this as they strolled.

"Not really. My mother is, well, you know the mom from *Mary Poppins*?"

"The votes-for-women lady?"

"Yeah."

"Sure."

"Okay, now cross that lady with Meryl Streep from *The Devil Wears Prada* and you have my mom."

Kylie furrowed her brow. "That makes no sense. Those characters are opposites, pretty much."

"Exactly." Tyler laughed again. "My mom is super flighty, but also extremely opinionated. And I guess you could say judgy. Of everyone but herself. She has this perception of how life is and should be, and it's really far from reality."

Kylie was quiet for a minute, hopping over someone's pizza slice that had landed facedown on the sidewalk. "Arthur sure knew how to pick them."

Tyler looked down at Kylie in surprise. It was the first time he'd heard Kylie refer to their father by his first name. Tyler always called him Dad.

"Apparently." He paused, feeling like he was revving an SUV at the edge of an ostensibly frozen lake, wondering how far he could make it across. "I don't know your mother very well. What's she like?"

Kylie quirked an eyebrow up at him, her lips pursed. "She's an asshole who abandoned me."

Tyler's blood froze. He figured he could retreat and change the subject, or he could serve up a fresh, hot, steaming pile of platitudes. And then he remembered what he'd promised himself. Right. He was going to be *himself* around Kylie. Screw the obligatory small talk.

"Well, obviously," he replied, a little smile on his face. She looked up at him in surprise, her lips quirked up. "I meant describe her the way I did my mom. Like, if you crossed two characters."

"Oh. Okay. If I crossed two characters..." She continued to stroll, thinking, and paused in front of a burger joint that was closed for the holiday. "You ever had truffle fries? This place has great truffle fries."

Charmed by this confident version of his sister, Tyler raised his eyebrows and nodded, like she was teaching him something new, when in fact he'd been eating truffle fries from that joint since before she was born.

"Two characters," she mumbled to herself again and kept strolling, peeking in all the darkened store windows. "I guess she'd be a cross between Jessica Rabbit and Jabba the Hut."

"Yikes," Tyler said immediately and made Kylie laugh.

"Maybe that was too harsh?"

He shrugged. "I won't tell if you don't."

He'd met Lorraine a handful of times, and in his opinion, that was not too harsh.

"What two characters do you think Dad would have been?" Tyler asked, hoping his voice was light as they strolled along, his gloved hands in the pockets of his coat.

"Stop calling him *Dad*, Tyler. I hate that."

He was quiet for a second, trying to interpret the warring feelings within him. Old, normal Tyler wanted to push back on that. New, meek Guardian Tyler wanted to acquiesce and give her whatever she wanted. He split the difference. "You call him Arthur, and that's cool, Ky. But I call him Dad. To me, that was his name. I...think it's okay that it's different for the two of us."

"How mature."

Her tone, dry with just a dash of venom, made Tyler wince. He suspected that he might be in the part of the horror movie where the dumbass who wanders off by himself realizes that he's walked right into the murderer's trap.

"It...hurts you when I call him Dad?" he floundered.

Kylie was quiet as they squished to one side of the sidewalk to let a huge, chattering family walk past, their loud voices reminiscent of a flock of geese heading south for the winter. When all was quiet again, she sighed. "He wasn't my dad, Tyler. Never. He was only around a few weeks a year. I barely knew him."

"I—well. Honestly, that isn't all that different than the way that *I* knew him either. He wasn't exactly present for my childhood either, Ky. He wasn't even interested in talking to me until I started becoming successful in my profession and even then, it was never about anything that mattered, not really."

"So, first he abandoned you and then he abandoned me, and you're just fine with that now?"

He took a long breath. Too careful was bound to piss her off; too careless was bound to hurt her. "No, of course I'm not fine with it. But it's been a long time. I'm kind of over it. I got over it."

She turned her head away from him and tersely adjusted her stocking cap, but he caught a half second still frame of her face in the passing shop window. There were tears in her eyes. His insides shrank at the idea of Kylie crying, but also, he welcomed it. He preferred almost anything over her blank indifference.

"You *got over* it?" Her voice was quiet, but that was the only hint of emotion that remained when she finally spoke again, a block later. "The man had a secret second family that he never told you about. You didn't find out until he fell over dead! And you're just over it?" She snapped her fingers. "Like that?"

He bumped shoulders with her. "First of all, don't talk about yourself as a second family. The man barely had a first family to begin with, and more importantly, you're not *my* second family. You're my primary family, Kylie. My *only* family when I'm really doing the math."

She darted her eyes up to his, shiny but not brimming over. She looked like he'd just offered her a trip to Spain and she was examining the plane tickets, trying to figure out if they were real. "Your—your mom?"

"Hasn't called me in months. Even when she knew that I'd just become your legal guardian. Even when she knew that this was bound to be one of the most challenging points of my life. Not even a phone call, Ky." He bumped shoulders with her again. "Who eats dinner with me? Who? Who meets my friends? You, Kylie. You're my primary family. Not just because of who you are and who your father happens to be. But because of everything you've done since we got tossed together. You're a *good* family member."

"Don't," she said in such a small voice that Tyler immediately stopped talking. If she'd yelled, he might have kept going. "Don't say anything else."

"Ky—"

"I helped with the window display." She cut him off with a nod of her head.

They'd stopped in front of Fresh, and Ty looked into the darkened windows. He had so much more to say but decided he'd driven far enough out onto the ice for one day.

The shop was closed, just like most of Court Street, but Fresh didn't have that abandoned-on-Christmas look that many of the other darkened storefronts did. The security gate was pulled down, of course, but Mary had left some of the lamps on, giving the store a homey, ambient feel.

Tyler complimented the window display, which really

did look cheery and bright. The conversation they'd just had was humming through him, the adrenaline brought on by the subject matter making him feel hollowed out. He was cold in his peacoat, but still, a line of sweat marched its way down his back. He wanted to push. He wanted to retreat. Instead, he just stood next to Kylie and looked through the window to the furniture display. "Clever how she did that," he said eventually. "With the opened presents around the tree, making it look like people really had Christmas morning in there."

"That was my idea," Kylie said quietly.

When Tyler glanced down at her, her fingers threaded through the slats of the security gate, he saw that she looked a little nervous.

"It's brilliant! It makes the shop look so much more lively than all the others on the block."

It might have been the cold, but he was almost positive that Kylie had flushed with pleasure at his compliment. She took a deep breath and he knew it for what it was. The end of their last conversation. This was her way of asking to move on. It was the least he could do to oblige her.

"The shop *always* looks more lively than the other shops on the block. It's the best shop on Court Street," Kylie said vehemently and again Tyler found himself observing her profile.

"You're sad to be done working there," Tyler guessed.

She shrugged, unthreaded her gloved fingers from the security gate and began walking back the way they'd come.

"Did you ask Mary if you could become a permanent employee? Not just a seasonal one?"

Kylie's cheeks flamed, and she stared at the ground as she walked. "No."

"Why not?"

Kylie shook her head. "I...don't want her to say no."

"So instead you're just not going to ask and let the dream die?"

She made a noise of annoyance, and he tugged on her coat, making her face him. He made sure she saw him roll his eyes. "Kylie, that's the dumbest. It's like walking up to the boy you want to go to prom with and telling him that you'll never, ever go with him in a million years."

Now she was the one rolling her eyes. "Topical. Way to take that problem and really put it into terms I'll understand."

He had to laugh at the healthy dose of sarcasm dripping from her every syllable. "Okay, fine. That was dumb, I admit. How about this then? You miss a hundred percent of the shots you don't take."

She pursed her lips but he could see her attempt not to smile. "Sports metaphor notwithstanding, I see your point."

"Besides, I doubt Mary's answer will just be no." He'd see to that himself. If he had to secretly pay Kylie's salary out of his own pocket, he'd do it. "She might cut your hours or something. And I know she usually has a lull in January so maybe you'd start again in the spring. But I know Mary loves having your help at the shop. She told me herself you did twice the work of the full-time guy she brought on."

"Jonah was useless. He spent more time Instagramming than he did helping. I walked in on him in the bathroom and didn't even apologize because he was sitting on the sink Snapchatting."

"I—" Tyler had no words for that. He wasn't entirely sure what people used Snapchat for. "I'm assuming he had his pants on."

Kylie laughed. "Yes. He did."

"Then... I guess no harm, no foul?"

Tyler could see the subway stairs two blocks ahead of them, but the truth was, he wasn't ready for this day to be over. They'd go underground, be surrounded by people, and their conversation would stall out. Then they'd get home and there was a really good chance she was just going to go to her room.

He thought fast.

"Listen, the holiday trains are going to be murder going home. But there's this really good Korean barbecue just past Gowanus. We could take a cab back from there after we eat. Up for a long walk to dinner?"

It was a little early for dinner, not even six yet, but it would take them an hour to walk there, and he was sure they'd be hungry by the time they made it.

"I've never had Korean barbecue."

"You're in for a treat. Seriously, it's one of my favorite food groups, and this place does it so well." He shivered just thinking about it.

Kylie laughed. "I'm not sure barbecue is a food group, but sure, I'm game."

Tyler shoved his hands in his pockets and led the way, pointing out the canal as they went, the changing neighborhoods, talking about Brooklyn, about nothing at all.

Turned out, Mary did want Kylie to continue working at the shop even after the Christmas rush. So, it was in mid-January that Kylie ended up taking Fin up on the offer to stay over for the night.

It was a Friday, and Fin had been by Fresh to help reorganize after the New Year, showing off just a little for Kylie. Ty was at a game that was going late and wasn't going to be home until around one. Fin figured she could either wait for Ty to come home to his house, stewing in that sock maniac's golden energy all night, or she could retreat to her own turf and not have to worry about it.

Since Fin had seen the videos of Tyler dancing, since the sock incident, she'd been avoiding being alone with him.

Because she had a problem. A major problem.

She kinda, sorta, maybe just a little bit had feelings for him.

And she had no freaking idea what to do about it.

She'd never experienced this before. He'd texted her the other day to invite her to a women's soccer game with him and Kylie in February and it had taken Fin an hour to craft a text back.

An hour.

And all the text had said was Sounds fun, let me check my schedule.

So, of course, two days later, he'd called to ask her if she'd checked her schedule yet. But she hadn't answered the phone. She'd been on the way to meet a client, saw it was Ty calling and just jammed the phone back into her bag. Then, even worse, she'd held her breath through listening to the entire voice mail.

She barely recognized herself! She was suddenly swamped with sympathy for all the lovesick clients she'd ever worked with before. Having feelings for someone was the pits. She felt like one of those shivering chihuahuas in turtlenecks whenever she thought of him, totally unprepared for life on this planet. Worst of all, every third thought was about him. It was a nauseating combination of exhausting and exhilarating.

She was constantly remembering something he'd said, or wondering what he was up to or what he'd think about something she'd heard on the news…ugh. How mortifying.

She hadn't, however, let herself watch those YouTube

videos again. Those things were potent and had screwed up her life for a month. The last thing this stupid crush needed was fuel.

Which was why she didn't want to wait on his couch for him to come home from work, rumpled and tired and friendly. She didn't want him to slip off her socks and give her new ones. She didn't want to see whether he'd sit on the armchair or on the couch right next to her this time. She didn't want to find out what his end-of-the-day scent was. Whether he would still smell like deodorant, or if he'd be a little sweaty, a little musty. She wasn't sure which she was rooting for.

Wait! She wasn't rooting for either.

Which was why Kylie was currently snoozing in Fin's guest room. In the morning, she'd walk Ky down to the sidewalk and hand her off to Tyler with a wave and a smile. Problem solved.

But when the morning rolled around, Fin really didn't feel like the problem was solved. She hadn't slept well and was already sucking down a cup of coffee on her couch when Kylie emerged from the guest room, scratching at her messy hair and stumbling to the bathroom.

"You're up early."

"Yeah, Ty already texted me this morning. Woke me up."

"What'd he say?" Fin hoped she sounded casual.

"Oh. That he was bringing bagels over." She squinted at the clock on the wall. "He should be here in about ten minutes."

"Here? As in my house?"

Kylie's eyebrows raised. "Yeah. He's picking me up and bringing bagels for breakfast."

"Okay." Fin forced herself to remain sitting, holding her mug of coffee and looking as serene as possible. What she really wanted to do was run in a tight circle with her arms waving over her head, but somehow she thought she might lose some of Kylie's respect if she did that.

"It's probably a good thing he's bringing food," Kylie said lightly, peering into Fin's kitchen. "Since you don't use your kitchen as a kitchen."

"Hey!" Fin argued. "I microwave popcorn in there!"

Kylie laughed. "I'm gonna get dressed."

As soon as she'd left the room, Fin rose, surveying her space. It was clean, as she'd done a thorough wipe-down of dust only three days ago. She'd also vacuumed and mopped. But it wasn't the neatest it had ever been. A stack of journals skewed haphazardly on her bookshelf from where she'd been leafing through them. Her lampshade was askew, a pile of unfolded laundry melted halfway off an armchair and two dirty cereal bowls sat stolidly on her coffee table.

She dealt with the journals first. Once they were neatly back on the shelf, she quickly did the dishes and surveyed her kitchen. The indoor herb garden she grew on her kitchen table was healthy-looking and smelled delicious. The series of crystals on her windowsill were sparkling in the sun. The herbs that were hanging on racks to dry looked a little unusual, but she wasn't about to disturb them now.

She was just going back to her room to change out of her pajamas when a knock came on her door.

She froze midstep, almost comically. He was here already. And she was wearing bunchy pajama pants, no socks, a sports bra and an oversized bright teal zip-up sweatshirt. At least she'd brushed her teeth and washed her face. Her hair, however, was in a nest piled on top of her head that she hoped would pass for a bun. She wished that she was wearing at least some of her rings and bracelets and necklaces. But nope. She didn't sleep in them. So here she was, feeling as naked as a jaybird, pulling open the door for a grinning, lazy-faced Tyler leaning one shoulder on her doorjamb.

"Morning!"

"How'd you know which apartment was mine?"

"Ky told me. Can I come in?"

She stepped aside and swept her arm out like a game-show hostess.

He grinned down at her bare feet. "I take it this is a shoes-off apartment?" He was already sliding his loafers off and setting them neatly next to Kylie's sneakers.

How could this have happened? How could Fin have a crush on a man who wore *loafers*?

"Yup," she said.

"That's good, because I brought you something." He reached into the pocket of his coat and fished out a brand-new pair of purple Smartwool socks. Fin gaped down at them as he held them out to her, but his eyes were already across the room, landing on Kylie. "Hey, kid. How'd you sleep?"

"Like a rock. Fin's guest bed is the most comfortable thing ever."

"What kind of mattress is it?" he asked Fin, waggling the socks at her when he realized that she still hadn't taken them.

"What? Oh, it's just an old futon." She finally took the socks and felt the jolt of warm energy that coursed off them. It went all the way up to her elbow and back down to her fingertips. Not every gift that someone gave her made her feel this way, just the really thoughtful ones, the ones where the buyer had held her in their heart when they'd purchased it. And right now, her fingers were tingling as she clutched the socks.

It was just a pair of stupid socks. Nothing to get twisted

up over. Socks were the kind of gift that women normally complained about getting. They shouldn't be making her heart do this weird half-step thing in the cavity of her chest.

"I brought bagels, and then we'll get out of your hair, okay?" Tyler strode toward the kitchen, stopped in the doorway of it, looked and then turned back around to Fin. "There's no kitchen in your kitchen."

She couldn't help but laugh. "Your sister said almost the exact same thing. I usually eat in here."

She got them plates, poured Tyler a cup of coffee and arranged everything on her coffee table.

"So," Tyler probed as he set out bagels and cream cheese and a few other spreads. "You don't cook, like, at all?"

"She microwaves popcorn," Kylie put in helpfully, her mouth already full with the bagel she'd added a borderline disgusting amount of cream cheese to.

"Kid. The mouth, the food, the words, for the love of God, swallow that trough of cheese before you speak to me again."

Kylie crossed her eyes at Tyler but did as he asked.

"No wonder you think I'm such a good cook," Tyler said to Fin. "If the only thing you use your kitchen for is herbs and popcorn, the standard isn't very high."

"You *are* a good cook," Kylie said, reaching for her juice. "Better than my mom at least. All she ever did was heat up frozen meals. Or if she was having people over, she'd order from a fancy restaurant and put it on plates like she made it."

There was a momentary lull in the conversation and Fin knew they were in dangerous territory of making Kylie feel funny about what she had just shared.

"I did that once. Pretended I cooked a meal that I'd bought."

Tyler swung his head over to Fin. "Really? You?"

She shrugged. "It was for this big date, and I was really nervous. I wanted to impress the guy."

"Really?" Tyler said again, this time incredulously. *"You?"*

Fin laughed and shrugged again. "What? I was young. He was hot."

"Did it work? Did he buy it, get super impressed and fall madly in love?"

Fin pursed her lips and shook her head. "No. Well, sort of. He was super impressed with the food. But I didn't know that he was kind of a foodie. So he kept pumping me for the recipe. Eventually I had to come clean."

"Let me guess," Tyler said dryly. "He was so enamored with you trying to impress little old him that he didn't care one bit, and the date went well anyway."

Fin narrowed her eyes. "So?"

Tyler opened his mouth to retort, but Kylie's phone rang from her pocket. "It's Mary. I'm gonna answer."

She scampered away into the other room, her bagel still in her hand.

Kylie came bopping back out of the room again, but this time with her backpack over her shoulder. "Mary's main weekend help just called in sick and she wanted to know if I'd come help for a little bit this morning."

Tyler's brow went down. "You can only work fifteen hours a week."

"I only worked twelve this week. And if I get more than three, then I'll count them toward next week. It's Saturday! Come on. Saturday straddles the line between the two weeks."

"You're seriously this excited about work on a Saturday morning?"

"You're seriously going to jump up my ass for being excited about work on a Saturday morning?" She put one hand on her hip. "Would you prefer I sneak off to do drugs on an abandoned playground? Or have unprotected s—"

Tyler groaned and held up a hand to stop her. "Please don't continue. Let me just get my shoes and we'll go."

"That's okay. I can take the train."

Kylie was already slipping her own shoes on, setting her bagel down just long enough to get her coat zipped up.

"You mean alone?" Tyler looked surprised.

"Sure. Ty, the trains aren't rocket science. I'm only going to Cobble Hill."

"How would you get there, then?" he quizzed her.

Kylie paused. "I'll take the Q from the Prospect Park station," she turned to Fin. "Unless Parkside is closer?"

Fin shook her head, her mouth filled with bagel and her eyes bouncing back and forth between Ty and Ky. "Nope. Prospect Park is closer."

"And then I'll transfer to the bus that goes up Atlantic. Boom. I'll be there in half an hour."

"Weekend trains," Tyler protested weakly.

"You know, Ty, I happen to be in high school and this may come as a shocker to you, but I can actually read signs. If there's any wonky weekend trains, I'll change my route or I'll call you, okay?"

"I—" He was standing, one hand in his hair, looking befuddled. "Call me when you get there?"

"I'll *text* you when I get there," she amended. "Thanks for breakfast, and thanks for the guest room, Fin!"

The front door slammed and then Tyler and Fin were alone in her apartment, only a plate full of bagels as a flimsy excuse for him to be there.

Still standing, his hair a mess, Tyler looked down at the

bagel in his hand, at his shoes at the door and then at Fin. "I'll go."

"Don't be ridiculous. Sit down. Finish your breakfast." She ignored the fact that her heart was doing its best to pump jittery Kool-Aid down to her fingertips.

He sat again and this time, with no Kylie to distract him, his eyes wandered her apartment.

"I like your place."

"Really?" She was surprised. She looked around at the copious potted plants, crystals and baubles hanging in the windows, the deep colors and antique furniture. "It's really not your style."

"Yeah, but it's really *your* style. And I like your style. It works." He took a big swig of his coffee. "Some people have these outrageous style choices, and you can just tell that they're doing it almost to convince themselves that it's who they are. But you? Nah, this is the genuine article. It works because it really is who you are." He paused. "When we first met, I didn't get it."

"What didn't you get?"

"Well, I guess I didn't get why a woman who looked like you wasn't trying to get famous somehow. You never wear makeup, you have, like, pirate princess hair, you don't wear designer clothes. I'd...never met anybody like you. I thought you must have an angle, and it drove me nuts trying to figure out what it was."

"Pirate hair?" she asked, her eyes widening with insult.

He laughed. "I said pirate *princess* hair. You know, long black hair all the way down your back. Hasn't seen a pair of scissors in about a decade."

"I get haircuts!"

He laughed, dropping his face into his hand. "I'm botching this. I'm trying to pay you a compliment. I *like* your hair. It suits you. In fact, your whole life suits you. And I like that about you."

When her affronted posture melted back into a relaxed one, he continued on. "There's no game. What you see is what you get, all the way down to your mismatched socks." He grimaced and shrugged. "It's rare. Everybody else cares about their image too much."

Fin took another bite of her bagel and glanced at Tyler. The bongo drum in her chest made her want to look away immediately. Because there was something about his long face, the easy way he chewed, the shadow of dark blond stubble.

Everybody else cares about their image too much.

An unexpected truth came through the parted clouds, one that surprised Fin, even as she said it out loud. "You don't care about your image any more than I do."

Tipping her head to one side, she analyzed him through new eyes. He wore a collared shirt, as usual, his face shaved, his blond hair long enough to flop onto one side, but cut stylishly. She could see the muscles in his forearms peeking out from the folded cuffs of his shirt, the sharply ironed line in his trousers. Everything about his appearance implied that he deeply cared about his image. Yet...

He looked at her in surprise. "I thought you thought of me as James Spader, image-obsessed '80s villain."

"I did," she said thoughtfully, her chin on her fist.

He laughed at her candor but she continued on.

"But now I think I'm wrong. I think that this whole thing you've got going on, it's more for the socks reason than it is for what other people think."

"Socks reason?"

"Yeah. You present yourself this way because it lends order to your life. There's rhyme and reason, and that reassures you. I think you look like this more for yourself than for anyone else."

His face quirked down, the corners of his lips pulling into a frown as he considered her words. "Maybe you're right. I hadn't really thought about it that way. I definitely like things the way I like them. And, yeah, I guess what other people think about it doesn't bother me too much." He chewed and swallowed the last bite of his bagel thoughtfully. "My dad was über image-conscious. He was always talking about how this or that would reflect on him, on the family. He always had the newest, sleekest stuff. But it was all ugly. No style, just money. I think that gave me sort of an allergy to the whole image thing. Besides, if my childhood didn't do it, then Kylie's would have. Our father's precious image was the reason he kept Kylie a secret."

"He didn't want people here to find out about his second family?"

"I guess. Lorraine is…not like my mother. I mean, my mother's no peach, but her blood is blue. You can drop her into any rich, hobnobby Long Island room, and she'll swill vodka martinis and make eyes at the pool boys with the best of them."

"But Kylie's mother isn't like that?"

"No. She's crass. She hits on everybody." He grimaced. "Including me."

"You're kidding me."

"Nope." He popped the *p*. "After I found out that I had a sister per my dad's will, I went to Columbus on the first plane I could catch. Unfortunately I spent the entire trip warding off Lorraine and barely got to know Kylie. Ky and I would text or email a little bit. And we had a weekly phone call. I visited a few more times. But I really didn't know her before this fall. Not in any way that actually ended up mattering."

Tyler sighed and dropped his head, his palm smoothing over the back of his neck. Fin had noticed this tic of his and had wondered over it before.

"You're getting to know her now."

"Yeah." Ty's head came back up, his navy eyes lit with something like satisfaction. "I think we're actually in a pretty good place. I just wish…"

"You could stop worrying about Lorraine."

"God…" Ty stared at her. "I know that you do this for a living, but it's freaky how good you are at knowing what I'm thinking."

"Well, then, allow me to show off a little." Fin cocked her head to one side and looked at Tyler, really looked. She observed the play of his own energy off of itself, the busy rush in some places, the calm swirl in others. She pushed her bongo heart to the back of her mind and really tried to understand the topic at hand.

"You're not worrying about Lorraine as much as you're worrying that she'll be able to get back into Kylie's life."

Tyler shifted uncomfortably. "Uh. Yeah. Makes me feel like an absolute asshole for saying it out loud. But pretty much the second I realized the way Kylie had been living I thought to myself, God, I hope that Lorraine stays gone." He gave her a wry look that she knew was covering up a deeper feeling. "You know I never wanted to be responsible for a kid. Not my style. But yeah, Kylie wasn't just some kid. And I figured that even as unprepared as I was, I could give Ky a better life than Lorraine could."

"I don't think you should feel like an asshole for that," she said quietly, internally wincing over the memory of the ball game. Her harsh words. Was he admitting that they'd been, at least at that point, partially true?

"The kicker is that Lorraine *isn't* gone. She's fighting legal battles to keep her ass out of jail. And honestly, I'm not really rooting for her to succeed. Shouldn't I be hoping for the kid to work things out with her mom?"

"Trust me, moms aren't always the safest place for a kid to be."

"Oh. Right. You, ah, came to live up here with your aunt, is that right?"

"Yeah. And she ended up raising me in all the ways that counted. All the ways that my own mother couldn't."

He paused for a second, his navy blue eyes on hers, a quiet expression on his face. "Is your mother alive?"

"I...don't know," she answered with a naked honesty that shocked her. "I haven't heard from her since I was fourteen." Fin popped her chin onto her hand and looked vaguely out one of her windows. "She was into drugs so it's possible she's gone. But she's also one of those people who lands on her feet. I guess I wouldn't be surprised either way." And just like that, she'd told Tyler more about her life than anyone besides Via knew. How had he done that? Gotten the truth from her like that? Fin cleared her throat, avoiding his eyes and steering the conversation into safer waters. "Trust me, if Kylie is anything like me, which she is, she stopped hoping for her mom to transform into mother of the year a long time ago. I think for better or worse, Kylie has accepted the reality of who her mother is. Whether or not she's accepted the reality of who *you* are, I'm not sure yet." She made a face. "Sorry. You didn't ask for a session. I'll stop now."

"No, it's interesting. I like watching you work."

A moment of silence passed between them and Fin was

aware that they were no longer eating, and their coffee cups were empty. Tyler had run out of reasons to be in her house. He seemed to realize the exact same thing at the exact same moment.

If she knew him at all, he was going to hurry himself out the door, not wanting to seem like he was pushing into her space.

"Uh, all right, well. I guess I'll get going then." He stood and picked up all the plates. "Bagels are yours, obviously. Hope you enjoy them. And thanks again for taking care of Kylie last night. It was a lifesaver for me, because it ended up being a late work night. So...okay." He reappeared from her kitchen, where he'd set the dishes. "I'll get out of your hair."

He strode over to his loafers and toed into them, pulling his stylish coat on and flipping the collar out.

Fin had never been particularly susceptible to men and their wiles. She'd rolled her eyes at shirtless ad campaigns and merely smirked at pretty-boy Instagram accounts. But, yeah, it was also true that a weakness of Fin's was watching a man adjust his clothes. She couldn't exactly explain it. But there was something about the tying of shoes, or the buttoning of pants, or the side-to-side adjustment of a tie that just *oofed* her. And watching Tyler fiddle around with the collar of his coat was no exception.

To her horror, Fin felt a blush rising in her cheeks. *Get ahold of yourself! It's not like you're watching him undress! It's a winter coat, for god sakes.*

And then, he was all dressed with nowhere to go but out of Fin's house. She found that, as much as she hadn't wanted him to invade her space, now she didn't want him to leave. She didn't want him to leave *at all*. He was getting dangerously close to her front door and there was that

CARA BASTONE   215

familiar voice, the one she almost always listened to, that was speaking so clearly inside of her. *Stay, Tyler*, the voice said. *Stay here.*

"Tyler."

He stopped and turned. And now, standing there, trying to see him, she felt as if she were squinting through yards of gloomy muck. There, at the bottom of the muck, was that golden energy she couldn't ignore anymore.

Stay, Tyler.

How could she get him to stay?

The thought struck her blindingly clearly, like a flash in the dark. She almost blinked against the intensity of it.

Her bathtub! The forgotten ask. How many times had she meant to ask her superintendent to swing by and fix it? And how many times had she forgotten? And now she knew exactly why her brain had let that information slip away time and time again. Because the superintendent wasn't the person who was supposed to fix the leak in her tub.

Tyler was.

She cleared her throat. He still waited there, patiently. Apparently he'd become accustomed to these long pauses in which she balanced her psychic life with her physical one.

"Do you know anything about bathtubs?"

CHAPTER FIFTEEN

TYLER WAS IN the best mood he'd been in in over a year. Kylie had gotten her grades back recently for the first semester, all Bs and a lone, glorious A. He'd take it. She'd started studying at the desk he'd set up in the living room. She almost always called him Ty now, she was holding down a job, singing to herself when she folded her laundry and had even started clearing the dishes after dinner.

That wasn't the only area where Ty's life was going swimmingly. He had a meeting coming up with his editor next week to convince him to let him take his column in a new direction, which might in turn free up some of his nights and weekends. He was currently on his way to play basketball at the Y with Seb and Matty. And best of all, he'd gotten asked out by the cutie behind the counter at his coffee shop this morning.

He bounced the basketball on the sidewalk as he jogged around the corner toward the Y, earning some dirty looks from a group of older ladies in large hats, stepping out of a church. He picked up the ball and tipped an imaginary hat to them. "Excuse me, ladies."

Two of them smiled at him, but one just frowned even more, rolling her eyes at the floppy-haired goofball grinning at them. That made Ty grin even harder. When he was far enough away from them, he started dribbling the ball again.

"What are you grinning at?" Sebastian called from where he and Matty were waiting in front of the Y.

"Got asked out by a hottie at the coffee shop this morning." He held his hand out to Matty. "Slap me some skin."

Matty gave him a whopping good high five and then jumped in a 180, facing away from Ty, holding one hand in the air. "No-look high five!"

Laughing, Tyler slapped hands with Matty again. That wasn't exactly what people meant by a no-look high five, but still, the kid had flair.

"So, when's the date?" Seb asked as he checked in at the front desk, handing over a few bucks to bring Tyler in as a guest.

"What date?" Ty asked, peeking in at the courts on the way to the locker room, seeing if there was enough room for them to just shoot around or if they were going to have to join a pickup game.

"Your date with the coffee shop hottie."

"Oh. I didn't say yes."

Tyler had his coat already locked into a locker by the time he turned around and saw his best friend gaping at him. "You...said no to a date. With a hottie."

Tyler grimaced. "You make it sound like it's a sign of terminal illness or something. You know I haven't been dating for a while."

"Sure, but things are finally evening out with Ky, I just figured..."

"I'd wanna get back in the saddle?"

"You ride horses, Uncle Ty?"

Tyler looked down at Matty's blunt face, his innocent expression, and swallowed down his own laughter. "No. I do not. It's an expression. It means to try something again even if you're out of practice."

"Thank you for the PG explanation," Seb muttered once Matty had scampered forward, out of the locker room and onto the courts.

"Mickey Rooney, think fast!" Tyler launched the ball over to the kid, nearly smacking him in the face with rubber, but Matty dodged at the last second, laughing like a maniac and chasing the ball down. "I'm not going to corrupt your kid by explaining that it's not horses I ride."

"Gross. Done. We're done with that topic."

Tyler laughed. He'd always known how to push Seb's buttons.

"So, that's really it? You said no because you're just not dating right now?"

"I guess." She'd asked him out before but had seemed unavailable since he'd gotten back from Columbus. Apparently she was available again. Honestly, Tyler hadn't really thought twice about saying no to the date. It had just sort of happened and he'd moved on.

"Because of Kylie?"

"Yeah. And—" Tyler cut himself off immediately when, to his confusion and horror, it was Fin's face that popped into his mind. The image of her laughing and sitting on the closed lid of her toilet while she handed over tools for him to fix the drain in her tub last weekend. He'd been happy to help; he'd done something similar with his own tub a couple years before. And maybe, just maybe, due to the smiley, blushy mood she'd happened to be in, he'd taken a skosh longer with the task than was strictly necessary. Maybe, just maybe, he'd fiddled around for an extra half hour because it had been nice to joke with her about nothing, her sagey smell filling the small bathroom around them, her cute-ass feet perfectly wrapped up in the socks he'd bought for her.

But that wasn't the reason he'd refused the date.

It couldn't be. He'd gone down that road before. That feelings-for-Fin road that led to nowhere but humiliated at a baseball game. How many times had she made it clear that she wasn't interested in him? Hell, the last month she'd obviously been making arrangements so that she could hang with Kylie without having to see him as well. If that wasn't a hint, then he didn't know what was. It was extremely dangerous to let himself start this silly crush up again.

"And…" Seb prompted.

"I don't know. Things are going well. I just don't want to rock the boat."

A court opened up, and the conversation stopped as the play started. The game alternated back and forth between Seb and Ty attempting to shove the ball down each other's throats and lifting Matty up onto their shoulders so that he could dunk. Ty was thrilled to see that Matty's ball handling had improved a lot since the last time they'd played together.

"Hey, Dad, can I have money for water?"

"Water is free."

"Not the kind I want."

Sebastian rolled his eyes and peeled a five-dollar bill out of his pocket. "Get one for me and Uncle Ty too."

"No strawberry flavor for me!" Ty called at Matty's retreating back.

Seb turned to Ty and passed the ball to him. "Any news?"

Ty didn't have to ask what kind of news Seb was prying after.

Ever since Kylie had come to Brooklyn, there'd been pretty much crickets on what the hell was happening with Lorraine. As much as he'd called his lawyer, Kylie's social worker, they always said the same thing: nothing to report yet.

Today, however, was different. "Actually, yeah. Got a call from our lawyer with an update."

"And?"

"And she's not going to get jail time." Tyler took a shot; it banked off the rim and went wide. Seb caught the rebound and popped it in the hoop, chest-passing the ball to Ty when he caught it again.

"I…have no idea how to feel about that," Seb said after a minute.

Tyler laughed, because it was the only thing he could do. "Join the club. Part of me wanted the judge to lock her up and throw away the key. After what she did to Kylie? Jesus. It'll be years before Kylie can fully sort through all this crap."

"But another part of you was relieved?"

"Yeah. I mean, she's Kylie's mom. I don't want her to go to *jail.*"

"So, what was her sentencing?"

Tyler sighed, shot a three-pointer that sailed gracefully through the net. "Time served, three years' probation and six months of mandatory rehab."

"Oh, the wonders of what having a little money in your pocket can do for you."

"I know. If only my dad knew that all his money was going toward keeping Lorraine out of jail…" Tyler paused, stared at nothing for a minute. "Actually, I have no idea how he'd feel about that."

"What does it all mean for Kylie? For custody?"

"Well, that's the good news. It'll be at least a year and a half before Lorraine can appeal the courts for custody. Under the judge's orders, she has to ace rehab, get a job and keep her nose clean for at least that long. Sounds like once she's out of rehab, we'll have to do mandatory visits to Columbus once a month so that they can see one another. But beyond that?" He shrugged. "Pretty good news, I guess."

Seb was quiet for a minute, jogged to one side of the court, peered down the hallway for Matty and jogged back, shaking his head. "Kid's stuck in, like, a ten-person line." He held his hands out for the ball. "So, you have her for at least eighteen more months."

"Thank God."

"Thank God," Sebastian echoed, studying Tyler closely. "I'm glad you think that's a good thing."

"A good thing? Oh, jeez. I know I was freaked out before, Seb, but I always knew I was a safer place for Kylie than Lorraine. I don't care if it's been hard. If worst comes to worst and I lose custody of her in eighteen months, I'll move to Columbus until she's eighteen. I'll, I dunno, rent the house next door. Be there for her and hope to God she wants to go to college in New York."

Tyler suddenly found himself the recipient of a disgustingly sweaty hug from his best friend.

"Dude. Space." He shoved away and then got a look at Seb's face. "Are you *crying*?"

"It's just cool is all," Seb said, brushing a tear or two off his face with the inside of his elbow. "You used to have such distance between you two. All those stilted phone calls, neither of you knowing what to say to the other. She seemed like such an obligation to you. I guess I'm just saying that it's good to see you care this much, Ty. It looks good on you."

Speechless, Tyler just sort of stared at his best friend. "I— Okay."

Sebastian glanced back at the hallway where Matty was waiting.

"Okay, quick. Tell the truth, dude. Are you pining after Fin again, or what?"

Apparently now that the little pitchers with big ears had gone to get fancy water, the dad could ask whatever the hell he wanted to ask.

Tyler frowned. "I never pined after her."

"You were tongue-tied around her for so long. Then you asked her out, got rejected and could barely even be in the same room after that."

"That is not what happened."

"Ty, you basically ghosted me and Matty because you were so torn up over her!"

Tyler stepped back from Sebastian. "You think I *ghosted* you?"

"Ty," Seb said gently right before he took a shot. "You were barely answering my calls. I spent the first forty years of my life barely able to peel you away for a day or two and then suddenly I can't even get you to text me back."

"I— It wasn't— That wasn't because of Fin." Tyler rebounded the ball and took his own shot, frowning at his best friend. "That wasn't exclusively because of Fin. And I wasn't torn up over her, exactly. More like, I was torn up over what she said to me."

"What did she say? I mean, Via told me that the conversation was pretty harsh, but I never got the details, really."

Tyler rebounded the ball again, not wanting to repeat it but also knowing it would be good for him. It was important that he remember exactly what she'd said to definitively end his crush on her.

"She basically told me I was a pathetic man-child who clung to you guys instead of growing up. That my proclivity toward the single life was abhorrent and that I was the last man on earth she would ever be interested in."

"And you believed her," Seb said flatly.

"For a while at least." Ty paused.

"Ty," Seb said, just staring at him. "I know she's all mystical and clairvoyant and spooky, but you're honestly telling me that it didn't occur to you to tell her to shove her idiotic theory where the sun don't shine? I mean, I love the woman, but she shouldn't have spoken to you like that!"

"I hate to admit it, but a lot of what she said really stuck with me. Maybe it wasn't all exactly right, but the truth is, if I hadn't been quite so haunted by it, I might not have risen to the occasion with Kylie so much, you know?" He dribbled thoughtfully, putting the pieces together as he went. "I spent the summer trying to prove to myself that I wasn't a hanger-on to your life and, yeah, it kind of made me want a life of my own. I didn't think that would come in the form of guardianship over my little sister, but when it did..." He shrugged.

"When it did, you took the chance." Seb was quiet, took a shot. He paced away and back, his hands on his hips. "I never thought that maybe your relationship with me and Matty was holding you back in some ways."

"My relationship with you guys has been one of the brightest spots of my life."

Sebastian grabbed the ball, dribbled it and then held it against his hip. He eyed Tyler. "But has it kept you from doing your own thing? I mean, I'm never going to complain about the years you helped me raise Matty. But I never really thought that maybe it was at your own expense."

"Nah, come on, I wouldn't change it."

"But those were years you could have been starting your own family. And instead you were—"

"Seb, we both know that I don't want my own family. Kylie is as close to my own kid as I'm ever going to want.

And helping you and Matty during that time, moving home, didn't keep me from growing up, it *forced* me to grow up. I'm a better person because of that. I don't want Fin's words to belittle one of my proudest accomplishments."

"All right, all right," Seb said, passing him the ball. "No need to get your panties in a twist."

Tyler dribbled the ball for a minute. "What she said, it bothered me a lot. And, yeah, it killed my crush on her."

Seb watched him for another long minute and then rushed to rebound the shot. "Fair enough." He took a shot. "Want to come over for dinner tonight? Via's making some stew thingy."

Tyler laughed, letting some of the tension seep out of him. "As much as I love stew thingies, we're gonna eat at home tonight. Kylie has some kid from her class coming over to work on a project."

"Strawberry-kiwi for dad, peach for Uncle Ty and cherry for me."

Matty came running up victoriously, almost bobbling the three plastic water bottles in his arms.

"Nuh-uh," Tyler said. "I want the cherry."

"No way!"

"You take the peach. No one likes peach."

"You said you didn't want strawberry. Not peach."

"Let's split both, then."

Matty narrowed his eyes and put his hands on his hips, one of them encumbered by the bottle of flavored water. "No deal. I don't want your germs."

Tyler laughed and cracked the top on the disgusting peach water. "You drive a hard bargain, kid."

CHAPTER SIXTEEN

"RACHEL," FIN SCOLDED in a stern voice through the thin door that separated her client's living room from the bedroom. She knew that Rachel was listening at the door instead of folding the laundry the way she'd claimed she would.

"Sorry!" Rachel shouted. "It just sounded like you two were really getting somewhere!"

Enzo, where he was sitting on an armchair, hands crossed over his gut and his feet propped up on his coffee table, laughed, low and guttural. "See what I mean?" He raised his voice to call through the door. "Woman can't mind her business!"

"And that's one of the things you love about her the most," Fin gathered, from the way his energy had swelled toward the sound of Rachel's voice.

Her sessions with Enzo had relocated out of the sterile office space to his fiancée's homey brownstone in Red Hook when they'd moved in together last month. The setting change had made a big difference in Fin and Enzo's sessions. They were really starting to trust one another, something that so rarely happened with her male clients.

Today, after a long session talking about Enzo's relationship to his work and to the uncle who was his boss, the two of them stood up and stretched.

She felt energized.

She knew it wasn't only her prowess as a spiritual counselor that was making this happen. She knew that at least some of the credit was due to the changes in her own life. Being around Tyler so much lately had...softened her.

"Your phone is buzzing," Enzo said as he stretched.

"Oh." She dug through her purse, her stomach giving that familiar electric jolt when she saw it was a text from Tyler.

SOS, was all it said. Her stomach went from jolting to dropping.

What's wrong? she texted back immediately, her bottom lip caught between her teeth and a line of worry between her brows.

She'd never stared harder at a set of thinking bubbles in her entire God-given life.

"Something wrong?" Enzo asked, making Fin jump. She realized that she was only halfway into her coat, clutching her phone and scowling like a crazy person.

"I'm not sure. My friend just texted—" Her phone buzzed in her hand and she cut off, devouring the text. Immediately, her face relaxed, her eyes rolled and a groan, part annoyance and part relief, left her chest. "About something that is absolutely not a crisis."

Kylie has a boy over and I need backup. I have tacos. Bring beer.

You're ridiculous, she texted back. This is not an SOS situation.

I'm about ten seconds from going out there to sit between them on the couch. So for the love of God, come over here and stop me.

"Rachel totally called it," Enzo asked, a smile on his face. "You've got a new man."

"What? No." She shoved her phone in her pocket and pulled her coat the rest of the way on, grabbing her messenger bag. "He's just a friend."

"Mmm-hmm," Enzo said skeptically at the exact same time that Rachel did from through the door.

"In my professional opinion, you two need to get a life," Fin called. She left them both laughing as she exited their apartment with a wave and jogged down their front steps to the train.

On my way, she texted and then paused. To save Kylie from the humiliation of having her older brother ruin a first date.

She came aboveground forty-five minutes later and gave the weekend doorman at Ty's building a friendly wave.

She only got in one knock on Tyler's door when it flung open. She hated the fact that her breath caught at the sight of his normally floppy hair that was standing on end from where he'd been tugging at it. It was ridiculous to find someone's nervous side so freaking cute. "What took you so long? Bad weekend trains?"

"I was coming all the way from Red Hook."

She stepped inside and tried not to freeze up when he reached for her messenger bag to help her out of her things. "What were you doing in Red Hook? Shit, I didn't screw up Saturday-night plans for you, did I? Holy God, what do you have in this bag, rocks?"

She laughed at his rapid-fire questions, trying to let mirth dispel some of the tension from his nearness. "I was working with a client. And to answer your question," she said as she flipped open the flap of her messenger bag to show him the ten rather large crystals she had inside, "Yes, I do have rocks in that bag."

He laughed and carefully set the bag in his coat closet, eyeing the crystals with interest. She was kicking off her boots when he stepped back to her and, in a move she'd only seen him execute with Mary and Via, helped her off with her coat. It was a gentlemanly thing, something she wasn't sure anyone had ever done for her before. It was brisk and practiced, there was no lingering, no crowding, no brushing against her neck and shoulders. He merely helped her peel her coat off and then hung it on a hook.

Feeling both flushed and a little silly, Fin crossed her arms over her chest and turned toward the living room.

"Where are they?" she whispered.

"Finishing dinner in the kitchen," he whispered back, leaning in just a bit and causing even more color to rush to her cheeks. "They'll be back out when they're done."

He nodded his head toward the coffee table in between the couch and TV and Fin did a double take. "Tyler. There are textbooks on the table."

"Right."

"They've been studying?" she asked, giving him a dry look.

"Yeah. They're working on a project together."

Fin groaned and dropped her head into her hands. "You sent me an SOS because Kylie has a school project with a boy?"

"What?" he asked obstinately, his hands raised. "Half the making out I ever did in high school was thanks to school projects. Besides, I'm not completely nuts. They've been…vibing."

Fin burst out laughing. "Vibing? Is that energy lingo you're using? Am I rubbing off on you, Ty?"

He scowled at her. "Did you bring the beers or not?"

She walked to her coat and pulled two beers out of the deep inside pockets, wagging them at him.

His scowl softened into humor. "Couldn't spring for a whole sixer? Had to just grab two loosies like a guy on a street corner?"

"Hey, I was already carrying a bag of rocks. You expected me to carry an entire six-pack as well?"

They walked back to the kitchen in time to see Kylie and her study partner clearing up their plates.

"Thank you for dinner, Mr. Leshuski."

"You can call me Tyler, Anthony," Ty said, pulling himself up to his full height.

But even though Tyler was tall, over six feet, Anthony towered over him. At least six five, at maybe fifteen years old, the kid had that bowed look of someone who'd grown too fast. But he had a wide, crinkly smile, and lots of black, curly hair that fell into his face and perfectly set off his ochre skin.

"Fin!" Kylie said as she turned around. "I didn't know you were coming over tonight."

"Just thought I'd stop by."

"Uh-huh," Kylie said suspiciously, her eyes dancing back and forth between Anthony and Tyler. "Come on, Tony. Let's try and finish that project."

She tugged at Anthony's hand and Fin felt a familiar wave of heat-ice radiate off the boy. He was having a big internal reaction to Kylie touching him and it was just about all he could do to hide it.

With chagrin, she had to admit that the exact same thing had just happened to her when Tyler had taken off her coat.

Tyler watched them go with narrowed eyes and then, with a shake of his head, started opening up the remaining takeout containers. He'd ordered enough food for a Thanksgiving feast and Fin was grateful. She hadn't eaten since lunch and it was almost nine o'clock now.

She sat down quickly, before he could do something swoony, like pull out her chair. He sat down too, and held up both of the beers she'd chosen, peering at the labels. "Which do you want?"

"Either. I went with Mexican beer because you said tacos."

"Perfect. Oh, this one needs a bottle opener."

She grabbed the bottles from him before he could stand again and used one to leverage the cap off the other. Then she twisted the cap off the first and held them both out, letting him choose which one he wanted.

He just gaped at her. "I…have never seen a woman do that before."

"Little something I learned growing up in Louisiana."

He shook his head, like she'd totally befuddled him, and selected a beer. "You never cease to amaze me, Fin St. Romain."

She already had a mouthful of an *hongos* taco, so luckily, she didn't have to respond.

"So," he continued on. "I didn't realize you worked on Saturday nights. Actually." He paused to consider. "I pretty much don't know anything about your job."

She took a drink. "I have about twenty clients who I see on a regular basis. Most of them once a month, a few of them twice."

"Holy shit. That's a lot of clients."

She nodded. "Yeah. The business has grown a lot over the last two years especially. After Via moved out, I wanted to keep living in my apartment, but that meant having to pay the rent on my own, so I really kicked things into gear."

"How'd you find all the clients?"

"The first few I found through the internet. I have a website. They reached out to me. I got a handful of clients I really trusted. And from there, it's all been referrals."

"That makes sense." He considered. "You meet these people in their homes, right? You'd want to make sure you could trust them."

"Actually, at first I meet all of them in this little office space I rent for the occasion. My neighbor's sister is a therapist and has a little annex attached to her office that I rent by the hour while I'm still learning about a new client. After a few sessions, I can tell if I trust them enough to meet at their home."

"And if you don't trust them enough?"

"I drop them as a client. Life is hard enough without inviting people I don't trust into it."

Ty's eyes dropped from hers and she guessed immediately what he must be thinking. The baseball game. The way she'd so effectively cast him out of her life, like he wasn't even worth the few minutes it would have taken to let him down more gently.

Her stomach cramped and she got up to get a glass of water.

She turned back after sipping her water and saw that his eyes were still downcast. He was still mulling over her words at the baseball game, she was sure.

But what, really, could she say now? *Tyler, I was wrong. You're not selfish. You're interesting and generous and kind, and now I'm the one crushing on you?* No. No way. There was no way that she was going to muddy the waters between them. She'd never forgive herself if she let this silly crush get in the way of what she was building with Kylie.

But that dulled look on his face as he worked his way

through his rice and beans was just killing her. And she was the one who'd put it there.

How could she make this better?

"You know, I've been kind of having a breakthrough with the client I saw tonight. And I think I have you to thank for it."

This was a delicate bridge to walk. Barely a few inches wide, with rushing water on either side.

His head came up. "Me? Really?"

"Yeah, this client, he's a man. I don't usually take on male clients."

He nodded. "Makes sense. Especially if you'd have to be in their houses alone with them."

Something smooth and hot seemed to wrap itself around her. He really understood what she was saying. She sat here, eating tacos and drinking cheap beer with him, the same way she might have done with Via. And he wasn't thinking she was overvigilant or silly when she explained her reticence to work with men. He simply nodded in understanding. It was new. It was refreshing. It...almost hurt, it felt so good.

"So," he said when she was quiet for a moment too long. "How was it that I helped?"

"Right. Yeah." She cleared her throat. "It was our friendship, I guess, yours and mine, that helped more than anything." She couldn't help but notice that his eyes had softened on the word *friendship*. "See, a while ago, when Kylie first got here, Mary mentioned something to me."

"She's been known to casually drop truth bombs."

"Exactly." Fin pointed her fork at him and took a long sip of beer. "She's kind of a Jedi master when it comes to that."

"Mary Poppins. Spoonful of sugar."

Fin grinned. "Anyway, she told me that I have a blind spot when it comes to certain things."

"Right," Ty agreed easily. "When it comes to men."

For some reason, when Mary said it to her, it had been illuminating. When Tyler said it to her, it was just plain annoying. "Oh, what do you know about it?" she huffed.

Ty pushed back from the table a bit and crossed his arms. "I know that you wrote me off the second you could tell I was attracted to you. Like it was some sort of fatal flaw. Right from the very beginning. It was like you pulled a big velvet curtain between the two of us. And the one time I tried to pull the curtain back, you just about katana-ed my head off. All because you could tell I wanted you."

He stared down at his plate. The fire in his eyes sort of leached away and a kind of sheepishness took its place. He uncrossed his arms and scraped a hand over the back of his neck. Maybe, she guessed, he was wishing that he hadn't brought up just how much he'd wanted her back then. "I'm gonna check on the kids."

He was up and into the living room. Fin heard their muffled voices stutter to a stop when Tyler entered the room.

She tried to regain her equilibrium.

He was back in the kitchen a second later. "She's sitting in the armchair, not on the couch," he reported with palpable relief.

Fin laughed. "Really, Ty, I don't think you have much to worry about there. He seems like a nice kid. And she doesn't even realize he has a crush on her."

Ty's eyes narrowed. "He has a crush on her?"

"Didn't you sort of have a crush on every girl whose house you went over to for school projects?"

Tyler looked for a second like he was going to argue, and then his face relaxed. "Touché."

He polished off his remaining taco. "So, if you instantly reject any man who's attracted to you, it leads me to this question. Which men actually *do* have a chance with you?"

"Only the ones who aren't attracted to me, apparently," she replied dryly with a lift of her eyebrows and a swig of her beer.

He batted his eyelashes at her. "Does such a man exist?"

"Anyway," she said with a pointed eye roll, though internally she was relieved that he was playing around again, "After Mary said that, I've tried not to—"

"Use the velvet curtain?"

"What is it with you and this velvet-curtain metaphor?"

"I dunno. Maybe it's because all your clothes look like an old lady's curtains?"

He was grinning dumbly at her, and she couldn't help but laugh.

"Ever since then I've tried not to be quite so blind when it comes to you," she barreled on. "And, yeah, I guess it's helped with a lot of the men in my life. Enzo, my client, said I've been different. Nicer, I think he meant." She shrugged, wanting to make this seem like not quite so big a deal. "So. Thanks."

When she looked up from her plate, his teasing expression was long gone. In its place was a contemplative look she wasn't sure she'd ever seen him make before. He was studying her. His eyes finished traveling her face and just looked directly into hers. It wasn't a long moment, but it was a loaded one. His navy eyes were momentarily unguarded, open. She felt as if a braided steel rope connected them, as if all she'd have to do was give that rope a tug and he'd move toward her.

"Ty? Can we watch that gymnastics meet you DVRed?"

Tyler jerked his eyes away and toward Kylie, leaning

in the doorway. "What? Oh. Sure. It's pretty old, though. Probably a month or so."

"That's okay," Anthony said as he came to appear in the doorway as well. "I haven't seen it and I like gymnastics."

"Do you do any yourself?"

"Used to when I was younger. But then I got more into this coding club and my mom said I had to choose one."

Fin hid her smile. She liked the way Anthony said *mom*. There was nothing grudging or embarrassed in his tone. It spoke a lot about their relationship.

"Usually I only get to watch it during the Olympics because we don't get very many sports channels."

"Well, I get all the sports channels. Just have Kylie ask me and I can record whatever you want."

Now the smile Fin was hiding became the grin that Fin was hiding.

Tyler went out to help them cue up the program, and when he got back, Fin let her smile free.

"What?" he asked as he sat back down.

"Got a soft spot for gymnasts?"

"Huh?"

"Oh, come on, Ty. All the kid had to do was tell you that he used to play a sport and you completely dropped the overprotective act and straight-up invited him over again."

His brow furrowed before his expression broke open. "Huh. I guess you're right." He laughed at himself. "I guess I'm an easy lock to pick. I used to do some gymnastics, so maybe it was a perfect storm."

"A gymnast and a ballet dancer?"

He froze, his beer bottle halfway to his mouth, his eyes narrowed. "Who told you? Sebastian?"

"Ky."

"*Kylie* knows?"

"She googled you when she first found out about you. She showed me the videos."

"She showed you the videos," he repeated numbly. "Oh, Jesus. The internet deserves to get punched in the nuts. Is nothing allowed to die? Ever?"

She leaned her elbows forward, impossibly charmed over his embarrassment. "Why are you so concerned with hiding it? It's really cool."

"Yes, I agree. Ballet is really cool. It's an exacting and demanding sport slash art form. And it's not like I'm ashamed of it or anything. But come on, would you want to see videos of your much younger self doing a bunch of crap that you were only marginally good at?"

"*Marginally* good at? Tyler, you were an incredible dancer. Seriously. I was really impressed."

He blushed, looking up at her through embarrassed eyelashes. "I mean, I loved it. Even though I got mocked for it my entire high school career. But in the end, I just didn't have the chops to make it professionally."

She shook her head. "The dance world must be cutthroat then, because from what I saw, you were incredibly gifted."

Again, charmingly, he went quite pink. "I auditioned a bunch at the end of high school, for all sorts of companies and troupes. But got nothing but a series of 'good try, kid.' Writing was another passion of mine, so I went to journalism school and danced with a few clubs for a while. After that, I tweaked my knee pretty bad and I realized that I might permanently injure my body for something that had become just a hobby. So I quit halfway through college."

"Do you ever dance at all anymore?"

He opened his mouth and then clapped it closed. "Uh. Yeah, actually. Before Kylie I was renting some studio time over by Union Square for an hour a week. Sometimes I'd stay for the class right after. Just messing around really. Trying to stay in shape. Stay flexible. Yoga is too slow. Pilates is too boring. So, mostly, in my normal life, I run, shoot hoops with Seb and Matty and—" he cleared his throat "—dance."

"But not since Kylie came to live with you."

"Right."

"You know I'd hang out with her if you still wanted to do that, Ty. It's just a couple hours a week. You could probably even plan it for when she's in school. You don't have to put your whole life on hold. I'm sure she doesn't even *want* you to put your whole life on hold."

He lifted his eyebrows and didn't look convinced.

"Honestly," she continued, "it wouldn't even be that big of a deal to leave her at home alone sometimes. She's a trustworthy kid."

"With Anthony the gymnast sniffing around? I don't think so."

Fin laughed and shook her head.

He groaned, his eyes tracing up to the ceiling. "I can't believe you've seen the ballet videos."

Seen them? I practically licked them.

"We need more beers," he decided. "I'm gonna go ask my neighbors real quick."

Fin cleared up the kitchen while he was gone, washing their plates and boxing up the leftovers. He came back with two more beers under one arm and half a cake balancing on a plate in the other hand.

"Medovnik cake for dessert," he said, hefting the plate up and setting it on the table with a flourish. "Courtesy of Ivetka and Kamil, my neighbors two doors down."

"Oh, yum. I haven't had this in years! Are they from the Czech Republic?"

"Yeah. She teaches at a few CUNY schools, and he works at a restaurant in Queens. Czech food that'll make you punch your grandma it's so good."

She laughed, which proved just how much of a crush she had, because that was not the kind of joke that would normally make her laugh.

"Beer and cake?" he asked. "Beer first, cake second?"

"Beer first, cake second."

"Good choice." He sat down, twisted the tops off their icy beers and peered thoughtfully at the label. "You were really popping beer bottles in your preteens back in Louisiana?"

"I was popping *coke* bottles in my preteens. And maybe, like, three or four beer bottles once when Tammy Wegren stole some beer from her mama and we got drunk while she was at work."

Tyler laughed, took a swig of his beer and squinted thoughtfully into his own past. "Let's see. The first time I ever got drunk, Seb and I were sixteen and trying very hard to be cool at this hot senior girl's party." He cleared his throat. "We did not end up being cool."

"Lampshade dancing?"

He laughed. "No. But there was definitely dancing of other kinds. That was the first night I ever freaked a girl on the dance floor. And then I had to run out of the house to go puke in the bushes. Seb basically carried me to the train. Then, he puked in a trash can on the platform, and I basically carried *him* home from the train."

Fin laughed. "Classic? I guess?"

Tyler joined in her laughter. "No, not a classic for us. We actually didn't party that much in high school. I was the kid who did ballet, and Sebastian had yet to grow into that giant head of his."

Fin thought of how handsome Seb was now with his blunt face and big body, but she could easily see how those large features would be pretty burdensome midpuberty. "Think Matty's in store for some awkward teen years?"

"Oh, I'd put money on it. It's gonna be a long and painful decade of teendom when he shoots up like a beanstalk and realizes that he's in love with Joy."

"You think so? I'm not sure they're in love."

"Trust me. They love each other. If it didn't make me feel like a perv, I'd put money on them losing their V-cards together."

"Oh, God." She squinched up her face and shook her head. "Why? Tyler? *Why?*"

"What? I'm sure they'll be over eighteen, and there'll be plenty of rose petals. Does that make you feel better?"

"No, you sicko. And I wouldn't wish rose-petal virginity losing on my worst enemy. Too much pressure."

"Bad experience?" he asked, blatant curiosity written in every line of his face.

"Not bad. Just awkward. I was kind of old. Twenty. And I'd been dating this guy for a few months. I was kind of like, *eh, why not?* Meanwhile he was like—"

"Drawing you a bath and serenading you with Boyz II Men?"

"Pretty much, yeah. He did the whole nine. Champagne. Flowers. Chocolate-covered strawberries…"

"And then you had really terrible, awkward first-timer sex?"

"Yup." She popped the *p.* "We didn't last as a couple much longer after that. It was pretty clear we weren't on the same page." She took a swig of beer. "How about you?"

"My first time? Let's see. I had you beat. I was twenty-one."

"Late bloomer?"

"Sort of? I think people thought I was gay because of the ballet thing, so I'd often go on a date and then the girl would be like, 'Hold on, is this a date?' Not exactly an aphrodisiac."

"Was she your girlfriend?"

He grimaced. "No. Just a nice girl I met at a party. We did it in somebody's bedroom and then got walked in on by a drunk kid looking for the bathroom while my pants were still around my ankles."

She grimaced too. "Ouch."

"You said it."

"You think anyone's first time is like, amazing?" she asked.

"Probably?"

"Doubts." This conversation was making them both a little giggly, and something about the way she said "doubts" made them both burst into loud laughter. It was the kind of laughter that picked you up and shook you out. The kind of laughter that made you feel like you'd just sprinted around the block in the fresh cold air. The kind that made it very hard to stop smiling afterward and made everything else seem funny simply by association.

The kind that made everything it touched sort of glitter.

She was still glittering an hour later, after they'd split the cake, when she and Tyler walked Anthony down to the curb and put him in a cab. She was still glittering when Tyler waved down another cab for her, held the door open for her.

Still glittering when, to her surprise, he reached down before closing the door and gave her shoulder a good, firm squeeze.

"Night, Fin."

"Night, Ty."

And then he did that thing. That thing where a man

knocks twice against the roof of the cab to indicate that it's time to pull away.

She figured she had to add that to the list along with tie-adjusting and helping a woman take a coat off. Because Fin just sort of crumpled back into her seat, her eyes closed, savoring the glitter of the moment the way someone might savor the first sip of truly great whiskey, or a fresh strawberry still warm from the sun, or a first kiss.

CHAPTER SEVENTEEN

A WEEK LATER, Tyler was trying not to be disappointed as he stood in Via and Seb's kitchen, Matty and Mary chatting away at the counter, Seb canoodling with Via while she attempted to wash lettuce for their salad.

Fin wasn't there. And now, only in the face of the brick wall of his disappointment could Tyler admit that he'd maybe been kinda, sorta looking forward to seeing her there tonight.

They hadn't seen one another since he'd put her in that cab last weekend.

January had slammed the door on its way out, dumping eight inches of snow, followed by two hours of freezing rain, and then plunging New York into what felt like subzero temperatures for almost a week straight. Everyone in the city was living in enough layered clothing that it took at least four minutes to undress for bed each night. Tyler hadn't seen his own skin in five days. Well, except for showers.

And now, here they were in February. The grayest, coldest month of the year, where all there was to look forward to was fudging on New Year's resolutions and maybe happening to see Fin at a friend's dinner. Where she then didn't show up for no good reason at all.

Well, maybe she had a great reason. But he'd be damned if he'd ask.

"Where's Fin tonight?" Mary asked, looking up from the puzzle she and Matty were dominating on the kitchen table.

Tyler could have kissed her. Not wanting to appear too eager to hear the answer, he walked to the fridge and helped himself to a beer.

"She...had other plans," Via replied. Was it his imagination or had Via's eyes flicked over to him?

"She had that date," Kylie called from the front door as she came in from the cold. Tyler did everything in his power not to freeze and cock an ear. He really did not want to look like a wolf scenting an enemy on the wind. He wanted any mentions of Fin and dates to leave his fur decidedly unruffled. "Remember, Mary? She told us about it this week at the store?" Kylie came into the kitchen, her nose pink and Tyler's red stocking cap clashing gorgeously with her coppery hair. She was holding a fresh bottle of olive oil in her hand.

"Thanks for going to get that, Ky," Seb said, taking the olive oil from her and immediately shoving a cup of hot cider into her hands. "Even if you don't want to drink it, just hold it in your hands for a minute—I'm getting cold just looking at you."

"He always says that to me too," Matty groused without looking up from the puzzle. "It doesn't make sense. You can't get cold from looking."

"You can when you're looking at pink toes on freezing-cold linoleum," Seb replied in an equally grousy tone.

"I'm sensing you've had this conversation before," Kylie said, a small smile on her face as she sipped her cider and went to the table with Matty and Mary, peering down at the puzzle as she sat.

The date! Tyler wanted to shout. *Am I the only one who*

hasn't lost my mind here? Why isn't anyone asking about this freaking date?

But alas, no one asked. Either all of them already had the info on said date, or they just plain didn't care.

Who didn't care about the dates their friends went on? he demanded angrily in his head as he helped set the table, carted plates of food into the dining room and then as he stabbed at the manicotti Via had prepared. Everyone else chatted happily over dinner while Tyler stewed. What kind of friends were these people that they didn't even ask? Fin could be on a date with a psycho right now and they'd all just be dipping bread in olive oil and quizzing Matty on state capitals like a bunch of…like a bunch of normal people who weren't in danger of being much too interested in Fin, he eventually had to admit to himself.

There wasn't something wrong with every other person at this table. There was something wrong with him. Because Fin was a thirtysomething woman on a date. It wasn't a national headline, for god sakes. It barely even registered on the gossip Richter scale. The only reason it mattered to Tyler was because he was the idiot who was somehow still letting shit like this matter.

Even though she'd told him in no uncertain terms that they weren't and would never be a match. Even though she was only hanging out with him these days because she and Kylie were becoming closer. Even though she laughed and ate cake and drank beer and laughed and smiled and blushed and locked gazes with him with those huge, gorgeously icy eyes of hers and— *Wait!*

It was that last part that was getting him all confused over manicotti. It was the last part that had him stewing over her going on a date. It was that last part that he needed to freaking forget about. Because it was that part that was screwing with his life.

Tyler knew, even seconds after he had the thought, that he wasn't going to be able to forget it. She was just too *Fin* to forget it. And nights like they'd had last weekend were too rare in a person's life. Nights that seemed like they were painted in a different palette of colors. So. Yeah. He wasn't going to forget it. But that didn't mean he had to keep on clutching the balloon string either. He could let it go. Let it breeze away. He could even wave goodbye if he was feeling sentimental.

He stabbed at more manicotti, trying not to frown.

No matter what, he had to let it go.

FOR ONE JOLTING SECOND, Fin thought the text was from Tyler.

How's the date?

But no. Of course, it wasn't. It was from Via. She was checking in that the date she'd talked Fin into taking wasn't a monumental disaster.

Luckily, said date was currently in the restroom so she didn't feel like a complete ass answering a text at the table. She thought about her answer for a moment, looking around the cozy little restaurant. It was a dark pub in Brooklyn Heights that he'd chosen for their date. She liked the stubby, droll candles on each table, the saloon doors that separated one part of the restaurant from the other. She liked the stuffy portraits of famous people in thick gold frames that lined the walls. And she'd really, really liked her thirty-dollar burger. But the date?

Shrugging to herself, Fin typed, Good.

Wow, Via texted back. Sounds like he's really knocked your socks off.

It was dumb that even the word *socks* made Fin's pulse feel like it was racing backward for just a second. She thought of strong hands on her ankles, tugging her just so, competently stripping an article of clothing from her body. She thought of what it had felt like to wear an article of Ty's clothing, how that pair of his wool socks had looked draped over the rest of her clothes in her hamper later that night. She scowled. How irritating. "The man doesn't have a monopoly on socks," Fin mumbled to herself. "Socks are a normal thing."

"What's that?" Donovan asked as he came around the back of her chair, his hand grazing her shoulders, as he slid back into his seat.

"Oh. Nothing. Everything all right?" He'd been gone for over ten minutes. Which was kind of a long time to be in the bathroom on a date.

"Yes." His maple-brown eyes tightened with chagrin as he traced a hand over his dark, buzzed head. "Look. I wasn't in the bathroom. I was taking a work call. I know that's a really shitty thing to do on a date."

"Yes," Fin agreed immediately, making him smile. "That is a shitty thing to do on a date. But Winnie told me just how busy you are. I've been warned."

Winnie was one of Fin's clients and apparently one of Donovan's good friends. She'd been the person to set them up.

"Right. But I'm still sorry I had to take that call. It's a sad day when I'm too busy to pay attention to a beautiful woman at dinner."

Fin knew it was a compliment. But there was something about his wording that got under her skin. Did that mean that if she were an unbeautiful woman it *wouldn't* be a sad day if he were too busy to pay attention to her?

Was she just looking for a reason to be annoyed by this guy? Was it a bad sign that she found his bad-boy attractiveness kind of grating? Would it have killed him to iron his shirt before this date?

"I'm gonna run to the bathroom," she said, bolting from the table and noting the fact that he hadn't stood up when she had. She marched into the bathroom and pulled up Via's phone number. Leaning back onto the counter, she dialed the number.

"You were right," Fin said without preamble the second Via answered. "I mean, you never actually said it out loud, but I knew you were thinking it. And. Yeah. You're right."

"Uh. Hold on." There were the sounds of chatting in the background that faded away when Via closed a door on her end. Fin remembered that her friends were all together right now at Seb and Via's. She'd shirked on the invitation in order to go on this dud of a date. "Sorry. Okay, go on. What am I right about?"

"I'm into Ty."

There was dead silence on the line for an excruciating ten seconds and then a victorious, very unladylike whoop that Via generally only made when she was romping the competition during a softball game. "I *knew* it."

"I just said you knew. We both know you knew it. Now can we please move on to what a huge problem this is?"

"Uh. Not seeing many problems here, Finny."

Fin hopped down from where she was sitting on the counter and listened to the sound of her winter boots clomping around the tile bathroom. "How about the fact that I'm on a date with another man right now?"

"Well, see, Fin, there's this thing called dumping someone? It tends to work really well when you want to stop having dinner with them."

"No. That's not the point." Fin tossed her braid over her shoulder, ignoring her own reflection as she paced past the mirror. She didn't need any additional assistance confirming the fact that she did, in fact, look like was losing her marbles. "The point is that this guy, Donovan, is *really hot*. Brown eyes. Short, dark hair. Deep voice."

"Just your type."

"Right. But I can't stop thinking about how his shirt isn't ironed."

"Since when do you care if a guy irons his shirt or not?"

"Exactly," Fin hissed, scaring the crap out of an older woman who'd just swung through the door. The woman averted her gaze immediately and scurried into a stall.

Fin sighed, tried to calm down and pinched the bridge of her nose. "I have never, in my life, cared about ironed shirts, or hair gel, or plaid welcome mats, or matching cuff links, or opening cab doors or any crap like that."

"And then you went and got a crush on Tyler and you found you kind of have a taste for it."

"Via, we both know that Ty is a piece of work. He's douchey, he's—" But suddenly, Fin found that she actually *didn't* have a list of complaints against Tyler. She had a list of fictional complaints against him. Things that she'd thought were true when she'd turned him down for a date. And maybe they had been true back then. But in the last few months of getting to know him, had she ever really seen him be selfish or thoughtless or douchey or entitled? With the exception of the floppy blond hair and the plaid doormat? No.

"But…" Via prompted.

"But he's a really caring person and he shows it in a

hundred different ways, and I am not interested in a man who's not even going to iron a shirt for a date with me. And that's *Tyler's fault.*"

"You're blaming him for raising your standards?"

"I don't want standards! I don't even want a man! I just want to—"

"Finny, at some point you're going to realize that having a true connection with a man, the right man, isn't the end of the world. Maybe, just maybe, Ty's presence in your life doesn't prevent you from having the life you're supposed to have. Maybe it *provides* you with the life you're supposed to have. If he's really the man you're supposed to be with, then he's going to help you build a family, not stand in the way of it."

"Via," Fin said, sagging back against the counter and ignoring the curious stares of the other bathroom-goer who was just now washing her hands. "This is a lot."

Via laughed sheepishly. "Okay. Yeah. You're right. I'm sorry. Some of us get a little self-righteous when we're in love. I'm just saying that when I was falling in love with Seb, I had all these reasons why I shouldn't, and your advice was basically for me to get out of my own way and let the good times roll. And that's my advice for you. Dump the wrinkly hottie and quit beating yourself up about having a crush on a really good guy."

"A really good guy who isn't my type at all," Fin said, because she was feeling obstinate.

"Types only mean something until you really get to know the person. And then they don't mean shit."

Fin laughed despite herself. It was always something when Via DeRosa took it upon herself to drop a curse word. "Good point."

"As always."

Fin rolled her eyes. "As always."

"I heard you roll your eyes."

"Love you, sister."

"Love you too."

They hung up and Fin, alone in the bathroom, finally turned to the mirror to really take a look at herself. She looked past the bright, befuddled, wild expression on her face and let her eyes fall to her jewelry. She gripped at the pendant she wore. She could barely remember putting this on. It was a heavy black stone that hung from her neck. Obsidian. A protection stone. And on her ears, two onyx studs, also black, also meant for protection. She wore her silver bangles with a matching black tourmaline bracelet on each wrist. *Protection, protection, protection.* And then her clothing. Not a stitch of color on her. Black tunic, black leggings, black winter boots.

She was basically Tyler's heavy-velvet-curtain metaphor in human form, blocking all light and possibility. She looked down at herself and saw no joy. No anticipation. No excitement of any kind.

She'd dressed for battle.

Why the hell was she even here?

Turning on her heel, Fin marched back to the table, saw that the plates had been cleared and breathed a sigh of relief.

"Look, Fin," Donovan started as she slid into her seat.

"I'm not available," she interrupted him. "I'm sorry. I know that Winnie said I was. She thought I was. But my situation changed over the last few weeks. I have feelings for someone, and I'm only here in order to avoid seeing him tonight. So. Yeah. I'm sorry for wasting your time."

"Wow. Um…" Donovan narrowed his eyes and quickly looked down at the table, like he had a dirty look to give, but didn't want to give it to her. "Okay."

"You seem…" Fin started, but then stopped. He seemed what? Great? They'd talked about nothing, he'd ditched her to make a phone call and then she'd ditched him to make a phone call. He didn't seem great and neither did she. They seemed like two velvet curtains who went out to dinner thinking they might have velvet-curtain sex sometime in the future.

How romantic.

Donovan chuckled when she didn't finish her thought. "It's okay. Really. You don't have to stroke my ego. No harm, no foul. He's a lucky guy, whoever he is." Donovan finished his wine in two gulps, setting the glass down with a *clink*. "Can I just ask though, if you like him so much, why are you avoiding him? Is he married or something?"

Fin laughed because it surprised her so much, the idea of Tyler being married to someone. She'd simply never thought about that possibility before. Tyler getting married. Tyler in a black suit, navy eyes, pulling perfectly folded vows out of his coat pocket.

"I feel sick," she muttered, covering her eyes.

"Ah. So he is married."

"He's not married. He's just not my type."

"Types are bullshit."

She blinked up at Donovan in surprise. "You're the second person to say that to me in less than five minutes."

He gave her a droll look. "Have a heart-to-heart through the bathroom stall, did you?"

She pursed her lips. "I called my friend while I was in there."

He held his hand up for the check. "We both snuck away from a date to make phone calls. Are you sure we aren't meshing? I kind of think we're a match made in heaven."

She laughed this time, liking Donovan a lot more now that she wasn't going to have to see him again.

"Trust me, we're not."

Donovan handed over his card after a quick perusal of the check. "You're the psychic. I suppose I'll just have to trust you."

CHAPTER EIGHTEEN

Is my purple bag still in your guest room?

FIN LOOKED DOWN at her phone and again experienced that disorienting up and down of thinking a text was from Tyler and then realizing it wasn't.

Normally, Fin wouldn't leave her brew on the kitchen stove unattended. It was a special tincture she was making for Matty, who'd come down with a stomach bug and still wasn't 100 percent. But Fin could sense the palpable anxiety emanating from Kylie's text and she figured that if there were such a thing as a purple bag emergency, Kylie was currently in the throes of it.

She jogged to the bedroom, checked and then jogged back, eyeing the tincture critically and deciding that no harm had been done.

Yup. It's here. Do you need it tonight?

Instead of texting back, her phone rang.

"Hey," Fin answered.

"I'm such an idiot," Kylie groaned.

"For leaving a bag behind? Trust me, little sister, that does not an idiot make."

"No. I'm not an idiot for that. Well, yes, I am. But mostly

I'm an idiot for thinking this stupid trip was going to be fun."

"Ah." Kylie's class was taking a two-night trip to Albany to see the state capitol, among other things. And though Kylie had been pretty excited about it not two weeks ago, ever since they'd gotten their room assignments, she'd been a wreck. Apparently, she'd realized that Anthony was her only friend, and she had nothing in common with any of the girls with whom she'd be rooming. And she didn't have the purple bag. Which was, apparently, the last straw. "Okay, well, I don't think the lack of a purple bag will ruin the trip."

"No, but my lack of having any friends will."

"You have friends, Ky."

"I have old-people friends. No offense. But you and Mary are not going to be on this trip with me. It's just going to be me and a bunch of catty fifteen-year-old girls talking about bras and blow jobs and TV shows I've never even heard of."

Fin opened her mouth to deny the probability of those actually being the topics of conversation, and then she reflected on her own teenage years and conceded that Kylie was probably right.

"Ky, you don't have to make friends with all of them. Just make friends with *one* of them. You said you're staying in a room with three other girls. I guarantee that at least one of them would rather talk about books or movies than blow jobs."

"Maybe you're right."

"Bring your headphones and your Kindle. Worst comes to worst, you'll just end up being the antisocial chick who is super into music and reading. That's not the worst rep a girl could have, all right?"

"Fin, none of them *know* about me."

Ah. Now they were really getting to the heart of the matter. "None of them know about your mom, you mean."

"I really, really don't want to be a freak anymore. Not like I was in Columbus."

Fin, who had a glass to the door of most people's energy, happened to know that everybody was a freak in some way or another. But she didn't think that was what Kylie really needed to hear right now. "You're not a freak, Ky. Your mom kind of is, but you're not."

Kylie laughed, knowing Fin's story about her own mother and not taking offense to Fin's words. But the laughter dimmed quickly. "You know the worst part, Fin? That *I* don't even know the story."

"What story?"

"She left…to go do drugs? With a new boyfriend? Was she part of a cult? Did she just give up? Hate Columbus? Hate me? What was it? These kids at school find out that my mother abandoned me and that I hid it for all those months. Can you even imagine the stories they'd make up about it? And the worst part is that I couldn't even deny them. Because I don't know what actually happened."

"Ky—"

"Mothers leave kids sometimes. That's not that freaky. But do kids usually hide it from social services when they get abandoned? No. If they find out at school what I did… *I'm* the freak. No question. And I just…don't want that. It's been cool to be the boring new girl from the Midwest."

"Kylie, little sister, please trust me when I say that you leave high school and you start to realize that *you're* the only one who gets to decide what you are. Freak or not. It's not up for debate with your peers. I know it's excruciating to not know what the hell your mother was thinking, that you're still waiting to understand. But just know that even if she wrote you a fifty-page letter explaining every last detail, the only thing that you can ever really know is your *own* story. Your own experiences, your own choices and reasons. You don't have to explain why you did what you did to anyone but yourself. Tyler is here to help you with figuring it out. I'm here to help you with figuring it out. But you're the only one who gets ownership over that story. Not gossips at school, not me or Ty, not even your mother."

Kylie was quiet for a moment. "Maybe you're right. But, God, this trip is still gonna be a disaster."

"But just remember what I said, Ky. One friend. All you need at a time like this is one friend. Trust me. Via was my only friend for like a decade."

Kylie took a deep breath. "Okay. Right. Kindle, headphones, one friend. I can do that, I think."

"I can bring your bag over if you want. You need it for the morning?"

"Are you sure? I know it's a pain in the ass, and it really is just a bag. There's just a few books in there I was hoping to bring and my favorite lip balm and—"

"Ky." Fin laughed. "I'll bring it over in an hour or two."

"You're the literal best."

Fin said goodbye, laughing and shaking her head. She finished Matty's tincture and set it aside to cool, spritzed her herbs with water she'd infused with moss agate and went into her bedroom to choose a few crystals for Kylie.

She chose an amethyst necklace because you can never go wrong with amethyst. She also chose a blue agate ring for attracting friendships and a small green malachite key chain for confidence.

Getting dressed herself, Fin gave herself a single, smiling shake of her head when she caught sight of her flowy royal blue pants she'd paired with her emerald green turtle-neck, turquoise scarf and rough-hewn garnet earrings and necklace. Her hair was loose down her back, wild and, yes, she could admit, a bit pirate-princess-ish. Could she have looked any more different from her date with Donovan? She didn't think so. She was practically a different person standing there.

The garnet, which she'd chosen without too much thought, was a stone that sought balance. It was an energy cleanser. And with any luck, it would keep her thoughts from getting too muddied if Tyler was home.

Which he might not be. Apparently, Kylie had told her, Ty was trusting her to get home from school on her own a few times a week. Which occasionally meant that she had the house to herself for a few glorious hours here and there.

Fin wondered if Ty had started doing that because she had mentioned it.

She grabbed her red coat with the hood, Kylie's bag and an umbrella on her way out. Half an hour later, she was resurfacing in Tyler's neighborhood, pleasantly surprised that there were still long, thin lines of pink in the sky left-over from the sunset.

She watched until she had to admit to herself that she was stalling and then crossed the street with a wave to the Camry that slowed down to let her pass.

The doorman was on his break, so Fin went straight up to Tyler's floor, knocking when she got there.

Tyler flung the door open, a crisp T-shirt over perfectly fitting jeans and a dish towel tossed over one shoulder. He held a carrot stick in one hand and obviously hadn't been clued in that she was coming over because the curiosity on his face immediately gave way to genuine delight at seeing her standing there. "Fin! Hi! What's up?"

She held up Kylie's bag. "I've been summoned to drop the forgotten bag."

"Oh my *gawd*," Tyler said, sounding just like Kylie, his delighted expression melting to one of complete horror. "My sister called you and asked you to trek across town to drop off a backpack? Of which she has *three*? I could have come and gotten it. Jeez." He shook his head in disgust. "Please, for eff's sake, come in. Do you want a beer? I made dinner. Let me feed you. At least, for the love of all that's holy, tell me you're hungry and that I can feed you."

Fin laughed and stepped into his apartment, setting Kylie's bag down and holding her breath while Tyler helped her strip her coat off. "It's not that big of a deal, Ty. Besides, when I agreed to bring the bag, I *may* have assumed that there'd be a free dinner at the end of the line."

He turned back from adjusting her coat on the hook, a smile on his face, which fell the second he looked at her. "Wow. You look…" He cleared his throat. "You have a date tonight or something?"

"Oh. No." *Just dressed up to see you.* Fin's mouth opened and closed, having no idea what to say.

"Fin! You're a lifesaver!" Kylie came bounding into the room, red hair flying, and saved Fin from having to come up with something—anything—to say.

"No problem." Fin handed over the bag. "And I added some crystal jewelry to the little pocket in front that'll help with the friends thing if you want to wear it."

"Score," Kylie said solemnly, and it warmed Fin's heart to know how seriously Kylie took her work.

"Hey. Kid," Tyler cut in. "Please don't ask our friends to trek across town to bring you stuff."

"She volunteered!" Kylie insisted, looking up from the jewelry she'd already dug out of the bag.

"Based on how much like a kicked puppy you sounded, I'm assuming?"

Kylie looked like she was going to argue for a second and then bobbed her head to one side, apparently conceding the point. "All right, fair enough. Fin, I'm sorry. I should have just sent Ty for the bag."

He burst out laughing. "Not exactly what I meant, but good enough, I guess."

"What's for dinner?" Fin asked, not even caring that she was a hopeless mooch.

"Baked chicken, mashed potatoes, green beans and salad."

"That explains the carrot."

"What carrot?" Tyler looked down at the carrot he still clutched in his hand. "Oh. Right. I guess I should go put that in the salad."

Fin watched him go and went to sit on Kylie's bed and help her finish packing. At dinner, they talked about the school trip, about the soccer game they were all going to next week, about Fin's birthday—

"Your what?" Tyler demanded.

"My birthday," Fin said calmly, a little mystified at the cloud of energy that had descended over Tyler's head like thick, soupy weather.

"It was really fun," Kylie cut in. "I didn't mention it, Ty? Mary closed down the store early, and Via came over. It was just us."

Tyler's eyes snagged on Kylie's face, and Fin hoped he could tell just how important it had been to Kylie to have been included in Fin's birthday celebration. And though Fin usually didn't celebrate, she'd had to admit that Mary had thrown her a really good party. It had been fun.

Some of his soupy energy abated just a bit, but she could tell that Tyler had feelings about said birthday.

After dinner, Kylie had homework, so she hugged Fin, thanked Tyler for dinner and disappeared back into her room. Fin rose and automatically started putting extra food in Tupperware, her standing at one counter and him kitty-corner. They were a foot apart, but she could feel him there. It wasn't heat exactly. It was more like a static disturbance. Her energy was touching his energy. It was a prickling awareness that cat-walked itself up her spine. She used to feel this all the time. Tyler's energy mixed with hers. Until the baseball game when she'd severed it like she was dead-heading an errant daisy.

But right now? In the kitchen, a delicious tension between them, she was feeling it again, even with his back turned to hers.

Is it coming from me? Or from him? she wondered, her pulse racing backward as she tried to keep her breath steady. Was she the only one putting out vibes? She couldn't tell. Not over the bongo of her own noisy heart.

"When was your birthday?" he asked, quasicasually. She felt him turn to her. "So that I don't miss it again next year. Put some of that in a small Tupperware for Kylie on the bus tomorrow, please."

Fin quietly, calmly, boxed up a lunch for Kylie and then turned to face Tyler, who was still facing her, carefully watching for a reaction.

"You're mad I didn't invite you to my birthday?"

"I'm not mad," he said, his brow battening down in confusion. "I'm kind of hurt. I thought we were friends."

"And birthdays are a measurement of friendship to you?"

"Well, hiding a birthday certainly says something about the level of friendship two people have."

She rolled her eyes at him. "Believe it or not, but my issues with birthdays have nothing to do with you. I...don't celebrate my birthday usually. Mary found out about the date and threw me a very small surprise shindig at the store. If you have issues with the guest list, take it up with Mary."

She turned back to the Tupperware and realized she had no more food to put away. She started carting empty dishes to the sink, stepping around him and holding her breath. There were straight-up goose bumps on her forearms at this point.

"Why don't you celebrate your birthday?"

Fin dunked the plates in the soapy water and reached for a sponge, sighing, knowing he wasn't going to let this go.

"It lost meaning for me as a kid because I never celebrated with my mother." Fin sighed again, knowing she was embarking on a sad, pathetic story and wishing she didn't have to. "She didn't know the exact date of my birthday. I was a home birth and it actually took a long time for her to report my existence to the state. By the time I actually had a birth certificate, she couldn't remember the exact date I'd been born. But she thought it had been January and she knew I was an Aquarius. So, January 26th it was. Like I said. Celebrating just seemed arbitrary to me. Cue the violin. Preferably a tiny one."

There was silence behind her. She waited for the sympathy. The requisite hug that she was going to have to grit her teeth through and pretend that his nearness didn't melt her knee joints and his pity didn't make her skin crawl.

But all that came was a firm squeeze to her shoulder. "That's an *awful* story. Jeez. Terrible. But it's also beside the point. Because at some point, you have to realize that birthdays aren't about you, they're about the people who love you getting to show you. But you know what? You're a birthday novice. So, I'll let it slide this year. Prepare your-self for next year, though. January 26th. Okay."

She heard a scratching sound and turned in time to see him adding her birthday to the calendar that hung on the wall on the far side of the kitchen.

She blinked. An unexpected, stinging tension gathered at the top of her nose, spread to her eyes. He was adding her to his calendar. Making sure that he wouldn't forget her birthday for next year. Because it was important to him that there was a day celebrating her.

She watched, his back turned to her, as he carefully wrote out her name.

She had the strangest feeling that even though he was writing *her* name, he was signing some sort of contract. In some grand, cosmic way, he wasn't just jotting down a date to remember, he was signing Fin into his life. Her name, in bold blue ink, was a casual reminder to himself to celebrate her next year. She watched as their friendship went from a few shaky months of growth to suddenly, at least, lasting another year.

She realized, watching him cap the pen he hung on a neat string next to the calendar, that she'd been picturing their relationship as a hallway with a door at one end. She'd known, in her pessimistic heart, that that door was locked up tight. Once they got to that door, there'd be nowhere else to go for them. Relationship over. She'd thought they'd reached that door at the ball game last spring. But Kylie's presence had somehow telescoped the hallway a bit farther. Fin and Tyler had kept walking. Fin had assumed they were going to reach the door again at some point.

But there Tyler was, writing her name into his calendar like locked doors didn't exist. He wrote her name down in careful handwriting as if all *he* could see at the end of the hallway was light. Maybe a corner that led in a new direction. Maybe even a quiet, comfortable room where it could be just the two of them.

"Don't you want to ask when my birthday is?" he asked as he turned, a smile on his face that slid off the moment he caught her expression. "Shit, are you crying?"

He strode toward her, his eyes wide, his hands suspended in the air like he was ready to catch her should she fall off into space.

"No," she answered in a husky voice, thick with emotion. "I mean yes. Yes, I'm crying. No, I don't know your exact birthday." Her last few words were muffled by the shoulder and neck that were suddenly pressing against her face, her breath stolen by the arms that banded around her, yanking her into his chest.

Here was the hug that she thought she'd been dreading. But why would she ever have dreaded something as warmly sparkling as this? He had one palm cupping the back of her head, his other hand spread, fingers in a perfect star, against the middle of her back. She was buried against him, her brow pressed into his collarbone, halfway covered by the collar of his T-shirt. She felt stubble against her temple, and when his breath huffed into her ear, she knew that he'd bowed his head down.

She should have known that Tyler was not a back patter. She should have known that he hugged with his entire body. In fact, on an intuition, she moved her socked feet an inch to either side and encountered his socked feet. Even his feet were hugged up against hers.

The sting of her tears gone, her temple brushed his cheek. "I don't know your birthday," she whispered. "But you're obviously a Gemini."

He laughed, and she felt it in his chest. A rumble of vibration and sound and heat that, for a moment, pressed them together even more intimately. She liked the way his sound felt against her. Coming from deep inside him, rumbling through her. She wanted more of it. She wanted him to speak while he held her so tightly.

"June 12th," he said, and she got her wish. She felt the rumble of his voice. Was it her imagination or were his arms even tighter around her?

Her arms were still pinned between them, and she didn't want them there. She started to move them and he loosened his hold against her. He thought she was breaking the hug and the idea panicked her. Quickly, she slid her arms out from between them and around his back, gripping her own wrists as she held him just as tightly as he'd been holding her. Instantly, his release on the hug was ruthlessly eliminated and she was back to being embraced fiercely, her front pressed to his.

"How'd you guess that? My sign?" he asked.

This time, she wanted to see his face. As long as they weren't looking at one another they could kind of pretend that this hug wasn't happening. So, she tilted her head all the way back and he lifted his an inch or two.

This, she knew, was the kind of embrace that balanced on that skinny bridge she'd been walking for so long with him. This was not how friends embraced. But that didn't make them lovers either, just because they were breathing each other's air and gripping the shirts on one another's backs.

Mostly because she knew, without a doubt, that she'd warned him away so well in the past that he had no confidence on whether or not she was actually inviting him back in, even when they were heartbeat to heartbeat, her toes gently laid over his. She knew what she had to do.

"I know you're a Gemini because you're curious. Adapt-able."

She felt his energy change. It was subtle. Where it had been skating around in confusion, now it just sort of slowed, like the motion of a cloud swirling lazily across the sky.

"Affectionate," she continued, listing his characteristics that absolutely slayed her the most. And now his energy slowed and swirled even more. She felt those goose bumps again. Whether he knew it or not, he was tangling himself with her, allowing some part of himself to get lost in her.

"Gentle," she whispered. "Generous." Her eyes dropped down, unable to keep from looking at his mouth. "Passionate."

When she lifted her eyes to his navy blues again, she felt his energy shift completely. Irrevocably. Moving as one, they eliminated all but an inch of space between their mouths, and she was overwhelmed by his energy, the delicious mixing of the two of them together.

She was liquid lightning, her blood slicking backward through her veins, her heart beating madly against his. She knew, without a doubt, that whether she'd meant to or not, she'd just busted the lock on a treasure chest of feelings that he'd meant to keep locked up forever. She could feel him, helpless against the onslaught of desire between them, but still desperately trying to cling to yesterday, when everything had been easier. When none of this had even been an option.

"It won't be easy," she whispered, her lips a breath from his.

His eyes widened and his nostrils flared. "You read my—" But she cut his words off when they pressed their lips together.

CHAPTER NINETEEN

THE SECOND, THE VERY SECOND, their lips touched, Tyler knew how well and truly fucked he was. It was like that horrible first millisecond after stepping off a high dive at a public pool. There was nowhere to go but down. And down he went. Fast.

He tumbled into her mouth, pressing smoothly against her plush lips until he caught, finally, the elusive flavor of her. He'd expected something earthy, sagey, herby. But no. Her flavor was surprisingly light, open, with hints of vapor and ozone. Tyler made a soundless groan, gripping her tighter, and slid his lips along hers.

His temperature was all off, the heat of the air that touched his skin as stifling as strips of steamed fabric laid over him. He gasped for breath and he breathed only color. Rivers of multicolored paint seemed to start at their feet and slow-motion tornado their way up. His eyelids pressed closed so hard that he saw his own heart, hidden in the lightless black cave of his chest, pumping colorful blood maniacally fast.

Her delicate hand, her grip surprisingly firm, traced up his back and they both jumped when static electricity shocked them where she touched him.

She made a noise into his mouth, just a soft little "hmm," like she was both curious and overwhelmed by what was happening. The noise pleased him so much his mouth opened and so did hers, their tongues meeting in a glancing, tracing movement that had them both, all at once, pulling their heads back to catch each other's eye.

They breathed hard, his muscles starting to protest at how tightly he clutched her. Their eyes bounced back and forth, trying to read one another. He could see nothing but her desire for him. Couldn't see past it. Maybe because it utterly shocked him. She'd spent so long putting distance between them and now here she was, her fingers tangled in the back of his shirt, her tongue tracing her bottom lip, tasting his flavor that he was sure still lingered there.

Affectionate, gentle, passionate. Her words describing him were on a loop in his head, taunting him. Confusing him. He'd become so used to the idea of her barely tolerating him that the idea of her *admiring* him didn't compute.

He tore his eyes from her gaze and stared directly at that mouth of hers. Her white teeth peeked out. Her lips, so plush and pouty, but he knew, viscerally, just how goofy that mouth could be when she was smiling, really smiling.

Her hand moved on his back and again, there was another jolting shock of static electricity. This time he even heard the snap of it, like a starting gun at a footrace. They both dived back into the kiss, wasting no movements with pleasantries. Her tongue tasted his once, twice, drew back, inviting him into her mouth.

She made that noise again, and Tyler let one of his hands trace up to cup the back of her head; his other hand finding the small of her back. In this way, he held her, told her in every way he knew just how badly he wanted her. Had wanted her for so long.

Might always want her.

The idea left him gasping as he turned his head to one side, breaking the kiss. But she took his chin and pressed her mouth to his again, soft and fierce at once, sucking his lower lip. Her teeth were just starting to scrape along his lip when they both heard footsteps coming down the hall behind them.

They instantly sprang away from one another, and as their bodies came apart, three or four sparks of almost painful static shock zapped between them. Whether it was punishment for separating or for having come together in the first place, Ty had no idea.

Fin turned before he could catch her expression and plunged her hands back into the dishwater, rifling through the dirty dishes. Tyler turned and picked up the Tupperware, marching mechanically to the fridge.

"Hey, Ty?"

"Yeah?" he responded. Knowing Kylie was leaning in the doorway of the kitchen, he stuck his head behind the open door of the fridge and took a few deep breaths, surreptitiously fixing his hair, hoping he didn't look too indecent when he looked up at her. Meanwhile, he could still feel Fin's hot mouth pressed against his, the imprint of her long body, softer than he'd expected, banded against his own, his colorful blood still high-speed chasing itself through his veins.

"One side of my headphones isn't playing. I think they're broken."

"Oh." He closed the fridge door and stood up, concentrated on his sister's words. "Crap. We just bought those."

"I know." She grimaced. "Think we can return them?"

"Sure."

"But can I take yours for the trip?"

He blinked. She'd never asked to borrow anything of his before. Hell, it had taken her long enough to even appear comfortable using his cups. She used to just fill and refill her own water bottle.

"Oh. Sure. No problem. Let me grab them." He padded back to his bedroom and took a minute just to sit on his cool bedspread.

"Holy shit," he muttered to himself, dropping his head in his hands. "Holy *shit*."

Fin had kissed him. No. Wait. He'd kissed her? Damn. The details suddenly seemed extremely important. He hadn't pushed it, had he?

He thought of her face right before they kissed, her eyes on his mouth, how hard she'd gripped his shirt. He winced because the memory of it was so potent it hurt, like a hard suck on a lime.

He stood, gave himself a mental shake and dug through his desk drawer, pulling out his headphones.

He walked back out to where Fin and Kylie were chatting in the kitchen still. He saw that Fin had finished the dishes and was drying her hands.

"Here you go," he said, handing over the headphones. "Make sure to leave yours out so that I can return them while you're gone."

"All right," Kylie said with a yawn. "I'm gonna hit the hay, I think. Remember that we have to be at school early tomorrow."

"Right."

She gave Fin and Tyler a quick hug each and then her door closed down the hall.

A few excruciating seconds ticked past as Tyler's hands found their way into his pockets. They both looked anywhere but at one another, and Tyler fought the almost irrepressible urge to whistle something. Anything.

"I…guess I should go?"

She was asking?

Hold on. He'd been waiting for her to bolt out of here. He could practically already read the text he fully expected to receive sometime in the next twenty-four hours: That was a mistake. Let's be friends.

Shouldn't she have left a Roadrunneresque trail of dust in her wake already?

Yet, here she was, shifting her weight from foot to foot, her eyes pointedly looking at his chest instead of his face.

Was this what a nervous Serafine St. Romain looked like?

Tyler felt like he'd walked into a room only to find all the furniture had been glued to the ceiling.

Was she nervous because she regretted the kiss but didn't want to get kicked out of Kylie's life? Was she nervous because she was just as confused as he was? Was she nervous because she'd liked it?

Was there any chance in hell, even an ice cube's worth, that she wanted to do that again?

"Um. Okay?" was his genius response. He turned it into just as much of a question as she had, hopefully letting her know that he had just as little idea what to do next as she apparently did.

She nodded, once, twice and then walked through his living room to where her coat and boots were.

"I'll walk you down," he said to no one. Just talking because it seemed like the thing to do.

It wasn't until they finally had their coats and boots on that Tyler cracked a smile. "You look like Red Riding Hood in that coat," he informed her, letting his eyes snag on hers.

"I get that a lot."

She was smiling too, just a little bit, and Tyler felt a miniwave of relief wash over him. At least he had that tiny buoy to cling to while he figured out just how bad the damage was.

They walked silently down the hall, endured a painfully quiet elevator ride and then they were out on the sidewalk. It was warmer than he'd thought it would be on a random February night. And a thin sheaf of clouds had pulled over the sky, almost like a veil separating the earth's face from the eyes of the moon. Tyler felt oddly protected by it, even if it was only a thin layer of cloud.

He dragged his eyes down from the sky and onto Fin, who stood, her breath in misty puffs in front of her, her hands in the pockets of her red coat.

"Crap," Tyler said, making her eyebrows rise in surprise. "I didn't call you a cab."

"Let's just hail one."

"At this hour?"

"There's one right there." She pointed down the street.

"But its light is off, it's probably off duty—oooooofffff course." He laughed to himself wryly when the second Fin put her pretty hand in the air the cab driver flipped his light on and pulled a U-turn to get to her side of the street.

She gave him a sideways smile, with just enough smugness for him to know that everything was going to be okay eventually. Their kitchen kiss hadn't ruined anything.

They'd have to talk about it at some point, of course. He just hoped that this time she'd let him down easier than she had at the baseball game. That wasn't exactly something he was clamoring to endure again anytime soon.

He opened the cab door for her. "Well…"

He expected her to duck down into the cab but instead, she turned in the circle of his arms, went up on her toes and sucked his bottom lip into her mouth again, as if this were merely a continuation of their kiss upstairs. She made that soft little "hmm" again and then his tongue was in her mouth. He banded an arm around her waist and yanked them together, stepping her back until she was flush against the cab. He tasted and tasted her, feeling instantaneously drunk, like he'd slugged back a cup of what he'd thought was water but had turned out to be tequila.

There was something about kissing her under the moon-lit clouds, with that water vapor mouth of hers that just—

"'Scuse me!" the driver's loud voice had them breaking apart, their foreheads pressing together, huffing curlicues of breath against one another's mouths. "You coming or going, lady?"

"Right," Fin muttered. "The world still exists."

Her eyes were fuzzy and nervous and…happy. Would it just be the stupidest thing ever to assume that this had been a positive experience for her?

She stepped back from him, loosening his grip, and folded herself into the cab. "Night, Ty."

"Night, Fin."

He closed the cab door and she popped her head into the window, lit in an orange stripe by the streetlamp overhead. She gave him a small smile and one quick glance of those eerily light eyes of hers before the cab pulled away from the curb and off they went.

He stood on the curb and watched the cab go. Even though they'd said very little to one another in the last half an hour, he couldn't help but feel like she was leaving smack-dab in the middle of a conversation.

Fin was lucky enough to have back-to-back appointments with clients in two different corners of Brooklyn the following morning. It meant that she didn't have the time to dwell on Tyler. Or to dwell on what had promptly become the best kiss of her entire existence.

Her first client, a noob to this whole energy thing, had been exhaustingly gung ho, asking a million and two questions about how it all worked and chattering so compulsively that Fin had demanded the client, Ana, get quiet. Fin then balanced crystals on several different points of her body, hoping it would calm her down a bit. Her second client, someone Fin had been seeing for years, had been much calmer.

But when, just after three p.m., Fin locked her apartment door behind her, she found that there was not much else to think about besides Tyler at that point. It was almost as if her brain had tossed a sheet over him for the morning and now that she'd pulled the sheet away, she could see that he'd been there the entire time.

She'd eaten lunch between clients, her indoor herb garden was tended, she was up-to-date on tinctures and teas, all her crystals were cleansed. She sighed. There was nothing to do but to clean the house.

She strode back into her room, slid all her jewelry off, changed into some leggings and a baggy T-shirt for cleaning and gathered her hair into a high ponytail to keep it out of the way.

Four minutes later, she was staring around her living room, realizing that the place was already perfectly clean.

In a huff, irritated at herself and at her stupid clean house that didn't offer a single distraction, she finally admitted that it might be time to reach out to Tyler. There was nothing more she could reasonably do without her actions tipping down into avoidance territory.

She went back into her room and took her phone off the

charger on her nightstand and plunked down on the edge of her bed, opening a text window to him.

Can we talk?

She deleted it. Too ominous.

Hey.

She deleted that too. Too juvenile.

How are you?

Delete. Too formal.

Got any free time today?

That one she stared at for a while. It was a solid *maybe*. But she still wasn't sure.

There was a knock on her front door, and Fin automatically flung her phone away from her, open text box and all, as if it had somehow summoned a visitor.

She took a breath, closed her eyes and knew exactly who it was. She'd recognize that energy across a football field. In a rainstorm. With her back turned and her fingers stuffed into her ears.

Well. She'd attempted to climb inside his skin in his kitchen and it was time to actually discuss that particular phenomenon.

She strode through her living room, took a deep breath and swung open her door. And there he was.

His peacoat was unbuttoned—she still couldn't believe she had feelings for a man who wore peacoats—his hair flopping to one side. He was breathing through his mouth, like he'd taken the stairs, and the expression on his face looked downright curmudgeonly.

"Tyler," Fin said warily, not quite able to pin down his mood.

He stood practically in the middle of her hallway, three feet away from her, his hands loose at his sides and looking a little untethered from the bonds of gravity. She wouldn't have been surprised to look down and see his shoes untied. They weren't. Because this was Tyler, but still. The man looked a little off-kilter.

"Did you know that I talked my editor into letting me write more freely?" he asked without preamble.

"Oh. No. I didn't know that. You mean that you won't have to write the play-by-plays of the games anymore?" She squinted at him, trying to keep up with the unexpected beginning to an unexpected conversation.

"Right. I mean, I'll still have to keep up with the team. But I get to write a lot more of what I want. Not exactly *whatever* I want. But pretty damn close. It's probationary. Contingent on me actually having something to say."

She cocked her head to one side, leaning in her own doorway, trying to figure out why the hell he was backing away from her. He was almost standing on the welcome mat of the door on the opposite side of the hall at this point. "Ty, you wanna come in?"

He barreled on as if he hadn't heard her question. "And Kylie's gone for two days, so I figured I'd have no interruptions. I'd bang this article out, knock my editor's socks off and I'd be well on my way toward this new facet of my career. You know, a beat writer who waxes philosophical on the role of sports in our society."

"Ty."

"Do you know how meaty that subject is? Especially in this day and age? There's so many angles. Athletes as celebrities, influencers. The role of an athlete in his or her community. Political movements. Whether or not professional athletes should be taking a stand when it comes to the exploitation of college athletes. Racial politics in sports. Gender inequality. God, there's enough there for me to write novels!"

He dragged a hand through his hair and then put both hands on his hips. That curmudgeonly look was full force, and his eyes were narrowed as they finally zeroed in on her face. "You know how much I've written today, Fin?"

She knew a trick question when she heard one and wisely kept her button buttoned.

He answered the question for her. "Nada. Zero. No, that's wrong. I wrote two words. I wrote my fucking name at the top of the Word doc like it's my sophomore-year book report."

"Tyler."

"Did I kiss you or did you kiss me?"

Ah. And here they were, at the heart of the matter. Speaking of hearts, Fin's had decided to flip upside down in her chest.

She let out a sound, a "who knows" sort of exhalation and watched the look on his face turn even more confused.

So, maybe she didn't know what she wanted from Tyler, but she had a pretty good idea of what she didn't want. And him standing in her hallway looking freaking bamboozled was what she didn't want.

"Tyler, why don't you come in out of my hallway, all right?"

To her surprise, he took another step backward. Any

farther from her and he'd be ringing her neighbor's door-bell with his tookus.

"No." He shook his head. "Nuh-uh. I'm staying right here."

Now he wasn't the only one feeling bamboozled. She put her hands on her hips, drawing her brow. "Someone's feeling particularly obstinate today."

"No. This isn't obstinance." His voice, in order to reach her across the hall, was a touch louder than it should have been in her normally quiet hallway. "I— If *I'm* the one who kissed *you* then I'm sure as hell not barging into your house and demanding information from you. I'll demand information from you out here in the hallway where you can slam the door in my face if you want."

He...was giving her an out. He'd come all the way over to her house for answers but wasn't going to push her for said answers. He was shouting to her across the hall so that he wouldn't crowd her. How ridiculous. How Tyler. Her heart flipped back over, but somehow she didn't think it had landed back in quite the right place.

"Let me get this straight," she said slowly, still leaning in her doorway, her arms crossed and one foot balancing on the other. "You're yelling about our personal business in my hallway, in front of my neighbor's door, in order to make me *more* comfortable?"

He let out an adorably exasperated huff, tugging a hand through his floppy hair again and making it stand up straight for just a moment before it flopped right back down. "Well, when you put it *that* way."

She couldn't help but laugh. She'd never seen him so flustered and she kind of loved it.

"Tyler, come into my house. I promise I'll have no problem kicking you out if I want you to leave, all right? You don't have to worry about crowding me."

A reluctant expression on his face, he seemed to weigh his options out there on her neighbor's doormat. After a moment, he sighed and then walked into her apartment, sliding his shoes off and hanging up his coat. He wore a V-neck sweater and slacks, and even with that ornery expression on his face, looked like he'd just come from a shoot for some business-casual magazine. His picture would be featured over an article entitled: "From Boating to Business, 8 Pairs of Loafers That Can Do It All."

She closed the door and when she turned back to him, he was looking at her, really looking, and the ornery expression had faded.

"What?" she asked, trying to decipher that helplessly pained look he was wearing.

"You have a ponytail."

"Oh." She put her hand up to the high hair tie and fiddled around with it. "I was just going to do some cleaning when you stopped by."

He looked away from her hair, his eyes bottoming out on her yoga pants, and his expression got even more pained. He jammed his hands into his pockets and turned away from her, going to sit down in the armchair on the far side of the room.

She took a moment to get some iced tea for each of them and then joined him in the living room, sitting cross-legged on the couch and leaning forward over her knees.

"Please," he said after a moment, dragging his hands through his hair again. "Please, just put me out of my misery and answer my question."

She fixed him with a stare and spoke slowly. He was extremely hard for her to read right now and getting harder by the moment. "You want to know who kissed who."

"Yeah," he said gruffly, dropping his hands from his face. "I do."

"Who do you *think* kissed who?"

"Fin!"

She laughed. "All right, all right. I don't know, Ty. We kissed each other."

He screwed up his face in frustration.

"That can't be true. It's never true," he insisted. "That's like when people say a breakup was mutual. It's never real."

She rolled her eyes. "Of course those things can be real. Rare, maybe, but real. Ty, did you *want* to kiss me last night in your kitchen? Did you lean in?"

He cleared his throat and slanted a look at her with those navy blues of his. "Yes."

Her heart feebly attempted to get back into its normal position and grotesquely failed. She took a steadying breath. "Okay, then. There's your answer. We kissed each other."

"So." He stopped, leaned forward over his knees and attempted to brush his hair down as he stared at the floor. "You leaned in too."

She balanced her chin on one fist. "Considering it was this side of twelve hours ago I was literally sucking on your lip, I'm not sure how much clearer I can make this, Tyler."

He stood and paced to the far side of the living room, absently touching the rainbow-making baubles that hung in her window. "Okay. Okay, so I kissed you and you kissed me."

"You know when you say a word over and over again and it starts to lose its meaning?" she asked dryly, her chin still on her fist. "Kisskisskisskiss. Doesn't mean anything anymore."

He turned from the window, his face serious, his voice low. "It meant something to me, Fin."

Her blood did that backward thing again. "I can see that," she said in a voice equally low. And she *could* see it. She'd never seen his energy so chaotic. So out of whack. He was scrambling as fast as he could, trying to make sense out of their kiss while also trying not to ruin everything. She rubbed a hand over her breastbone, trying to make her heart settle back into its normal position, but she just couldn't make it go.

"Okay," he said again. "Okay. Normally, I'm a see-how-it-all-turns-out kinda guy. But I've got Kylie and that's hard enough even when I've got my head on straight. So, I've got a few things to say, I guess." He strode back over to the armchair and plunked down in it, rubbing the palms of his hands over the knees of his slacks. When he looked up at her, there was something in those navy eyes of his that she hadn't seen since that day at the ball game.

"Look," he said. "It's obviously no secret that I used to have a big thing for you. And it's not like I'm at home writing your name in my diary or anything. But still. You've helped me out so much with Kylie. I honestly don't know what I would have done without you these last few months. And… God, I can't believe I'm saying this to Serafine St. Romain." He tossed his eyes to the ceiling for a moment but then they were back on her, more confident than they'd been out in the hallway. "But that—last night—it meant something to me. And confused the hell out of me. And if it didn't—doesn't—mean anything to you, then we can't do it again. Okay?"

Fin, sitting on the couch, her chin on her fist, let her eyes drop for the first time since they'd sat down in the living room. She felt chastened, and a little silly, and extremely humbled. Here she was, making wry jokes, deleting texts to him, dancing around her feelings. And there he was. In person. Admitting how he felt. Asking questions. Being honest.

She suddenly felt like a cad of the first degree. Protecting oneself from actual harm was one thing, and she'd had to do that a thousand times in her life, warning off men on the street, blocking people on the internet, that kind of thing. But this? This dance she was doing with Tyler right now was simply protection as *habit*. It was a hard-worn groove in her internal hardwood floors and she was walking it simply because that was what she knew how to do. Meanwhile, he, for the second time, was putting himself right out there. Even after the first time he'd done it she'd eviscerated him like a pasture-raised chicken carved up for market.

This right here, staring at her in a V-neck and slacks, was what bravery looked like. This was what it looked like to ask for what you needed. And, damn, it looked good.

Fin found herself looking at her own hands folded in her lap, her thumbs playing an in-house thumb war tourney.

What's it gonna be, Finny? She was surprised by the voice she heard then. It wasn't her own intuition. No. That was Jetty's voice. Challenging Fin, knowing just how good she could be if she tried.

What's it gonna be?

"And if it did mean something to me?" she said quietly, and forced her eyes up to his. "If it meant something when I kissed you, could we do it again?"

His eyes went from round nickels to half-moons to almond slivers in a matter of a few breaths.

She rose up from the couch and his energy did the same thing it had done in the kitchen last night. It went from a mad, swirling storm cloud to a slow-motion tumble, everything just a touch away from being frozen in time.

"No," she said. "On second thought, don't answer that. Let me make this really clear. Ty, it was special. I want to do it again."

"Special," he murmured, his eyes locked on hers, his expression completely bemused.

"Would you like some proof?"

"I—" His mouth clapped closed again. "Yes."

She took a few steps closer to him and by the time she was at the foot of the armchair, she could see the pulse dancing the tango in his throat. His hands were on either of the arms of the chair and his face was tipped up to hers. She could feel his nerves, his reticence, his ever-present confusion. And if she hadn't felt that zapping lick of hope radiating off of him, she might have stepped back. If she hadn't felt the words *hell yes* materialize out of thin air and just known that they were from him, she might have given him his space back.

Mindful of her long legs and the tight squeeze of the two of them in that chair, Fin folded herself sideways onto Tyler's lap, her eyes bouncing back and forth between his. He wasn't leaning in, but his arms instantly came around her, one hand sliding up her back, the other making itself at home over top of her knees, hooking her to him.

Their eyes were connected in that time-bending, steel-rope sort of way, and when she leaned forward, so did he. Their eyes stayed linked even when their lips brushed.

"Ouch."

They leaned back as one, her hand going over her mouth to rub away the zap of static shock that had just sparked between them.

"Why does that keep happening?" he asked.

"I have no idea."

He narrowed his eyes. "Shit. You're, like, *actually* a witch, aren't you?"

She rolled her eyes at him, laced her fingers in his hair and tugged him forward. This kiss was not tentative. Not exploratory. This kiss had a purpose. Fin wanted Tyler to leave this kiss and know exactly how much she'd meant to kiss him.

She used her mouth to open his mouth and joyfully swallowed the groan of appreciation that reverberated from his chest. Fin flattened a hand over his heart, reveling in the race of his heartbeat, in the rumble of the sounds he was making as she kissed him. He gripped her even tighter against him, and she had a flash of intuition. Ty, she realized, was tactile. She was sure he was just as turned on by visuals as the next guy, but he was also a true toucher. Which was something that was rarer than it seemed. In this day and age of internet porn, it seemed to Fin that most guys were more into the visuals of sex than how it actually felt. All the popular sex positions these days had minimal body contact, people just kind of forking each other, their only contact being between their tines.

But not Ty. She knew without even having slept with him, just from this kiss. He momentarily stopped to shift her higher on his lap, to nuzzle his nose under her chin, to smooth her ponytail down over her back.

When they kissed again, it was just as needy, but somehow even softer. She felt every swipe of his palm over her thigh, every rough adjustment of his forearm over her back, the tight set of their bodies against one another. All of it was heating her up. But in a languid way. Like the difference between heating butter in the microwave and setting it out to warm in the sun.

Her neck was cricking, kissing him sideways like that, so she reared back and swung a leg over his hip, straddling him and facing him head-on. He automatically widened the set of his knees and had her fitting even more snugly against him. She smiled at him smugly, but he leaned forward and kissed the smile right off of her mouth.

This kiss had been meant to knock his socks off, to clear up some of his confusion, but she hadn't quite calculated for just how good of a kisser Tyler was. She'd never, in her life, been kissed like this. Him bending her slightly backward, cradling her head in one hand, taking her weight so that all she had to do was open wide and receive him.

And receive him she did. He was a tongue kisser for sure. But not in that tone-deaf, domineering way that so many guys were. He wasn't invading her mouth, planting a flag, taking. No. He was tasting her. Warming her. And, she had to admit as she lunged up and didn't let him retreat, he was opening her right up.

CHAPTER TWENTY

FIN OUTRIGHT LAUGHED when she came back from the bathroom. Tyler supposed he must look ridiculous. He knew his hair was a mess, his sweater tugged to one side and the expression on his face could only read: stupefied.

He leaned against her kitchen counter, one hand covering the bottom half of his face while his eyes rested on the takeout menus she'd fanned out for him to choose from. But he didn't see a thing. He was still stuck in the land of twenty minutes ago when she'd been straddled across his lap, his hands lost on the oasis of her body, her heat grinding desperately into his aching lap, her mouth taking and giving, remaking him into a different person.

Even though it had just been kissing, Tyler felt different. Very different.

He felt newly hatched. Like a very nearly middle-aged man who'd just pecked his way out of a shell he hadn't known he'd been wearing.

"I feel like I just woke up from a coma," he told her when she leaned against the kitchen door and just stared at him from across the room, that goofy smile on her face.

"No luck on choosing takeout, then?"

"I'm pretty sure I left my ability to read somewhere in your mouth."

She laughed again. "Feeling a little befuddled, Ty?"

He dragged a hand over his face, hearing the scrape of

his late-afternoon stubble. "And you're not?" He'd seen her face when they'd realized it was time to peel themselves off of one another. They'd both known that, at that point, it was either strip down or get up. Tyler hadn't been sure his blood pressure was ready for the strip-down option yet. They'd both opted for ordering some takeout and seeing where the rest of the evening led them. Either way, she'd been dozy-eyed and exhilarated and just as baffled as he'd been.

She smiled at him, light eyes through dark eyelashes, one of her fingers tracing her lips. "I'm definitely...something."

"Come over here," he told her and was downright shocked when she listened. He'd fully expected her to argue, to get him to come to her, which he totally would have done. On his knees. Over rusty nails. But instead she sauntered on those long, long legs across the kitchen, her palm skimming over the tops of her indoor herb garden as she walked past, her eyes pinned to his.

He gulped. Luckily, his body knew what to do. The second she got close enough, he reached out and caught her by the waist, tipped her weight forward so that her hips knocked into his, her soft chest sinking forward into his rib cage. He laced their fingers together on both hands and something caught his attention.

"You're not wearing any of your jewelry." Now that he was really looking, it was strange to see her without it, like the bejeweled tiger had decided to take off her stripes for a while.

"I usually don't when I'm at home."

"I thought jewelry wearers generally wore their things all the time. Bed, the shower, that kind of thing."

She shrugged her shoulders. "Maybe some do, but I don't wear my jewelry absently. I wear it with a lot of purpose.

Meaning. And that meaning usually goes away when I'm at home."

"You mean you wear it for protection when you're out of the house?"

"Sometimes." She nodded. "Or for courage, or creativity, or luck. Mostly, it just helps me to interface with the world. I know which crystals I'm wearing, what they're purported to be good for, and it helps me put my best foot forward. But when I'm at home—"

"There's no world to interface with."

"Exactly."

He lifted her hand and absently kissed her palm. "If you'd known I was coming would you have worn some?"

"Definitely."

He caught her eyes and was pleased to see her looking lazily aroused by the sight of him kissing up her wrist, making tracks toward her elbow. "What would you have worn?"

She considered his question with a solemnity that made her look momentarily regal. "I have a necklace with a spirit quartz pendant I might have put on."

"What does spirit quartz do?"

"Protects innocent women from scoundrels."

He stopped midkiss at her elbow and quirked her a look. "Is that right?"

She laughed. "No. But it banishes fear."

He stopped kissing her then, and for a moment, just nuzzled his stubble against her inner arm. He let her hand drop and laced his fingers around her waist. Her stare was always intense, with those icy-light eyes and that unblinking intake thing she did. But he was starting to be able to read the nuance there. If he looked, really looked, he could just sense the edges of her vulnerability. She could have just made a joke about what the crystal did. She didn't have to answer the question honestly, but she had.

"Fear?" he asked gently. "Am I scary, Fin?"

"Am I?" she asked, arching that emoji eyebrow.

"Good point," he conceded. But his mind was chewing over her admission and it was important to him to clear something up. "Fin... I hope what you mean is that me, as a concept, is scary. Not me as a man. As the person standing in front of you." She opened her mouth but he pressed one finger there for one moment, needing to finish. "Because I know that you've had to grow all sorts of weapons and armor just to be able to live your life in peace, and I hate that. I hate that for you. I wish it weren't true. And I guess I just want you to know that if you ask me to leave, I'll go. Simple as that. You don't have to shove me away. I'm not going to push you, Fin. I'm going to listen. If you talk, I'll listen."

"If I talk, you'll listen," she repeated, looking at him like he'd just spoken Finnish.

"Simple as that. I promise you I will." He ducked his head from one side to the other. "I'm stubborn. So, there's that. But I don't ever want to make you feel unsafe. Ever. In any capacity. Obviously physically. But I mean that emotionally as well. Mentally." He paused, searching for the right words. "Psychically? Mystically? I don't really know what you'd call it. But I know you well enough now to know that you're operating on a different plane than I am sometimes. And if I'm ever doing something wonky...with my energy. Just clue me in. Give me a chance to fix it."

She took her eyes away and pressed her forehead to his collarbone. He could feel her fingers plucking at the hem of his sweater. "You're asking for communication."

"Well." He adjusted his grip around her waist and rested his chin on her head. "I'm a talker. Just ask Sebastian."

She laughed, tilting her head back and catching his eye again. "But you're so bad at communicating with Kylie."

He laughed now. "Ky seems to kind of be the exception to my rule. But she and I are figuring out how to talk to one another. For a while, you were an exception too. I had no idea how to talk to you. But I wanna figure it out. Even if, in the end, we're just friends who made out a few times, I wanna be able to really talk to you, Fin."

She plunked her head back down and spoke into his sweater again. "You're saying you want to know me. Really know me."

"Bingo."

She sighed and mumbled something he couldn't quite hear. But he could have sworn he caught the words peacoat-wearing feelings-haver and maybe even Hamptons hair, but he couldn't be sure. When she looked back up at him, she was chewing her bottom lip. "All right," she said. "Let's order takeout."

THEY ATE TAKEOUT SUSHI for dinner, sitting on her living room floor. Tyler asked questions about her work, and she asked questions about his. She made them tea and Tyler tried very hard to drink his with a straight face but she saw right through him, laughing and getting up to add cream and sugar to his.

They hadn't turned on any lights in the apartment and by the time Tyler mentioned that he should probably get home, she was simply a blue shape on the floor next to him, silhouetted only by the dim natural light filtering in from the kitchen.

She agreed to walk him to the train, and they got bundled up in the dark, neither of them wanting to turn on any lights, knowing it would burst the bubble of the warmest, most exhilarating afternoon he could ever remember having. When they got out into the February air, it was fresh and crisp, all of yesterday's low fog long gone.

"The moon is even smaller than yesterday," he observed as they strolled along, his hands in his pockets and her arm crooked through his.

"It tends to do that," she said with a smile.

She chatted to him about moon phases and different cultural beliefs about them. Neither of them said anything at all about the fact that they'd bypassed the train stop and headed straight into Prospect Park. They strolled the pedestrian path, and a dry, crisp snow began to lightly fall. There was something exciting and renewing about this particular snowfall. It was nothing like the usual stomach-plummeting, face-palming dread that typically accompanied a February snow in Brooklyn.

They turned back and exited the park, walking along the cobblestone sidewalk that lined one side of Ocean Avenue. They were headed back toward the train, sure, but also back toward her house.

"Weirdly," Tyler said. "I'm kind of hungry again."

Fin glanced at her phone and laughed. "You are never going to guess what time it is."

"10:45."

"It's 8:15."

"What?" Tyler confirmed the time on his own phone. "Jeez. We let the light fade naturally in your apartment and it got me all turned around, I guess."

"We ate that sushi at like 5:00 and called it dinner."

"And then took a three-mile stroll. No wonder I'm hungry."

"Ty?"

He looked down at her, snow in her hair, an innocent question on her lips, cars honking and revving past on one side, the park, dark and peaceful on the other side. And he knew two things then, unequivocally. One, his feelings for her last year had not just been a crush. They'd been real and intense and meaningful. And two, she hadn't extinguished them with her speech at the ball game. Nope. She'd just locked them in a back room, and he'd mistaken them for gone. But here they were. Intact and restless after all that time locked away. It was all he could do to try to shush those feelings, calm them, soothe them, convince them that he wasn't going to sequester them any longer.

"Yeah?" he said gruffly, hoping that everything he'd just discovered wasn't served up on a platter for this psychic to see.

"Wanna come over for dinner?"

He laughed and nodded and they headed back to her apartment. When they got there, she immediately turned on some lamps, turning her apartment moody and, to Tyler's mind, sexy. Her casual cleaning outfit was even more devastating to his senses when she was revealing it bit by bit. Unwinding her woolen scarf from around herself, unbuttoning her winter coat. He slid the coat off her shoulders, and she whirled around, a look in her eye that was somehow fierce and soft all at once.

"It just kills me when you do that."

"What?" he asked.

"When you help me with my coat."

"Oh." For some reason, he felt his cheeks heat. "I...didn't even think about it. I guess it's reflex."

"You also open cabs and hold the elevator doors open like they might slam closed and chop my head off."

"Well, I—"

"It's very cute," she said, stalking forward.

He took a step back and found the front door up against his back. She went up on her toes and rubbed her cheek against his. Knowing just how much stubble she'd be finding there, Tyler winced. He was closing in on his necessary second shave of the day.

"Annoyingly cute," she said, dropping back to the flats of her feet. "I tried not to have a crush on you, but then you just kept helping me with my coat."

She turned on her heel.

"How about Italian?" she called over her shoulder. "I'm feeling carby. And I think I have a bottle of red."

She disappeared into her kitchen, and he was left staring at the place where she'd just been.

Crush.

Crush.

Crush.

"Fuck," he whispered to himself. Over the year, in order to save his own sanity, he'd convinced himself that she wasn't into him. He'd made the landscape between them as barren as possible, determined not to let hope bloom there, knowing just how lethal that could be for him.

But now here they were.

They had a glass of wine each with the Italian food that was delivered forty-five minutes later. They sat facing one another with their backs on opposite arms of the couch and when the dinner was done and Tyler had put away the leftovers, he came back and sat down again in the same way. Only this time he pushed one of his feet forward. She did the same, laying her toes over his and making his heart bang.

"You're wearing your purple socks," he noted.

"It's my favorite day of the week when I get to wear the socks you bought me."

"I'll get you more."

The wine had been just enough to make them both dozy. He thought of the cold, fresh snow outside and shivered, not wanting to ever leave the sexy, colorful cave of Fin's home. When she pulled the afghan over them, he didn't protest. When she slid down farther and tossed him a spare couch pillow, he certainly didn't say a word.

And when, roughly seven hours later, he woke up with one of her ugly-cute feet in his face, he just laughed.

"You always wake up laughing?" she asked, stretching and basically kneeing him directly in the ribs.

He grunted, kept laughing. "Only when I realize that I slept over at Serafine St. Romain's house and didn't score."

"Don't bro out on me now, Leshuski." Fin rolled up and stretched for real, yanking the blanket off of him as she stood. "I actually slept a little bit. Surprise, surprise."

"You're not a sleeper usually?"

She turned to him with that emoji eyebrow in full cannon. "Do I strike you as a good sleeper?"

He laughed again, sat up, grabbed her by the waist and dragged her back under the afghan, this time right side up, with her nestled against him. "Don't go anywhere yet. It's early."

"You have no idea what time it is."

"It's still dark out!"

"It's winter, it's always dark out." But she surprised him by snuggling into him all the same. She was warm and soft and pressing her forehead under his chin. Neither of them mentioned that her thigh was laying directly over a very awake part of his body. They were both adults, both understood the manner in which they wanted one another.

Tyler couldn't help but let his hand trace down her back, play with the top seam of her leggings.

She shifted against him. "You're a mountain man in the morning."

He groaned, dragging a hand over his face, scraping over his beard with chagrin. "Ugh. I know. I usually shave before bed to prevent this from happening. Otherwise it takes me twice as long to shave it off in the morning."

"I can't believe your beard grows that fast."

"So does my hair. I get it trimmed every two weeks."

"Between that and the gel, your hair budget must be through the roof."

She was biting her lips together, so Tyler was fairly certain she was teasing him. "I do not use hair gel."

Cue the emoji eyebrow.

"Fine," he huffed. "I might, on occasion, use a little pomade. But these are just good-hair genes you're witnessing."

"It's so strange how you and Kylie can look so different and so similar at the same time."

"I know." Guiltily, his thoughts traced back to Kylie for the first time in twelve hours. It was strange not to have been dwelling on her while she was on her trip. She'd been foremost on his mind for months. He instantly felt guilty, and suddenly nervous, like just because he hadn't been keeping her in his every thought, that something bad could have happened, and it would be all his fault.

"She's fine," Fin told him, doing that thought-reading thing she did so well.

"How do you know?"

"One, I'm in tune with her. If something terrible were to have happened, I'd have an intuition about it. And two, she'd text you if something happened."

"Or she'd text you."

Fin nodded in concession. "She trusts us, Ty."

A wind chime sound went off in her bedroom and this time Fin sat up for real.

"That's my alarm. I have a client meeting in an hour and a half up in Greenpoint."

"Eesh. You've gotta get going, then."

"There's a bagel shop on the way to the train if you wanna grab a bite with me."

Tyler finger-brushed with her horrible natural toothpaste and sat on her couch as he watched her pace around the house, getting ready for the day. Twenty minutes later he grinned at her as she scrabbled with the lock on her door.

"Still feeling befuddled, Ms. St. Romain?" he asked, leaning against the wall of her hallway.

He walked her to the bagel shop, and by the time they'd gotten their orders, it seemed she'd found her footing again. Wordlessly, she'd taken his coffee from him and fixed it with cream and sugar, just the way he liked. She was running late, so they got their bagels to go, slurping on their coffee cups as they walked to the train.

"You gonna be able to work today?" she asked.

"I'll head home and give it a shot."

"I—" She stopped walking so he did too. "I want to come over after my appointment."

"Yes," he said immediately. "Please do."

"Good."

He kissed her underground, after swiping into the train station, but it wasn't the kiss that stayed with him for hours afterward, it was the hug. Her arms clinched around his back, her forehead against his neck, his head bowed into the negative space above her shoulder. It was a seal on the end of their night together. A stamp saying, "We did this, it felt good."

They split ways to catch their separate trains, and Tyler was glad that her train came first. He hadn't known how good it would feel to watch her head to work, to see her off safely. It didn't make him feel left behind. No, it gave him purpose.

CHAPTER TWENTY-ONE

"CAN WE GO to your house?" Tyler asked the second he swung open his front door for Fin. She blinked at him. He already had a stocking cap and a scarf on, his jacket swinging from his fingertips, his shoes perfectly knotted.

She quirked her head to one side, trying—and failing—to catch his mood. He looked a little harried. A little guilty. "Why?"

Tyler glanced back at the apartment behind him, shifting on his feet. He was freshly shaved, and she could smell toothpaste and deodorant on the air. She suddenly felt like the fuzzy penny you sometimes find at the bottom of a purse. For once, she wanted to be as polished up as Tyler.

"It felt weird to be here without Kylie. And I think if I have you over…"

"It'll feel even weirder."

"Yeah." He shrugged. "Like I'm lying to her or something."

They'd been given the gift of forty-eight hours to explore this thing between them without having to explain it to anyone yet.

"I get it. When we're at my house, it feels like we've got a little stolen time to sort of chart the waters."

"Right."

"But when we're here it's like we're…cheating?"

Tyler grinned. "Exactly. I knew you'd understand."

He leaned forward, cupping her elbow and pressed his mouth to hers. "Damn."

He leaped back and so did she, one hand over her mouth.

"Seriously," he groused, rubbing his lips where they'd just been static shocked. "What *is* that?"

She shrugged. "My place?"

Tyler just kind of blinked at her for a moment. "It's really surreal to hear you say that to me."

She huffed and rolled her eyes. "You're not over that yet? I like you, Ty. I want you to come over and get under my afghan with me."

"Yeah," he said, shaking his head and tugging his coat on. "This is not a dream, Tyler," he muttered to himself, making her laugh.

They bumped shoulders on the way to the train. If it had been warmer, Fin wondered if they'd have held hands. But as it was, both sets of their hands were firmly ensconced in pockets. When they got on the train, it was midday and uncrowded, but still, they sat rather close on the bench seat. The train swayed and jolted, knocking his knee into hers. Fin stared down at their legs, that single point of contact. As she watched, Tyler pulled his large, booted foot back. He crooked it around hers, their ankles crossing, the entire sides of their boots touching. Fin caught her bottom lip between her teeth and looked up at him. His eyes went from where their ankles crossed to hers. His navy blues looked slow and lazy, like he was turning to her underwater.

They practically ran home from the train, both of them desperate to get out of the cold winter air and somewhere warm. Her house, her couch, under her blankets, against one another.

Tyler nearly vibrated next to her in the elevator up to her apartment. Neither of them spoke.

They speed walked down the hallway to her door, and Fin considered it a small miracle that she didn't drop her keys. The second the door was open, Tyler shouldered his way in, slamming it behind them, unwinding his scarf, unzipping his coat, yanking off his hat.

His hair stood up straight for one moment before it cascaded back down into its perfect fall. When he turned to her, she saw the need in his eyes, the nerves, the desperation.

And even in the midst of all that, he hung up his coat, folded his scarf, lined his boots up carefully.

She nearly didn't keep the groan contained. Why did everything about this man just kill her? She'd never been into neat freaks before. So why now? Why this preppy blond with his collar all but popped?

He helped her slide out of her coat, though she could feel the impatience thrumming through him.

"Remember when I helped you with your coat zipper?" she asked, surprised when her voice came out breathlessly.

"I remember," he said, just as breathless. "I held my breath while your hands were inside my clothes. I felt like if I so much as inhaled, you would have slapped the shit out of me."

"I don't touch people," she told him, turning around to face him as he hung her coat up. "Almost ever, Tyler. I don't really like it. It's too intimate, sometimes it's even invasive. But that day? Feeling the way your body heated up the air around you? I wanted to touch you. I wanted to press my chest to yours and zip that coat up around both of us."

"That can be arranged," he told her, stepping close enough for her to be able to see the large gulp that traveled down his throat.

"I like touching you, Ty," she confessed, the words

not much more than a rasp as they left her lips. "And I've wanted to, for a long time."

"You have no idea, love." He bent at the knee, landed palms on the backs of her legs and lifted her clear off the floor.

Fin, who was by no means short and by no means light, made an eeping sort of sound and clutched at his shoulders. But she felt the strength there. The tensile smoothness of his muscles. He took two long steps and dumped her backward onto her couch, following her down. Fin laughed, her hair flying everywhere, but the laughter stopped when his mouth came down over hers.

This time, they kissed right through that preliminary static shock, groaned into it instead of recoiling. They were in a pile on top of one another, her legs knotted underneath him and one of his feet on the floor to keep them both from tumbling into the coffee table.

Admitting to him that she liked touching him had popped some cork inside of her. Fin felt a rather giddy freedom when she tugged at his hair, used her thumb to trace the whorl of his ear, went palm-flat against his neck. His energy pulsed into her, so Tyler, so kind, so orderly, so unbelievably desirous of her.

She gasped and dropped her head back as his mouth opened up just below her ear.

Always, her whole life, she'd known that when a man wanted something, he took it. But today was different. Today she could feel the tremulous tornado of feeling that Tyler had for her. It was blustery and growing and sweeping them both away. But yet, he wasn't taking from her. No, his warm mouth was tracing a pattern against her pulse point; he was groaning into her skin, keeping his weight mostly off of her. She felt the slope of his nose against her chin. And then his cheek against hers.

Had he?

Yes, he'd just stopped sucking on her neck in order to give her a quick little hug and… Fin. Was. Finished.

She planted her palms on his shoulders and pushed at him.

He folded back immediately, his weight and heat lifting off of her and making her feel like she might float straight to the ceiling if she wasn't careful.

"All right?" he asked, panting and sliding a palm across his own chest like he was checking to make sure his heart was still working.

"Yeah," she panted back, unknotting her legs and propping her knees on the outside of his hips. "Sometimes you throw me off when you're so sweet. Like with that hug you just gave me."

"That throws you off?"

"Yeah." She shifted a little. "Most guys don't do that. Hug in the middle of making out."

"Too busy trying for a homer?"

"Something like that."

Tyler stared down at her, his palms on his thighs, his eyes both seeing her and not seeing her as he worked his jaw, deep in thought.

After a moment, he disentangled them and went to stand, his hands sliding into the pockets of his slacks. Much as he had yesterday, Tyler made a circuit around the living room, touching the crystals she kept on the bookcase, running a hand over the top of one of her photos on the wall. He flicked on a lamp, looked out the window and then turned back to her, his hands back in his pockets.

"I like you, Fin. In a big way."

She could taste the bright, metallic electricity of his nerves all the way across the room.

"I'm not trying to take something from you. I wasn't back then and I'm not now." He cleared his throat and leaned against the window. "At some point, I hope you'll get used to that."

Fin sat up slowly. Her hair cascaded around her shoulders, and because she was immediately too grateful for the curtain between her and Tyler, she started braiding it back, knowing instinctually that she needed to be open now. Bared to him.

"Tyler, are we going to tell her?"

"Kylie? Yes."

Fin tossed her braid back over her shoulder. "You want to tell her tomorrow?"

He shifted against the window, hands still in his pockets. "Yes."

"That what? That we're together?"

He took a big breath, strode across the room, slid onto the couch and used one hand to hoist her legs over his lap. It was like he was using her body to pin himself down to the furniture. "Only if it's the truth," he said quietly.

Cocking her head to one side, Fin regarded him. "Maybe we should sleep together before we decide what this really is."

Tyler stilled, his hand on her knee, his brow furrowed. "Fin." He paused for a second, seemingly needing to gather his thoughts. "Are you asking me to *audition*?"

She burst out laughing. "No? Yes? Kind of? Sexual chemistry is important, Ty. What if we tell Kylie, and then realize that this whole thing is a big fat nothing? Not worth it."

"Fin, you literally shock me every time we kiss. You think this thing is going to fizzle when we get naked together?"

She paused. "I'm not saying— What are you doing?"

He'd stood up and was yanking buttons on his shirt, untangling his belt from the waist of his slacks, tossing it aside. "What does it look like I'm doing?"

"You're getting naked."

He bent down and divested himself of one sock and then the other. She knew how much he meant business because one of them flew over one shoulder and the other across the room.

"I'm pretty sure I've been offered the chance to get naked and show you how I feel. So, I'm freaking taking it."

His shirt agape, barefoot, Tyler leaned down and then Fin was wrapped around him again and lifted into the air. "Ty!"

"No?" he asked, pulled his face from the crook of her neck, his eyes clear and calm.

She grinned. "Yes."

He strode forward into her room, his mouth pressed against hers, his tongue doing this slow slide that made her lose the feeling in her legs. She was snaked around his body, his hands leaving a permanent imprint on her ass.

His shoulder knocked against the doorjamb and then her back was pressed, rather too firmly, into her dresser. He whirled around, and his shin banged the chaise longue.

"How is your room even put together?" he asked, panting, as he yanked his mouth from hers. "It's a freaking corn maze in here!"

She couldn't help but laugh and then even harder when he turned them sideways again and banged his elbow into her dresser, making all the jewelry tremble on the jewelry trees.

"There." She pointed over her shoulder.

"The bed," he sighed. "Safety."

He launched them sideways and they landed in a heap. But it wasn't quite the proffered safety he'd hoped for because her leg got caught in his leg and her knee jammed hard into his thigh, dangerously close to the goods.

He grunted, shot her a glare and pushed her knee away. He rolled to his back with a laugh. "Holy *crap*, that was close."

Her heart galloping, turned backward and upside down in this new position it called home, she crouched over him, eyes wide. She was torn between laughing and begging for forgiveness. Fin opened her mouth to apologize but found herself already tugged over top of him again, their mouths clashing and opening, those lazy, half-open eyes of his just *doing* things to her. She twisted herself on top of him, pushing against his hardness at her belly, wanting *more more more* of everything.

"More," she told him, feeling suddenly like it was the only word in her vocabulary. And what a useful word it was, covering such a wide manner of sins. More skin. More tongue. More bed-creaking grinding. More moaning into his mouth. More. Of. Everything.

His hands were tight on her back, pinning her down to him, twisted in her clothing. She had to push back hard against his grip to sit up. Once she was there, she grinned down at him. He looked wrecked, and she liked it. The most disheveled she'd ever seen him.

She reached down and yanked her tunic off over her head, tossed it aside.

"Holy mother Bethlehem," he groaned, his eyes as wide as daisies as he looked for the first time at her chest, naked except for a bra. "I didn't know. You always wear such loose clothes. But fuck. I—had no fucking—"

He stopped talking and sat up, his hands automatically tracing the hourglass of her hips and his eyes bottoming out on her breasts.

Okay. So apparently he was a boob guy. Which she'd never really known because of her clothing choices. He dropped his forehead against her breastbone and, for just a moment, pushed his whole face into her cleavage.

She couldn't help but laugh.

"Okay, so you're *really* a boob guy."

"You have no idea."

It was then she registered the scrabbling fingers at her back. He was yanking at the clasp of her bra, and she could feel the tremble in his hands. He put his arms all the way around her, hooked his chin over her shoulder and peered down her back. "Who the fuck designed this bra? The military?"

It was then, pressed flush against him, that she felt the wild, almost rabid, beat of his heart. With just one wincing snap, he finally stripped her bra off of her. She pushed him back, so that they were both on their knees on the bed. She grabbed two handfuls of his open shirt and yanked it over his head. But she pulled too fast, and his armpit and wrist got caught.

"Wait. Oomph. Crap." He pulled it off himself, and then there was nothing left to do but just look at one another.

His chest was wider than she'd thought it would be. It was covered in a mat of light hair, muscular but not bulky. He still had that same dancer's build as he'd had in the videos she'd seen. His shoulders capped his body off in a round, strong way, rolling sinuously as he leaned forward. He balanced on his knuckles, kissing her again. She noticed that he was keeping his hands to himself, and so she did the same. She could feel the raw heat from his skin, but their only connection point was their mouths. When he pulled away, his eyes were even lazier than before, somehow relaxed and urgent at the same time.

"Let's each do our own pants," he suggested, which she thought was a grand idea. They both flopped onto their backs to lift their hips and shimmy their pants down in identical fashion. They peered sideways at the exact same moment and burst into laughter.

"This might be the least smooth seduction I've ever been a part of," he muttered to himself.

"Including when you lost your virginity at a party and a drunk kid saw your butt?"

He laughed. "Why did I tell you that? And yes. Less smooth than that." Both of them pantsless now, he rolled over her, and her braid got caught under his weight.

"Ow."

"Sorry."

Shaking his head at himself, he rolled again, pulled her on top of him and let their bare legs tangle together as her weight settled onto him. He groaned and planted his hands over his face.

Huh. Sitting up so that she straddled his hips, his hardness pressing quite firmly into her panty-covered ass, she tugged his hands away from his eyes.

"Everything all right down there?"

He let out a long breath, his eyes stuttering on her chest, his hands compulsively going to the dip at her waist. "I just want you so badly, Fin. And you're so—so—you hurt to look at. You're like Helen of Troy or something. Seriously, if you'd been born in an earlier century, people would have worshipped you."

She frowned.

"But that's not even—" He tried again. "Fin, I've wanted this for a really, really long time with you. I had that major crush on you for so long. And then that went away. But then I got to know you again, and I wanted you in a different way. A stronger way. But I don't think I even realized it. Because I wasn't letting myself hope for it. I wanted it so badly that I knew it was idiotic to hope for it. And now I'm here and you're naked and sitting on me and looking like *that* and, yeah... It's a lot."

It never ceased to amaze her, the kind of personal magic that words held. As soon as he said the words out loud, she could just stop guessing about it. His heartbeat had told her he was nervous, but now that she knew for sure, it was easier to understand. To quantify. And she could admit it herself.

"For me too."

In case he didn't believe her, she lifted his hand from the curve of her waist and pressed it to her chest so that he could feel her own heartbeat.

"I haven't had sex in a long time," she admitted to him, and then, deciding that since she was already straddling him, almost buck-ass naked, there wasn't much point in holding back. "And I'm not sure I've ever had sex with someone who makes me feel...this."

He sat up so that they were almost nose to nose. "Makes you feel what?"

Well, she wasn't quite prepared for those kinds of dec-larations. She lifted one shoulder and dropped it. "Stuff," she said stubbornly.

He smiled that easy smile of his and Fin felt some of her nerves abate. "I feel stuff for you too," he whispered.

"That's good."

"I feel—" he held up two hands like brackets "—'insert noun here' for you."

She laughed, cocking her head to one side and slowly unbraiding her hair, wanting to feel wild and unrestrained with him.

"I really really verb you," she whispered.

They both laughed and he pulled her into an easy hug. Or, effortless, she should say. Because there was nothing easy about the place where their hips were joined, an incredible heat between them, begging for friction.

His eyes dilated to almost completely black and he licked his lips. "I don't have any condoms," he rasped.

This bit of information intrigued her. He was a forty-two-year-old sex-haver who didn't have condoms on him? "Really?"

"Yeah. I used to keep one in my wallet, but then with Ky… Sometimes I'll ask her to grab some cash out of there. I keep her medical cards in there. It just felt weird."

Fin face-palmed. "God, you're cute."

She hoisted herself off of him and was two steps away from the bed when his arm came around her waist. "Where are you going?"

"To get condoms," she said, rolling her head to one side when he kissed up, over her shoulder to just under her ear.

"Mmm," he groaned. "There's time."

He tugged her back so that she sat at the edge of the bed, between his spread legs. She could feel his hardness pressed against her ass, straining against the fabric of his briefs. Tyler's hands started a slow journey down her legs to the backs of her knees. She couldn't stop staring at their legs pressed up against one another like that.

"You have long legs," she gasped as he drew a line up the inside of her thigh.

"So do you," he said, nibbling on the curve of her shoulder. He hooked his chin over her collarbone, peering down her body. "And killer tits."

Fin burst out laughing. "No. Just no. Never. You are not allowed to say *killer tits* when you have your hand between my legs. Or ever, for that matter. Strike it from your vocabulary."

He was laughing too, his smile pressed into the side of her neck. "Thought you'd like that. Figured it would fit my '80s villain image."

She turned her head to one side, caught his eye. "You know I don't think of you like that anymore."

"I know," he whispered. "You verb me."

"I do."

This time when they kissed, her head twisted, his head over her shoulder, it was slow and long and spanned on and on. He had one hand pressed to the soft skin halfway up one thigh and the other hand palm down over her belly. Fin absorbed the slow, caressing nudges of his tongue, warming her, liquefying her. It wasn't until she started wiggling in the cage of his arms that he finally moved his hands.

"Tyler," she whispered, letting her head drop back as one of his warm, rough hands smoothed over her breast. His heart danced against her back.

Tyler weighed her in his hand, his thumb strumming across her nipple once, twice, and the third time she arched her back and pushed into him. His hips pushed forward into her ass and she made a sound she hadn't expected to make. Turned on, desperate, tight and relaxed at the same time.

"Tyler," she whispered again and he hooked his chin over her shoulder again. Just watching his hand play with her breast.

"I really had no idea you were shaped like this," he breathed, letting his other hand come up and join in the fun. He was firm and gentle; he molded her and plucked and pushed her together, creating a deep crevasse of cleavage that immediately made him groan. He picked up her hands and made her hold her own breasts together while he dipped his fingers into the dark place between. He pulled her hands away and kissed her palms, one and then the next, guided her hands behind her, to his hair, making her body arch like a crescent moon.

"I might accidentally yank your hair," she whispered, flexing her fingers against his scalp, feeling every impossibly silky strand against her fingers like some kind of liquid fire.

"You just do whatever you need to do, love," he whispered, one of his hands still plumping her breast and the other one back on her knee. He drew that same straight line up the inside of her thigh and her leg swung free like a door. *Knock knock*, his fingers seemed to say.

"God, yes," Fin replied, answering his unspoken question. His hand hesitated only briefly, his eyes still looking down her body, watching himself touch her.

And then the flat of his palm was laid over her, giving her his heat. His energy. She made a guttural sound. The man had no idea how potent he was.

"All right?" he asked, stilling.

"The hands," she gasped, "have a certain kind of energy. Different than other parts of the body. Can you feel it, Ty? What you're putting into me right now? God." She tossed her head to one side. Even through her underwear, his hand over her heat was like mainlining him. It was a river of Tyler Concentrate all streaming in through her body, arousing her, overwhelming her, inundating her. She realized her hands were in fists in his hair, but couldn't relax against the feeling. "Close your eyes," she instructed him. "Do you feel it? What's there between you and me? Even if you don't believe, can you feel it?"

He did as she asked, his hand still and firm between her legs, his eyes clamped closed. She could feel him trying.

Feel him searching. And that too touched her. After a moment, his breath hitched. "Wow. I think… Yeah, I think I
can feel it. It's like a flow. Like a river."

"Exactly," she gasped. He lessened the pressure against
her but she chased him forward with her hips. "More."

He didn't need more urging than that. Tyler's hand
slipped up her stomach, his fingers pressed to that temp-
tation of a line where her underwear cut across her skin.

"More?" he whispered.

"More," she answered.

His fingers slid underneath her underwear and found
her wetness. "Ohholymotherfuckdammit."

She would have laughed if she hadn't been too busy
twanging with energy and sensation, her body coiling
against the place his fingers rested. She hadn't expected
him to be so cursey during sex. It charmed her.

His fingers slipped, not making a pattern so much as
exploring her. Her eyes were glued to the sight of his wide
hand underneath her tiny underwear; she knew he was
looking in the exact same place.

Her hands came down from his hair, releasing him, and
she planted them onto his legs, feeling his coarse hair, the
heat, the tensing of his muscles.

He let out a long breath she hadn't realized he'd been
holding, and this time, his fingers did trace a pattern
through her wetness. A sort of figure eight that had her
pushing forward, her eyelids heavy, her chest heavy with
breath and heartbeat.

"Wow," he whispered. "Wow, dammit."

He started a soft little strum with his thumb, and she
let her head fall back. He caught her eyes for a moment
and then directed his gaze back between her legs. He was
touching her softly, learning her.

"I—" She gasped. "Take work," she warned him. "Don't have—" She gasped again. "A quick trigger."

He grinned. "You act like I don't know you, Fin."

And the featherlight butterfly of his touch didn't increase in pressure but it did increase in speed. He was teasing her, his fingers tracing her, guiding her. She was chasing that feeling, rising. This didn't feel anything like it usually did when she touched herself, but she couldn't stop her eyes from rolling back.

She was losing herself in the touch of him, choking out his name when he pressed two fingers inside of her, his thumb still strumming. But she hadn't lost track of time; she never did during sex.

She tried to turn, to press against him, move to the next act. But he put one hand on her hip and held her still.

"You'll get carpal tunnel," she protested.

He tilted her chin, looked in her eye, searched her expression. "Does it feel good?"

"God, yes."

"Then be patient." He pressed her back down and resumed, his fingers scooping inside of her, his thumb strumming, his breath hot on her neck, his hand sculpting her breast.

And again Fin was chasing sensation, losing her breath, gasping, writhing against him, one of her hands in a fist in the sheets, the other gripping his knee.

But again, time got its nails into her hair and Fin felt herself yanked back to reality. She tried to twist in his arms for the second time and this time he let her. She panted as she straddled him, her panties soaked, her mouth seeking his. He kissed her fiercely for a moment before he tugged his head back and searched out her eyes.

"What just happened?" he asked gently.

"Um, foreplay?" she said, a little bit of snark racing in to cover up the nerves that had started to wake up again in her gut.

"No. Why'd you have me stop? It felt like you were close."

She cleared her throat and tried to lean in for a kiss again, but he raised his eyebrows. She held, just a breath from his lips, and sighed. "I told you I'm not a quick trigger. It can take a really long time to get me there."

His hands traced the hourglass of her, a small smile making the corners of his mouth catch the blue in the waning late-afternoon light. "Good thing we have a long time with no obligations right this very second."

His expression, light and sweet, clouded a moment later as he read the look on her face.

"Hold the phone. Are you saying that you don't want me to even *try* to get you off?"

Fin felt her mouth twist up. She resisted the urge to slide off his lap and get under the covers, where she wouldn't be quite so naked.

"It's…been the source of a lot of frustration in the past."

His brow furrowed. "For you?"

After a moment, she shook her head. "Usually for the guy. They get irritated when nothing they do works. But it's not that big of a deal. I can almost always get there by myself during sex."

Tyler's mouth dropped straight open. His eyes went wide as he flopped backward onto the bed, his arms flinging up over his head.

"Wow," he murmured to the ceiling. "Wow. It all makes sense now."

CHAPTER TWENTY-TWO

"WHAT MAKES SENSE?" Fin, still straddled across Tyler's lap, poked at his chest. He gritted his teeth because she was extremely wet and extremely warm and even through their two pairs of underwear he could feel her in excruciating detail.

"You," he told her honestly. "No wonder you had no interest in me pursuing you. No wonder you distrust guys who want you so badly. Because they pursue you relentlessly, usually insulting you if you turn them down, and when you *do* say yes to one of them, apparently he's not even patient enough to get you off? Jeez, I'd have kicked my ass to the curb too, if that had been my experience."

Her brows were down, watching him like he was some alien creature who was trying to communicate in another language.

"You say that now…" she said after a minute. "But forty minutes of fruitless canoodling later, and you might be singing a different tune."

He sat up so that they were nose to nose. "Absolutely zero canoodling is ever fruitless. If I wanna canoodle you, trust me, I'm doing it for the sake of canoodling. And orgasm should not be viewed as the only destination. That's a total *orgasm killer.*"

She cocked her head again to the side as if she were still

actively trying to figure out what language he was speaking. "You're serious."

"Dead." He brushed his nose over hers. "Something I learned as I got older and got better at sex is that pressure to perform is not sexy. Ever. Dudes usually figure this out in relation to their boners."

"What do you mean?"

"I mean a watched pot never boils."

She threw her head back and laughed and he silently thanked God that the furrow between her eyes was gone. "You mean that if everyone is just sitting around and waiting for the boner to rear his head—"

"Then six more weeks of winter it is."

She laughed again before her smile gave way to an inquisitive look. "You think the same theory can be applied to my orgasm?"

He gave her a droll look. "Fin, if you're counting down the seconds to when I'm going to get frustrated and give up on your elusive orgasm, you are literally *never* going to have said elusive orgasm. Also, if the *only* reason I'm touching you or going down on you is to get you off, then I'm probably going to get frustrated if you don't get off. The point is that we're supposed to be enjoying each other. Reveling in each other. And if we're doing that, pressure free, then usually that leads to the happy fireworks times."

She raised an eyebrow. "And if it doesn't lead to the happy fireworks times?"

He shrugged. "Then you get yourself off during sex. Or we use a vibrator. Or I give you ten minutes alone in the shower to take care of business. I dunno. I'm just saying that if we're actually considering having sex with each other regularly, relationship-style, then there's gonna be times that you don't come or my boner takes a coffee break or whatever. If we just kind of accept that we can still have good sex even if we're not checking every box every time, then we'll *actually* have good sex. Where I'm not praying for boners and you don't have one eye on the clock waiting for me to tell you there's something wrong with your hoo-ha."

Her face changed from one emotion to the next, but Tyler wasn't sure he was accurately interpreting any of them. She looked confused. And hopeful. And trepidatious. And excited.

"That actually makes a lot of sense."

He propped his hands behind his head. "You know, I'm not the worst."

She rolled her eyes and rubbed herself against him. "So, what happens now?"

He gulped and pressed his eyes closed for a moment against the image of a topless Serafine St. Romain straddling him. He deserved the medal of honor for having that conversation while she was naked.

"Uh," he grated out. "We have sex?"

She laughed. "Good idea."

And then the weight of her was gone as she scampered to the bathroom and back, condoms in hand.

She held out a hand to him and he took it. She yanked him up to his feet. "I like your theory about pressure. Beds are a lot of pressure. Let's go to a less sex-havey place." She tugged him a few feet to the side, and they both sat down hard on top of the chaise longue that took up one wall of her bedroom. It was romantic and curvy and entirely too small for two people. It was perfect. Her body was jammed up between the wall and his body, her breasts in his face, her legs twisted with his.

Tyler leaned forward and took one of her nipples in his

mouth, testing her, suctioning, nibbling. He kept his promise and reveled. He lost himself in the piano keys of her ribs, the plush paradise of her breasts.

She kissed at his ribs, dragged her hands through his chest hair. Just when he was about to ask her if his chest hair bothered her at all, she rubbed one cheek against it and bit his pec. That was a yes to the chest hair, then.

They grappled together, sweaty and cramped on the chaise longue. She dragged her foot up the back of one of his legs, pushing her toes underneath the leg of his boxer briefs. He grunted and tucked his thumbs into his waistband, tugging them down over his hips. She reared back and helped him get them the rest of the way down.

Her eyes landed between his legs, and she surprised him by breaking into a wide, lustful smile.

"You look like you have some very evil, very dirty plans in store for me," he said, unable to keep from tracing the shape of her hourglass with his hands.

"I'm just smiling because your dick kind of looks like you."

"What?" Tyler laughed and looked down at the appendage in question. "What are you talking about?"

She was sitting on his thighs, her hands on his hip bones. Before she answered, she leaned down and pressed a kiss to his tip, almost chaste. Tyler's hips jutted upward of their own accord and, holding his eye, she gave him one hot, glancing lick before she lifted her head again and answered his question.

"I'm not sure how to explain it. But he looks like you. Preppy. Masculine. But with all this desire he keeps on a very short leash."

"I'll take your word for it," Tyler said, unable to keep himself from reaching a hand down, readjusting himself.

Fin batted his hands away and reached for a condom, opening it and expertly sliding it down his length. "Sorry," she grimaced. "I'll get bigger ones next time."

"These'll do," he grunted, counting backward from nine thousand at the feel of her tight, confident grip against him.

The very second she was done fussing over him, he reached up and toppled her back down, over him. He tipped them to the side again so that she was pinned between the wall and him, his body on the chaise longue just far enough not to fall off. Her leg was over top of his hip, her eyes snagged on his, her breasts smashed against his chest. She was completely pinned and open to him with the exception of her underwear.

Pulling them off of her would require him to disentangle the two of them, and there was not a penguin's chance in hell of that happening. So, Tyler simply reached down and yanked her underwear to one side, baring her to him. Fin's pupils dilated and she jutted her hips forward, her light eyes almost hypnotizing him. Tyler found her with his fingers first, and she was the same heaven she'd been over on the bed. Warm, impossibly wet, ready for him. Open and tight and perfect. He guided his hardness straight toward the promised land, pressing himself just half an inch inside of her and waiting, his entire world trembling like those first disorienting few seconds of an earthquake.

"More," she whispered, moving her head so that their mouths were pressed together, not kissing, just smashed together and breathing, her arms around his rib cage, their chests pumping in and out. He planted the flat of his palm against her ass and held her still as he pushed himself forward.

Not too fast, not too slow. Tyler pushed in halfway,

pulled back out and then thrust forward and let himself sink to the hilt.

He said words. Lots of them. He felt like she was pulling them out of him with those eyes of hers. He had that familiar hypnotized feeling as he felt himself get lost in the light blur of her gaze. Her arms were a hard cage around him, their noses and mouths smashed together. He placed one hand between her back and the wall, reared back and thrusted again. And again.

The chaise longue scratched her wooden floor as it moved an inch or so at a time. Tyler was dimly aware of planting a foot against the wall for leverage. On their sides like this, they didn't have a huge range of motion, but neither did they seem to need it. He could feel her pleasure point smashed against his pubic bone, the same way her breasts were smashed against his chest. He could hear her voice, begging directly into his mouth. He reveled in the tight, almost unforgiving clasp of her body. He felt her begin to rhythmically clench around him as she rose, chased her own fire, lost herself the way he was losing himself.

"Ty," she chanted. "Ty. Oh, God. I'm gonna—" And that was all the warning he got before her fingernails raked across his back, her arms clamping hard around him, her head getting thrown back as her entire body went tight and writhing and pressure, pressure, pressure around where he needed her the most. White light spread into the corners of his vision as he endured the most pleasurable pain of his life. There was nothing like this. Nothing better than this moment right here.

He stopped thrusting and just held inside of her, letting her feel him there. He'd been close, but hadn't come yet and suddenly, he found he wasn't quite ready to. Though pulling out of her heat went against every law of nature known to mankind, Tyler did just that.

"Mmm," she groaned, tossing one arm over her eyes. "That was—" She cut off and looked up when he gripped her knees and swung her around on the chaise longue, opening her up to him where he knelt on the ground. "What? You don't have to— Oh, shit."

He knew he didn't have to. Which was part of why he wanted to so badly. He hoped that one day she would understand this. That sex without unwritten sexual obligation was the highest plane of adult fun that anyone could ever reach. It was like the secret hidden level at the end of an old Nintendo video game. Not everyone knew it was there, but once you found it, you refused to settle for less.

He opened his mouth over her wetness, kissed her there like he had her mouth. Slow and unbothered and joyful. He could still feel her aftershocks from her first orgasm and he chased them, used them like a roadmap, let himself find where she was sensitive, where she was too sensitive and which places made her yank his hair. He held her open with his hands and let himself lose track of time. He wasn't completely converted on this whole energy thing, but he did his absolute best to nonverbally communicate to her that he was having a blast, that she should forget about time, that this was perfection.

He nuzzled and kissed and nipped. But it was the suckling she liked best. The no-nonsense, concentrated, he-didn't-come-to-play suction that had her in that crescent-moon shape again, nonsense words that dissolved into a kind of hoarse scream as she trembled, vibrated, clamped down on the two fingers he'd slipped inside.

She reared up and he barely recognized her. She'd never looked more like Cleopatra than she did in that moment.

She was fierce and glowing with whatever the nonangry version of anger was. She had it in spades. She tumbled forward, off the chaise longue, and knocked him back onto the floor. He caught himself on the heels of his hands, his legs spread out before him with Fin kneeling in the triangle they made. She aggressively ripped the condom off of him, leaned forward and swallowed him down.

Apparently she hadn't come to play either. Because did she tease him? She did not. Did she experiment? She did not. Did she play? She did not. She merely attempted to get the roof of his head to blow off in cartoon steam.

He collapsed backward onto his elbows, thrust his hips up into the fisted hand she'd brought into the mix, and simply stopped holding on to reality. White claimed his vision then as pleasure, needle-sharp and ruthless, was summoned forth from him in an unstoppable cyclone.

He was shocked to feel echoes of that same palm energy she'd encouraged him to feel earlier. This was like that but multiplied by the earth. This was grounded in pleasure, in giving. He knew, without question, that he was giving something of himself to her. Not just his ecstasy, but a piece of who he was. He was riding on the impossible euphoria of handing himself over to her. Hers for the taking.

I'm yours.

The words popped into his consciousness out of nowhere as she sucked him through the most life-altering orgasm he'd ever experienced. And when he huffed and fell backward, and she continued to lap at him affectionately, he knew another truth: wherever this static-shock-having, possibly psychic, magic-doing, potion-brewing witch woman wanted to lead him, he was going. He'd go with her into the beyond. The next world. The next life. Beyond, beyond, beyond.

TYLER WOKE UP alone on the floor of Fin's bedroom. The sky outside the window was a deep blue but he lay in a triangle of orange light glowing in from the living room. There was a pillow under his head and a sheet tossed over his hips. He moved one hand down and confirmed that he was still very much naked.

He didn't usually enjoy sleeping on a floor, or really anywhere but his Serta mattress and Egyptian-cotton sheets. But so far with Fin he'd slept a night on a crappy antique couch and taken a very satisfying catnap on the rug on her bedroom floor. Had he ever felt more refreshed? He didn't think so.

He sat up and something rolled off his forehead. Squinting in the dark he found it with a soft grin. It was a clear, almost round crystal that she'd laid there. He held it in the palm of his hand and gazed down at the little rock. It was warm from his forehead, but he almost felt like it was warm from her. Like although she'd gotten up, she'd left a piece of herself behind. He stood, stretched and found his pants, remaking her bed from the mess they'd torn it into earlier. He took one last look around the room that he was quite certain had changed the path of his life before he went to look for Fin.

He found her in the kitchen. Her hair was knotted in a huge pile on top of her head, and she wore his button-down shirt and her purple socks. There were miles of leg in between. Her back was to him as she slid something chopped up and orchid-purple into a pot on the burner. He heard her say something but couldn't quite make it out. Something moved over him, almost like a static shock without the shock.

He watched quietly as she chose herbs from her drying rack and those went in the mixture too. Almost instantly, a fragrance curled out into the air, riding on the back of the steam.

"Smells good in here," he said, stepping toward her.

She jolted under the touch he smoothed over one of her hips, but softened immediately, leaning back into him, letting her head fall back onto his shoulder as he wrapped his arms around her front.

Holding her like this just felt right. It had fond memories attached to it, considering he'd held her like this the first time he'd touched her naked body, just hours ago. But there was something about them sandwiched together like this, both of them facing forward, that made him feel allied with her. Like they were staring down the future together.

He kissed her temple, rested his chin on top of the messy pile of her hair. "Whatcha makin'?"

"Uh, it's a kind of celebration tea."

He knew instantly that she wasn't telling him the whole truth. He leaned forward, over her shoulder and sniffed the pot. "Smells...sexy."

It was true. Something about the scent was romantic, made him think of dark rooms and whispers and warm, smooth skin.

She said nothing, just turned the heat down, put a dash of something in the pot and put the lid on.

"What's it called?" he urged her, catching a view of one pink cheek of hers and feeling beyond intrigued.

She shifted her weight from one foot to the other. And look at that, he had nervous Fin in the circle of his arms, her breasts resting on his forearm, the cradle of her head pressing into his shoulder. He suddenly felt giddy with holding her.

She turned all at once, her light eyes defiantly on his, but her cheeks still tantalizingly pink. "It's...it's called love tea, okay? It promotes relaxation and calm, but also celebration for when—" She mumbled the rest, but he didn't need her to say it clearly.

He twisted a fallen strand of her hair back into her bun and finished the sentence for her. "It's for when you've just made love to someone."

She nodded tersely, her eyes on the notch between his throat and chest. "For when you're happy about it. It sort of seals it all in."

He jolted, as she had, when she landed one palm on his chest. He knew now that she was showing him her energy, her palm energy. But she was also messing around with his chest hair. He felt giddy and nuzzly and ridiculous.

"Some people smoke cigarettes after sex. You brew magic tea."

She smirked up at him.

"I want a glass," he told her.

She frowned, but he could tell that it was simply to hide her pleased smile. "It'll be ready in a few minutes."

"Are you hungry?" He glanced around then, realizing he had no clue what time it even was. "Jeez, your house is like a wormhole where time bends and means nothing anymore."

"It's 6:45 p.m.," she told him.

He shook his head and laughed. "It's so weird to spend time with another adult at this time of day. Well, not so much right now, but we started hanging out at like two in the afternoon. On a weekday."

"Yeah." She scratched at her head and made the whole mess of her hair move as one organism. Tyler felt obscenely charmed by this. "I don't know anyone else who's freelance."

"Our weird schedules mean we're going to start eating dinner at five every night."

"At least we could benefit from the early-bird specials."

He smiled. "I wonder how Kylie will feel about that."

His smile faded as he considered his own question and truly did wonder how Kylie would feel about that. About all of this.

Fin, one eye on him, tilted back toward the stove and lifted the lid. "One thing at a time, Ty. Tea's ready."

She poured two cups of the tea, which was a surprising shade of pink. Tyler eyed it somewhat dubiously the moment her back was turned, smiling wide and innocent when she turned back. She led him into the living room, where they piled onto her couch, their limbs tangling, most of her weight on his lap. He winced and lifted and yanked one of her heels out from under his thigh. He liked how uncareful she was with him. She was womanly and graceful as she moved through the world, but get her alone and she was suddenly coltish and slightly clumsy. It felt like a secret that only he knew and he could feel himself locking it tight within him, somewhere that no one else would ever find it.

He eyed the tea. "So, do we say a prayer or something?"

"A prayer?" she asked, looking confused. "Like, bless me, father, for I have—"

He cut her off with a loud laugh. "No! And that's not exactly a prayer. That's what you say when you go to confess your sins. I meant, like, is there a spell we're supposed to say?"

Now she was the one laughing and rolling her eyes. "No, Ty. The magic is in the sitting and drinking. You and me together. There's nothing hocus-pocus about it."

Holding her eye, he leaned forward and took a sip, readying himself not to wince against the flavor. But to his surprise, it actually tasted good. A little like taking a bite out of a flower bouquet, but there was cinnamon in there. It was warm and light and she'd made it for him. Love tea. He'd have drunk a gallon of it if she'd asked.

CHAPTER TWENTY-THREE

THE NEXT MORNING, Fin could feel Tyler's anxiety before she even opened her eyes. She'd slept again, which was unusual for her. With a man in her bed, which was even more unusual. She couldn't remember that ever happening before.

It's because you trust him.

Jetty's voice in her head. Her aunt, who had known so much at a glance. She'd probably had more clairvoyance than Fin's mother, who'd worn silk scarves and sat on a curb chirping ominous warnings to passing tourists in the French Quarter. Her mother, who hadn't ever minded parting a dope from a dollar. Who'd had the gift and abused and ignored it at every turn. Who'd let it drive her straight to that half-hinged life she'd barely held on to, like the edge of a sail in high winds.

All these years later, the common-sense intuition in Fin's head still sounded just like her stolid aunt. It was still Jetty who was trying to keep Fin from running from herself.

Tyler's anxiety was bright and specific, like how lime green was almost never just called green. He was worried about Kylie. Fin could feel it. It was a personal worry and Fin knew, without having to ask, that it wasn't one he'd talk about if she asked. Not right now.

No. Right now he needed a distraction.

"I don't know how to trust a man," she said into the morning light that she still hadn't opened her eyes to see.

She stayed behind the comforting, warm curtain of her eyelids and felt him turn toward her, the blankets pulling tight against her breasts and then loosening when his warm hand traced over the plane of her stomach.

"I didn't know you were awake over there."

"Doing some early-morning worrying, just like you."

He chuckled, pressing his lips into her hair. His soft, warm lips transformed into a sharp bite over the lobe of her ear, and she jumped, her eyes flinging open, his smiling, sleepy face filling her vision.

"Morning," he whispered.

"So it is," she whispered back.

"Why don't you trust men?" he whispered to her, his face light and open and playful.

"Because I never knew any," she said simply. "No father. My mother never had boyfriends. No uncles. No friends. No cousins. No brothers. My mother was very clear that all they do is take and never give. That they wreck you."

"And your aunt?" Tyler asked, his voice still low, but the playful whisper long gone. He painted a picture over her hip bones with the palm of his hand, but it was more soothing than arousing.

"Never married. They'd had a brother who'd died when they were little, Jetty and my mother. But my time with Jetty, in her home, it was very female. Just me and Jetty and Via. And after Jetty passed, it was just me and Via."

"You dated."

Fin nodded. "Yes, but sort of in the same way that someone visits a zoo."

Tyler laughed and absently snuggled her closer in a comfortable way. "Out of curiosity?"

"And because you know for sure that the animals stay locked in their cages. They can never really get to you."

"Ah." The mirth in his eyes dimmed. "Have I gotten to you, Fin?"

"Ty, you never even had a cage." She traced his eyebrows, so light in color sometimes she forgot they were even there. "That's why you were so scary to me. You were always a wild animal. All I knew how to do was hurt you enough to keep you very far away."

"I don't want to be far away."

She sighed and looked at the ceiling of her apartment, her haven, her fortress. It was at that moment that the weak morning sun finally peeked around the edge of the neighboring building and hit her window, an orange cloud of light that turned her room into a candle.

"Have you ever done this before? A relationship?" she asked him.

"Yes and no. I dated a woman for a few years after college. Sam. She was sweet and never nagged me about my weird hours. I was doing an a.m. sports radio show at the time and had to leave the house at 4:30 every morning. I was usually in bed by 8:00. Not exactly a ton of fun in your midtwenties. We called it quits when it became clear that she was waiting for me to ask her to marry me. And later I was regularly seeing a woman, Alicia, back in California, but when Seb's wife died and he needed me, I called things off and moved home."

"You were relieved to leave her behind," Fin intuited, fascinated, despite the pacing feeling in her gut, to hear about Tyler's past.

"Yeah. Or rather, I was relieved to have a good reason to leave her. She was a cool person. There was no reason that it wouldn't have worked except for the fact that I just didn't care that much. And leaving town to go take care of my best friend made it so that I never had to tell her how little I cared."

He slid up a few inches and nudged her back so that they could both share her pillow, their noses just a few inches apart, that steel rope braiding itself between their eyes again. "But I've never done *this* before, Serafine. I've never waited and waited for someone I wanted so bad. Well, it's not want exactly. It's...attraction."

The lonely teenage girl who still lived somewhere in her heart immediately deflated. She'd thought he might say love.

"No, don't get me wrong," he laughed as he read her expression. "I don't mean attraction in the cheap, shallow sense of the word. I mean it in the...magnet sort of way. Wherever you are, I want to be. When you move, something in me follows you, even all these lonely months, when I haven't let it be my eyes that follow you, something in me still followed you. Attraction. I was, am, stuck to you. I don't know how else to describe it."

"Energy," she whispered. "Our energy knew how it felt about each other before we did. I could sense that all the way back since the first time we met. It was instant for me. I just didn't like it."

"I didn't like it much at first either. I didn't want to chase you. But, then, yeah. I did." His eyes went distant for a moment, the murky orange room glowing all around them. Fin got the strange feeling that the room had detached itself from the apartment building. They were simply floating haphazardly toward the sun. "So, what do we do about this trust thing?" he eventually asked her. "You're not used to trusting men. Neither of us know much about relationships. How do we keep from driving this spaceship straight into the sun?"

She smiled, hearing his words. He'd been thinking about crashing into the sun the same way she had. *Explain that one, universe.*

She went to groom his bedhead, realized that his villainous hair was already falling in that perfect way that it usually did. Frowning, she moved her hand to his beard instead and was soothed by the imperfection there. The beard that had grown in overnight, even though she'd sat on the edge of the bathtub and watched him painstakingly shave it off not even nine hours ago. She liked the incongruous nature of it. Perfect hair, pesky beard. Something about that was perfectly Tyler.

"We go very slowly," she said, the answer coming to her from somewhere in the heart of their glowing morning room, almost as if there were a spotlight shining on them and them alone, of all the people in the world. "And we make it up as we go along, even if it only makes sense to the two of us. And Kylie. This doesn't have to make sense to anyone but us."

He nodded, his eyes closing in contentment for a moment before they shot back open. "Fin, are you a, uh, marriage type of person?"

She laughed at his obvious discomfort, charmed that he'd made himself ask. "Ty, up until about seventy-two hours ago, I wasn't even a sleep-the-night-in-the-same-bed-as-a-man sort of person." She nipped his lips with hers. "This is what I meant by taking things slow."

He nodded, somehow managing to look both soothed and argumentative at the same time. "I get that. But we haven't really taken things slow at all, love. You know what I mean? Because I'm in your bed. While you're naked. We're about to tell Kylie about us. Three days ago, we hadn't even kissed."

"Sure, but we've both had feelings for a long time. And what do you mean *I'm* naked? Are you not naked?"

Instead of lifting the covers, she explored with the pads of her fingers, harrumphing in disapproval when she reached the band of his underwear. He grunted when she gently snapped the band against his hip bone. "I can't sleep naked. I always end up thinking, what if there's a fire and I have to run outside in front of all the neighbors?"

She laughed and ducked under the covers, relishing the sudden darkness, the closed heat of the cave of blankets, his chest hair against her cheek. She couldn't hear his heart beating, but she could feel it, racing against the morning, his breath sprinting to catch up as she slid his underwear to his knees and rested her head on his thigh in the darkness under the blankets. She found his hardness with the palm of her hand and pushed it to one side and then the other, giving him a lazy, wet kiss on the crown and making him bend one of his knees up, almost as if he were protecting himself against the sharp pleasure of it all.

He said her name, *Serafine*, the whole name. Fin got the same feeling she had as she'd watched him sign her birthday into his calendar. Her full name, her given name, was a contract of sorts. He was signing her into his life with every desperate groan, his hands reaching under the covers, finding her forehead, her hair, her ears. His fingers traced the circle of her lips where she was stretched around him as if he wanted, needed, to feel the place where they were connected.

She took him hard to the back of her throat, swallowing around him and then blinking at the sunlight that was suddenly everywhere as he threw off the blankets and sat up. Taking her by the chin, Tyler sat her straight up, his tongue in her mouth and his hand scrabbling for the condoms on the nightstand. They scattered onto the floor and Fin dived for them, draping herself over the side of the bed. One of his hands snaked up her thigh and she felt the firm press of his thumb between her legs, testing her, teasing her, marveling. She sat up, tore the condom open and sheathed him tightly before crawling forward onto his lap. She gasped as she sat down on him, taking him in faster than she should have, the pinch of discomfort she felt somehow emphasizing just how intimate it was to do this with another person, to invite a man into her body. She would have chased that discomfort, ridden him too hard and too fast, just to understand it all better. But Tyler held her hips still and let her adjust to the raw size of him. His stubble scraped over her nipple, her collarbone, her neck, her temple. His arms were steel bands around her back. She could feel the individual press of each finger as he finally started to move underneath her.

Fin tipped her head back to stare blindly at the glowing ceiling and felt his hands tangle in her hair, trapping her there so that his lips could trace her pulse, so his teeth could gently test the elegant length of her throat.

But there was nothing elegant about the way they ground themselves together, barely pulling apart, just deep and then deeper. He was barely withdrawing and she reveled in the desperate, inarticulate nature of it. There was something unschooled and primal about all that skin, the tight grasp of him. It was uncouth and overwhelming and so ungodly *personal.*

It was that thought that ignited the quickening deep inside of her. Just how personal this man was.

"I was so wrong," she gasped, pushing him backward and planting her hands on his chest, riding him hard enough to slam the bed against the wall.

"What?" he asked, his eyes squinting through his own pleasure, trying to make sense of her words on the other side of it.

"I thought you were shallow and superficial, Ty."

He banded an arm around her waist and tumbled her to her back, disconnecting long enough to have her huffing in frustration, only to sink back into her so fast she tightened and groaned and kept chasing that quickening.

"Dowehavetotalkabouthisrightnow?" he choked out, burying his face in her hair, inhaling sharply, trailing his teeth down the side of her neck, pinning her hands onto the mattress.

"Yes!" she moaned, both in answer to his question and because the hip-twist thing he was doing was just so good. "Because you're not shallow. You're so *personal*, Ty. Even the way you have sex. No one does it like this. Just you. Oh!"

"Say that last part again." He stopped thrusting, his mouth open, her hands pinned, his body buried deeply inside of hers. He held, held, held, panting, his pupils expanding and contracting, trying to capture the light, the moment, the very image of her.

"Which part?"

He released her hands and went down to his elbows, his forehead against hers. He caged her in gorgeously, keeping the rest of the world out. There was nothing but them. "The part where you said it was only me. Is it only me for you, Fin? Just me?"

He was asking her for words, but she couldn't oblige him just then. There were no words for this feeling. She locked her ankles around his back, her wrists over his shoulders. She was hugging him so tightly she was doubling back and hugging herself. And wasn't that just the way it was supposed to be? Wasn't loving someone like this supposed to involve loving yourself? Wasn't that what Via had been trying to explain all those weeks ago? You couldn't logjam one part of your heart and expect the other rivers to flow freely.

"All or nothing," she eventually gasped, not even capable of caring if he understood what she meant. *Just you.* But it wasn't just him. It was *only* him. "All. Everything."

A deep, almost helpless sound was coming out of him as he worked himself against her, his forehead dropping to her collarbone as his back curved hard into a C over and over again. She felt the rough scrape of his leg hair, the desperate tug and slide of his hand up and down the curve of her body. She whipped her head to one side and watched him ball up her pretty purple sheets in one white-knuckled hand. His movements went tight and jerky and then he was saying her name again. Her full name. His arms were all the way around her, all his weight on her chest as he spent himself inside of her.

His weight seemed to increase as he fell into what she could sense was a rather meditative state. Fin was, herself, familiar with the postorgasm haze and didn't begrudge him one second of it. She couldn't, however, breathe.

She gave him a light back scratch, slow and sweet, meant simply to remind him that he was a part of the world. But it was almost as if she'd static-shocked him. His body went rigid, his weight was gone and then she was being dragged under the covers, the blankets sloppily blocking out the light as he sealed them both into her bed. She blinked into the sudden stuffy darkness and then gasped when her knees were pulled apart and a warm mouth licked between her legs.

"Tyler."

"Shh," he said, letting his voice rumble into her. "Just pretend I'm not even here."

She laughed. How could she pretend he wasn't there? He had his tongue between her—

"Oh, lord." Fin arched up and a slice of light almost blinded her where the covers pulled free and the morning invaded. She clawed them back down.

This was too much. Too good. But also too much pressure. It was too transactional; there was too much pressure for her to come.

"Ouch!" she yelped when he bit her sharply on her thigh.

"Quit thinking up there! If you come, you come. If you don't, the world is not going to end. Just lay back and let me start my morning off right, all right?"

Not exactly loving being told off, Fin crossed her arms over her chest. But any rigidity she'd been attempting to hold on to simply melted away as he started to pet her with his tongue. Each of his strokes somehow both deep and soft.

"Personal," she whispered, mostly to herself. The air under the covers was stiflingly hot, and it felt good. They were sweaty and slipping against one another as she started to rock against him. He held her down with one forearm over her hips, but his other hand explored and slid and pressed deeply inside of her.

She wanted so badly to let go...but just couldn't. Everything he was doing felt so unbelievably good, but he'd already come and she was taking so long and he must be getting bored and—

"Fin," he said, his lips against her thigh again. "Read my energy. Read me. Be honest with yourself. How am I feeling right now?"

As his tongue came back to draw circles around her clit, Fin let herself reach out and find his energy. It didn't take much. The man was loud. Which made Fin realize just how hard she'd been working to block him out before.

How hard she'd blocked out everyone she'd ever slept with.

She sucked air in through her lungs, let her eyes close in the stuffy blackness of the blankets and let herself feel him. His energy hit her like a wall of light and sound. She was flung sidelong into his golden sphere of life and feeling and...contentment. There were other emotions there as well, of course. Every human was a complicated tapestry of thousands of feelings, each of them struggling to top-dog the next. But there, loudest of all, in Tyler, at that moment, with his head between her legs, was contentment. Followed closely by a lingering arousal that hadn't leached from him after his orgasm.

He gave her a potent, twisting kiss, and Fin could not, for the life of her, scent even a trace of impatience in the man. He was fully in his body, in the experience of her. Her back arched when he kissed at her again.

"That's it," he muttered.

Light slanted in again from the side, momentarily blinding her as she arched for him, cried out, twisted at his hair. She let his golden glow take her away as her heels dug into his back, just trying to hold on to the bounds of the earth.

When the orgasm swept over her, she'd never known another one like it. This was jet stream and ozone on the air, clear blue sky, plummeting upward at the speed of light. She lost her grip on the sheets, arrows of cracked light burning her eyes as her body slashed its way through pleasure.

She fell back, her top half limp even as her legs still trembled. She'd probably have the imprints of his ears on her thighs, she'd been gripping him so hard. She must have been gasping for breath, there was blanket in her mouth, her own hand over her forehead, her hair everywhere. She felt Tyler fighting with the blankets and then light surrounded them on all sides, no longer orangey and glowing, but a glaring full-morning slice that told her just how much time had passed since they'd gone under the covers. She waited for the requisite guilt to swamp her that it had taken that long for her to come. But it didn't come. Maybe it was the lovely buzz that still reverberated through her limbs, maybe it was Tyler, grinning at her from her shoulder, the blankets in a hood over his hair, his big feet waving happily from the foot of the bed.

Either way, the guilt didn't come. But laughter did. Fin threw her head back and laughed her heart out.

She grabbed Tyler's neck and hugged him, realizing that so many other times his energy had mixed with hers, she'd attempted to grab it by the scruff of the neck and leave it on the curb. But why? Why, when it felt this good to let it course through, in her blood like a stiff drink drunk too fast? She hummed with it, reveled in it and knew, in her heart, he was experiencing the exact same thing.

CHAPTER TWENTY-FOUR

FIN WENT TO pick up some groceries while Tyler went to pick up Kylie from her school. It was already almost 6:00 when the charter buses rolled down the street, finally back from their field trip. As he watched Kylie jump off the bus, chatting back over her shoulder to Anthony, he was glad that he got these few minutes alone with her. It had been strange to say goodbye to Fin, even just for an hour or two, after the intense togetherness they'd experienced for the last few days.

But now, watching Kylie's red hair bob among her classmates as she searched the block for Tyler, he was grateful to be picking her up alone.

Because this wasn't anything nearly as simple as a hierarchy. There was no comparing Kylie or Fin and their roles in his life. He hoped that Kylie would never ask him to. He knew that he would have to balance time between them. Time for Kylie. Time for Fin. Time for all three of them. Time for just the two of them.

He waved at Kylie—a small one so as not to embarrass her—and as he watched her make her way toward him, he realized that for the first time since he'd become her guardian, he wasn't utterly terrified of messing up. He was certain that someday she'd be able to write an entire memoir on all the mistakes he'd made and was going to make, a whole library even. But he wasn't scared of them. They were inevitable. Natural.

He thought of his journey with Fin, filled with mistakes on either side. But that was how they'd gotten here, to today, where she was headed to pick up groceries for the three of them. Where he was allowed to whisper in her ear before they fell asleep. Where they felt a true connection together. The mistakes were part of that connection.

"What's that look on your face?" Kylie asked as she approached him. He reached for the extra overnight bag she had over her shoulder and she handed it off without a second thought.

"What look?"

"I dunno. You tell me," she said as she eyed him skeptically. "You look kind of...dopey."

Well, he'd been thinking of Fin so it wouldn't surprise him in the least if he looked like the biggest dope in New York City. Part of his heart hadn't stopped whirring like helicopter blades in seventy-two hours. If he didn't concentrate on Kylie, he might lift off from the ground by his spinning tail, hearts in his pupils like a Looney Tunes character.

"Don't I always look dopey?" he quipped. "How was the trip?"

Her curiosity over the look on his face immediately tempered as she shrugged. "I dunno. Good."

They walked twenty more feet before Tyler realized that was really all she planned on saying about it. "Come on, you've gotta be kidding me. I've been waiting for two days to hear about this thing." He bumped her with his shoulder. "Gimme the *deets*."

She smiled, frowned and then glanced around them quickly. "There are no deets. And don't say *deets*!"

He laughed. "At least tell me if you took Fin's advice."

He also took a glance around to make sure that none of her classmates were in hearing distance as they jogged down the stairs toward the train. "Did you make at least one friend?"

She glared at him like she was attempting to turn him into a sewer rat with simply the power of her ire, her teeth gritting together. "Yes."

"Great!" He modulated his glee immediately, knowing it wasn't welcome 'round these parts. At least not when it came to rooting for her to make friends. Nothing was more annoying than that, he was certain, but still, he had a tough time wiping the silly smile off his face. He searched for a topic change. "Fin's gonna come over for dinner. She's picking up groceries right now." He glanced at his phone. "She should be getting there about the same time as we are."

"Mmm," Kylie said listlessly, looking at her own phone. She obviously wasn't listening to a thing he'd just said.

"Hello?" he said loudly, turning a few heads on the train and intending to embarrass her a *little* bit. "Anyone out there? Dear diary? Can you hear me?"

"Shh!" She shushed him with an elbow to his ribs. "I was listening before. Fin's coming over for dinner. Let me just answer this text and then I'll put my phone away."

Oh. She was answering a text. He surreptitiously attempted to glance at her phone. Not spying exactly. He just wanted to know if she was texting with this Anthony kid. And if she was, he wanted to know if any pictures of any kind were being sent. He'd read the headlines. He knew what kinds of things kids were using the internet for. And the last thing he wanted was a googlable picture of Kylie—

Thank the good Lord. He sagged backward. She was in a group text with two people. One of whom was named Luna and the other was Aceda. Those were girl's names.

And she was in a group chat. Most likely nothing seedy would happen in a group chat. Right?

She slipped her phone in her pocket and narrowed her eyes at him. "Seriously, what's wrong with you?"

"Other than the fact that I definitely didn't put enough deodorant on this morning, I'm fine." He was a sweaty wreck, but he'd make it to the other side of this subway ride.

They were quiet until they were walking the few blocks back to the house, aboveground, the streetlights already buzzed on, most of the town houses and storefronts they passed looking buttoned up for the night even though it was only 6:30. This was how it was in February. Come May, there'd be people on every other street corner chatting and playing music until ten p.m. at least. Every winter Brooklyn was a well-mannered seventy-five-year-old. Every summer, she was a teenager again, bucking curfew and wagging her tongue at the adults.

Speaking of teenagers, Tyler glanced down at the one who was walking next to him. "You're not…like…sexting, are you?"

Kylie stopped altogether, turned on her heel and started speed walking in the other direction.

"Hey!" Tyler jogged after her. "Where are you going?"

"I'm taking a different route home. We are not having this conversation."

He took her by the shoulder and turned her back around. "Come on. You know I have to ask, right?"

"I already know about the birds and the bees."

"Yeah, but these days the birds have high-speed internet access, and the bees like to convince you they'll only think you're cool if you send naked pics."

"Oh, Jesus. Kill me, Lord. Just end this mortal misery."

She raised her face and palms to the sky, looking so sincere Tyler had to laugh.

"Stop that." He slapped her palms back down to her sides. "Bad karma."

"Karma? Jeez. Fin is really getting to you."

Tyler's mouth clapped shut. She had no idea.

"You're blushing," Kylie was kind enough to point out with her pointer finger an inch from his cheek. "Tyler, this leads me to one question and one question only. Have *you* been sexting?"

"No," he snapped. "I have not." Which was an oversight that he was quickly going to be rectifying. "And don't change the subject."

She sighed. "What do you want me to tell you? I watch Netflix, go on BuzzFeed, read manga and now I have like three friends who text me. I don't even have a Snapchat, Ty. You lucked into the one teenager on earth who uses her phone like a grandma."

"Grandma Nora used a rotary phone until the day she died, so she actually had you beat there."

"Oh. Right." Kylie looked momentarily perplexed. "I forgot how old you are. You actually knew her."

Tyler cleared his throat as they waved at the doorman and got on the elevator, thankfully without an audience. "Well. Yeah. I'm glad to hear that you're not using the internet for…sex stuff."

Part of him wished the elevator cords would snap and just end this horror.

They stepped off onto his floor. "Ky…"

She stopped, her eyes on his feet, not on his face.

He cleared his throat again. "I hope you'll talk to me if you ever have questions about this stuff. I mean, I'll wear a ski mask, you'll wear a ski mask, we'll never have to look at each other's faces, I swear."

Thankfully, she laughed. "Tyler, I promise I'll talk to someone, okay? Just…maybe not my older brother."

The elevator dinged behind them as Tyler unlocked the door.

"Whoa," Fin said, her arms full of groceries. "Hell of a vibe in this hallway."

"It's his fault," Kylie said, pointing her thumb at Tyler. "Hi, Fin."

Kylie ducked into the apartment and Tyler raced back toward Fin, taking the groceries and making sure the coast was clear before he kissed her cheek.

For some reason he didn't understand, that made her blush. "What?"

"Nothing," she whispered. "I just think it's sweet that you go for the cheek kiss even after we…" She glanced toward the open living room door. "Never mind."

He laughed and hauled everything inside. As he made dinner, he kept an ear perked toward Kylie's room, where she and Fin were chatting easily about her trip. Kylie regaled Fin with the horrors of the sexting conversation she'd just had with Tyler. But Tyler didn't mind. *Mistakes are part of it*, he reminded himself, holding Fin in his heart like a talisman.

Forty-five minutes later, the three of them sat down to broccoli chicken casserole, beers for Fin and Tyler, bread on the table. He let them continue their conversation without adding much. It was nice to hear Kylie chatter away, something she did more freely with Fin than she did with Ty. The disparity didn't bother him. He hoped that this wasn't any more a hierarchy for her than it was for him. It wasn't about comparisons. It was about having a balanced diet of people in her life. And he and Fin balanced one another.

The conversation lulled, dinner was pretty much over and Fin's socked foot nudged at Tyler under the table.

"Uh, Ky." Tyler pushed his plate aside. He'd always hated the stomach-dropping introductions to hard topics. The *I have something to tell you*s. *There's something we should talk about*s. The *we have to talk*s. So, he simply didn't use one. He jumped right in. "Fin and I are together now. Romantically."

He wasn't sure what he'd been expecting Kylie's reaction to be. But he'd kind of assumed there'd *be* a reaction. Her face didn't change a whit; her eyes went from Ty to Fin and then to the table. "Okay."

The longest three seconds of Tyler's life passed. "Um. Nothing is going to change, really. We might see Fin a little more than usual. But for the most part, it'll all be the same."

"Right."

"If you have any questions?"

"It's not exactly rocket science. I know what it means for two people to be together. I'm gonna finish my homework and check in with Mary about my schedule for the rest of the week. Thanks for dinner."

She rose up, leaving Fin and Ty in her dust. She cleared her plate and was gone. There was nothing left on the table to even show she'd been sitting there. It was like Tyler and Fin had been alone at the meal. All he could feel was the gaping cavity where she'd just been.

"Shit." He dragged a hand over his face.

"Yeah. Shit." Fin stared down the hallway, her hand finding its way into Tyler's.

"Was that as bad as I think it was?"

"I haven't seen her this closed off since Thanksgiving."

"I don't get it," Tyler mumbled, picking up Fin's hand and pressing it flat against his cheek, barely registering that he was seeking the feeling he got when their energies mixed. "I kind of thought she'd be excited. She's made comments here and there about us getting together."

"To me too. But I'm sure the reality of it is way different than the dream of it."

"I'm gonna try again."

"You want me to—"

"No." He shook his head with certainty. "I think it needs to just be me and her."

Tyler stood up, took a deep breath and strode to Kylie's closed door. "Ky?" he called, knocking twice and swinging her door open.

He froze, all the blood leaving his face when he saw her sitting halfway on her bed, clutching something in her hand.

"What the hell is that?" he asked, his voice hoarse. It was a ridiculous question considering he'd already easily identified the thing in her hand as an obscenely large wad of cash. His eyes wide, his throat closing, he tried a different question. "Where the hell did you get that?"

"I—" Her mouth opened but no words came out. The money was halfway shoved back into the little fabric envelope, like her body was rejecting the idea of having it out in the wide open.

On some sort of autopilot, he strode forward, holding out his hand.

He didn't even have to tell her to hand it over. With a look half terrified and half irate, she slid it gingerly into his grip.

"You can't just come into my room," she said, but her vehemence was undermined by the childish wobble of emotion in her voice. She was still frozen on the edge of the bed, like she didn't want to move and make herself even more visible.

Tyler felt the blood pinprick down out of his arms and legs as he ruffled through the cash. "There has to be— Jesus—three thousand dollars here. Kylie..."

"I didn't steal it."

"Well, I know that Mary isn't paying you in cash, so you better explain, fast, what the hell you're doing with thousands of dollars hidden in your room."

"Mom gave it to me."

Tyler instantly felt sick, his heartbeat banging all the way down to his toes, pumping nausea and adrenaline to the four corners of his earth.

Her mother gave it to her? When? Had Kylie had it the whole time? Brought it from Columbus? Or, God, had Lorraine been contacting her secretly? Mailing her money... for what? To run away?

"She left it for me, I mean," Kylie said, her shoulders caving. The only thing keeping Tyler's heart from squeezing down into a raisin at that moment was the fact that Kylie looked perfectly miserable. Like there was a chance, *a chance*, that she understood just how screwed up this whole thing was.

"When she left earlier this year," Tyler said slowly, scrabbling for clarification. "She left you a bunch of cash."

"Spending money. So that I could order food. That's what..." Kylie folded forward and looked even more miserable. "That's what she always did. When she'd leave for a weekend or something, I'd come home and there'd be two hundred bucks on the counter and I'd know I was on my own for a bit."

"This is *not* two hundred bucks."

"It was six thousand when she first left. So, I knew she

was going to be gone for a long time. I was careful with it. I didn't order in. I got cheap stuff from the grocery store so I wouldn't run through the money."

"Because you had no idea how long she was going to be gone for." His voice sounded strange to his own ears.

He thought of the sheer quantity of Easy Mac and cereal that had been at that house. He thought of Kylie's nest of blankets in the upstairs bathroom where she'd been locking herself in, terrified to sleep alone in the house. He thought of her getting ready for school every day. By herself. Making her own lunch. Catching the bus. Coming home and turning on every light in the house. Eating shitty processed food and counting cash. Rationing.

Even now, Tyler could look back and see how she'd been rationing *everything* since he'd met her. Money. Her energy. Even her affection. He'd naively thought that it would just take time to get her out of her shell. Like a turtle who needed to get comfortable with the temperature of the water. But now he saw the money clenched in his hand was a harsh physical symbol of reality, that it had all been so much more complicated than that.

She wasn't ever going to give more than she thought she could. Because this kid had been taught to protect herself at every single turn. Because there'd been no one there to protect her.

"Kylie," he asked gently, sagging backward to sit on the edge of her desk. "Why were you counting it just now?"

She eyed him, like she knew a trap when she saw one. "…I wanted to know how much was there."

"Why would you need to know how much cash you had when I'm the one who pays for everything for you? Why now?" He knew the answer but he needed her to say it out loud.

She glared at the floor, her face red, her breaths coming fast and then faster. He wished she'd move, pace around, throw her hands in the air. But she just sat there.

"I was hoping this would happen, Ty. I wanted you to get with Fin. I saw how much you liked her right away. And her, you. It wasn't as obvious, but I thought, *maybe she likes him.* And pretty soon, that became pretty freaking obvious too. I showed her the videos of you dancing because I knew she'd like them. I talked you up because I knew she was stubborn and didn't like to see the softer side of you. I basically *pushed* you two together. And I always knew what would happen next. Okay? So. Congrats. Congrats to you two, congrats to me. It doesn't have to be some big reveal. I get it."

"Kylie, the money. Why were you counting the money?"

Still frozen, she spoke in a low, composed voice that was so much worse than yelling.

"I just wanted to make sure I knew how much freaking money I have to my name before you sent me back."

He thought maybe his brain had just cracked in two, cleaved cleanly down the middle by his irrational sister.

"Hold on. Just stop talking. Everybody stop talking!" Tyler yelled, although it was just the two of them and he was the only one talking. "Send you back? Send you back *where*? To what? You think that just because Fin and I are together now, that I won't want to be your guardian anymore?"

She shrugged, her angry chin pointed at the floor, her arms finally coming unstuck from her sides and crossing over her chest. "No one wants their kid sister around when they're starting the life they really want. You're gonna want to get married, Ty. Have kids. I'll be in the way—"

"I don't *want* kids!" Tyler shouted. "I— You're— I'm

not fucking sending you away, Kylie. And not as a matter of principle. But because you live here. *You live here.* This is where you live. With me. In this condo. I want you to stay here."

"Oh, stop it!" She put her hands over her ears, and it was then that he saw how bright her eyes were, like she'd accidentally rubbed hot sauce into them. "Don't insult me. I know *exactly* how excited you weren't to drag me back to Brooklyn. I know exactly how much you didn't want your sister taking up your home office. I heard you in Columbus, Ty. 'Please let Lorraine come back. Please let Lorraine come back.' You didn't want me then. And I'm just supposed to believe that you magically want me now?"

Tyler blanched, realizing that she'd heard his pleas to a higher power. His highly personal mantra for that horrible time in his life, in Kylie's life. "Yes!" he roared. "You're supposed to believe it. Because it's true!" She was as still as an ice statue, but he paced from one side of her room to the other. "Yes, I wanted your mother to come back. No, I wasn't prepared to be your guardian. No, I didn't want your entire life to get turned on its head. But you know how long I felt that way? About one freaking week. And then you know what my new mantra became? 'Please let me get custody of her. Let me take her back to Brooklyn.' You know how many times I said that to myself? Probably about a thousand times a day. Dammit!" He tilted his head to the ceiling and shouted a question at the universe. "Why the hell couldn't she have heard that part?"

"You didn't want me," she said stubbornly. "You told me so yourself."

He sagged backward onto the desk again. "What? When the hell did I tell you that?"

"You told me, point-blank, that you're as much *at the*

whim of the judge as I am. You only did this because you had to."

He remembered her confusing reaction to his statement. That she'd blanched, winced back like he'd slapped her. He hadn't understood it at the time because it had never even occurred to him that she'd take it so far from the way he'd meant it.

"Kylie, that is not what I meant. I didn't mean that the only reason I was taking you was because the courts were making me. The judge didn't hold a gun to my head. He simply said, 'Look, Tyler, it's you or the foster system.' And I said me. It's me. It'll be me and her. *That's* what I meant."

She said nothing.

He had no idea if now was the time to be quiet or keep talking, but because he was Tyler, he kept talking. "I admit I was freaking terrified at the beginning. My feelings about having you here have evolved. Are you going to punish me for that? I want you here. I want the two of us to live here together. We make a good family."

"No!" She sprang up, moving for the first time since he'd come into her room. She didn't look as furious as she had a second ago. Worse, she looked overwhelmed, desperate, wild. "Don't say that. You said that before. You said that I was a good family member. And I don't get it." She covered her wild expression with both hands. "I don't fucking get it."

He knew she was crying behind those hands and he moved toward her. "What don't you get?" he asked softly.

"I don't get the pattern. But I've never understood the pattern, and I'll drive myself insane if I try. I don't get it. I don't get it."

"Kylie." He moved toward her and took her by the shoulders. Her hands stayed firmly over her face. "What don't you get?" He repeated the question.

"You say I'm a good family member?" Her hands finally dropped, and shiny tears had trailed down her cheeks, her lips pulled down at the sides almost like an infant's would. Her hair was wispy at the temples but brushed back over her shoulders, making her look both young and mature at once. She gasped for air over her jumping breaths. "You say that I care about your life and your friends and eat dinner with you. You think that makes me worth keeping around? Makes me good family? Well, you think I *didn't* do any of that for her? You think I didn't try my ass off to be good for her? Kind to her? Easy to be around? I did everything. Everything! And still! All she leaves me is a note and that."

Kylie pointed toward the wad of cash on her desk. She shook free of Tyler's hands and strode over to the money, carefully rolling it back into the neat wad it had been in before Tyler had ruffled through it. She stared at the money in her hand.

Tyler watched helplessly as tears dripped from her chin and onto the front of her zipped sweatshirt.

"I can't figure out what it is that I did that made her leave, Ty." She was whispering now, like there was no more voice left inside of her. She wiped her tears with the back of her wrist, still talking to the money and not facing Tyler. "I mean, I know, I know. I've been to the therapy. It's not my fault. Blah blah blah. But logically, Tyler, I had to have done *something* that put her over the edge."

"Kylie, *no.*"

She cut him off. "She wasn't a good mother. I get it. She's not patient with me. She doesn't like whenever I made things hard. It makes her so mad. But I knew that if I just went to bed when she told me to and ate what she put on the table and didn't complain or ask for too much then she was gonna at least keep being there. At the very least. And I don't *get it*. What was it? I don't understand what I did that was the last straw."

"Do you know what arbitrary means?"

She glared at him. "Yes."

"It basically means something that doesn't correlate with anything else, right? It's almost random."

"You're saying she *randomly* chose to leave me?"

"No. I'm saying the reasons she chose to leave were not ones you could have predicted. If she was going to leave, she was going to leave and there was nothing that you could have done."

"Because I'm a kid?" She finally tossed the money back down and faced him. He took her place on the edge of the bed, feeling the adrenaline from their fight course through his system like a drug. His legs felt jittery; his heart pounded in his throat.

"Because nobody can control anyone else," he said quietly. "Because you can't make someone do anything. Ky, if Dad taught me anything, if my mother taught me anything, shit, if *you* taught me anything, it's exactly that. You can't control someone. There's nothing you could have done to keep her there if she didn't want to stay. Not cleaning the house every day. Not getting good grades. Not winning the freaking lottery."

Her face collapsed like a kicked-in tin can. She took a shuddering breath and scraped her eyes on the inside of her elbow, making the fabric of her sleeve dark with her tears.

"Don't tell me that it's all random, Tyler. Don't tell me that there's nothing I can do but wait for people to just leave. I *have* to be able to do something about it."

She reached over and shoved the money to the ground,

spiking it like a football. The rubber band that had been holding it snapped and half-curled bills spiraled across the floor. "Shit!"

She slid down the side of the desk, folded up and sank her forehead to her knees.

The guardian in him wasn't sure if he should stay away or not. But the human in him, the brother in him, was crawling across the floor, arranging himself next to her so that their shoulders pressed together.

"Kylie," he said, pushing his weight into her. "I love you. I don't say that enough. I just want you to know that in this moment, when we're screaming at each other and everything is terrible, I love you."

She didn't move from her tortoised-up position, her face hidden.

"And I didn't mean to make you feel powerless. I'm just trying to make it clear to you that you are *not* the reason your mother is looney tunes. And I'm not saying that to you in some school-therapist sort of way. I'm saying that to you as a logical person who has looked at the situation and made a judgment. I *know* what shitty parents look like. I had two of them before Dad died. And now I have one. Just like you. Maybe I'm not supposed to say that to you about your mom. That she's shitty. But I don't know what I *am* supposed to say either. So, I might as well tell you the truth." He sighed and realized that her position actually looked pretty good. He rested his own forehead on his knees and talked to the ground, finally saying everything he'd been thinking for months.

"Leaving you the way she did makes her a shitty parent. And you know what? I hope to God she goes to therapy and parenting classes and rehab and turns her life around and can be a good mom to you. Because you deserve that.

You deserve a good mother. But I cannot sit here and listen to you thinking that your mother could have been better if you'd been better. Because that's just not the way it works. Please. If you can't believe me yet, can you please just trust me that at some point, you *will* agree with me? Just trust me. I promise. Please trust me."

"I can't trust you, Tyler," she whispered, dropping the bottom out of his heart.

"What?"

"I can't trust you because you won't tell me. Why won't you just tell me?"

"Tell you what?" He'd have told her anything she asked at that point. If he'd had a diary, he'd have read it to her front to back.

"Tell me what your last straw is."

"My last…" He groaned and banged his head backward a few times onto the desk behind him. "Fucking Lorraine," he griped with so much vehemence that Kylie's head popped up, blurry, red eyes and all.

"What?"

"Kylie, someday you're going to realize that what I'm about to say isn't a lie. Okay? Just, someday you'll believe me about this. But I don't have a last straw. Not when it comes to you. I mean, my temper has a last straw. I might yell at you. As evidenced by the nine-part opera that just played out in here. But please, kid, believe me. When it comes to loving you? Being there for you? Putting a roof over your head and food on your plate? I'm not measured in straws. Therefore, you're never gonna find the last one. There is no last one. I'm measured in, I don't know, whatever happened during the big bang. Some sort of material that is actually expanding. You're never going to reach the end of it." He sagged forward onto his knees again. "I'm not making sense, am I? My head is spinning."

Whether he was making sense or not, Kylie didn't answer. After a few minutes, he felt her lean back onto the desk, unfolding just a bit.

After a long, quiet minute, more characterized by dazed exhaustion than by discomfort, Tyler bumped their shoulders together. "Have you ever heard the phrase 'hurt people hurt people'?"

"No," she said after a minute, pulling herself out of whatever reverie had sucked her under and rolling her head so that she looked at Tyler.

"It means that people who are hurt end up hurting other people. And, I mean, I don't think it's right a hundred percent of the time, but pretty much, if you're ever wondering why one person hurts another, it can almost always be answered by the fact that they're in pain of some kind. And that's not an excuse. Plenty of parents are in pain and they don't leave their kids. But it helped me a lot when I was trying to understand my own mom. And Dad, for that matter. I'm not trying to make excuses for Lorraine, but I'm just trying to humanize her a little bit. She is a person. With problems. And a life. And a whole past filled with who-knows-what. If she were a happy person, with no pain and no problems, she probably wouldn't have left you, kid. It's as simple as that. *That's* why it's not your fault."

She was quiet for another long stretch. "Maybe say that last part to me again in like six months, all right? My brain is dead."

Six months.

It was the most rewarding thing she possibly could have said to him. It was a small acknowledgment that they would still be together in six months. That they might still be having conversations as meaningful as this one.

"You got it."

There was another stretch of silence, and Tyler wondered if it was time to get up, give her some space. He stared at the mosaic of curled bills on the floor.

Fin knocked on the doorway, and the two of them rolled their heads to look at her.

The expression on her face told Tyler that she'd heard everything; he just hoped that was okay with Kylie.

"Drink this." She strode forward with two coffee mugs in her hands and shoved one at each of them. "I had to make it from the stuff in Tyler's cabinet, so it won't be as potent or flavorful as if I'd made it from my own herbs. But trust me. You both need it."

Tyler and Kylie exchanged eye contact, peered at the steaming, reddish liquid and then simultaneously sipped from the mugs.

"Ohmygod."

"Shit, Fin!" Tyler yelped, coughing against the noxious flavor that threatened to resurrect the casserole he'd eaten for dinner. "What is that?"

"It's a trauma elixir. It helps level your adrenaline back out and calm you down. It's terrible, I know. But drink it."

She put her hands on her hips and gave them both a stern look. Tyler squinted at Fin, looking fiercely beautiful in the doorway, and attempted to communicate via brainwaves: *There better be a blowjob for this somewhere down the line.*

She quirked an eyebrow at him in such a knowing way that he wondered if she actually had heard his thoughts.

Tyler took a deep breath, cheers-ed Kylie and swallowed

the contents of the mug down in three great gulps. Kylie followed his lead, gasping and sagging to the side.

"Remind me to save our next fight for after Fin goes home," she panted, shoving the mug away from her.

He laughed. "And please remind me to sign you up for the debate team, because, kid, I think you've got the chops for it."

CHAPTER TWENTY-FIVE

FIN BASICALLY TUCKED Kylie into bed that night and then, when she emerged from Kylie's room and saw Tyler sprawled on the couch, his eyes practically spinning, she did the same for him.

"Stay," he murmured as she pulled a blanket up to his chin, her skin prickling at being near his neat, golden energy.

She chuckled. "Trust me. None of us are ready for me to stay over."

She leaned down, kissed his mouth to shut him up and scraped the back of her hand over his stubble. "I'll see you tomorrow."

She knew he was exhausted from his talk with Kylie, because it was the first time he didn't walk her down to get a cab. Fin took the opportunity to take the train instead. It was an easy ride, only half an hour, and she wanted to feel like herself for a little while. Like the young girl who'd learned the trains with Via at her side.

It wasn't until her front door was closed and locked at her back that Fin let the tears come. It wasn't often that she cried. But tonight there was no stopping it. She hadn't been able to keep herself from absorbing the emotions of the two people she loved. Normally, she would have gotten out of Dodge if she'd seen a fight like that happening. It was too dangerous for her. She knew that those kinds of emotions ran the risk of getting lodged inside of her, where she'd carry them until she could expel them. Tyler and Kylie almost felt trapped inside her heart, their pain and confusion, their loneliness and desperation. Fin clawed at the buttons of her coat and let it fall in a heap on the floor as great sobs collapsed and expanded her rib cage. She fell onto her couch, clutched a pillow and let the emotions come. She knew that fighting them made them worse. She had to relax into the pain; it was the only way to let it move through her unhindered.

She cried Kylie's tears first. And they were so familiar, because they were the same tears that Fin herself had cried as a young girl in New York City. Tears of abandonment, tears filled with questions, every tear a plea to the universe, *Please don't make me inadequate. Please don't let them leave me.*

And then came Tyler's tears. And these were tears of helplessness. Tears of utter disorientation, like he was plunked down in the middle of a desert and told, *Find Kylie water, her life depends on it.* She cried Tyler's tears of regret and anger. She cried tears of fear and frustration. Kylie's tears had been great wracking sobs, clear rivers down her face. Tyler's tears were fat raindrops that seemed unending, until, of course, they ended.

She was shocked when there was more to cry. She realized that this last batch of tears were hers and hers alone. Fin curled on her side, her knees almost to her chin, and gulped for air. Her own tears pooled in her eyes in great batches, blurring her vision before they fell away, sideways, into her hair. These were the tears of someone who was mourning the loss of a life she'd thought she wanted. A life she'd worked toward for years. A life she'd thought would always keep her connected to the woman who'd raised her. She thought of the nail-biting, hair-whitening process that she'd gone through to try to become a foster parent. She thought of how many no's she'd gotten from the state. She thought of Kylie, inviting Fin into her life. She thought of Tyler, of partnership, how much better they were when it was both of them together. Fin cried harder. She'd wanted to be a foster parent. She'd wanted it so badly, nothing fake or posed about it. And now she cried out her grief over having to say goodbye to it. Goodbye to that life because she was saying hello to another one, a different one. And the hello made her cry as much as the goodbye had. Saying hello to this new chapter was as relieving as it was painful, like those few seconds after a Band-Aid gets ripped off. *God, it hurts, but look, it's not the wound.*

When there were no more tears, when Fin shook with exhaustion, when she was carved out like a pumpkin, Fin lay weakly on the couch and felt what remained.

It was a swamping love. A love that had been filling up her heart for months, like water rising that she hadn't acknowledged until she was palms against the ceiling, her lips sucking for that last inch of air. All before she realized she could breathe underwater. Maybe not all water, but *this* water. Tyler's water.

Fin, as exhausted now as Tyler and Kylie had been when she'd left them, let her eyes close, and there was Tyler in bright, almost painful Technicolor, his navy eyes sparkling as obnoxiously as the lights of the Coney Island roller coasters behind him. His dumb, smug smile as he messed with Matty's and Joy's baseball caps. The image blurred and smudged and there Tyler was in Seb's backyard, his T-shirt sticking to him in splotches the size of eggplants as he engaged in hysterical water-gun warfare with Matty. Tyler, jaw shadowed, shirt pressed, eyes shell-shocked as he sat at Thanksgiving, Kylie looking almost identical in expression.

Colors blended, the world tilted as a young, svelte Tyler danced shirtless and graceful across the screen of Fin's mind. Even replaying it was potent magic. His energy undeniable, there was no going back from having seen it. Gold melted into green into navy blue, his eyes swirled out of nowhere, stern and laughing and a little insane as he stripped socks off of her, as he grinned at her from where he fixed her tub, kissed her silently in his kitchen, rose over her in the dark, scolded her about patience, made love to her with unabashed enjoyment.

And last, the images slowing now, the colors fading to the color of the inside of Fin's eyelids, she felt the cold wall of Tyler's hallway against her back, her hands clenched whitely under her chin, as she listened to his voice. As she listened to him parent Kylie. As she realized, for the first time, that the water had already risen, there was nothing she could do but sink down, watch the sunlight play at the surface and breathe.

FIN KNEW THAT she couldn't wait forever to tell Tyler how she was feeling, but that he'd also had a pretty intense time with Kylie and could probably use a bit of a break. Besides, it was important to Fin that Kylie get comfortable with their new arrangement. She didn't want weirdness between her and Tyler during this transitionary period. And there was always the chance that dropping the *L*-bomb on someone could make 'em feel a little weird.

So, a week turned into two, and Fin still hadn't explained to Tyler that she was pretty sure she was apples-over-applecart in love with him.

She came over almost every night, or Ty and Ky came to her house. Kylie was just starting to trust that Fin and Ty's connection to one another didn't, by nature, exclude her.

They went to that women's soccer match in New Jersey, the three of them. Fin was extremely charmed to learn that Tyler was a terrified, borderline incompetent driver. She'd kicked him out of the front seat of their rental car and initiated road-trip rules in order to have complete control over the music selection. He'd gritted his teeth through the showtunes that Fin had put on just to screw with him and then surprised her when he knew the lyrics to at least four of the Annie Lennox songs on the album she played next.

The soccer game was a blurry mess that Fin could barely concentrate on because she was so freaking happy to be where she was. She couldn't stop grinning.

"What?" he asked her, his mouth full of hot dog.

"Just thinking about the fact that I've been to a whopping three sporting events in the last decade."

He furrowed his brow. "But you've been to three of them with me."

"Exactly."

He held out his hot dog and Fin took half of it down in one bite. "Needs hot sauce."

"On a dog? You're a monster."

Unlike at the Nets game, Kylie could barely peel her eyes from the field. She was a terrible soccer fan. As in, she was terrible to sit beside. She yelled and groaned and complained about minuscule details of the game that Fin couldn't even begin to spot. Tyler just looked proud of his little sister.

And when Tyler made the big reveal that he could use his press pass to get Kylie to meet a few of the players? Hoo boy, the stammering and blushing commenced. Tyler and Fin both just gaped at this starstruck version of the girl they'd come to know quite well.

The drive home was quiet and comfortable, padded on all sides by the plush dark they drove through to get back home.

They spent Valentine's Day as a trio as well, with Tyler and Kylie throwing popcorn at the screen as Fin made them sit through two crappy rom-coms she'd sworn would convert them.

Tyler and Fin had sex during the daylight hours only, when Kylie was at school. Fin had never been more grateful to have a job where she made her own hours. The hours of one to three p.m. took on a dozy, sexy, lip-biting, sheet-pulling, color-blurring quality that Fin had never before experienced.

The end of February was surprisingly warm, and one week into March there were already tulips crowning in the tree wells. March was a notoriously cruel month in Brooklyn, known for holding out handfuls of candy to unsuspecting citizens and then snatching the candy away, only to shove six inches of snow down their pants. Or at least, that was always how it had felt to Fin.

But the ides of March came and went, and there was no sign of ice. One Saturday morning was warm enough, in the sun at least, that Tyler texted Fin asking if she'd like to join them for a good old-fashioned Prospect Park blanket day. It was a spring tradition after all.

Which was how Fin found herself stretched out on Tyler's king-sized (of course) picnic blanket, a box of bagels and cream cheese at her feet, a sparkling water in one hand, watching the clouds. Every twenty seconds or so, a frisbee floated through her line of vision as Tyler and Kylie stood on either side of the blanket and tossed it back and forth.

Snoozy from the sun, Fin watched the big cumulus clouds accumulate and puff away above her. It was one of the many things she missed about Louisiana: how tall the clouds were there. They were mile-high monstrosities that only seemed to move in one direction: up. They showed anyone who cared to look exactly the path to heaven. The clouds in New York were usually flatter, grayer, like a wool cap pressed too far down over a forehead.

But not today.

Today they were tooth-white and buoyant, making Fin feel just how small the earth really was.

She took it as a sign. Today was the day.

Who could keep love quiet on a day when the clouds flirted with the blueberry sky like that?

A shadow crossed her vision, something bumped her shoulder rather hard and then an apple crunched in her ear.

"Whatcha thinkin' 'bout?" Tyler asked as he sprawled out next to her, bouncing his foot across the opposite knee like a toddler at nap time.

She couldn't help but laugh. *Ladies and gentlemen, the man I love.*

"Hey, Ty?"

"Yeah?" he answered Kylie, who was kneeling on one end of the picnic blanket, packing her bag up and pointedly not looking at the way Tyler's head had decided to rest on Fin's belly.

Kylie generally played the blindfold game whenever Fin and Tyler were close enough to trade DNA.

"Tony just texted me. He and some other school people are up by the Grand Army Plaza entrance. Mind if I go?"

Play it cool. Fin tried her hardest to transmit this direct order into Tyler's brain. Not only was she about to go hang out with friends her own age, she was willingly asking Tyler for permission to go do it. *Don't blow this.*

Tyler lifted his head. "Is it a date?"

Fin nearly face-palmed.

Kylie blushed all the way up to the ball cap she'd screwed onto her head that morning. "*No.* Anthony and I are just friends."

"Oh." Tyler scratched at his stubbled chin and looked back and forth between Fin and Kylie, apparently trying to interpret the eye roll they were giving each other. "Okay. Just let me know if you leave the park."

"Bye."

Kylie turned on her heel and practically jogged up the bike path toward her friends.

"Something tells me I should feel like a doofus right about now," Tyler said, crunching the apple and resting back against Fin's stomach.

"I'm in love with you."

Tyler jolted, coughed up a bite of apple and rolled onto all fours. He loomed over Fin, blocking out the sun and framing himself perfectly in a crown of fluffy cumulus clouds. "Do me a solid and repeat what you just said."

"I'm in love with you."

He choked on the apple again. "You're going to kill me," he said dimly, sitting back on his heels.

"Well, quit taking bites of apple right before I tell you I'm in love with you." She sat up too, wondering if her smile looked as dopey as it felt.

He made a choking sound again, but this time there was no apple to make a threat on his life. "I—" His hands went to his hair. "Holy cow."

She raised an eyebrow at him. "I wish you could see your energy right now. Seriously, you look like an insane person."

Tyler laughed, a little hysterically, reached for her palm and placed it over his racing heart. The laughter fell away and left behind was unfiltered earnestness. She'd never seen truth look quite this handsome before.

"Fin—"

"Uncle Tyler! Auntie Fin!"

Their heads pivoted in unison to where—"Oh, good grief," Tyler muttered—Via, Sebastian, Matty and Crabby all made their way up the path.

"Well, this is one way to tell them," Fin said calmly, even though Tyler's heart under her hand had started beating triple-time.

"Tell them," he choked out awkwardly, either repeating what she was saying or asking that she be the one to do the deed.

They'd decided, a few weeks ago, to go easy on themselves. They wanted to have a relationship free of the fishbowl. Telling Kylie had been an easy decision, necessary, the right thing to do and neither of them regretted it. She'd been fine with keeping it under wraps for them, considering she was still figuring out how she felt about the whole thing.

Telling their best friends, however, had been one that they both had wanted to wait on. This wasn't like high school where every development with a love interest was supposed to be shared posthaste, or else go down in history as an ultimate betrayal of friendship. No. They were all adults here. Seb and Via had their own lives and—

"What the hell is this?" Via asked as they approached, delicate hands on her slim hips, her eyes immediately clocking the way Fin's hand rested on Tyler's chest, the way Tyler's fingers gripped Fin's hand. "Is this a *date*?"

Fin knew Via well enough to catch the giddy joy that was rising through her and to know that she'd just signed herself up for a very long spill sesh with her bestie sometime in the very near future.

"Who's on a date?" Matty asked, swinging his head around. And then standing almost on top of Tyler, pointing an accusatory finger about an inch from Ty's eyeball. *"Them?"*

"Watch where you're pointing that thing." Tyler batted Matty's hand away. "This isn't a date. We're here with Kylie."

Seeming to regain his faculties, he stood, brushed off his pants and held out his hands to help Fin stand.

"Well, where is she then?" Sebastian asked, looking for all the world like he was attempting to restrain himself from some combination of outright laughter and judgy eyebrows. The effect was rather constipating.

"She's with friends up the park," Tyler grumbled. "And we were just…"

The lingering pause at the end of the statement implicated them far more than the truth would have.

Fin sighed and leaned into Tyler's side. "I was just telling Tyler that I'm in love with him. For the first time."

"What'd he say?" Matty practically shouted.

"He didn't respond. You all walked up."

"Oh my god. Oh my GOD. Oh. MY. GOD." Via tugged at her own cheeks, delighted laughter tearing out of her. Fin had never known that phrase could have so many separate meanings. "We have to go. We have to *go.*"

Via tugged fruitlessly at her humongous boyfriend's hand. Sebastian just kind of stood stock-still for a moment, staring between Fin and Tyler.

"Seb!"

"Right." He shook his head, grabbed Matty by the collar of his shirt and started hauling his family away. "Right."

"Come over for dinner tonight!" Via shouted back over her shoulder once they were back on the path and practically tripping over her feet to get away.

"Fat chance," Tyler muttered, collapsing back down to the blanket and dragging Fin with him. "I'm ending my associations with those people," he mumbled. "They come over here and ruin the single greatest moment of my life. They'll be lucky if I ever darken their doorstep—"

"Ty?"

"Yeah?"

"You're mumbling to yourself."

He didn't respond, just lunged forward and flattened Fin against the blanket. "Super in love with you," he said, his lips against her lips. "Like a dumb amount. Ass over tits."

Fin burst out laughing. "How can you be so proper looking and so vulgar all at once?"

"It's a gift."

"Actually, it kind of is. It makes you unique, Ty."

"Everything makes you unique," he said, his lips still pressed against hers, his weight pinning her down, every word pushed into her mouth like they'd die if they hit fresh air. "You're the uniquest. I've never met someone else like you. And not just the psychic thing. It's the everything thing."

She was laughing harder now, attempting to peel him off of her. "You're like those fish that hold on to sharks with their mouths."

"Thanks."

"Ty, I'm not going anywhere. You can let me breathe."

He rolled onto his back and now Fin was the one pressing down on him, curled into his side the way they did when they watched TV on the couch together. She was sure they were making a spectacle of themselves and refused to care. The blueberry sky was their ceiling, the sun was just warm enough to have her feeling like they were snuggling into bed. Tyler was her home now.

"I know I'm a broken record but I still can't believe this

is happening sometimes. I mean, less than a year ago you kicked me off the island for being a sad, lonely loser who clung to bachelorhood. And now you're telling me you love me and I'm full-time taking care of a kid. What a world."

"I didn't say you were a sad, lonely loser clinging to bachelorhood." She pursed her lips and frowned.

"You *basically* did. It's okay. I'm over it now. But you told me that you could never trust me because of what my priorities were. That I put myself before everyone else and that wasn't your jam."

Fin pushed up on her palms, an urgency pulling strings tight all across her body. Something had just occurred to her that never had before. "Tyler, you know I was wrong, right?"

Her eyes searched his and with a plummeting stomach, she realized that he still believed some, if not all, of the horrible things she'd said to him that day.

She reached out and gripped the sides of his face, needing him to hear her.

"Tyler, that speech I gave you had, like, nothing to do with you. It was completely about me and my own fears. It was so inaccurate. I mean, I called you selfish, Ty. You! You're so generous and sweet and caring. You always have been. You've given years of your life to Seb and Matty. And that entitledness I was so fond of pointing out? It wasn't you feeling entitled because of your status in the world, it was you feeling entitled because of your place in their lives! You'd spent years basically being Matty's other parent and then Via came along and you were displaced and totally unsure of what your role was anymore. I get that now, Tyler. But I was completely wrong at first. I had you down as sulky and entitled, but that was just dead wrong."

Slowly, he came up to a sit as well, his hands clasped over his knees as he looked at the ground, the sky, Fin. His navy eyes seemed to reflect the entire world in that moment. All the way down to the trees lining the path next to them and two tiny Fins living in his pupils. "What changed your opinion of me?"

"I mean, getting to know you better, allowing myself to give you a chance."

"It wasn't Kylie?"

Fin frowned, getting the sense that this question was actually many questions all rolled into one. "Seeing you with Kylie was what allowed me to soften toward you in the first place. The way you worked to make her fit into your life, the love and tenderness you obviously had for her. I got to see who you really were from the way you interacted with her."

Tyler turned away then, his elbow on one knee, his chin in his palm. "Fin...my position as Kylie's guardian is tenuous. In just over a year, her mother could get her back."

"Wow." Fin sat back on her haunches and watched the clouds for a second, feeling all her rising giddiness and adrenaline freeze in place. "I—I'd thought she was with you until she was eighteen. But I guess that was only because that was how my own custody arrangement had worked, and I just sort of superimposed it."

Tyler was quiet and for the first time since she'd seen the ballet videos of him, his energy was completely unreadable to her. He was closed for business in a way she'd never seen before. It frightened her. Fin reached for his hand and to her immense relief, he immediately laced his fingers with hers.

"Would you—" His voice scratched and he cleared his throat, took a deep breath. "Would you still want me if I wasn't a package deal anymore?"

Sudden understanding nearly whipped her hair back from her shoulders, and in the stiff wind of it, she felt an instant, biting sadness that he'd misunderstood her feelings so badly.

"Tyler... I don't love you because you happen to come with a kid. I love you because you having that kid showed me who you really are. You think I can ever unsee that? God, every time I look at you, you're practically standing in a halo of gold, holding your heart on a silk pillow, mine for the taking. Whether or not the courts award you custody of Kylie has nothing to do with that."

His eyes were bright with shiny emotion as he let out a long breath, rested his forehead against his knees for a moment. "But you want kids so bad, Fin. And I love Kylie, want her in my life forever. Hell, she'll probably be the person who buries me. But babies? Little Leshuskis?" He grimaced. "You weren't completely wrong about me at the baseball game. I don't want a house full of screaming kids and dirty diapers. I'm not exactly sure what it is that you want. But I hope that me having Kylie in my life doesn't imply to you that I've done a complete one-eighty on this issue. Being a dad... It's not exactly my thing. It probably never will be."

TYLER, FEELING VERY much like his heart was on that silk pillow she'd just mentioned, watched the woman he loved with his breath caught in his chest. This was a truth that he'd been holding inside, shifting from one side to the other for weeks. He watched her face and saw a complicated expression cross there. Confusingly, she landed on something that looked an awful lot like guilt.

"You know I've been trying to become a foster parent for a few years now."

"Right."

"And every time my application has been denied. Over

and over." She paused, looked out over the field that yawned wide before them. Brooklyn really showed out for the first reliably warm Saturday. Frisbees abounded, and picnic baskets, and makeshift badminton, and kites on kites on kites. He had the feeling that she saw none of it. She might as well be watching a screensaver. She picked a piece of grass and worried it in her fingers. "When you're in the middle of these things, you look so hard for the *why*, that sometimes there's no chance of ever seeing it. I was looking with a microscope at every bullet point of my life, but I didn't just sit back in an armchair and use my own two eyes to see the full picture."

"And what was the full picture?"

"That I just wasn't ready." She laughed, but it was a complicated sound, filled with so much more than humor. "The universe knew. I mean, if I'd gotten a kid thrown my way, I wouldn't have screwed anything up too badly, I don't think. I have good judgment and a big heart. But all the reasons I wanted to be a foster parent, well, I was ignoring the biggest one." She looked up at him and for the very first time, Tyler thought of her eyes as more than light or ice. They were warm and open and inviting, like a blanket of sand seen through two feet of the clearest water. What color were those eyes of hers? It struck him then that he'd never even tried to figure it out before. This woman had so many ways of keeping others just one step farther away than they'd like to be. Her tiger eyes, her sharp words, that emoji eyebrow. He understood then, as clearly as he could see her, what she meant.

"You didn't want to be alone," he whispered.

"Exactly."

He tipped her chin up, had her meeting his eyes again.

"You don't have to sound quite so ashamed about that, love."

"I'm not ashamed about wanting a family. I'm ashamed to have been so sure that that *wasn't* the reason I was doing all this. To have transformed it into this wholly selfless desire in my head."

"Do you still want to be a foster parent?"

"Yes. I'm positive that it's part of the reason I'm here, on this earth."

Tyler knew better than to ask, "Then what's the problem?"

"You want to know what the problem is, then?" she asked, emoji eyebrow in full force.

He laughed and kissed her lips and then that eyebrow. "God, you're freaky. Yes. I do want to know what the problem is."

"It was two things, actually. Via's logjam theory and watching you talk through that fight with Ky last month."

"What's the logjam theory?"

Fin played with his hand, tracing the lines there. He wondered if she could tell his date of death. "That you can't expect to fully love with any part of your heart if some of it is dammed up."

"You're not dammed up!" he protested, instantly irritated on her behalf.

She smiled at his reaction. "Not anymore. Not since letting you in. Loving you. But I think I need to get used to it for a while. Loving you and Kylie. Using my whole heart. I have to build my muscles. It's like not having used my left arm my entire life and then suddenly someone hands me a firehose and says, 'Hold on!'"

"A firehose, huh?" He kissed her knuckles. "That's how much you love me?"

She rolled her eyes. "Listening to you fight with Kylie... Tyler, it was masterful. I know you don't want to be a parent. And that's fine. But as a mentor? A guardian? Jeez. I was blown away by how you handled that. With compassion and anger and honesty and so much love. You had all these tools in your toolbox. And it just hit me. *Tyler uses the whole toolbox*. And he has his entire life. You're equipped to deal with Kylie because you love with your whole heart, Ty. I accused you of being stunted at that ball game. But I should have pointed that finger at myself."

"Quit calling yourself stunted," he said grumpily. "You're perfect. End of story."

She laughed and shook her head. "Whatever you say."

"Is this your way of telling me that you're not sure you want kids either?"

"Biological kids?" She gave him crazy eyes. "Ah, no. We have that in common. I don't know, maybe it's because I wasn't really raised by either of my birth parents, didn't even know my father. But yeah. Not interested. There are so many kids in the world who need a hand and a home. That's what I want."

He was quiet for a long time and, somehow, they found themselves seated against each other, Fin's head tipped back onto his shoulder, their eyes watching the sky, using the other's body to keep their own upright. "Fin?"

"Yeah?"

"I'm not asking you to go full psychic on me or anything. But if you had to wager a guess, based on how well you know me, am I gonna be into fostering a kid with you at some point?"

"I don't see the future, Tyler."

"I know—"

"*But*, sometimes I get these images. Other people might

call them visions, but everything in the future is so subjective, always prone to change, that I don't usually put any stock in them."

"Do you have one about me?"

"I can see you a few years older, hanging up after a call with Kylie. She's at college, I think. Or maybe some kind of abroad program. You miss her so bad you kind of slump down over the kitchen counter. I'm there, and I ask if everything's all right. You give me this look like, *I have all this energy and love and time and nowhere to put it.* And we both kind of know that it's time to talk about fostering again."

"So…" he said slowly. "What color shirt am I wearing in this vision?"

She laughed and pushed back against him. "It's not a science, Leshuski."

He picked at the grass next to him and sighed. "It sounded right, though, didn't it?"

"Yeah," she said in a low voice that he could feel echo through the cavity of her body and into his. "If I were a betting psychic, I'd guess that in a few years, we'll have built the muscles we need to really do this the right way."

His stomach executed a perfect pirouette as he tugged a little too much grass out at the root. "Were we, uh, wearing wedding rings?"

She went still for a moment and though he knew he'd never be able to sense energy in the way that she could, he felt momentary tension that almost instantly melted away into humor and sweetness and warm sun on warm skin under white skyscraper clouds. "Are you telling me that you're a marriage type of person?"

He grinned, even though she couldn't see it. She'd thrown his own words back at him. *Marriage type of person.* What did that even mean? "I'm not sure. I never had a great reason to really ask myself that question before." He lifted his fist and let the grass go in the wind. "I'm an in-love-with-you type person. I'm a committed-to-you type person."

"Me too," she whispered, her head lolling back onto his shoulder. "Tyler?"

"Hmm?"

"It's okay that we don't know the rest."

"My favorite part of that sentence is the *we*."

She jolted and reached back to lace her fingers with his. A static shock sparked between their palms, but at this point, they barely even noticed. "*We* is a very powerful word."

"It can mean so many different things at once," he agreed. And propped up against the woman he loved, in a park he loved, in a city he loved, Tyler thought about *we*. All the different *we*s in his life. In this one park alone. He could almost feel a line of love arcing from him all the way to the north part of the park where Kylie sat with *we*s her own age. And down to the south of the park, where his best friend's family had made their own *we* into an unbreakable unit. And to the woman leaning into him. He relished the weight of her, the trust and challenge of it. He looked at the sky and felt their place in the world. The green, rolling mat of the park underneath them, like the face of a clock in a city grinding its gears all around them.

He looked at the sky and felt both massive and minuscule at once, a tiny cog in the universe perhaps, but imperative to the people who loved him. And what a relief. What a relief to need and be needed. What a relief to have created this happiness.

* * * * *

ACKNOWLEDGMENTS

FIRST AND FOREMOST, I'd like to say a with-cherries-on-top sort of thank you to my agent, Tara Gelsomino, and my editor, Allison Carroll. These two brilliant people not only helped me fine-tune this manuscript, but they also helped me chop out twenty thousand words. I can't even begin to describe how much patience, how much muscle, that requires. I can't thank you enough. Thank you to Michele Bidelspach. If Allison was the person who helped me get this book on the highway, you're the person who helped me parallel park it. Thank you to Gina Macdonald, your attention to detail is unmatched. I'm so grateful to you! To the entire team at HQN, you're a radiant and gorgeous group of people. You've got vision! Talent! You've got the juice!

As always, a huge thank you to my family for being so unstoppably supportive. To my husband, thank you for pretty much single-handedly moving us to a new apartment so that I could have an office to write this book in. How much I love you is in every page of this book.

Thank you to Jeanne and Vivian, the two people who have taught me what it means to see beyond the obvious, the physical, the proveable. You two have made my world so much bigger. Fin would not exist without you!

And finally, thank you to the reader. For so long, I wrote without knowing you, without ever expecting you to be a part of my books. And now that you're here, all I can do is step back, throw my arms out, and thank you for letting me into your life.

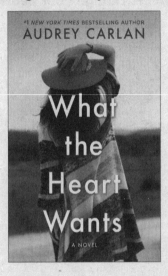

Get 4 FREE REWARDS!

We'll send you 2 FREE Books plus 2 FREE Mystery Gifts.

FREE
Value Over
$20

Both the **Romance** and **Suspense** collections feature compelling novels written by many of today's bestselling authors.